What the critics are saying...

৪১

Talking Dogs, Aliens and Purple People Eaters

EPPIE 2005 Finalist

eCataRomance Reviewer's Choice Award 2004 "Perfect! Pleasurable! Phenomenal! Talking Dogs, Aliens and Purple People Eaters by Shelley Munro is perfect summer reading, pleasurable from the first page to the last and phenomenally well written! Please treat yourself to your own copy of Talking Dogs, Aliens and Purple People Eaters." ~ *eCataromance.*

"Shelley Munro has taken a humorous, well-written, and interesting look at what could happen if little green men—or women, in this case—came to Earth. For a book that is amusing, sexy, sweet, and pretty much unforgettable, I highly recommend Talking Dogs, Aliens and Purple People Eaters." ~ *Romance Reviews Today*

"Talking Dogs, Aliens and Purple People Eaters is a funny romantic comedy that will have you in stitches when you read it. I found myself really enjoying this story; the characters were intriguing and it has a different type of romantic plot…I know you won't be disappointed. I wasn't." ~ *Just Erotic Romance Reviews*

Never Send a Dog to Do a Woman's Job

"*Never Send a Dog to do a Woman's Job* is a fun romp. With enough sexual action to satisfy any reader of Ellora's Cave books, there is also a tremendous amount of humor woven in. Ms. Munro has written an extremely enjoyable story that this reader finished in one sitting." ~ *Fallen Angel Reviews*

"Shelley Munro has written a book that is pure reading enjoyment…You can't miss these books; the whole setup kept me laughing all the way through. I hope Shelley Munro writes another book to this series. I'm ready to see more." ~ *Novelspot*

"Shelley Munro creates a delightful story. Her characters are endearing and entertaining. Both characters are all too human. Alex wants to be appreciated for more than his looks. Lily has low self-esteem. Killer, the talking dog, will make you chuckle. Prepare to laugh and enjoy Never Send a Dog to Do a Woman's Job." ~ *Coffee Time Romance*

Romancing the Alien

Shelley Munro

ELLORA'S CAVE
ROMANTICA PUBLISHING

An Ellora's Cave Romantica Publication

www.ellorascave.com

Romancing the Alien

ISBN 1419954989
ALL RIGHTS RESERVED.
Talking Dogs, Aliens and Purple People Eaters Copyright ©
2004 Shelley Munro
Never Send a Dog to Do a Woman's Job Copyright © 2005
Shelley Munro
Edited by Mary Moran
Cover art by Lissa Waitley and Darrell King

Trade paperback Publication October 2006

Excerpt from *Sex Idol* Copyright © Shelley Munro, 2006

Excerpt from *Make that Man Mine* Copyright © Shelley Munro,
2005

Warning:

The following material contains graphic sexual content meant for mature readers. This story has been rated E–rotic by a minimum of three independent reviewers.

Ellora's Cave Publishing offers three levels of Romantica™ reading entertainment: S (S-ensuous), E (E-rotic), and X (X-treme).

S-*ensuous* love scenes are explicit and leave nothing to the imagination.

E-*rotic* love scenes are explicit, leave nothing to the imagination, and are high in volume per the overall word count. In addition, some E-rated titles might contain fantasy material that some readers find objectionable, such as bondage, submission, same sex encounters, forced seductions, and so forth. E-rated titles are the most graphic titles we carry; it is common, for instance, for an author to use words such as "fucking", "cock", "pussy", and such within their work of literature.

X-*treme* titles differ from E-rated titles only in plot premise and storyline execution. Unlike E-rated titles, stories designated with the letter X tend to contain controversial subject matter not for the faint of heart.

Also by Shelley Munro

ဢ

Curse of Brandon Lupinus

Men to Die For *(Anthology)*

Scarlet Woman

Sex Idol

Summer in the City of Sails

Talking Dog: Romantic Interlude

About the Author

ဢ

Shelley lives in Auckland, New Zealand with her husband and a small, bossy dog named Scotty.

Typical New Zealanders, Shelley and her husband left home for their big OE soon after they married (translation of New Zealand speak — big overseas experience). A year-long adventure lengthened to six years of roaming the world. Enduring memories include being almost sat on by a mountain gorilla in Rwanda, lazing on white sandy beaches in India, whale watching in Alaska, searching for leprechauns in Ireland, and dealing with ghosts in an English pub.

While travel is still a big attraction, these days Shelley is most likely found in front of her computer following another love — that of writing stories of romance and adventure. Other interests include watching rugby and rugby league (strictly for research purposes *grin*), being walked by the dog, and curling up with a good book.

Shelley welcomes comments from readers. You can find her website and email address on her author bio page at www.ellorascave.com.

Contents

Dedication

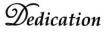

To my wonderful editor, Mary
for believing in Talking Dogs,
and for Paul.
He knows why.

TALKING DOGS, ALIENS AND PURPLE PEOPLE EATERS

&

Chapter One

&

"We're gonna crash. Buckle up."

"What?" Janaya spun around to gape at her aunt, Hinekiri. One look told her the truth. Hinekiri wasn't teasing.

Janaya gulped and scowled out a porthole at the rapidly approaching blue planet and muttered a succinct curse, trying to halt her escalating panic. Tendrils of icy fear curled around her insides. Her worst fear come to life. "I thought you said this…this antique had plenty of life yet." She fumbled with the harness straps and another weak curse slipped out when the ship plunged into white, fluffy clouds, sending her stomach swooping toward her toes.

"Ah, good." Her aunt's voice held satisfaction, despite their impending doom. "You worked your way through the Earth-speak tapes."

Janaya stared at her aunt, speechless for an instant, before her gaze slid past the porthole once more. She swallowed and imagined shaking Hinekiri until her teeth rattled and good sense reigned. The image didn't ease her panic any.

"We're gonna bloody crash!" Janaya shrieked. "Pay attention. What do I do? I don't know anything about flying this bucket of bolts. I'm a bodyguard."

"Yes, dear, and I'm very proud of you."

"*Hinekiri!*" The only reason she'd boarded this ship was because fear for her aunt's life was greater than her dislike of flying. She was beginning to regret her impulse big time.

"I said we were crashing," her aunt said. "I don't believe I mentioned death."

"You… When we land, I'm going to damage you," Janaya gritted out.

"Tsk-tsk." Her aunt waggled her forefinger while she nonchalantly maneuvered the manual steering controls. The ship groaned in loud protest and if anything, they picked up in speed. "I thought you stowed away to protect me from the bad guys." A teasing grin flashed, lighting up her lined face. "Not do their dirty work for them."

"Tell. Me. What. To. Do." They were gonna die. Janaya was sure of it. She'd never live to set foot on Dalcon again. She'd never get the captain's promotion she was aiming for, the promotion she'd earned by sheer hard work. And Santana would find someone else.

"Harness up and let me concentrate."

Tension seeped through Janaya's body, finding an outlet in her white-knuckled grip, as she watched her aunt calmly prepare to crash.

"I thought you said most of the Earth's surface is water," she blurted, her gaze darting from the porthole on her right to her aunt and back.

"That's right, dear."

"Are we going to land in water?"

Her aunt looked up from the panel of controls and frowned. "Can't you swim?"

Janaya bit her bottom lip to keep the curse that trembled on her tongue contained. "Yes, I can swim." The quirk of Hinekiri's top lip gave her away, and Janaya's shallow breaths eased out with a relieved hiss. Chances were good that her aunt was…ah yes…pulling her leg. When she stood with both feet firmly on the ground again, she'd feel more in charge. After an aggrieved glare at her aunt, she amended the thought. Maybe not.

"Assume crash position."

Janaya stared at her aunt. Then with morbid fascination, her gaze drifted to the bridge view port. Instead of the water she'd expected, she saw land. Flashes of green, trees then a sea of gold.

The initial impact jolted her body and clacked her teeth together. Behind her, something crashed to the floor—probably one of the stupid Earth-speak tapes her aunt had insisted she view and assimilate. The ship hurtled off the ground then hit again.

"Hee-haw!" her aunt shouted, one hand raised in the air, her wiry body riding the impact despite the constraints of her harness.

Janaya lacked the same exhilaration as they bounced across the ground barely missing a large tree. The sturdy branches gouged the protective outer shell of their ship as they zipped past.

"I'll try for up in those hills." Her aunt jabbed at the controls, and the ship responded sluggishly before hurtling to the ground again. Trees and hills passed in front of Janaya's horrified eyes.

What felt like hours later but was probably only a matter of minutes, they settled feet short of a dilapidated building up on the hill. The stench of metal fatigue lay heavy in the air.

"I need to stand on the ground," Janaya muttered. "*Now*. Is it safe?" Nausea worked up her throat. In a panic, clumsy fingers clawed at the restraining harness. In the end, her aunt leaned over to release the lever.

"No problems with the atmosphere here," her aunt said. "New Zealand, according to my charts. Clean and green."

Janaya needed no further urging. She stumbled out the door, dragging in huge breaths of fresh air until her lungs ached. Gradually, the panic attack subsided leaving her shaky and embarrassed. Make that mortified. Thank the Gods her aunt had been the only witness.

Hinekiri strode down the narrow exit steps from the ship and stopped beside her. She patted Janaya on the shoulder in a silent gesture of comfort. "Janaya, we need to camouflage the ship so the Earth people don't stumble across it."

"All right. I—" The small hairs at the back of her neck prickled to life. Janaya stilled, her eyes narrowing as her gaze swiveled to survey the area around the ship. Her hand slid toward her hip.

"Back on the ship," she snapped to her aunt as she pulled her weapon free. "Now."

To her right, the leaves of a fern shuddered. Janaya scented the air. Sweat. Torgon sweat.

"Come on out with your fingers poked inside your ears," she ordered, aiming her neutralizing weapon at the dark green bushes that had moved.

"That would be, hands in the air," her aunt said.

Janaya shrugged, not taking her eyes off the leafy plant. "Whatever. I have a weapon. Come out."

The fern leaves shook, dried leaves crackled underfoot. Janaya's outstretched hand never wavered, the heavy weapon still pointing at the bushes.

"Don't shoot." A black nose thrust past a lacy fern leaf.

Janaya's eyes widened.

A black face with black eyes poked into view. "Are ya gonna shoot?"

"Janaya, put the weapon down. It's a dog. Nothing to get trigger-happy about."

"Yeah," the little dog said. It stepped into full view. The dog stood below knee height and had white fur peppered liberally with black spots. It trotted closer, tail wagging. "Do ya have any food?"

Janaya reholstered her neutralizer and rolled her eyes. "Talking animals?"

"I never met a human who talked back," the little dog said. "Food? Do ya have any?"

Janaya glared. "The sooner we leave this blue planet the better. How long will it take for the ship to be repaired?"

"Two, maybe three—"

"Days? Cool."

"Months."

"Months!" Janaya saw her promotion chances slipping away. After five Earth days, she'd be missed. Especially with the big mission coming up. They'd declare her AWOL. Janaya swallowed her regrets. The protector would become the hunted.

"Parts are hard to get. Besides, I intend to sightsee while I'm here. I'm not slaving over a smoking spaceship without a little fun. And I'm not leaving Earth until I see what I came for."

"Yeah." Janaya sighed, having heard the refrain all the way to Earth. No matter how logical her arguments were Hinekiri never wavered from her goal. "The migration of the wildebeest."

"I didn't ask you to come. It was your idea to stow away."

"The Torgon want your galaxy exploration charts and your journals. And once they get them, they won't care if you're dead or alive. They've put a mercenary contract out on you."

"Contract, somtract. They've got to catch me first."

"Someone's coming," the little dog said. "Perhaps they'll have food."

Janaya scented in the direction the dog had lifted its nose. She felt a curious swooping pull that zapped all the way to her clit. Excitement sparked within. Her heart thudded and she shifted, uneasy with the sensation and the way her new Earth clothes clung to her breasts.

A steady, buzzing drone sounded. Janaya frowned, every instinct hyperaware of the new threat of danger. A clean scent drifted to her on the breeze, one that reminded her of the mountains and spruce forests of home. Then her eyes focused on a small dot on the horizon at the bottom of the hill. The dark blue dot grew steadily larger, her apprehension growing in direct proportion.

* * * * *

Hunger ate at Luke Morgan's insides. He pictured the medium-done steak he'd left on the kitchen table. One bite less in size than when he'd taken it off the grill. Luke squinted through the late afternoon light, wishing he was back in his kitchen raising the second bite to his mouth.

Flying saucers.

Mrs. Bates had been at the vicar's homemade wine again. He knew it. His second-in-charge knew it. But he still had to check it out. Sometimes it plain sucked being a cop. The grumbling protest of his stomach provided a great punctuation mark for the thought.

His radio blasted into sudden life. "Have you sighted the UFO yet?" Eager anticipation colored his receptionist's voice.

"No," he muttered. "Mrs. Bates said the North Ridge, right?" Luke figured he'd better follow procedure and do this thing right even if it was all wine-induced and a figment of Mrs. Bates' fevered imagination.

The rutted track disappeared, leaving nothing but native totara and karaka and a narrow track leading up to the clearing at the summit. Luke sighed, knowing he was going to have to hoof it. Luke coasted his Land Cruiser to a halt and yanked on the park brake.

Damned flying saucers.

* * * * *

Janaya squinted through the sunlight at the tall figure that climbed from the vehicle and tried to ignore the spark of anticipation. *Totally weird.* Especially since she couldn't wait to leave this God-forsaken outpost. Had to be a twenty-four hour bug. Her body ached all over. "What are we going to do? We haven't had time to hide the ship."

"I hope he has food," the little dog said, cocking its head to survey the approaching man.

"Is that all you can talk about," Janaya snapped, eyeing the creature with disfavor. "Aunt?"

Unbidden, her gaze slipped back to the male. He was tall, and even from this distance she knew he would tower over her medium frame. Dark brown hair, tousled and untamed, touched on his shoulders.

Janaya sucked in a deep breath. The same clean scent she'd smelled before bubbled through her senses like a sparkling tonic.

"Rather nice specimen, isn't he, dear?"

"Humph," Janaya muttered, trying to ignore the pounding of her heart and the flip-flop of her stomach, the sudden moist dampness between her legs. She ripped her gaze from the Earthman and tried to quell her aunt's smart-ass remarks with a frosty glare.

"I bet he has a nice tush. That would be rear end to you."

Heat suffused Janaya's face. "I have no interest in the man's front end or his back end. I have an agreement with Santana."

"Santana!" Hinekiri's mouth tightened to a straight line. "That male was a horrible child and he hasn't improved as an adult."

"You're not the one joining with him," Janaya snapped.

"Praise Lord Julian. If I were merging with a male, at least I'd check out the merchandise first."

Janaya whirled away from her aunt to stare at the approaching male. Unbeknown to her aunt, she'd already checked out the merchandise. She cringed as she recalled the fiasco. Then her shoulders squared. Next time she'd get the mating procedure right. Santana would have no complaints on that score. It was true that Santana wasn't as imposing as this male but he had good qualities. And she liked his family. Longing seeped into the region of her heart when she thought of the empty spaces that only family could fill. Once she'd secured her captain's bars and completed formalities with Santana everything would work out with her father. He'd realize she loved him and would recognize her worth. He'd finally accept her as blood daughter instead of calling her a nuisance.

"How do we hide the ship?" Janaya asked, changing the subject to avoid the fierce argument building within her aunt. Hinekiri could argue all she liked. Janaya had chosen Santana and her decision was final.

"Oh, didn't I say? There's an emergency camouflage button. The ship will appear invisible for as long as the power source lasts."

"Why didn't you—never mind. Do it. He's nearly here."

The little dog sniffed and sighed loudly. "He doesn't have any food."

"You're right. I don't smell any."

The dog wagged its tail. "You scent better than most humans."

Hinekiri pulled a small control box from her low-slung Earth trousers. Jeans, she'd called them when she'd handed a similar pair to Janaya. "Camouflage on."

Janaya glanced over her shoulder. The ship was still visible. "The system's failed," she whispered in a terse voice. *Was nothing going to go right on this mission?* Irritation with both herself and her stubborn aunt shot through her body finding vent in gritted teeth. Her right hand slid to the weapon at her hip, ready to defend her aunt.

"No, wait. Don't shoot him. Watch."

The man she'd seen earlier strode into the clearing where they stood. He didn't hesitate or even blink on seeing the ship, but continued toward them with a loose-limbed gait that reminded Janaya of a two-toed tigoth—sleek and well-muscled. Confident that he'd catch his prey. Janaya's skin tingled. The sensation crawled through her body, across her lips, tugging her nipples to tight peaks and finally settling low in her belly in moist feminine heat. She slid her weight from foot to foot in a slow fidget. Janaya froze when she caught the grin on her aunt's face.

"Something wrong, dear?"

"This damned G-thing you gave me to wear is right up my—"

"Hello there." The man's voice slid across her skin like soft, satiny monterey petals drawing her body tight with unexpected sensual need. Fascinated by the Earthman, her gaze drifted down to the column of tanned flesh showing in the V of his blue shirt. An urgent need to slide her tongue across the same path her eyes had taken gripped her mind. She took half a step forward to complete the action before her brain jerked into gear then screeched to an appalled halt. A soft choking noise drew her gaze northward to gleaming dark brown eyes. Hot eyes that simmered with an answering passion.

Janaya took another half a step to close the distance between them.

"Down, girl," her aunt muttered, placing one bony hand on her arm in warning.

The clear transparency with which her aunt saw her need brought a blush of hot color to her cheeks and that too, flowed down her body, converging in one achy spot. Janaya opened her mouth but all that emerged was an undignified croak. Instead of interrogating him, her mind drifted to wonder what his dark hair would feel like as it slid between her fingers, if the passion that arced in the air between them would translate to hot, uninhibited mating. There had to be more to the process than what she'd discovered so far with Santana. Aware of his laughing eyes scanning her face, her body, Janaya tried to dislodge the huge lump in her throat with a dry swallow. The throbbing silence stretched. Luckily, her aunt came to the rescue interrupting her frantic thoughts by taking the initiative.

"Good afternoon," she chirped. "And it's a great one, too. I'm Hinekiri Jones. And this is my niece, Janaya Smith."

False names, Janaya noted with silent approval.

The man halted in front of them and nodded politely. "Police Constable Luke Morgan," he said in a husky voice that plucked at Janaya's nerve endings. He grinned showing dazzling white teeth, and shared the grin between both of them before stooping to pat the dog on the head. Straightening, he said, "I know this is going to seem like a weird question, but I've had reports of an unidentified flying object. Did either of you see anything strange in the last hour?"

Janaya gasped. Her croak of denial turned into a cough. Did he not see the ship parked right in front of him?

"A UFO?" her aunt demanded, her violet eyes widening in excitement. "How exciting. If you find it, holler 'cause I'd love to meet one of those little green men."

The man chuckled. "Personally, I'd rather not come face-to-face with an alien but I'll keep your request in mind." After a brisk nod for Janaya and a wide grin for her aunt, the man—Morgan—strode past them, a mere two feet away from the ship.

"He didn't even glance at the ship. How come he can't see it and I can?"

"There is a scientific explanation, but I don't have time to explain. Your unauthorized presence on my ship has created a little problem," Hinekiri said. "You shouldn't have stowed away on my ship."

"I didn't stow away. I'm protecting you. What sort of problem? The crash wasn't my fault." Indignation dripped from Janaya's voice. Someone had to protect her aunt from the Torgon, and she didn't trust any bodyguard except herself. Apart from her estranged father, Hinekiri was all the family she had left and Janaya didn't intend to lose her to a butt-ugly Torgon.

"You didn't have travel inoculations before you left."

Janaya hated the smug tone her aunt used. Every survival instinct rose up and shrieked of danger. Her eyes narrowed. "What haven't you told me?"

"Earth's atmosphere varies from ours on Dalcon."

"The oxygen content is the same. I checked."

"Ah, but did you check the trace elements?"

The smugness had grown to a smirk. Janaya was beginning to really hate that smirk. "Tell me."

"The trace elements on Earth act like a booster to our systems. Inoculations counteract the effect."

"What? What effect?" It was like drawing teeth from Dalcon's national bird, the fodo.

"The senses are amplified."

"Hearing, sight you mean?" A relieved sigh eased through her lips. That didn't sound too bad. She could live with enhanced senses especially if it helped to keep Hinekiri safe. Janaya glanced at her aunt again. The smirk had turned toothy. Very toothy. And it stretched from one side of her aunt's wrinkled face to the other.

"What else?" she demanded.

"Sexual desire."

"You mean…" Janaya turned to study the figure of the retreating Earth male. Even with the distance between them Janaya saw how well the man's trousers cupped his buttocks. Her palms itched as she thought about fondling.

"Yeah, like I said before, nice tush. Pity Santana isn't here with you. He could take care of the emotional…ah…overflow."

Janaya wrenched her gaze from the Earthman's butt with difficulty. Her heart beat faster, and her breath wheezed from her lungs as though she'd only just finished a heavy training session. Her eyes landed on her aunt's face. The smirk hadn't lessened any. She bit back a groan. She may as well hear the worst of it now. "Out with it," she muttered. "Tell me everything." To enforce her request, she took two steps toward her aunt and set her face in a threatening scowl.

"No need to hurt a little old lady," her aunt chirped. "I'd like to point out that this is your fault for jumping before checking the consequences."

Janaya took another step, and this time she didn't have to force the glare. "Tell me the worst."

"There's no need to shout, dear. What I was about to say is that even if Santana was here, he couldn't help. I'm afraid you've imprinted on the Earth male." Her aunt beamed. "Nice choice, dear. If only I was a little younger. Perhaps I'll meet a nice Earthman while I'm here. We could double date."

Chapter Two

ॐ

Luke Morgan resisted a glance over his shoulder but it was a close thing. His brain pounded as though he'd tied one on the night before. Lust simmered through his body bringing his cock to unwilling life. Even if they hadn't told him he'd have guessed the two women were related—one glance at their violet eyes confirmed it.

"Hell," he muttered. "Keep your mind on the job." Mrs. Bates would expect a full report on his return. But when he compared Mrs. Bates' wobbling chins with the violet-eyed siren's long legs and smooth skin... Trim waist and rounded breasts... He shook his head to clear the red cloud of lust that fogged his brain and sent blood galloping to his cock. Nothing to compare at all. With luck, the two women and their dog were passing through Sloan instead of hanging about to taunt his self-imposed celibacy.

He didn't need distractions now that he'd finally got his act together. Stopped the booze and cut out his sexual antics trying to prove he wasn't a failure as a man.

"Come home to Sloan, son. Help me out of a spot while I take time off."

His father had presented a strong case and Luke had found himself in Sloan where life in law control was peaceful and he didn't have to see his ex-wife and his ex-best friend every other day. Fishing. Now that was a real occupation—one he'd reacquainted himself with since his arrival.

"Just as I thought. No damn flying saucers up here." Luke paused at the edge of the cliff that looked over the wide plains of Sloan below. At this time of year, wheat covered the fertile land down by the Gibson River. As far as he looked to the north, he could see golden ears of wheat waving softly in the breeze, almost ready for harvest. Not a UFO in sight. As he suspected, a wild goose chase. Luke turned away, eager to get back to his lunch. In his peripheral vision, he caught something out of place.

"What the hell?" He whirled back to stare out at the wheat fields in stunned disbelief.

Two perfectly formed circles showed in the far eastern wheat field. No tracks leading in. Luke squeezed his eyes shut then opened them again. Yep, just your average, everyday crop circles. A heartfelt groan escaped. Goddamned bloody crop circles. He could already picture the headlines in tomorrow's Sloan Gazette. Something along the lines of *Aliens from Outer Space Visit Sloan.*

After one last glare at the crop circles, he turned to stomp back to his vehicle. Mrs. Bates could take her UFO and—

"Holy shit!" Luke froze on the edge of the cliff, staring with half horror, half morbid fascination at the silver disc parked in the clearing not far from the old Rycroft barn. A hydraulic drone jerked his gaze to the lower portion of the thing—he refused to call it a UFO—and a narrow set of stairs slowly extended outward. Luke's heartbeat picked up. A warning inside his head told him to run but training held him firm.

"Janaya, wait," an elderly voice shouted.

"I *will* bond with Santana."

"It's too late, I tell you. There's nothing you can do to change fate."

"I want to hit something. You'd better hope a Torgon shows up because otherwise you're it."

Luke straightened. Aliens that spoke English?

"I don't want an Earthman. I want Santana."

Yep, definitely English. He'd understood the close panic in the young feminine voice.

"I didn't ask you to stow away."

"Someone had to protect you."

Bemused by the talk, Luke relaxed, letting his breath ease out slowly. They sounded more intent on attacking each other rather than picking on a Kiwi cop.

Footsteps thumped closer. As Luke watched a pair of slender legs encased in tight denim appeared. Being male, Luke couldn't help but imagine what the rest of the package would look like. Before he could even start to join the dots, the female materialized at the bottom of the steps. *Oh, baby.* It was the younger of the two women he'd met earlier. His lips pursed in a silent whistle of appreciation. Janaya Smith—if that was her real name—was young but not too young. A light blue midriff top hugged generous curves. Dark blonde hair was pulled back in a braid and hung over her left shoulder. Lust reared its ugly head again. His cock stabbed against his uniform trousers in a demand for playtime. Pissed with the sensation and with himself, he cursed.

The woman spun and lifted a weapon from a holster on her hip all in one smooth move. Before Luke could react, she fired.

Luke dived to his right and found himself over the edge of the cliff, falling into empty space. His hands snatched at rocks, a scraggy plant. Anything to halt his fall. He grabbed at a flax bush. His shoulders strained as his body jerked to a sudden halt. Small pebbles rained down on his head.

Hinekiri Jones peered over the edge of the cliff. "Are you all right?"

"I'm hanging on the edge of a cliff," Luke said trying to keep his voice calm when he felt like cursing a blue streak. "I'd rather have both feet on the ground."

"You sound just like Janaya."

Looking up, Luke saw the dog appear beside the old woman. "Any food down there?"

He'd fallen down a damn rabbit hole! Luke's arms throbbed and felt as though they were being separated from his shoulders, tendon by tendon. And he worried for his sanity. Little green men and talking dogs. Yep, he was losing it. "Are you going to help me or not?" Okay, he was starting to sound a little testy. Must be something to do with the psychosis he'd suddenly developed. The woman disappeared from his sight but Luke could hear her issuing orders to the younger one.

At the top of the cliff, Hinekiri glared at Janaya. "Help him." Then she fixed her glare on the dog. "And you, shut up about food. We'll find some later."

The dog wagged its tail. "Shutting up right now."

Janaya gaped at her aunt. "How can I help him?" She wasn't going anywhere near that cliff edge.

"*Janaya.*"

The crisp no-nonsense tone of her aunt's voice had Janaya moving like the well-trained protection officer she was. Swallowing, she inched closer to the cliff edge. Instantly, vertigo made her head swim and she jerked back to safety. "I can't."

"You're a bodyguard. Go guard his body."

Janaya's guilt grew. She'd been that rattled with her aunt's revelations about bonding with the Earthman that she hadn't thought first. She'd merely reacted to the noise and fired her weapon. A failure of a basic bodyguard principle—confirm target before discharging weapon.

"Are you gonna bloody help me or not?"

He sounded irritated and she could hardly blame him. She'd have to help him. She couldn't let her aunt put herself in danger and Hinekiri would go over the edge if Janaya didn't do something quickly. Janaya sucked in a deep breath and pushed every scrap of fear to a compartment at the back of her mind.

"Oh for goodness sake," her aunt snapped.

Janaya felt a shove in the middle of her back. She stumbled forward and fell headlong over the cliff. A panicked screech emerged as her arms windmilled. Somehow, she slowed the fall and her body righted itself. "Hinekiri!" she cried, her heart pounding so loudly she could hardly hear herself think. "What's happening?"

"I'm here." Her aunt's wrinkled face peered down at her. "Fly," she ordered. "Use your strength."

Fly? Her aunt had flown her bucket of bolts too close to the sun!

No sooner had she thought about flying then she hovered in the air beside the man. Janaya looked down. Terror jerked her into a frenzy of movement. Her hands shot out to clutch at the man's waist. Their combined weights strained the flax bush. Dirt pelted them and the plant roots made a cracking noise as one by one they released their grip on the cliff. Janaya screamed. The Earthman cursed fluidly with words she'd never heard before.

"Janaya! Drag that man back up here this instant. Don't make me come down there."

"No! Stay there!" Terror made Janaya tense. Please let her aunt do as she was told for once.

"Do you have a rope?" Luke shouted up to her aunt. He didn't believe Hinekiri's assertions any more than she did.

"Janaya, move your butt. *Now*." Something in her aunt's voice told Janaya to obey. Without looking down, she thought about flying again. Traces of panic shimmered through her mind as she clung to the man and raised her head to look up at her aunt's encouraging face.

"That's it, Janaya. Think about moving upward. Imagine solid ground beneath your feet."

"Get a rope," the man gritted out, his hands gripping a fist full of flax leaves so hard that the color bleached from his hands. "Don't listen to your damn-fool aunt. That's a hundred foot drop below."

Janaya looked down. She gasped and clutched at his shirt. Janaya was very aware of the Earthman's hard muscles pressed against her breasts, her belly, her thighs. His clean scent teased her nostrils making her heart beat faster. Then remorse surfaced at the direction of her thoughts. She was promised to Santana.

"Sweetheart, as much as I'm enjoying being personal with you this is neither the time nor place." For an instant, dark eyes held a hint of amusement along with masculine interest. Then his eyes glinted with determination to survive. "A rope. *Now.*"

Janaya jerked her hands from behind the Earthman's neck and pushed against his chest. Instantly, she dropped several feet down the cliff. A screech squeezed past her lips.

"Center your mind, Janaya," her aunt hollered. "Pretend you're training."

The words pierced her rising panic. In a leap of faith, Janaya loosened her grip on the out-jutting rock she'd clutched. She pushed away from the cliff and found herself hovering beside the Earthman. Unattached to anything. For an instant fear strangled her. She grabbed for the nearest handhold. Sharp spikes pierced her palms, and she let go as quickly as if she'd grasped flames. A masculine hand grabbed her outstretched hand.

"Concentrate, dammit," the Earthman growled. "At least fly up to the top and get a rope so you can haul me up."

Fly to the top. Huh! *Ungrateful lout.* Janaya grabbed the Earthman by his shirt collar and hauled upward. They shot upward like a cork from a bottle of sizzling cacjuice. At the top of the cliff, they barely missed her aunt. Janaya twisted her body to compensate. The Earthman flew through the air like a lightweight trainee. Janaya glanced down at the ground. They were hovering half a body's height above the ground. And Janaya wanted to stand on solid ground. *Desperately.*

No sooner had she thought the image then they plummeted to the ground. The Earthman hit the ground first and Janaya dropped on top of him. He groaned.

"Are you all right?" Janaya demanded. Guilt gripped her mind as she pushed up on her elbows and ran her hands across his chest, shoulders, and arms.

"Stop," he gasped out.

"Tell me where it hurts," Janaya demanded. Before he could answer, she ran her hands down his legs.

The male let out a husky groan. His eyes fluttered open to look right at her. His sensuous mouth turned up slowly into a grin. Dark eyes shone with warmth and distinct humor. "Keep that up, sweetheart, and we could get real cozy."

Janaya froze, her right hand on the Earthman's upper thigh. His hands curled around her shoulders and lifted her off him. His eyes crinkled at the corners in silent laughter. She felt answering warmth in her cheeks. The heat intensified when she heard her aunt's cackle.

The dog growled suddenly, a low deep rumble that raised the hairs at the back of Luke's neck. Luke leapt to his feet as two figures in lilac one-piece suits sprang from beneath the drooping leafy strands of a rimu tree. They charged Hinekiri, shiny weapons the size of a handgun extended in front of them.

Janaya thrust Hinekiri behind her and faced the alien mercenaries.

Luke gaped up at them. It was hard not to. The lilac duo stood at around six foot, with long white-blond hair and equally pale skin. Their faces seemed to bleed into their hair making it look as though they had no face. Their pale white eyes reinforced the nothingness. Luke had no idea what sex they were. But he knew one thing. The sneers on their colorless lips were mean and he agreed with Janaya. They didn't intend to leave survivors.

"Give us the charts and the journals and we'll let you go," Luke heard a guttural voice order.

"Bite my arse," Janaya snapped. Balanced lightly on her feet, she held her hands in a defensive position. Luke stepped up beside her, thinking he'd love to bite her ass along with a few other parts.

"Take Hinekiri and lock yourselves inside the ship," she said without taking her eyes off the aliens.

"I'm not leaving—"

The lilac duo rushed them. Luke pulled out his gun but Janaya moved even faster. She spun about and let rip with a kick at one of the weapons. It glinted silver as it flew through the air. The other alien fired. The violet flash from the weapon was blinding, close enough to sear his eyeballs. But it missed.

Janaya closed the distance between them in one bounding step and smashed her knee into the alien's face.

"Go, Janaya!" Hinekiri cheered from behind him.

"Get her in the ship," Janaya snarled over her shoulder.

Luke gestured at Hinekiri with a jerk of his head. "Do as she says. Let Janaya concentrate on what she needs to do."

"We may as well," the dog complained. "They don't have food."

Once he was sure Hinekiri was inside the ship, he turned back to Janaya. She feinted a move to the right then lashed out with another lethal blow with her right foot. She landed a kick. Luke heard the crack of bones as one of the aliens crashed to the ground. Janaya pointed her weapon at the still form and calmly pulled the trigger. The alien disintegrated before his eyes, leaving nothing but a pile of smoking embers.

Luke stared, shock holding him immobile. Janaya stalked the other alien.

It backed up then fumbled for its weapon. Luke noticed the weapon shook despite the alien's scowling bravado.

"Police," Luke shouted. "Put the weapon down." Healthy fear slithered through his veins as the alien's cold gaze sliced through him, rampant with the promise of retaliation.

"Stay out of this," the alien snarled, brandishing his weapon at Luke.

Luke froze, glancing at the pile of dust that was all that remained of the dead alien. He didn't want to end up like that.

Behind him, the dog barked. Luke watched it dart into the low scrub to the right of the spaceship. Seconds later, the dog shot out behind the alien and sank sharp teeth into the back of his calf.

"Get the devil creature off," the alien shouted and shook his leg vigorously, kicking out and swinging the dog through the air.

With the alien distracted, Janaya jumped him, hitting out with her fist. Off-balance, the alien wobbled then toppled to the ground with the dog still attached to his leg.

Janaya didn't hit like a girl, Luke thought pursing his lips in a silent whistle of admiration.

A sharp bark erupted from her lips. The dog let go of the alien's leg. Then Janaya snatched up the alien weapon. A bright violet light blinded Luke and when he was able to see again he saw the second alien had burnt to a crisp. All that remained was a pile of purple-tinted dust.

Luke blinked. Janaya pushed past him and hurried to her aunt's side.

"You all right?" she asked her aunt.

"Good job, dear. Where did they come from?"

"I told you they'd follow."

"Do I get food now?" the little dog asked.

Janaya stooped to scratch behind the dog's ears. "Do you have a calling name?"

"My former owners called me Annie. Don't like that one. Want a new name."

Janaya grinned at the little dog's disgruntled tone. "All right. What would you like us to call you?"

"Killer," the dog said with a decisive bark.

Janaya nodded, biting back a chuckle. "Killer, thanks for the help."

"Would you like to tell me what's going on?" Luke demanded. He eyed the dog uneasily. He'd understood every word of that conversation and he didn't like it one bit.

Janaya whirled around. Luke had witnessed everything. How would he judge her now that he'd witnessed the brutality that was her life? She was good at her job and she wasn't going to apologize for it. "Torgon," she said curtly to cover her trepidation. Her heart pounded, the blood roaring through her veins at the intent look in his dark eyes. Without thinking, she lifted her hand to cup his jaw. The dark stubble felt rough beneath her fingertips. Warmth from his skin sizzled through her hand and up her arm. Janaya's gaze tangled with the man's and a brief shiver of awareness rippled through her sensitized body. She moistened her lips.

"You gonna tell me what you eat for breakfast?" he whispered. "Just so I'm prepared."

Somehow, Janaya wasn't sure when, Luke had moved even closer. Every inch of her skin tingled, craving his touch, the sensation of his hands running across her bare skin. His clean scent teased at her nostrils making her want to press her nose to his neck and breathe deeply.

His dark eyes seemed to soften and he lowered his head, his lips stopping a whisper above hers, his eyes still holding her gaze. "Right after you tell me what the hell just happened."

"Janaya stowed away without inoculations."

Janaya's head jerked in the direction of her aunt's voice. She scowled. Subtle her aunt wasn't, referring to the way this man had imprinted on her. Janaya took a step back and looked up at Luke from a safer distance, where she couldn't succumb to temptation and touch him. The way his lips had set to a determined line told her he'd demand answers until he got what he wanted.

"Let me check your hands," he demanded. "You're bleeding."

Janaya didn't think it was a good idea to let him touch her, not again while her willpower was at an all time low. The need to rip off his clothes and service him shocked her rigid. She glanced at her aunt and caught a teasing smile of understanding.

"You could always kiss him, dear. That's my suggestion."

Give in to the desire.

Heat suffused Janaya's cheeks at the thought, and she hurriedly thrust out her hand for Luke to look at. A gasp escaped as his fingers curled around hers. The gesture felt too intimate, too personal.

"Although I'm tempted, I don't require a kiss at the moment." His dark eyes held amusement tempered with something more. Something she didn't want to investigate too closely. "I want answers. Am I going to have aliens in lilac popping up all over the town?"

"I...ah..." Janaya glanced at her aunt.

A small box attached to Luke's belt squawked. "You can tell me in a minute." He plucked the box off his belt and pressed a button. "Yeah?"

The tinny voice was clearly discernable to all three.

"Mrs. Bates wants a situation report. She says her sister sighted the UFO over Ted Morrison's wheat field."

"Oops," Hinekiri said. "Sounds like the cloaking device is out as well as the landing gear."

Luke stared at Hinekiri then Janaya. "I'll look into it." After pressing a button on the handheld radio, he said, "Tell me this is a dream—overactive imagination. Confirm my suspicions about Mrs. Bates drinking the vicar's wine."

Janaya tore her gaze from Luke's somber face to glare at her aunt.

"That depends."

"That's what I thought," Luke snapped. "You are the little green men."

"Uh-huh. Wrong sex," her aunt chirped.

Luke's eyes swept down Janaya's body and back up. Her skin prickled beneath her clothes and it felt as though he'd physically touched her.

"Figure of speech. I can see you're both female." He swept a hand through his hair making it tousled rather than merely

33

windswept. "Hell." His jaw clenched and suddenly he seemed to come to a decision. "You'll have to come with me."

"Ohhh! How exciting, Janaya. We're under arrest!"

Luke scowled. "You're not under arrest."

"Then why are we going with you?" Janaya demanded. As she spoke, she stooped to pick up the remaining Torgon weapon, pushed the reducing button, and placed it in her hip holster.

Luke backed up, keeping a wary eye on the weapon. "Easy. Let's keep this friendly."

Janaya wanted to laugh out loud and the impulse startled her. Bodyguards were trained to kill with the latest techniques. Janaya had no difficulty in taking care of herself and her aunt. And she didn't fear Luke. However, the concept of friendly had many meanings. The Earth clothes her aunt had produced for her to wear suddenly felt tight like a pair of manacles and chains. By St. Christin, she hated this out of control sensation.

"What did you have in mind?" Janaya pushed the words past gritted teeth while her fingernails dug into her palms to stop her from reaching for him again. Caressing him.

"I want to keep an eye on the pair of you. You've only just arrived and you're already creating problems." Luke cupped Janaya's elbow and propelled her down the dirt track. When they reached the spot where her aunt stood, he also gently shunted her into movement. Janaya noticed Killer fell into step behind.

"Why me?" she heard Luke mutter under his breath. "No stress. Is that too much to ask for?"

Chapter Three

🔊

After a terse, silent drive back to his house, Luke pulled up out the back of his father's white weatherboard home. He switched off the ignition.

"Home," he said. "I'll get you settled then I need to check in at the station and write up a report." *And work out a plan to keep his sanity.*

"What are you intending to write in the report?" Janaya regarded him with her cool violet eyes.

"I'm not sure. I'll probably stick to the truth as close as I can and fudge the rest."

Puzzlement marred the smooth brow for an instant. "Fudge?"

"He means he's going to gloss over some of the facts," Hinekiri explained with a chuckle.

Janaya nodded thoughtfully as if she was filing the expression for later use. Luke bit back a grin. If she needed help working out the way things were done on Earth, he'd certainly be willing to teach her a thing or two. His penis danced a jig at the thought. "Okay, I'll give you the quick tour." He opened the door to the rear of the house and stood aside, silently daring Janaya and her aunt to step in front of him. After another of those pissing contests that he was coming to enjoy, she gave a clipped nod and gestured at her aunt to enter.

"Kitchen, dining room, downstairs bathroom." Luke's gaze was drawn to Janaya's slender form and her economical movement as she prowled the passage. Hinekiri showed interest but the cop in him saw that Janaya scanned for exits, for possible escape routes in the event of an attack. Her wary surveillance pricked a healthy curiosity. A bodyguard. Luke's stealthy gaze took in her curves, her deceptive fragility. He'd already witnessed her strength, her speed and her coolness under fire when she'd faced the Torgon attack. He tried to ignore the way she'd saved his butt because he still wasn't sure he believed it himself. The woman was superhero material. All she needed was the skintight red suit. Luke's cock jumped again at the idea and he hurriedly reined in his wayward thoughts. Talking to aliens was madness. Having sex with one would be suicide. Besides, he had no idea if she had the requisite body parts.

Hell, who the fuck was he trying to kid? He ached for her.

"The bedrooms are upstairs. Mine is the one right at the far end of the passage. There are three others to choose from. Take your pick. Clean linen in the cupboard over there. If you want to wash up, there's clean towels in the bathrooms. If you're hungry, there's plenty of food in the kitchen."

The dog pricked its ears. "Food?"

Luke frowned, deciding to ignore the issue of a talking dog. That was the least of his problems at the moment.

"What about parts?" Janaya asked. She sounded as eager to leave as he was to have her leave. Unaccountably, the fact rankled. Every time he looked at her, he wanted to know what she tasted like. Her lips. The tender skin just beneath her ear. The warm, softness of her breasts. The feminine juices that signified her arousal.

"Parts?" she repeated with clear demand.

Luke suppressed a smirk as he tried to keep his eyes above neck level. "Hinekiri can make a list and we can go from there."

Janaya scowled. "As soon as possible."

Luke nodded, understanding her need for a means of escape. Under the same circumstances, he'd feel the same way. "I'll be back as soon as I can," he promised and left them standing at the bottom of the stairs leading to the second floor.

* * * * *

Luke arrived back at the house after dark, cold, hungry and pissed as hell. Mrs. Bates was convinced she'd seen a UFO and nothing he'd said had swayed her mind. Luke hadn't liked lying to her, but he could imagine the kafuffle if the locals found out there was a UFO parked up on the ridge and he was host to a couple of aliens. He'd never see his favorite fishing spot and he'd end up more wired than what he was now.

Luke shuddered inwardly, imagining the spotlight of publicity. Newspaper stories. Television reporters thrusting microphones in his face, probably digging up his past and his very public marriage breakup in the process. No privacy. History repeating itself when all he wanted was peace.

Hell, he could definitely live with his lie to Mrs. Bates if that was the alternative.

Luke parked the car at the rear of the house. Crickets chirped in the old, gnarled pohutukawa tree as he strode past and headed up the narrow footpath to let himself in the kitchen door. Without turning on the lights, he dropped his car keys on the bench top. The old floorboards creaked as he climbed the stairs and turned toward his bedroom. A yawn cracked his jaw. Damn, he was tired. Without bothering about lights, he pushed the door of his room open and after placing his gun and wallet on the dresser, started to shuck his clothes.

"Do ya have any food?"

Luke's heart leapt halfway up his throat as he scrambled to get the light. He blinked at the sudden surge of brightness then glared at the small dog curled up in a tight ball on his bed.

"What the hell are you doing in here?"

The dog yawned then dropped its head to rest on its paws. "You told us to make ourselves comfortable."

"I also told you that the end bedroom was mine," Luke muttered.

Just his luck. He lusted after a woman, one particular woman with violet eyes, and he got a dog. True, it was a dog with attitude but he didn't feel like conversation. He wanted Janaya.

After a heavy sigh, Luke striped off the rest of his clothes. He switched the light off and padded over to his bed. "Move over," he muttered, too tired to argue about bed space tonight. It was a little dog. It wouldn't take up much space in his king-sized bed.

A soft noise woke Luke. His eyes popped open as he strained to hear the foreign sound again. He moved a few inches to the left and met empty air. Off-balance, he hit the hard, wooden floor with a loud thump. A curse spilled from his lips as he sat up and rubbed his bruised hipbone.

"Whazup?"

In the dim light, he made out Killer's head poking over the edge of the bed. Luke glared. "You pushed me —"

Then he heard the noise again. A feminine screech rent the air. Luke grabbed his gun and leapt to his feet. A corresponding male curse made Luke pick up the pace.

He sprinted to his father's bedroom and skidded to a halt at the doorway. Two forms sat up in the bed.

Hinekiri. And his father.

Luke squeezed his eyes shut. This was a figment of his imagination. This was not happening. His father was safely in the South Island visiting his old army mate, George. Convinced he was dreaming, Luke opened his eyes.

There were still two people in the bed. Hinekiri clutched a pale blue sheet to her chest while his father just looked plain confused.

"Poke your hands in your ears," Janaya ordered from behind him.

That was all he needed — a trigger-happy niece to add to the pot. Luke squeezed her arm in warning, not letting go until he was sure he had her attention. "Don't shoot."

"But my aunt screamed."

"The man in bed with her is my father," Luke said dryly. "He was the one doing the cursing."

"Your father?" Hinekiri said with a great deal of interest. "Well, hello sailor," she chirped, batting her eyelids.

His father looked shell-shocked and he didn't even have all the pertinent information yet. Just wait until he heard he was in bed with an alien. On second thought, perhaps he'd keep that little gem to himself. "Dad, what are you doing here?"

"I live here," his father spluttered. "The question is what are you doing?" His father glanced at Hinekiri in bemusement before turning back to Luke, his gaze sliding stealthily past to check out Janaya.

Belatedly, Luke realized he was naked and from what he'd noticed, Janaya wasn't wearing much more than him. The pink-colored chemise thing was a bit on the skimpy side. "Back in a sec," he muttered, wheeling about to head back to his room for clothes. Before he'd taken two steps he came to a halt. Janaya had that silver weapon in her hands. He'd seen firsthand the damage it could do and although his father's sudden appearance presented a problem, he didn't want him to end up as a pile of smoking embers.

"Janaya, come with me." Giving her no choice, he grabbed her forearm.

"But my aunt—" Janaya dug in her heels and Luke felt his feet leave the ground.

"Quit that," he snapped in a fierce undertone. "You're meant to blend in, not stick out like boils on a man's backside."

Janaya glanced back at the elderly couple sitting in the bed. They hadn't noticed her slip since they were too busy sizing each other up. Her aunt didn't seem upset. In fact, judging by the gleam in her eyes, Luke's father was the one in serious trouble. She shuddered inwardly as her aunt's words about double dating came back to bite her on the bum. She needed to get them home to Dalcon—sooner rather than later.

Chagrined at the slip, Janaya set Luke on his feet. "Sorry. I…" Her words trailed off as she became conscious of his bare skin and something jabbing her in the stomach.

"We need to talk," he said. "In private. Come with me."

The man had no clothes on and he wanted to talk?

Janaya nodded while her gaze drifted down his body on a scenic journey as he walked away. Broad shoulders tapered down to a trim waist and tight buttocks. Her mouth watered. She wanted to sink her teeth in, to taste, to mark him then soothe the stinging love bite with her tongue. She wanted—What the heck was wrong with her? Why was she lusting after this man when she had finally captured Santana's attentions? Santana was the one she should concentrate on. Wrinkling her brow in a fierce frown, she tried to dredge a vision of Santana's face from her memory.

And failed.

Luke turned, waiting patiently for her to follow.

Unbidden, Janaya's eyes swept down his body—the front view this time—then back up past his sensual mouth to his eyes. The roguish glint she encountered drew a gasp.

He was watching her.

One dark eye closed in a wink and a slow, cocky grin curled across his lips. The knowing look brought a surge of color to Janaya's cheeks. Fool! She had the attention span of a fodo. *Concentrate on Santana.*

"I thought you wanted to talk?" What would happen if she said yes? Yes to the silent question in his gleaming eyes. She wanted to.

"Coward," he mocked.

The soft taunt stung and without thinking, she moved toward him. Stalked him. Her fierce frown should have made him move but he stood his ground, almost daring her to do her worst. His bottom lip quivered as though he was biting back a chuckle. Janaya's eyes narrowed. She closed the gap until nothing separated them but his skin and her clothes. Her first impression was one of heat then she heard the rapid beat of his heart. He wasn't as confident as he seemed and that made her feel a whole lot better. An echoing grin spread across her face. Two could play this game. She lifted her right hand and trailed her fingers over his shoulder and down the golden skin that covered his biceps. His intake of breath fueled her courage and she stood on tiptoe to press her lips to his, to taste and satisfy the curiosity that burnt within. His breath tickled her mouth — a pleasurable sensation that made her thirst for more.

"Living dangerously," he murmured.

Maybe, but for once, she found she didn't care about doing things by the rules. Perhaps there was something of her aunt inside her after all.

Her tongue slid across the seam of his lips, demanding a taste of the dangerous. And Luke didn't hesitate to grab the invitation. He opened his mouth, nibbling, beginning a sensual exploration that made her knees soften. Luke wrapped his arms around her shoulders pulling her flush with his naked body. A shiver worked down her spine, lodging low in her belly. Her breasts thrust against the skimpy Earth clothing her aunt had provided, the smooth fabric creating a delicious friction against her sensitive nipples.

Breathing hard, Luke tore his mouth away from hers and Janaya couldn't prevent a moan of disappointment at the separation. She had never felt this sizzling emotion with Santana. Never. Janaya didn't want to stop. If her aunt was right and it was too late for her now that she'd met the Earthman, she might as well crash and burn like a shooting star. They wouldn't be on the blue planet for much longer. As soon as the ship was repaired, they would leave — if Janaya had her way. She had a promotion to score and a joining ceremony with Santana to complete.

Luke grabbed her hand and tugged her inside a room. Once she was inside, he shut the door.

"Did ya bring some food?" Killer asked.

"Hinekiri has food for you," Luke said, opening the door a fraction.

"Oh, boy!" Killer bounded off the bed and nearly head-butted the door in her haste to leave.

Luke shut the door then snapped the lock home. "Alone at last."

A shiver of nervousness had her retreating. Janaya knew she could defend herself. She could throw the Earthman through the air using one hand. She could hurt him, yet she was the one who felt vulnerable. Imprinting didn't happen that much on Dalcon. Conditions had to be right. The trouble was that they varied from couple to couple. Janaya had never paid attention, not when she'd set her sights on joining with Santana and becoming a member of the Marachi family. When all she craved and wanted was her father to tell her he was proud of her, proud to call her daughter.

Janaya trod unfamiliar territory and she didn't like it. According to her aunt, this was fate. Janaya studied Luke's bare toes as a delaying tactic.

"Come here," he said.

His feet were large but nicely formed like the rest of him.

"Don't tell me I frighten you," he murmured.

Janaya finally risked a look. Yeah, he frightened her. He made her feel like a raw recruit again.

"I want to strip that sorry excuse of a nightie off you, throw you down on my bed and blanket you with my body," he drawled. "And that's just for starters."

Janaya swallowed, the words that she'd formed in her mind drying up in her throat. She tingled. Every inch of her body trembled with need and all he'd done so far was kiss her. Dampness soaked her G-thing at the thought of doing more.

"If you don't want the same thing I do then you'd better leave. If you stay you won't get a second chance. I intend to keep you in my bed for a long time."

Janaya heard the anxious thud of his heart as he offered her a way out. It sounded like the slow pounding of waves on a rocky beach. Hypnotic. Her heart picked up the pace to beat in unison. Did she want to go?

Wimp.

The Earth word whispered through her mind then repeated a little more forcefully. It sounded so much like her aunt lecturing her that Janaya glanced over her shoulder to check that Hinekiri wasn't standing in the doorway behind them.

"Your answer?" Luke stood before her waiting. His need was clear in his face, his burgeoning erection and the taut stance.

"Yes," Janaya whispered. "Just until the ship is repaired."

He froze on hearing her whisper but his eyes glowed hot. Dark and full of sensual promise. "Come here to me."

She knew what he was doing. He was making her go to him so later she couldn't cry coercion. Janaya took half a step forward. This stupid bonding business felt like coercion, she thought grumpily. It was as though she'd been injected with a powerful drug. She hungered for him. She needed him and it felt as though if she didn't join with him soon, she'd burn from the inside out. Heck, she'd probably do that anyway.

Chapter Four

ะ

Luke's heart stuttered in protest as Janaya hesitated.

Hell! She wasn't going to change her mind?

Fighting the need to seize her, to haul her into his arms using brute force, made him tremble. His body ached and his erection jutted outward like a damn pointer dog scenting prey.

Oh, yeah. He knew what he wanted. And he prayed like hell she desired him with the same compulsion that rippled through him. Because if she left, he'd have to drive into town and pick a fight at the Red Fox pub to handle the pent-up need that slammed his body. A feral grin stretched his lips at the thought. Guy could get arrested smacking another man for no apparent reason. But on the other hand, he could hardly bash his father. A hole in the nearest wall wouldn't help either since he'd have to fix it.

Luke's eyes roved over her curvy body and settled on her breasts with their tight coral nipples that peeped through sheer silk. They cried out for suckling.

He was the man for the job.

She took another baby step toward him. Luke clenched and unclenched his fists instead of acting as his lower brain ordered. He didn't know why but he sensed it was important she came to him of her own free will.

Come into my parlor, said the spider to the fly. Silently, he urged her to close the distance between them. His gaze traveled away from her breasts, downward past the trim waist he wanted to measure with his hands. The pink-colored confection that was her only covering ended mid-thigh, screening treasures he wanted to explore. Frustration burned his gut afresh and made his shaft twitch. *Come to me, baby. I need you.*

Luke started to count backward from one hundred to pass the time and counteract the burn that pulsed like fizzy champagne through his lava-hot blood. One hundred. Ninety-nine. Anything to delay the impending explosion down south... Ninety-eight. Ninety-seven—

Janaya ran the final two steps and slammed into his chest, knocking him off balance. He closed his arms around her waist and savored her sandalwood scent. Success! His eyes slid shut as he held her, just enjoying being close and holding the woman next to his skin.

Thank God she'd stayed.

A sweet pain pierced Luke's heart then the sensation dissolved, blindsided by the firm weight of her breasts pressing into his chest and the feel of her lower body rubbing against his throbbing erection.

Luke gritted his teeth against the pleasure and smoothed his hand up her arm to her shoulder. He paused to tug on the shoestring strap of her silk nightie. "One of us has too many clothes on." His voice came out low and husky and full of need.

"I'm guessing that would be me." A smile tugged at her lips. Janaya stepped away from him and grasped the hem of her nightgown. In one smooth move, she swept it over her head and stood proudly before him dressed only in a hot pink thong. Violet eyes met his unflinching, almost daring him to find fault.

But how could he? Luke's breath held while he catalogued the smooth skin and supple curves. Sleek feminine strength delineated with grace and confidence. "You're beautiful."

Her lack of self-assurance, hesitation or whatever had slowed her decision seemed to have seeped through the floor, sloughed off as easily as her nightgown. Luke wondered at the reason for her choice but didn't voice his thoughts. Only an idiot would make her second-guess her decision. His Dad hadn't raised no fool.

Full lips curved into a pout. She tossed long strands of blonde hair over one naked shoulder, thrusting firm, round tits into prominence. "You're all talk."

It was the sort of pout that goaded a red-blooded man to action. And his blood definitely rated as red. Luke reached for her, pulling her into a casual embrace.

Set the boundaries first, boy.

His father's words of wisdom, uttered years ago when he was a teenager, floated through his mind. He didn't want her to think he was committing to anything more than the next few weeks. "Are you sure about this?"

Bloody hell! Hadn't he decided not to question her decision? *God, where was his brain?* His cock chose that moment to snuggle in the V of her thighs, cuddling up to the silk of her panties. The heady sensation that ripped through him answered the question. Engaged in a hormonal moment. That's where his brain was at. He cleared his throat. "Are you sure?" he repeated.

"I'm here, aren't I? Hinekiri and I are leaving as soon as the ship is repaired."

Luke nodded. Good. Nothing long-term. They were both on the same page.

He grinned suddenly. "Okay. I'm done with the chit-chat." He curled a hand around her nape and drew her to him. Luke intended to take this slow and draw out the enjoyment for both of them. He dipped his head to take a kiss, caressing her lips slow and easy, tasting and sipping in a get-to-know-you kind of way.

Janaya allowed the exploration then without warning used her teeth.

Luke jerked back in surprise, his lip smarting from the sharp nip. "What was that for?" He fingered his bottom lip, probing for blood but his fingers came away clean.

Mischief lurked in her violet eyes. "I've done this before. I'm not fragile."

Luke wanted to laugh. She did that. Kept coming up with quips that tickled his amusement. "Glad you've made that clear." Narrowing his eyes, he used his bulk to herd her to the bed.

Still smirking, she backed up until the bed stopped her retreat. She toppled back on to the mattress and Luke sprang, pinning her with his body in a move reminiscent of the wrestling shows of his boyhood. So she wanted action.

So did he.

He took her mouth hard, nipping and tasting before thrusting his tongue into the warm sweet cavern beyond. The taste of spearmint delighted his tongue. Man, she tasted good. A man could get used to this—a soft woman under him to plough. Maybe this celibacy kick wasn't such a shit-hot idea after all.

Janaya bucked beneath him even as their tongues dueled, rubbing, jolting body parts together with exquisite friction. She wasn't passive like his ex. Luke pulled back to feather kisses across her jaw. The need to taste her breasts throbbed through him like the relentless pound of a waterfall but he wanted to do a little sightseeing on the way. Before he had time to blink and dive in for another kiss, she'd rolled them both over and lay on top of him, boobs jiggling in his face with each ragged breath. Her luscious, creamy curves, crowned with pebbled coral nipples taunted his willpower.

Bend down a bit further, sweetheart.

Janaya stared down into his eyes with a triumphant grin on her flushed face.

An answering smirk ached to burst forth. He should have felt resentful of her superior physical power but it turned him on. Made him impossibly hot. Sort of like the boot was on the other foot, he thought as he let the smile loose and grinned back like a loon. Or maybe it was the novelty factor. He was doing it with an alien. Whatever. Janaya was with him because that was what she wanted and it made him feel like a Greek god.

"Now who's stalling," he whispered, ensnared by her feminine strength and her hot violet eyes that promised pleasure, extreme pleasure for both of them.

Janaya grabbed both his hands and raised them above his head. Luke barely suppressed the shiver that shot the length of his body and made his engorged shaft twitch again and his balls draw tight. She studied his upper body silently, her gaze a soft caress then slowly she lowered her head to graze her teeth across one masculine nipple. The sharp sensation drew a rough gasp from deep in his throat and jerked his lower body inches off the mattress.

She froze, her gaze leaping to meet his. "Did that hurt?"

Luke cleared his throat, his eyes fixed on hers as he tried to anticipate what she'd do next. "No."

"I wouldn't want to maim you."

He gaped at her in shock. *Jesus! He didn't want that either.*

"You are not the same as San...the males from our planet."

Luke felt his eyes widen. She looked the same, but he wasn't sure he wanted to carry on with this...this...experiment. In fact, his male equipment had wilted dramatically, no longer interested in getting the job done. His brain scurried north while he pondered if he should panic and run.

"Small differences," she murmured with a half smile. "The most important parts seem the same." She bent her head to kiss a path across his chest. Her long hair hid her expression from him and he stretched out a tentative hand to touch the soft, fragrant locks. Maybe he'd play wait and see before he hit panic mode.

"Keep your hands above your head," she murmured throatily.

At least she hadn't ordered him to poke his hands in his ears. Whenever he heard her say that people—things—died. Luke followed her breathless order while he wondered what she'd do to him next. The anticipation made his hips shift restlessly, his heart beat stronger, faster.

Her breath washed across his skin as she moved down his body. Her hair fanned out across his belly and abdomen while her warm, moist breath left a trail of goose bumps. Luke swallowed. No problems in the equipment department now. *Yes, sir!* Ready and rearing to go.

A hand trailed down his cock sending his heart racing with expectation. He ached to hold her, to explore her in the same way. Before the thought was half formed, he moved his hands.

"Don't move. Not yet. I want this to last."

Luke smothered a groan. It would be good if she actually started. His heart pounded against his ribcage like a crazy thing and begging words started to cram his mind. He closed his eyes and his world narrowed to one of pure sensation. Small feather light strokes down his shaft made his body jerk off the bed again. Insistent hands gripped his hips holding them firm. Luke felt as if he might explode. His balls ached for action. This was torture. Then her tongue replaced her fingers. And he really wanted to beg.

Satisfaction filtered through Janaya. Luke's face showed open pleasure, so much so that Janaya was actually enjoying herself. This was proving much more fun than when she'd serviced Santana.

"That's it. I can't take any more," he gasped.

Janaya froze. Surely, he wasn't complaining about her performance? "But you were enjoying it," she blurted.

This time he stilled. He pushed up on his elbows to stare at her. "Of course, I'm enjoying it." He gestured at his erection. "Does that indicate a lack of interest?"

Janaya wrinkled her brow in confusion. "Do you do things differently here on the blue planet?"

Luke stared, then his mouth kicked up in a cocky grin so infectious that Janaya found herself smiling back. "How about letting me take things from here and then you can tell me how the sex differs?"

Janaya hesitated. The few times she had done it with Santana had been painful, but something inside drove her to nod in agreement. When she was near this man, her skin itched and the G-thing she wore became sodden and damp. Perhaps her aunt was right and she was missing a link. Perhaps Luke was that link.

"Okay?" Luke quirked one dark brow.

"Yes."

"If I do anything that you don't like, tell me and I'll stop," he added.

Janaya noted that he didn't mention her superior strength but the knowledge shimmered in his dark eyes.

He kissed her, tasting her fully while one hand trailed across her breast, circling the nipple but never settling, never touching. Janaya arched toward his touch, aching for hard pressure. She wanted to purr and suspected Luke knew it. His mouth slid from hers and trailed kisses across her jaw, down her neck, exploring the dips and curves of her collarbone finally ending at her breast. After teasing her for mindless minutes until she felt like grabbing him and giving pointed directions, he finally sucked her nipple into his mouth and drew hard. Arrows of sensation marched from her breast to her lower belly. She caught her bottom lip between her teeth to bite back a moan. That felt so good. Right now, the fabric of the G-thing felt so wet it was a wonder the silky apparel didn't slide right down her legs. She groaned as he suckled her other breast and continued to taunt the first, applying pressure right where she needed it, pinching and tugging the pouting nipple. His hand crept across her belly then lower sending quivers running the length of her body. Luke slid his hand between her legs to encounter damp fabric.

"You're so ready for me," he murmured, running his fingers along the edge of the elasticized legs. She shivered. He dipped his fingers underneath then looked up at her with a boyish grin. "Let's get rid of this."

Before Janaya could formulate an answer with her sluggish brain, he yanked at the thin strip of material. Fabric ripped and dropped away baring her fully to his sight.

Janaya's gaze leapt to his face, her heart jumping through hoops and over hurdles as she studied his reaction. Santana had… *Never mind, Santana. This is for you. Enjoy the moment.*

"No pubic hair," he murmured, tracing fingers across the smooth, hairless skin that shielded her pussy. "Nice."

He looked…hungry. His eyes dark and intent like a man starving for a feast.

Janaya swallowed the lump that had bloomed in her throat. He made her feel worthy, beautiful, instead of a ritual to perform to make a mating legal. Nothing like the way Santana… Janaya tensed.

Stop thinking of the man!

His hand stilled. "Do you want me to stop?"

Stop? Was the man crazy? Janaya cleared her throat but when she tried to speak nothing emerged but a strangled croak. She shook her head.

"Stop?" He sounded disappointed and she shook her head frantically from side to side.

"No!" The word exploded past her lips. "Don't stop!"

"Thank you, God," he breathed. The cocky grin sprang to life again. "I'll carry on then." He moved down the bed until his face was level with her mound. "Man, I'm gonna enjoy this."

Janaya swallowed, wondering what he intended to do. The mating ceremony with Santana had been quick. Then he'd studied her through his pale eyes and said he supposed she was adequate. Only two more ceremonies to complete.

Luke gripped her thighs. "Stop that, sweetheart. Whatever you're thinking about." He smiled lazily, resting his chin on her mound as he stared up at her. His breath tickled her tummy, sending a shiver of awareness galloping back to her clit. Her pussy quivered. He exerted enough force to let her know he wanted access. Free access to her cleft.

Trust him.

She thought about it. Something about the Earthman's eyes encouraged trust. Janaya let her legs relax and fall apart.

"Close your eyes," he whispered. "Concentrate on where I touch you. Concentrate on how you feel."

Janaya's eyelids drifted shut. Her senses heightened yet narrowed to focus on his touch. She heard the beat of Luke's heart, the soft tick of a clock. Anticipation simmered. A ribbon of awareness sped through her stomach, radiating outward. Lower. Her blood thickened. Nipples tightened even further to achy, rigid buds. Something wet stroked across her pubic bone. Janaya bit back a moan. The Earthman had barely started yet her heart thundered as if she were in a race. The sensation repeated. Her heart leapt in her chest. Cool air blew across her mound then lower. Janaya felt her juices weep down the inside of one thigh; she felt the prickle of whiskers against the tender skin of her inner thighs. She stirred restlessly, her breath coming in harsh pants, her head tossing from side to side on the pillow.

"Steady, sweetheart." Amusement coated the masculine purr. "We haven't started yet." He swiped his tongue over her clit.

Janaya's pulse bounded away like a startled unilope fleeing a tigoth. Her eyes snapped open and her pelvis thrust upward seeking more of the pleasurable stimulation. The tang of her arousal filled the air.

"Can't I trust you to follow orders?" He chuckled and slid from the bed leaving her panting hard and tingling from head to toe.

Janaya's head turned to watch him stride across the room. Buttock muscles flexed with each step. She sighed. Maybe if she followed orders she'd get a chance to scrape her teeth across that tempting expanse of flesh. Then she'd lick the sting from her touch and move on to lick her tongue down his cock to the plum-colored head. Yeah. Good plan.

Luke bent to rifle through the top drawer of the wooden dresser. She caught a glimpse of his cock as he bent and her mouth watered, suddenly desperate to taste.

"Don't even think about it," he said, his voice low. Sexy. "Shut those pretty eyes."

Janaya found herself obeying, euphoria shooting through her veins to settle in a low, pulsing hum in her pussy. Her head tossed from side to side. She heard the drawer shut with a snap. Her insides pulled with renewed anticipation. The intimate darkness behind her closed lids heightened her arousal.

The mattress depressed as he joined her on the bed again. She turned toward him listening for each move he made, imagining him watching her, his gaze traveling the length of her body. The scent of cleanser—Earth soap—on both her and him filled her nostrils. Her acute ears heard the slither of silk. Luke lifted her head, smoothing her hair down, tucking it behind her ears. Material covered her eyes making the blackout permanent unless she exerted her physical strength and pushed the issue.

This time, Janaya parted her legs without being asked. Cool air brushed her nether region. Dampness seeped from her cleft. Keen expectation held her still.

"Right, now where was I?" Luke murmured. He brushed a kiss over her lips and she tasted her juices on his lips.

"Tasting me," Janaya blurted. She felt the blaze of color in her cheeks. The heat sank to her breasts.

A soft chuckle sounded. "So I was," he mused. "Then let's get this party on track again."

Janaya held still, waiting. Anticipating. What would he do next? Raw heat rolled over her while her remaining senses worked hard to compensate for her blindness. Touch. Luke's callused fingers parted her folds and massaged her clitoris, sending lightning arcing through her veins. "More," she gasped, driving upward to meet his lazy fingers.

"My pleasure," he said in his masculine purr. One finger sank into her pussy. She groaned. Another finger slid into her slick cunt, stretching her while his thumb brushed over her clitoris. She writhed, wanting more of the delicious friction. Harder.

"More," she said, the word ending on a groan of pure appreciation. A tingle started. She moaned, thrusting up to seek direct stimulation. The tingle spread, radiating outward, culminating in several crashing waves of sensation that shot down her legs to her toes.

"Ohhh!" she moaned, still riding his hand to milk the orgasm of every sliver of sensation. *That* hadn't happened before. Janaya dropped her hips back to the bed, boneless with satisfaction.

A third finger pushed deep into her nectar-slicked vagina. Her belly tightened at the renewed spike of pleasure. So good, she thought, her senses reveling in the heightened awareness the blindfold bestowed on her.

"Your cock," she demanded. The deep, full marvel of his cock thrusting into her body would ease the ache that had sprung up again. "Please."

"Yeah," Luke murmured. He flicked his tongue in a teasing pass over her clit that left her desperate for more. "I'm thinking I'd like that too. And since you asked so nicely."

Janaya heard the seductive rustle of cotton sheets as Luke worked his way up the bed and kissed her deep and hot with lots of tongue action. He continued to explore her mouth while he reached for something with his hands. A crackle of paper sounded. Janaya felt Luke roll to his side. Muscles flexed in his arms before he rolled back to remove her blindfold.

"I want to see your eyes when you come," he said and pushed into her pussy. Hard and fast with delicious friction. They both groaned.

Janaya clung to him, her hands wound around his neck while their lower bodies strained together. He felt thick and hard inside, the sweet pleasure filling her as she arched into his thrust. His right hand tweaked a nipple, each tug sending a corresponding jolt through her pussy.

"Wrap your legs around my hips," Luke whispered tersely. His breath came out in sharp rasps and with her enhanced hearing she heard the rush of his blood through his body. His free hand curved around her hip and then lower to touch her leg, guiding her as to what he wanted. Needed. Tormenting her with each onslaught.

She followed the order blindly, without argument, and was glad she did. The angle of his thrusts changed, taking him impossibly deep until it felt as though he hit her womb with each drive into her.

All the while, he watched her, dark eyes searing into her soul, silently urging her to freefall with him into carnal pleasure. Janaya wanted the ecstasy, a repeat of the pleasure surge, as much as his burning hot eyes told her he did.

Janaya clenched her inner muscles experimenting with the technique she'd learned at the joining class on Dalcon. The move wrung a strained groan from Luke so she did it again.

"Yes," he hissed. He withdrew his cock only to hammer into the depths of her cunt. The exquisite shimmer she'd experienced earlier sent greedy longing through her. More. Now. Janaya gasped. Luke drove into her. Short, hard strokes that repeatedly bumped against her clit. The shimmer coalesced into a stream of pulsing waves that wrung a soft groan from her throat when they peaked in a crashing finale.

Luke thrust again, maintaining eye contact, his dark eyes reflecting her pleasure-filled gaze. Once. Twice. Before the elation of orgasm fell away, she felt the pulse of his penis deep within her as his seed spewed from him in climax. She clutched him tightly, grateful and awed. She hadn't known mating could be like this. Extreme. Inspiring. Invigorating. *Fun.*

When the hammer of his heart finally hushed, he bent to kiss Janaya's lips in a soft, open-mouthed kiss.

"That was amazing," he said, his tone sincere and almost in awe.

"Yes," she murmured. Simply the best mating she'd ever had. Janaya cuddled up close to his sweat-slicked body, savoring the closeness after the most amazing experience of her life. If this was bonding, the same bonding that Hinekiri lectured on, then she was all for it.

* * * * *

A thump on his bedroom door jerked Luke from a lusty dream. He cracked his eyes open to find some of his dream true. Janaya lay wrapped around him like a ribbon on a Christmas gift.

"Luke, you coming out of there anytime soon?"

Beside him, Janaya stirred. As he watched, her eyes flickered open.

"Morning, sweetheart." Luke ran a possessive hand across her hip, savoring the smooth skin. He lowered his head to snatch a kiss.

Janaya swept a lock of blonde hair away from her face and peered up at him. The sleepy look sent a spear of lust straight to his cock.

"Luke!" The doorknob rattled impatiently.

"Coming," Luke snapped.

"You haven't got time," his father hollered through the door. "Dammit! All hell is breaking loose out here."

Luke sighed and nuzzled the soft skin behind Janaya's ear one more time. He knew that tone. Seriously rattled.

Even though he sensed things were dire, he was loath to leave the warmth of his bed and the woman he held in his arms.

"Luke!"

Muttering to himself, Luke dragged his hands through his hair and swung his legs over the edge of his bed. Well-used muscles winced at the movement, causing a snicker to emerge.

Damn. He'd enjoyed last night. And the early hours of this morning. *Several times.* The second snicker held definite satisfaction.

"Stay there," he said. "We didn't get much sleep last night."

"No." Janaya stood decisively and stretched her hands above her head.

Every thought in Luke's mind stalled. On second thought, perhaps he'd stay here with Janaya. Plenty to keep him occupied. His hands reached for her breasts even as the thought formulated.

"Luke, get your butt out here now!" Heavy masculine footsteps retreated but Luke knew if he didn't appear soon his father would take an axe to the door.

Luke sighed with real regret. So much for that idea. He grabbed a pair of jeans and yanked them on. "Go back to bed," he murmured. He unlocked the door and sauntered down to the kitchen whistling.

"Good of you to join us," his father grunted.

Hinekiri pushed a coffee mug away from her and stood. "I'm off to look for parts."

"Parts for what? Maybe I could help," his father said.

Luke cut off his whistle mid-bar. "I don't think that's necessary. I know exactly what Hinekiri needs." It was bad enough that his father had turned up here unexpectedly and found him shacked up with Janaya and her aunt. He didn't need him to find out they were aliens.

His father gestured at the newspaper that sat on the kitchen counter. "You have enough to do without running around after vehicle parts."

"What—?" The insistent ring of the phone cut into Luke's reply. He snatched up the receiver after giving his father a hard glare. "Yeah?"

"We've had reports of strange men wandering around the old junkyard. And Mrs. Bates wants to know what you're going to do about the aliens. She says that the reports in the paper are proof that she was right. We could do with your help. Will you be here soon?" Tony, his second-in-charge demanded. Underlying the request was a trace of panic that told Luke things were bad.

His father held up the front page of the Sloan Gazette. The headline was enough to start a burning sensation in Luke's gut.

"I'll be there in ten," he snapped into the phone.

Luke placed the phone down and reached for the paper. The headline was just as bad as he'd feared.

Alien Crop Circles in Sloan

The accompanying story was worse.

"We're going to have every nut in the neighborhood out in those wheat fields," he muttered.

"They're already there," his father snapped back. "That's what I've been trying to tell you. Look lively. You're in urgent need of damage control."

Luke whirled about and headed for his room. Janaya sat up in bed and watched him in silence.

"The mayor's rung," his father hollered after him.

As Luke snagged a denim shirt from his wardrobe, he scowled. He shoved his arms in the sleeves and buttoned it up.

"And that reporter's rung too."

Marcie Montgomery. He sighed, knowing already that this day would suck big-time. Well it could just wait until he had a cup of coffee. Luke stomped back to the kitchen and grabbed two mugs from the cupboard. Soft footsteps behind told him Janaya had followed. He turned to give her a quick grin, disappointed to see her fully dressed. Violet eyes glowed and a soft flush swept over her cheeks. His heart gave an answering little blip before he turned back to the coffeemaker. Deciding that Janaya looked like a black coffee kinda girl, he filled the mugs and handed one to her.

He took a sip of coffee and regarded his father with trepidation. How did he get rid of him without making his father suspicious? "You coming back to work or are you heading off again?"

"Might hang around for a bit," his father said, taking the seat at the table next to Hinekiri. His gaze wandered off Luke to touch on Hinekiri and lingered. "I promised to show Hinekiri some of the sights."

A mouthful of coffee sprayed from Luke's mouth, hitting the table and both Hinekiri and his father.

"What the hell's wrong with you today?" his father roared leaping to his feet.

"Sorry," Luke muttered, grabbing a towel. He offered it to Hinekiri who smiled.

"I think Luke's a little shook up about the aliens in town," Hinekiri said.

Luke speared her with a glare but it didn't dampen the mischievous look in her violet eyes. No wonder Janaya looked ready to do bodily harm to her aunt at times.

"Load of cog wash," his father snapped. "Probably some fool kids egging each other on. It is almost the end of the school year."

"Okay," Luke said, thinking rapidly. "How about you going off to investigate the crop circles and I'll go and sort out things at the station? I can drop off Hinekiri and Janaya on my way."

"Sounds good to me," Hinekiri chirped.

Luke frowned. The woman looked as angelic as a kid about to stuff a big, black weta in the teacher's desk. The prehistoric grasshopper-like insects had really put a scare in the girls when he'd been at school. Hinekiri had the exact expression of a prank-setting boy. He absolutely refused to let her go off with his father. He looked to Janaya. She could keep her aunt under control.

"But what about our sightseeing?" his father asked.

"I really need to sort out…some things first," Hinekiri said.

To Luke's relief she kept things suitably vague. "Right." He placed his cup of coffee down on the bench. "Let's go."

They exited the house via the kitchen door before his father could muster an argument. Luke held the rear door of his vehicle open for Hinekiri then opened the door for Janaya. He was unable to resist the urge to run his hand over the rounded cheeks of her ass. His cock stirred with a joyful tallyho. God, he thought with real sorrow when he shut the car door. He could be in bed with her instead of chasing fictitious aliens. They'd barely started their erotic journey. And since she was leaving soon, there was no time to waste.

"I don't like the sound of the strangers hanging around," Janaya stated the instant Luke climbed behind the wheel. Her body felt pleasantly relaxed, as if she'd had a session at Dalcon's Refurbishment Club. Blood and enthusiasm zinged through her veins in a way it hadn't for a long time.

"It's probably—How the hell do you know there were reports of strangers hanging around? I never said anything. Tony told me during the phone call."

"She has powers," Hinekiri chirped from the rear seat.

"What sort of powers?" Luke gritted out. Janaya noticed the way his hands gripped the driving wheel, the way his jaw tightened. Heck, she could even hear his teeth grate backward and forward.

"I—"

"She's learning them as she goes along," Hinekiri offered.

Silence fell. Luke jerked the gear controls and the vehicle shuddered before driving smoothly. Finally, he took a deep breath and glanced at her.

"Do you mean to tell me that you have supernatural powers? You can do more than fly? New supernatural powers that you have no control over?"

"No, I—"

"That's right," Hinekiri said. "And it wouldn't have happened if she hadn't tried to interfere."

"Will you let me speak?" Anger coursed through Janaya's body. Hinekiri was so stubborn. The information that had surfaced on Dalcon came from a reliable source. If she'd had longer, Janaya would have extracted the truth from her informant but with her aunt's departure imminent, she'd run out of time. And that had made her nervous. Janaya sent a glower at her aunt, trying to glare her into submission. Instead, a fierce heat collected behind her eyes. Janaya squinted, seeing a bright violet light in front of her eyes. The light grew brighter. She blinked. Thin rays of violet light shot from her eyes.

Hinekiri screamed.

Luke swore.

The vehicle swerved then ground to an abrupt halt.

Janaya gaped at the huge hole in the rear seat—right next to her aunt. Smoke wafted upward and a noxious odor filled the vehicle. Horror bled into trembling. She'd almost done the assassins work for them.

"Sorry," she whispered, unable to look her aunt square in the face.

Looking at Luke was just as difficult. There was a huge hole in the rear of his vehicle. The road was visible through what had once been a perfectly good seat. Janaya thought about the number of credits in her safe box. Probably not enough to purchase a new one for Luke.

"If you want to damage something, try the purple aliens outside. Any time now would be good."

The urgency in Luke's voice made her spin around. Three Torgon assassins stood in the middle of the road, their weapons extended in front of them. Janaya opened the door.

"Seat belt," Hinekiri muttered.

A metallic clang indicated she'd released the harness while she issued the reminder.

Shelley Munro

Janaya heard her aunt lean forward to peer between the front seats. "Do you have your weapon?"

"I don't think she needs a weapon," Luke countered in a dry voice. "Just do that weird eye thing again and they'll run for the hills."

"I'm not sure I can," Janaya muttered, not taking her eyes off the Torgon. She slid from the car. "There's someone coming."

"Hell." Luke gunned the engine. "Do something. Quick."

Luke's panic beat at her mind, distracting her for an instant. One of the Torgon fired. The shot singed the top of her head.

Janaya yelped. She heard the hoarse, grating laughter of the Torgon and the rapid clicks as they communicated their glee and their plan of attack. By the sword, what was she going to do? She had no weapon. Another bodyguard rule she'd broken. But she'd been that rattled by what had happened last night with Luke she'd forgotten to pick up her weapon. Unfortunately, her mistake would get an innocent Earthman killed. And who knew what they'd do to Hinekiri to force her to give them her precious exploration charts.

The rattle of the approaching vehicle sounded louder now. As was the voice of the man who muttered under his breath. "It's your father," she said in horror.

"Bloody hell." Luke pulled a gun from his glove box. He released his seat belt. "I'm not sitting here waiting for you to do something."

Fury ignited inside Janaya and she directed it at the impossible Earthman who was forever trying to order her about. His pretty face and his sexual prowess didn't mean he could walk all over her. She was a bodyguard in the Imperial force.

Her aunt gasped. "Don't look at Luke!" she shrieked. "Aim at the Torgon."

Even as her aunt gave the warning, Janaya felt intense heat building up behind her eyes.

Luke fired his gun.

62

Purple light filled her eyes making everything shine with a lavender haze. Panic struck. She was still looking at Luke. Concentrate. Dammit, she was going to kill him if she wasn't careful. And hellfire, she wasn't done with appeasing her appetite!

Hinekiri pointed. "Janaya. Over there."

Everything moved in slow motion—the approaching vehicle, Luke shooting at the Torgon, her aunt's frenzied hand movements. Then Hinekiri slapped her hard on the side of her face. Her head jerked toward the group of Torgon. Fury galloped through her mind, pressure built and suddenly purple light shot from her eyes in a concentrated beam.

"It's a strike," Hinekiri roared behind her as one Torgon burned down to a pile of ash.

Beside her, Luke fired again. The projectile from his weapon caught a Torgon right between the eyes. He exploded like a hot ball fish, spraying purple gunk the distance of two bodies lined end to end.

"Yes!" Hinekiri crowed, punching her fist in the air. "Get the last one, Janaya."

Janaya concentrated, channeling her anger at being attacked. When the heat developed behind her eyes and the purple light returned she knew she'd managed it by herself without Hinekiri or Luke. She focused her eyes, shot. And missed.

"Where'd he go?" Luke demanded.

"Into hypermode back to where ever they left their ship. They never hunt alone, always in packs," Janaya said in disgust. Ready to attack another day.

"Great." *We're going to have purple aliens popping out of the woodwork.*

"Not if I have anything to do with it," Janaya muttered.

"What?"

Janaya froze. *He hadn't said that out loud.* "Aunt?" Clear panic sizzled through her voice and she didn't mind admitting to the emotion. How was it possible she could read his mind?

"The two of you mated last night?" Hinekiri made it a question.

Luke stared at her in silent accusation. "If you mean had sex then yes, we did. What else aren't you telling me? I'd rather know it all up front so I can protect the people of Sloan. I don't want any more nasty surprises today. Two are enough."

Hinekiri's teasing grin smoothed out to concern on seeing Luke's apprehension. Janaya didn't blame him for his snappy questions. Quite frankly, she wanted to get her aunt alone and commit the physical damage she constantly threatened her with. And then she'd turn her over to the Torgon. Hinekiri had never mentioned a word of any of the possible symptoms when she'd discovered her presence on board ship.

"I've never heard of a Dalconian imprinting on an Earthman before," Hinekiri said. "I can give you a broad idea of what to expect but then again, I might be wrong."

"What's the worst that can happen?" Luke demanded.

Janaya lifted her head to stare in the direction they'd come from. "Your father will arrive in a few minutes."

"Quick. Before Dad arrives."

"The bond will become stronger each time you join. Dalconians mate for life," Hinekiri murmured.

"Okay." Luke closed his eyes, an almost pained look skipping across his face. "We won't have sex again. We'll keep away from each other."

Janaya thought of how beautiful it had been last night. How connected she'd felt to Luke. It had been nothing like servicing Santana. The thought of never feeling the slide of his mouth against her naked skin again made her want to cry.

Chapter Five

ഇ

Luke's father braked and pulled along beside them. "Is there a problem?"

"No problem," Luke said. But although his voice remained even and controlled, Janaya read a myriad of emotions on his face. Irritation. Distrust. Regret.

It was the regret that stirred an answering response within her.

Killer jumped from the passenger seat onto Luke's father's lap and stuck her head out the driver's window. "Did ya bring any food?"

"I hope you don't mind me taking your dog out. She jumped in while I wasn't looking and I didn't have the heart to leave her at home."

Janaya leaned closer to Killer and scratched her behind the ears. With a soft growl, she told Killer to protect Luke's father.

"Woof!" Killer swiped a pink tongue across Janaya's face. "Will ya give me food?"

Janaya laughed. "It's a deal."

Luke's father shook his head. "I don't know why you're talking to Killer as though she can understand. Well, if you're sure that you're fine then I'm off to the wheat fields."

He drove off leaving an uneasy silence behind.

"How come I can understand the dog and Dad can't? The sex thing?"

Janaya glanced at Hinekiri and then back at Luke. "It's because I imprinted on you when I saw you. Somehow you've acquired some of my powers."

"But not all of them."

"No."

"Great." Luke jerked his head at the dead Torgon ashes. "At least Dad didn't notice the debris. Get in. Tony, my second-in-command, will be tearing his hair out by now if he's dealing with Mrs. Bates."

Janaya nodded and climbed back into the car. They drove along in silence, Janaya staring straight ahead. Part of her longed for the old days when the worst she needed to cope with was kicking bad guys in the butt. This situation with Luke was messy because they'd talked, they'd had fun together. Emotions had happened. A frown puckered her brow. She couldn't remember anything like this happening before, especially not with Santana. They didn't see each other much and that seemed to work much better.

"Hinekiri and I will find alternative accommodations," Janaya said.

"No!" Hinekiri screeched from the rear.

"Over my dead body," Luke snarled. "I'm keeping you both in my sight so no one gets hurt."

Janaya sucked in a calming breath and forced away the sudden vision of her being in *his* sight. The idea of being crushed in his embrace... And this licking business he'd introduced her to—she wanted more. Her body heated and she found herself fidgeting and squirming in the leather seat. Janaya glanced at him. The solid, clenched jaw jerked her back to reality. She'd stayed in his vicinity last night and now look at the mess they were in.

"But we can get the ship mended and leave quickly if you would let us," she argued.

"I'm not going to squabble about it. I'll lock you up if I have to."

"Sounds kinky. Do you think your father has handcuffs?" Hinekiri asked.

"No!" Janaya said tersely, jerking around to glare at her aunt in the backseat. "You stay away from Luke's father. Luke has enough problems as it is." Janaya cursed under her breath. Her instincts had been right. Hinekiri was interested in Luke's father. No telling how stubborn she'd be about leaving. She was still muttering about seeing the bloody wildebeest creatures in some place called Africa. Why she'd want to see a weird gnu run from point A to point B, Janaya had no idea.

"We're here," Luke said with clear relief in his husky voice. He turned the vehicle right into a wide street flanked by palm trees and colorful gardens. He waved at the drivers of each car they passed before turning left into a narrow road and coasting to a stop in a graveled parking area outside a brick building.

"Stay with me and don't talk to anyone." Without another word, he climbed out of the vehicle and waited impatiently for them to follow.

Luke strode up the steps in front of the square building. A lopsided sign fronted the façade. The faded words proclaimed the building a police station. Two men and a woman stood on the footpath outside the hardware store next door. Spirited chat complete with hand gestures ensued. When they saw Luke, they fell silent.

"Fascinating, isn't it?" Hinekiri whispered in her ear, immediately making Janaya frown. She hoped her aunt didn't do anything stupid and attract attention.

"Are you coming inside?" Luke demanded, holding the door open for them.

Janaya decided to pick her fights. She'd go along with the grumpy, arrogant male for now. "Hurry," she said, grabbing hold of Hinekiri's forearm and dragging her through the open door. At the last moment, she remembered to temper her strength but Hinekiri still winced. "Sorry," Janaya whispered. "I keep forgetting."

Janaya and Hinekiri trailed Luke through the crowded room.

A tall, slim woman with long blonde hair and glasses pushed in front of Janaya. "Luke, about time. I want your comments for the paper."

"Slept in, no doubt," a large woman in an ugly orange floral dress said. "I told you there were aliens but you refused to listen."

"There are no aliens," Luke snapped.

"Oh, dear," Hinekiri whispered. "What are we going to do? We have to help Luke. That large woman looks meaner than a Torgon."

"I think Luke would prefer us to stay out of the way," Janaya countered.

Several men and women leapt up off wooden benches and converged on Luke at once. Janaya heard aliens mentioned several times. A frown creased Luke's face, tugging at Janaya's inner guilt. She should have listened to her gut and kept away from Luke and his father. Luke seemed to sense her gaze and glanced across the crowded room at her. Instantly, a dizzying current raced through Janaya followed by intense longing to service him despite the crowd. A shiver of awareness shot to her pleasure points as she imagined them naked. Alone. Janaya sighed, quashing the inclination. They couldn't join together again. The consequences were too dire. For both of them.

"Constable, do you know where the spaceship is?" a thin, bald man demanded.

Luke brushed past the determined throng, tight-lipped. "I'll talk to you soon and answer any questions you have."

"What's wrong with now?" Marcie Montgomery said with an arch grin.

The reporter, Janaya thought. Her mouth firmed when she saw the drift of the blonde woman's eyes to Luke's masculine attributes. Had the woman no shame? She felt the subtle build up of heat behind her eyes. Holy St. Francis! She couldn't put holes in any of these people. What should she do? Panic seemed to make the heat intensify. A faint tinge of purple blurred her eyesight.

"What's wrong?" Hinekiri whispered.

"I think—Holes."

"Don't you dare!" Hinekiri snapped, taking in the threat of danger at once. She grasped Janaya's forearm and dug her fingernails in until they bit into her flesh painfully. "If you get us in trouble I will take you to the nearest cliff and toss you off. Don't think I won't. You might be my favorite niece but that won't stop me," Hinekiri warned in a terse undertone.

The anger bled from Janaya as soon as she visualized the scene her aunt described. "I'm your only niece," she murmured. She slumped back weakly against the painted wall, breathing deep and slow. Gradually the purple tinge in her eyes receded. The fight for control had zapped her energy, and she hoped like hell a Torgon didn't make an appearance. Even though she felt as weak as a newborn, Janaya tried to focus on their surroundings again, unwilling to commit another bodyguard sin—that of being taken unawares.

"Thank God you're here!" The young man behind the desk looked as though he wanted to hug Luke. His Adam's apple bobbed up and down. "Can you help Mrs. Bates? *Please.*"

Janaya propelled her aunt past the crowd of people and pushed her after Luke, following the path he'd cleared. She kept a close eye on her aunt. It would be just like Hinekiri to wander off the minute she found the opportunity. Mingling with the natives was her special thing. But somehow, Janaya didn't think that the Earth natives were ready for her aunt.

"Do you want me to process these two?" Tony asked. "I'll do it while you deal with Mrs. Bates."

"They're not under arrest," Luke said tersely.

Although Janaya couldn't read his thoughts this time, his body language told the story. *He didn't want them here.* The minute they were alone she'd insist that he let them go to source parts. They were both highly qualified and able to take care of themselves. Once the ship was repaired, they could move on and leave this planet. Then maybe Luke would find the peace he wanted.

"I insist you talk to me now," Mrs. Bates said. "Or else I'll ring the Holmes television show. They'll talk to me."

"Wait in the interview office," Luke said, praying for patience. No mistaking the threat there. Her face glowed with righteous indignation as she marched past him into the small interview room. She'd relish the spotlight if Mr. Holmes came to interview her for the Holmes show. God, what a mess. The last thing he wanted was the television media ferreting around in Sloan. "Mrs. Bates, please take a seat. I won't be long."

A roar of protest filled the room. The crowd surged forward, waving fists and shouting over the top of each other. Despite the vehement objections, Luke turned to herd Hinekiri and Janaya past the reception desk into his office. He shut the door and leaned against it as if to keep the protesters at bay.

"What parts do you need? Have you got a list?" Luke asked. He avoided looking at Janaya but temptation clawed at him anyway. A deep breath didn't ease the ache in his balls. Hell. He had to get a grip. This whole situation would escalate out of control if he wasn't careful. Luke pushed away the Technicolor scenes of Janaya that played through his head, replacing them with the worst passion-killer he could think of — Mrs. Bates and Marcie Montgomery with him in a threesome. His breath hitched in horror.

"Luke? What's wrong?" Janaya tugged on his shirtsleeve. "You've gone quite green."

"A threesome with Mrs. Bates and Marcie Montgomery will do that to a man," he muttered.

"Huh?" Janaya said.

In the interests of self-preservation, Luke edged away. He tried. He really tried but his gaze became entangled with Janaya's breasts. He knew what they felt like now, what they tasted like. "Breasts," he said. "We were talking about bre—"

Luke's face felt way overheated while a distinct pain seared through his chest. "Ah...parts for your ship!"

Hinekiri's brows arched. "I can give you a verbal list. Now let me see." A grin quivered across her lips. "We need a breastplate!" she chirped.

"He means parts for the ship," Janaya snapped.

"Did you?" Hinekiri asked. "I could have sworn—"

"Just give me a list of parts." Luke glared at Hinekiri. He liked a sense of humor as much as the next guy but not when it was aimed at him. And not when he needed to deal with the press. "I don't have time for this." He stomped over to his desk and yanked open the top right drawer. Damn, his head throbbed. His whole body ached come to that. Felt like he'd fallen down a mountain backward. Feeling the weight of a stare, he looked up from his search for a painkiller. Janaya gave him a tentative smile and the ache changed. It dived south, straight to his shaft.

The door burst open. Luke's father strode into the office. The roar of the crowd in the outer office followed and only receded when he slammed the door.

"Bad out there," his father muttered, shaking his grizzled head. "There were so many people out at the crop circles that the Sloan Woman's Division has set up a cake stall. And Ted Morrison is selling entrance tickets at his gate."

"That's the least of our problems." Luke rummaged for the painkillers again. When he found a sheet of tabs, he popped two and swallowed them down dry. "Okay. Dad, can you take Janaya and Hinekiri to Robbie's car parts? I have to see Mrs. Bates."

"Janaya will stay with you," Hinekiri said in a firm tone. She grasped his father's arm and looked up at him through a flutter of eyelashes. "Richard and I can handle the shopping."

Luke groaned inwardly. He didn't even have to think about this to know it was a bad idea to let Hinekiri go off with his father. He opened his mouth to protest but Janaya beat him to it.

"No. Absolutely not. I am coming with you. What if something happens to you? What if the Torgon arrive?"

A tense silence ensued while Janaya and Hinekiri fought it out in a duel of glares.

Luke froze sure he saw a flash of purple in Janaya's eyes. "Quit that. Hinekiri, are you sure you won't change your mind?"

Evidently, Hinekiri caught the same warning signals he did. "All right," she said in a snippy voice. "I'd like to point out that I've been managing okay on my own for some time. You sure know how to rain on a girl's parade!"

"Huh?" Janaya said.

"Never mind," Luke said. *He did not want to think about his father and sex in the same sentence.* "Just go. Out the back way. And take this." He handed Janaya a gun and then opened a second door that led to a corridor and the rear entrance to the police station.

"Told ya they'd try and sneak out the back," a short, skinny man crowed. He shoved a fluffy black microphone in Luke's face. "Can I have a comment about the aliens? What do they look like? Is there any truth that they have green suction caps all over their faces?"

His father groaned. "For God's sake. Will you people get a life?" He shoved past using his superior height to shoulder the reporter out of the way.

"Don't I know you?" the reporter asked, frowning at Luke.

"I don't think so. Dad, I'll see you back at the house." His father escorted Hinekiri past the waiting reporters while Luke grabbed Janaya by the arm for a quiet word. "Please, sweetheart. Be careful, huh? Try and keep a lid on that temper of yours. I can't afford any more attention. We have enough to cope with."

"I'll be careful. I promise."

And Luke knew she meant it. Sincerity blazed from her violet eyes.

"I do know him!" the reporter shouted. He grabbed his photographer by the shoulder. "Turn the camera on and keep filming until I tell you to stop."

"You're Luke Morgan. Married to Victoria, daughter of Sir Robert Paykel."

Aw, shit. Was his past going to follow him round for the rest of his life? Hadn't he paid enough?

"No comment?" the reporter said, his manner arch and a trifle sly. "Detective Luke Morgan was recently acquitted of heading a drug cartel in Auckland," he said for the camera.

"Luke?" Janaya stepped up beside him jerking his thoughts from the past and the hell he'd gone through trying to clear his name. "Should I help clear the area?"

Alarm exploded through Luke. "No." Hell, no! "I'm fine. Just keep an eye on Dad and Hinekiri. Keep them out of trouble. I'll be fine."

Janaya nodded and strode off without looking back. Luke couldn't have stopped his appreciation of the view to save himself. Sex appeal oozed from her with each gentle sway of her hips. The smooth stride and sensual flex of her butt tied his gut in knots. Man, he had it bad.

"Nice ass," the photographer said. "Can we get back to the subject at hand?"

Luke bit back his instinctive protest. If he didn't make a big deal then the reporter wouldn't pay any attention to her.

"Who's the broad? Does Victoria know you've replaced her already? Is it payback because Victoria played around with your best mate?"

The reporter's raised voice attracted the attention of others. Soon there were a pack of the bloody reporters all baying for his blood. Uneasiness hit him square in the gut. Luke felt the old dread, the sense of out of control and helplessness rising within him. His past was about to bite him in the ass. Knowing there was nothing he could do at this stage in the way of damage control, he decided to head back into the station to face Mrs.

Bates. He'd take one knotty problem at the time and suck in the rest. Pretend he didn't give a damn about the false drugs charges, his best friend's betrayal and the worst thing of all—his ex-wife's lack of loyalty when things got tough, her weird take on fidelity.

He moved purposefully inside and shut the door with a quiet click even though he wanted to slam it in frustration. At least Hinekiri and Janaya were with his father. Between the three of them, they'd keep out of trouble.

Then Luke thought about Hinekiri's propensity for mischief, Janaya's trigger-happy fingers and his innocent old Dad. Holy shit! Luke glanced outside the nearest window to check the sky for flying pigs.

"Luke! Please, I need help. There's so many people in the station we need crowd control."

Luke sighed and strode into the reception area to face the fray. The first person he saw was Mrs. Bates. She chatted to a reporter, waving her hands with great animation. Of course, she hadn't paid a blind bit of notice to his instructions to wait in the office. Too busy being nosy.

"Who are those women?" Mrs. Bates demanded when he stopped beside her.

"No one important," Luke said. He paused waiting for a bolt of lightning to strike him down. When it didn't happen, he gestured for Mrs. Bates to follow him to his office.

"I'll settle Mrs. Bates and then come back to get rid of the crowd," he told Tony. "Mrs. Bates, I promise I won't be much longer."

"About time! I'm a taxpayer, not a homeless dosser to brush off." Each of her chins wobbled with indignation.

Oh, yeah. He was in for a telling off. Luke resisted the urge to fidget. He hadn't suffered through a bad telling off since he and his best friend, Scott, had chopped off Melissa Hill's ponytail when they were ten.

His second-in-command looked distraught. His dark curls stuck up as though he'd plowed his hands repeatedly through his hair while he tried to deal with the large number of complaints and UFO sightings. Six people squeezed together at the reception desk, all talking at the same time. The loudest seemed to capture Tony's attention, a fact they'd cottoned on to since they were hollering loud enough to wake the dead.

"Who's the woman? The blonde? Why are you so protective?" his reporter nemesis shouted. "Is she on witness protection?"

"Witness protection? Who's on witness protection?" another reporter demanded thrusting his microphone in front of Luke.

Luke bit out a succinct curse. "Quiet!" he roared.

The din faded.

"What's that the boy said?" an elderly gent demanded.

"Quiet," his wife muttered, "then I can hear for both of us."

Luke resisted a roll of eyes but it was a close run thing. "We can't attend to your problems if you're all shouting over the top of one another. I want an orderly line and we'll deal with you one at the time."

"What time is the press conference?" someone shouted from the back.

Luke rubbed the sudden ache in the region of his chest and prayed for patience.

"Tell us who the blonde bird is and we'll leave," a reporter said.

"My cousin," Luke said folding his arms over his chest.

"If she's your cousin then why didn't you say so?" the smart-assed reporter retorted.

"Because my family has been through enough because of your muckraking in the papers." The ache in his chest intensified, not exactly painful but sharp enough to give him pause. Lord, he hoped he wasn't coming down with the flu. He didn't have time to be sick. "I wanted to protect my family's privacy."

"So what time's the press conference?"

When hell freezes over, Luke thought, but he wasn't dumb enough to spell it out. Past experience helped him along. "When we have anything of importance to report," he said.

Hopefully Hinekiri and Janaya would find the parts they needed and be on their way before any more damage was done. Luke sucked in a hasty breath as a jolt of pain pierced his ribs. Yep, that was the answer. He'd keep his father on the job, helping them search out the parts they required and they'd all avoid further messy entanglements with the press.

Chapter Six

ഔ

Janaya bent to study a sheet of rusted metal at closer quarters. She tugged it from a heap of antiquated Earth vehicle parts so she could get a better look. A sharp cramp bit into her side and Janaya dropped the metal with a loud clatter. Killer let out a startled yelp and ran to hide behind Hinekiri.

"Are you all right?" Hinekiri asked, attracted by the noise.

"No food there," Killer said. "I'll try over there."

"Fine." Janaya winced at a repeat flash but bore it in silence.

"Hmmm," Hinekiri said, planting her hands on her hips. She cocked her head to the side, a small smile playing about her lips.

Janaya glanced over her shoulder to check for Luke's father and to see what he was doing. "What does that mean?" she demanded in a harsh undertone. Her aunt had that annoying smirk on her face again. "Tell me instead of acting secretive. It's driving me nuts."

"Good girl. I'm proud of you applying yourself to language studies. It's very important to immerse yourself in local culture."

Oh, right. She was on to her aunt's subtle maneuvers. Janaya applauded in a slow clap of congratulation. "Very good. Now stop dodging the issue and tell me why you're smirking."

"How are you feeling, dear? A few aches and pains?"

"Is that another symptom of being on Earth?" Janaya said, feeling a swoop of relief clear to her stomach. For a fleeting moment, she'd worried she'd caught some insidious disease from this backward planet. "That's reassuring. I was starting to think I was ill."

Hinekiri's smirk widened to display a mouthful of white teeth. "Nothing wrong with you, my girl."

Janaya's warning antenna extended to full length. She concentrated on her aunt's expression trying to read the subtle nuances. "But? There is a but, right?"

"I never liked that Santana. The thought of being related to him —" Hinekiri broke off to give a theatrical shiver.

"Not that bonding rubbish again!"

"Yep," Hinekiri chirped. "Think about Luke and what you were doing last night."

Janaya felt her cheeks heat in a most unprofessional way. Thank the Gods that none of her fellow bodyguards were present. "No! I refuse."

"Humor me." Hinekiri's violet eyes glowed with silent laughter. "Just a little experiment. Is the cramping pain still giving you problems?"

Janaya nodded, wondering how her aunt knew. But then nothing Hinekiri did surprised her.

"Think of Luke," Hinekiri insisted.

Involuntarily, Janaya thought of Luke and how his body felt when he was buried deep inside her. Warmth flowed like molten dragon honey through her veins. Feminine juices moistened her G-thing. *Again.* A permanent scenario with that Earthman around, she thought with disgust. But that didn't mean she had to like the sensation.

"Pain gone?" Hinekiri prompted in a gentle voice.

Janaya frowned. The aches and pains had definitely eased. Could Hinekiri be telling the truth?

No! Just wait a Dalcon minute! She refused to stay here on Earth for a moment longer than necessary. Not when she'd worked so hard for her promotion to captain. No way, no how was she staying here on Earth at this godforsaken outpost called New Zealand. Her hands curled to fists. Dammit, she wanted to see her father's proud face when she received her captain's bars.

"I'm not staying here."

Killer tore over to them, barking insistently. "Purple people eaters! Purple people eaters!"

"Killer's right. Torgon," Hinekiri muttered in resignation. "I wish they'd take the hint and leave me be."

Janaya wheeled around to see a purple-suited trio heading their way. "Why does this happen to me?" she muttered with a trace of disgust. "Why couldn't they have stayed away while Luke's father is here with us?"

"With the situation between you and Luke he was bound to find out soon. This will be much easier for all of us. It's not good to have secrets from family."

"I am not staying here!" *That was not a hysterical note.* Janaya sucked in a deep breath before speaking again. "I'm going home to Dalcon as soon as the ship is repaired."

"Hmmm."

"Too late now." Janaya pulled out Luke's gun and shook her arm trying to get rid of the prickly pins and needles sensation. "Let me take care of this. And make sure Luke's father stays out of the way."

Luke's father sauntered up to them, the way he moved reminding her of Luke. The aches rapidly disappeared as a vision of Luke popped into her head. Naked, cock waving like a flag in the breeze. Horrified, Janaya shook the vision away.

"Hell's bells!" Luke's father muttered. "Get a load of the pansy purple suits those blokes have got on. They look like they're going to a fancy dress party."

"Richard," Hinekiri said, batting her eyelids in a flirtatious manner. "There's a sheet of metal down the far end of the yard. I need some help to move it."

"I'm the man for the job."

Janaya watched her aunt herd him away so his back was to the approaching Torgon. A nagging pain exploded through her chest, making her stagger. Concentrate, she told herself fiercely.

She fixed her gaze on the three Torgon and lifted her weapon. Another wave of pain swept down her arm and her heart picked up the pace. The weapon she held wavered. *She didn't need Luke.* No matter what Hinekiri said. They'd agreed to have a little fun while she was on Earth. Sex. Mutual pleasure. Warmth flowed through her veins again and her pulse slowed to normal. The hand holding the gun steadied. Control returned. Janaya stared the Torgon in the face, their intimidating stares having no effect.

"Hand over the galaxy charts and we'll let you go."

"I don't think so." Janaya squeezed the trigger. The Torgon on the right exploded into a mass of purple goo.

"Holy shit!" Luke's father had come up behind her.

"Stay back, Richard. Let Janaya handle this."

Janaya quit mucking around and sprang at the remaining two Torgon. A kick to the ribs crippled one while she calmly fired at the other. A third shot finished the last and piles of steaming purple goo were all that remained.

"It's safe now," Janaya said. "That seems to be the lot of them."

"How did…? Did you…? Does Luke know about you?" his father demanded. "And who were they?"

Janaya put her weapon away and turned to Hinekiri. She winced at the arrow of pain that shot across her chest and spread down to her stomach. "What else do we need in the way of parts? I want to leave so I can take my captain's exams. Once we leave everything will get back to normal."

"Not so fast, missy," Richard Morgan said. "You haven't answered my questions yet."

Janaya opened her mouth to tell him to quit giving orders but Hinekiri dug her in the ribs.

"I'll do the talking," she said.

"That," Janaya muttered, "is what I'm afraid of."

Hinekiri ignored her. So did Richard. Janaya shared her glare between the two oldies. If he wasn't so damned annoying

80

and the situation wasn't so wrong-time wrong-place, Janaya would have felt pleased for her aunt. Instead, pissed was the Earth word that battered her brain. And it sure fitted the occasion. She was well and truly pissed. She wanted to go home. She wanted her promotion. She wanted love.

"We're ready to leave as soon as we load this last sheet of metal on your vehicle," Hinekiri said.

"Good," Richard said. "You can explain things on the way home."

Janaya climbed into the back of the vehicle. A steady stream of pain circled her body, making her legs heavy, her body lethargic. The need to see Luke was like a craving for a heady drug. She knew the drug was bad for her but if she didn't have it, she thought she'd collapse and die.

"A spaceship!" Richard exclaimed. "Where's it parked? When can I see it? Did you make those crop circles?"

"I'd have to plead the fifth on that last one," Hinekiri said with a chuckle.

Huh? Janaya thought. Stupid Earth-speak. "I don't think—"

"That's right, missy. Don't think. Kids these days are all the same. Luke and my daughter, Lily, are always trying to tell me what to do."

Hinekiri sent her a speaking glare, one Janaya remembered distinctly from her growing up years. Janaya allowed an indignant sniff to show displeasure then she closed her eyes and started to recite the bodyguard regulations in her mind. The steady hum of anticipation that fizzed through her body ruined her concentration. The second regulation remained a mystery. All she could think was that she'd see Luke soon.

"Janaya, we're home."

Janaya's eyes snapped open to see Hinekiri's smiling face. Home? She focused on the strange gnarled tree and the white house with the garden of cheerful red flowers. *This was not home.* A shiver worked down her body.

"Janaya, let's get you inside. You need sleep." Hinekiri reached for her but Richard nudged her gently aside.

"You get the door, Hinekiri. I'll carry Janaya. Poor thing looks done in."

Janaya frowned. Something wrong. But she couldn't keep her eyes open. At least the weird tingling and the jabbing pains had subsided. She sighed deeply and breathed in essence of Luke. It seemed to surround them as Luke's father carried her inside the house. Janaya fought a yawn. Perhaps she'd sleep after all. Hinekiri would stay safe in the house.

* * * * *

By the time Luke left the police station, it was pitch-black outside. Once he left the township of Sloan and headed down the country roads leading to his house, the nagging headache he'd had all day lightened. Not surprising. He challenged anyone to deal with the crap he'd put up with all day and stay headache free.

Two battered vans were parked on the side of the road. Luke slowed and wound down his window. "You folks have a problem?"

"No problems," a longhaired man said. "Just stopped to have a snack for dinner and clear the head before we swap drivers."

Luke nodded. "Take care."

The strangers waved as he drove off.

The house was dark when Luke drove up the uneven driveway. Although it was late, the fact struck him as strange. His father didn't generally turn in this early. Ah, well. At least he could have a quiet beer to unwind. Luke parked and his groggy brain took in the fact that his father's vehicle wasn't there. His gut prickled and instincts shot to high alert. No way! His father would have rung if he intended to go off on his travels again especially since they had *guests*.

Had he rung work? Hell, Luke didn't know. He'd meant to grab his pile of messages before he left then promptly forgotten.

Had Janaya and Hinekiri gone?

The question fuelled a strange panic he didn't want to analyze.

Luke jumped from his vehicle and trotted up the path that led to the back door. It opened when he turned the handle but that wasn't out of place. Sloan was generally a crime-free town with few problems. Luke bent to remove his boots then stepped inside and switched on the light. The first thing he noticed was the small square package on the table wrapped in purple paper with a darker purple bow. The attached name-tag indicated it was for Janaya. Beside it sat a plain white envelope. His name was on the outside, written in his father's bold scrawl. The two things combined together made his gut jolt in renewed warning. The panic ratcheted up a notch. He reached for the envelope then tossed it aside.

Beer first then something to eat before he faced whatever was in the letter. The bad news could wait a bit longer.

Luke yanked open the fridge and pulled out a can. The can let out a hiss as he lifted the ring pull. Tipping back his head, he drank savoring the crisp taste of hops sliding down his parched throat. Someone had left a covered plate in the fridge, the remnants of dinner. Luke's stomach rumbled as he yanked the foil cover off the plate. Well-hell. His father had obviously gone all out to impress the ladies with his cooking. A roast beef dinner with all the trimmings. Feeling decidedly better, Luke shoved the plate in the microwave, set the timer then picked up the letter from the table. He ripped open the envelope and pulled out two sheets of paper. The familiar scribble told him his father had written one and he assumed Hinekiri had written the other.

Son,

Hot dog! When were you going to tell me we housed a pair of aliens? Some of those weird purple creatures attacked us when we were trolling for parts in the junkyard today. Then Hinekiri had to let me in on the truth. The good news is that we managed to fix the spaceship this afternoon. Evidently the damage wasn't as bad as Hinekiri let on to Janaya. Hinekiri's worried about that girl and she seems to think you can help. I know you're busy but do your best for her. After all, you seemed to be getting on okay this morning.

Luke grunted, imagining his father's sly smirk. Truth to tell, his father was probably relieved at the way he and Janaya were getting on. Luke knew part of the reason his father had gone on holiday was to get his son on track and interested in life again instead of trying to self-destruct. As much as he appreciated the help, he could do without a pair of matchmakers on his case. Especially since they had no concept of the trouble that sleeping with Janaya had caused. The woman had read his mind this morning and damn near killed them with that weird eye thing. He was wary about taking his vehicle in for repairs and had resorted to putting a stiff board over the hole to stop his stuff dropping out of the car. How the hell did he explain a hole in the backseat big enough that you could see the road out the other end? No, thank you very much but he'd choose his own bed partners without help. Luke went back to the letter.

We took the ship for a test flight.

"Which explains the two sightings over the wheat fields around five this afternoon," Luke muttered in disgust.

The ship handled well but Hinekiri wanted a longer test run. She said she'd come to Earth to do a little sightseeing and map the area for her chart collection. Evidently, she'd read about the migration of the wildebeest in the Serengeti National Park and wanted to see that. I thought, why the hell not? So, that's where we're headed. Not sure when we'll be back. Hinekiri said she's booked at a fancy lodge for a couple of weeks. It was all spur of the moment. Janaya hasn't been feeling well, something to do with travel inoculations, Hinekiri said, so she's staying with you. I'll ring if I have time to let you know what we're up to.

Love Pop.

The ping of the microwave jerked Luke from his thoughts— relief that Janaya was still here, trepidation at the thought of her reaction and a stirring of the old boy down south at the thought of a bit of playtime.

He reached for the letter from Hinekiri.

Hi Luke,

No doubt, Richard has told you we're off to deepest, darkest Africa. Can't wait since I've wanted to visit for a long time. Unfortunately, Janaya won't feel the same way. She'll feel as though she's failed in her job to protect me. She thinks the Torgon will get me and steal my charts if she's not there to run interference. I don't know where she got the idea I'm a helpless old lady.

Luke grunted. "Helpless? Huh! She's about as helpless as a platoon of soldiers." He smothered a yawn of exhaustion. Almost time to hit the sheets. Tomorrow would probably be every bit as bad as today. Luke sighed at the thought and continued reading.

But she's stubborn and won't change her mind once an idea is fixed. She wasn't too well this afternoon so we left her sleeping while we drove out to the ship and made repairs. She was still sleeping when we came back for dinner and didn't wake when we left.

I've been on my own for some time and I'm still in one piece to tell the tale. Anyway, I'm leaving it up to you to put Janaya's mind to rest. Give her a kiss from me. Welcome to the family, Luke.

Love Hinekiri.

P.S. I've left a package for Janaya — no for both of you really since I'm sure you'll benefit from the contents.

P.P.S. Killer decided she wanted to see Africa too so she's on board ship with us.

Welcome to the family. He stared at the words until they blurred. Welcome to the family. What the hell did that mean? Surely she wasn't still going on about that mumbo-jumbo regarding bonding. Load of crock. Luke glanced up to see the package sitting on the table beside his beer. He picked it up and headed up the stairs, deciding he'd better check on Janaya if she wasn't feeling well. He checked each bedroom he passed but didn't find Janaya until he reached his own room.

His heart clenched briefly. She looked so right lying in his bed with the moon shining through the open curtains highlighting her features. A frown creased his brow at the admission. His plan was to stay away from women.

All women.

Luke placed the purple package on the bedside cabinet.

She stirred and the blue sheet that covered her slithered to the ground, landing in a puddle of cotton. Janaya didn't wear a stitch of clothing.

His breath hissed out. A gentleman wouldn't stare but he couldn't tear his gaze away from the tempting sight. Luke decided he was no gentleman. His cock stirred with renewed energy as his eyes lit on her breasts. He used to think he was an ass and legs man but he was becoming addicted to her tits—the shape, the feel and definitely the taste. Luke's mouth watered as his gaze drifted over her curves and settled lower on her hairless mound. The urge to shuck his clothes and lie with her was an urgent pounding in his gut. He stepped closer.

Janaya whimpered, shifting restlessly on the bed again. Another soft cry escaped as though she were dreaming.

"Steady, sweetheart," Luke murmured. His hands went to the buttons on his shirt and he'd undone four before he realized what he was doing. The experience of having Janaya read his mind this morning made him hesitate, his hands on the fifth button. This bloody bonding business. The idea of never sliding into her body again made him aware of the vacuum in his life. At the moment, he existed. But with Janaya last night, he'd *soared*.

To hell with the consequences.

Reading between the lines of Hinekiri's message it was already too late.

Luke slid the last button free then stepped out of his trousers. Another whimper from Janaya told him he was doing the right thing. She needed him too, even if she fought the idea.

They needed each other.

Naked, he stretched out beside her. Janaya nestled up against his chest trustingly as though they belonged. Luke smoothed his hand over her cheek and couldn't resist dropping a kiss on slightly parted lips.

His cock loved the closer contact and snuggled close to Janaya. Hell, he wanted to sink into her so bad he trembled. But if she wasn't feeling well? Luke kissed her again and then pulled away intending to do the honorable thing and try to sleep.

Janaya's eyes flickered open. She gave him a sleepy smile that warmed him through and made his pulse race.

"Hi," he said. "How are you feeling?"

"Great," she whispered, reaching up to kiss him.

Luke groaned under her ministrations. *She isn't feeling well.* But he couldn't help kissing her back. Tongues dueled in a slow thrust and parry. He drew her even closer so they were pressed chest to breast.

"I love the way you taste," she murmured. "Salty. Spicy. Addictive." She punctuated each comment with a kiss that took him beyond rational thought.

"Open for me," he whispered, inserting his thigh between hers and exerting pressure until her legs splayed. Please, let her be ready for me, he prayed. He simply could not wait.

His hand slid down, past her breasts, over her flat belly, enjoying the smooth slide over silky skin. As before, her nude mound and baby-soft skin fascinated him. Time to explore further later. Luke slid his hand lower, holding his breath. Not that kissing and cuddling a little first to aid arousal wouldn't be pleasant but something inside urged him to claim her, to make her his. He couldn't have put up a fight if he wanted. The need to mate with Janaya and to brand her pounded relentlessly through his mind and body. A compulsion.

Luke made a light, passing move over her clit. She moaned at his touch. Damp, succulent warmth met his hand when he explored lower.

"Now," Janaya demanded, pushing against his hand. "I need your cock inside me now."

Eagerness burned in her too. Thank God, because he'd gone from zero to go so quickly he thought he might combust from the inside out.

Luke moved over her, craving the satiation he knew would come. He thrust into her vagina, impaling her with the force of his drive home. *Oh, man.* That felt good. So good. He withdrew and Janaya moaned a protest. Her hands clutched insistently at his shoulders.

"More," she demanded.

Luke was all for that. He rammed his cock into her. Once. Twice. His balls tightened. Pressure built but Luke fought his release.

"Fuck me harder," Janaya ordered. "Please. I need more."

Luke tried distraction with a slow, thorough kiss. For himself as much as Janaya. Despite the urgency that pounded through his blood, he wanted to make the sweet pain last. His tongue moved in and out of her mouth in time with his cock before his mouth slid away to nibble at the creamy skin of her neck. His fingers skimmed over her clit, wet and slippery with her juices.

Janaya hummed her approval. He changed the angle of his thrust slightly and pounded into her with an unrelenting beat. A gush of liquid arousal smoothed his way. Then a jolt of pure sensation zapped from his shaft. Janaya tightened her cunt around him, as if she sensed how close he was to spilling his seed. He thrust again, squeezing his eyes shut to concentrate on the euphoria that pumped through his veins.

Janaya gasped softly. He felt her pussy clench, grasping and massaging him. She gasped again and he lost it. Seed spurted from his cock in a pulsing stream. For long moments, his cock twitched and bucked inside her vagina. Luke's heart thudded. Pleasure suffused him and when he finally settled into his body again, Luke found he clutched Janaya so tightly it was a wonder she could breathe.

Luke slid his satiated cock from her and arranged her boneless body against his. He wondered if she was all right. Hell, he wasn't even sure she'd come. He'd been too busy with his own out-of-body experience.

"Thank you, Luke," she whispered against his chest. It was almost as if she'd read his mind again. Luke pulled away slightly and frowned, not comfortable with the lack of privacy reading minds might entail. An experiment, he decided, since he had to know. *Hinekiri and Dad have run off to the Serengeti.*

Luke waited for an explosion.

But nothing happened.

He settled his head back on the pillow and cuddled up to Janaya. This morning had been a fluke. That was a relief. He grinned a feel-good grin just because he could. Damn, he felt supremely excellent. Every tired, achy muscle felt rejuvenated and ready to go another round.

Janaya stretched in a languid move like a cat. Her breasts flattened against his chest. His hands rubbed up and down her back, pressing her closer. Each delicate move of her body hiked his pulse until his breathing sounded like a steam engine.

"Again?" she asked, arching her brows in a questioning move.

"Yeah."

Janaya moved away from Luke and sat up. She peered at him through lazy, half-open eyes. "I think I'll have a shower," she said. A playful laugh escaped when she saw Luke's disappointment. "I was definitely gonna invite you. I still need help getting everything to work properly." A lie, of course, but she wanted to encourage him. It seemed to her that a shower for two would be much more fun. Her gaze flickered down his body to light on his penis. Then she looked up and saw he watched her. Janaya licked her lips and hid a grin when she heard him groan. The Earthman was so much fun to tease.

Chapter Seven

&

"I could manage a shower," Luke said in a husky voice.

"We'd better be quiet or we'll wake my aunt and your father."

Luke clasped her hand and tugged her against his side as he led her down the passage to the bathroom. His palm was calloused from working with his hands. The contrasting texture sent a shudder through her just as it did when he touched her breasts or smoothed his hands down her flanks.

Janaya thought briefly about her aunt's assertions—that the more sex they had, the closer they cemented. She thrust the thought away, not liking the idea any more than when the subject had first been broached. She and Luke had talked about it. They had both agreed this was a short-term thing that would last until she left. With no regrets.

Hand in hand, they turned into the bathroom together. Luke switched the light on and shut the door after them and bolted it. Good idea, she thought in approval. She didn't want Hinekiri to walk in on them because it was so easy to picture that happening. That would be really embarrassing even if her aunt did approve. And she didn't like the idea of any other female seeing Luke's naked body. She stroked his broad chest, pinching one of the flat disc-like nipples as her hand cruised past. Her property, she thought with a trace of possessiveness she did her best to ignore.

"Do you remember how to turn the shower on?" Luke teased as he nibbled down her neck, lightly scraping at the tender skin below her ear.

Janaya eased away from Luke, ready to take the challenge. "Of course, I remember," she said loftily and she reached into the shower and twisted the tap. Instantly, cold water hit her mid-chest. She let out a surprised yelp while Luke had the audacity to laugh.

After tugging her out of danger, Luke crowded her against the white vanity unit. He lifted her up without warning and sat her on top, her back to the mirror.

"That's cold," Janaya said with a laugh. She tried to wriggle off the icy surface.

"But not as cold as the water, I bet." Luke stayed her with a kiss, his hands massaging her nipples to peaks. He bent over her and licked the droplets of water off her skin. "It comes from a spring and takes a while to run hot."

Steam started to billow from the shower creating a warm private haven. The mirror misted over and cold became a faint, discomforting memory.

Luke drew one nipple in his mouth. He pulled on it hard and the corresponding tug of sensation rocketed straight to her clitoris. Janaya hummed her appreciation. She really liked it when he did that. Santana hadn't liked to touch her anywhere except the joining place and from what she'd heard, the rest of the Dalcon males went about business in exactly the same way as Santana. Certainly gave a Dalcon female fodder for thought. She wondered if that was why Hinekiri had never mated and spent so many long months away from home. Somewhere, there was a business opportunity here for—

Luke let her nipple pop out of his mouth and Janaya groaned in disappointment. They both looked down at the moistened tip of her breast. A small grin played on Luke's lips.

"Just making sure you had your mind on the job," he said.

"Believe me, you have my total concentration. And why wouldn't you? You make me feel good. *Very good*," Janaya purred. She leaned her weight back on her elbows, thrusting her breasts forward in a silent offering.

"You know what?" Luke didn't wait for her to answer. He stood back and reached into the shower. Seconds later, the water stopped.

"Aren't we having a shower?" Janaya didn't have to pretend disappointment.

"We will," Luke promised, "but I didn't want a cold shower. That wouldn't have the right effect at all." He chuckled as they both glanced down at his engorged cock. "I thought we'd play a little first."

The wicked glint in his eyes sent her pulse soaring. Her heart missed a startled beat before it galloped away, signaling the excitement she felt to the rest of her body. "What did you have in mind?"

With his mercenary's smile intact, he slowly moved his hands downward, skimming either side of her body until he reached her thighs. "Open up, little girl," he whispered. "Let me in."

Luke tugged on her body so her ass balanced on the very edge of the vanity unit. With his masculine strength, he parted her thighs more insistently and stepped in between. Janaya glanced down to see his cock positioned exactly at her entrance.

"Are you ready for me, sweetheart?" His hands traced across her mound, lightly circling and pressing until she shuddered with anticipation. Luke parted her slick folds, his thumb skimming closer to her clit with each teasing pass. Moisture wept from her pussy, trickling slowly down her leg. Janaya wriggled, wanting Luke to hurry then it occurred to her he was enjoying teasing her. A quick glance at his eyes confirmed the fact. Janaya decided it was time for her to explore Luke a little more fully so she had experience to take home to Dalcon along with the memories.

Luke strummed across her swollen flesh with a soft pressure that was enough to tease and taunt but not enough to bring her into a toe-curling orgasm. "Do you like that?"

"Being teased?" she asked in a tense voice. Slowly, she leaned into him, her gaze enmeshed with his. Her nipples dragged across the light coating of hair on his chest. A smile appeared as she experienced a ticklish sensation that created an interesting side effect. Her nipples pulled to tight buds as she traced a round circle on his chest and Luke's fingers stilled. The man had a fascination with her breasts. She rubbed against him again, managing to wring a sharp intake of breath from him.

His eyes darkened and a slow, easy smile bloomed. "Are you making this into a contest, sweetheart?"

"And if I am?" A kiss. She wanted a kiss. Janaya twirled her arms around his neck and tried to concentrate on her own explorations of his body instead of the resumption of the teasing passes his thumb made over her clitoris.

"I'd say that since this is a win-win situation, do your worst."

Janaya's eyes narrowed at his challenge. Did he think she'd back off because she wasn't as experienced as him? Not likely. She loved a good dare. And she knew she'd win. She bent her head and stroked her tongue across one of his flat masculine nipples. A salty tang exploded in her mouth. She sucked lightly then nipped him. His engorged penis jerked against her belly. Score one for the visiting team, she thought with a trace of smugness. Janaya pressed against his shoulders, signaling she wanted to get down. In one smooth move, she leapt down and dropped to her knees before Luke. She ran her hands over the smooth surface of his penis.

He sighed heavily, his hand coming to rest on the top of her head, masculine fingers tangling in the loose strands of her hair.

She traced a vein that ran the length before circling the plum-colored head with soft, teasing pressure. A drop of clear liquid formed in the tiny slit at the end. Curious, Janaya flicked her tongue over the small slit to lick up the drop. It tasted salty and not unpleasant, but best of all her action made Luke groan. Hiding her smile, she traced the length of his hot, distended flesh with her tongue. Luke's fingers flexed in her hair and she glanced up to catch the look of rapture on his face.

Following instinct, she drew his cock into her mouth and sucked lightly in much the same manner Luke did when he drew on her breasts. She massaged his balls enjoying the knowledge they were hard and aching because of her. Luke groaned.

Her tongue swiped across the tip with delight. His hands tightened, tugging on a lock of hair. His hips jerked then he groaned again and thrust gently, his penis entering her mouth further. The blunt end hit the back of her throat before he pulled back. Janaya saw his eyes were squeezed tight and his large body shook. Fascinated, she sucked harder and when he thrust into her mouth again, she wanted to smile. The power she had over him turned her on, made her impossibly hot. Her feminine spot wept for him. If anything, Luke grew larger inside her mouth. She tensed for a moment then relaxed trusting him not to hurt her.

After another slow thrust, he suddenly withdrew and grabbed her around the waist. Janaya let out another startled yelp at the icy-cold sensation on her bottom as she hit the vanity again. Luke stepped between her legs and plunged his cock into her weeping pussy with one swift move that stole her breath. *Oh, yes.* This was exactly what she wanted. Luke withdrew and slammed into her open body again. Her back pressed against the misty mirror while her hands circled his neck and held on tight. Janaya arched into his next pumping thrust and the first greedy fingers of climax streaked through her body.

"Again, Luke," she half-pleaded, half-groaned.

One of his hands circled her breast then pinched her nipple hard to coincide with his next thrust. Pain and pleasure met. An euphoric rush swept through her body and Janaya screamed her pleasure. Luke jabbed into her rapidly with several lunges then stilled, the ripple of him deep inside bringing an answering pulse from her pussy.

Luke hugged her tight then pulled away to rub his sweaty forehead across her face. "I think you're gonna kill me," he said. "I know I need food."

His stomach rumbled loud enough for Janaya to hear. "Shower first," she said, "then food."

* * * * *

"Are you sure we don't need clothes?" Janaya asked. "What if Hinekiri or your father come downstairs to the kitchen? Their doors are shut—" Janaya frowned suddenly and Luke watched the process with fascination. The cute wrinkle of her pert nose made him want to kiss it, to kiss her and her worries away.

"You don't think they're…ah…together?"

Luke knew they were together and quite frankly, he didn't like to think too hard about his father's sex life. "They're old enough to know what they're doing. Hurry, I'm hungry."

"But what if—"

"They won't come downstairs," Luke said firmly. Guilt brushed against his conscience. He should tell her they'd left but knew it would upset her. It would sure put a screaming halt on his sex life and selfishly, he didn't want that so he intended to put off the bad news for as long as possible.

Janaya bit her bottom lip and instantly, Luke wanted to soothe it. He stepped close enough to brush his thumb across her mouth. Her subtle perfume, the scent of wildflowers and the tinge of sandalwood from his soap, jerked his thoughts to sex and how quickly he could shove inside her sweet pussy again. But this time, he held himself to a kick-ass hot kiss. He thrust his tongue deep into the warmth of her mouth, tasting and savoring her before finally pulling away.

He couldn't do it.

The lie sat like a heavy weight on his shoulders.

He sighed. "The reason I'm not worried about Dad and Hinekiri coming downstairs to find us naked is because they're not here."

"What?" Janaya shrieked. She jerked away from him and glared.

Alarm rose in Luke. "Please don't look at me like that, sweetheart. I don't like that dark purple in your eyes and I sure as hell don't want to explain to the medics why I'm naked as a baby and have a huge hole in my gut!"

To his relief, Janaya concentrated her fury on his father's favorite recliner chair. That was better. The chair needed recovering—hell, it would look better at the dump.

"Why didn't you stop them? You've seen the Torgon."

Luke hated the defeated wobble in her voice. "I didn't know. They wrote letters and left them for me. They're over on the sideboard if you want to read them."

Janaya covered the length of the kitchen in three strides. She plucked the sheets of paper off the wooden surface and scanned them. Then she glanced at him. "Okay. I can't go after them because I don't have transportation. All we can do is wait."

Luke nodded, accepting her reasoning as truth.

"Aren't you worried?" she burst out. "They might die and if they do the guilt will eat me alive."

"Of course I'm worried," Luke muttered. "My life has been like an adventure down a dark rabbit hole since aliens Smith & Jones hit Sloan. But Dad sounds excited in his letter so I'm going to try not to think about the things that can go wrong."

"I'm not going to make it back to take my captain's exam."

Luke's heart twisted at the anguish in her voice. "It's important to you."

"Yeah." She laughed but the sound held little humor. "I want to make my father proud of me."

"I'm sure your father is proud of you. Hinekiri is."

Janaya's shoulders slumped and her breasts jiggled but he tried to ignore that bit to concentrate.

"My father hates me."

"What?"

"My mother and brother died in an accident when I was young. My father and I survived. I've tried but I think he still misses them."

Luke thought he understood. Janaya was trying to prove herself to a selfish, self-absorbed man, one who didn't deserve her love and loyalty. "There's nothing we can do until Hinekiri and Dad return." He brushed a lock of blonde hair away from her face and smiled at her, hoping to ease her turbulent thoughts with a little banter. "Meantime, there's no reason why we can't have fun."

Luke reached past Janaya to open the pantry. He pulled out a bottle of runny honey and a can of aerosol cream. Then just in case Janaya preferred things a little tarter, he opened the fridge and grabbed a tub of yogurt. Strawberry yogurt—his favorite kind.

"What are you doing?"

Luke licked his lips, his cock leaping in hedonistic anticipation. "We're going to eat," he said. "Don't tell me you've gone off the idea of food."

Chapter Eight

"You don't have to come to work with me," Luke said. It wasn't difficult to see how restless Janaya was. He'd made the suggestion so she could keep busy. He wasn't gonna suggest doing housework, that was for sure. A man could get into trouble trying to pigeonhole women. No telling how an alien would react to the suggestion.

"Might as well," Janaya said with a distinct lack of enthusiasm.

Luke wished they could stay in bed. They certainly communicated perfectly there but, unfortunately, Janaya was like a kid trying to cross a sun-heated beach in bare feet. She jumped at every noise and some he didn't even hear. He made a pot of coffee and shoved a couple of pieces of bread down the toaster.

"Did you open the package your aunt left for you?"

Janaya nodded. "It was a book."

Luke grabbed two china mugs and poured coffee. He carried them over to the kitchen table and dropped into a seat opposite Janaya. A grin curled his lips as he shunted one of the mugs across the table to Janaya. His lover. Man, he liked the sound of that. Even if Janaya was determined to head back to Dalcon the minute Hinekiri returned.

"What sort of book?" He sipped his black coffee with a sigh of pure appreciation. Nothing like a cup of coffee and an armful of shapely woman early in the morning.

"The Kama Sutra," Janaya said.

Luke almost spat the mouthful of coffee at her. "Did you look at it?" he managed when he could breathe again.

"No. It's still upstairs. I'll look at it later."

"What's wrong? I told you not to worry about Hinekiri and my father. You admitted yourself that she's looked after herself for all these years."

Janaya's frown intensified to a full-out grimace. "Yes, I'm worried about my aunt. I admit it. But it's not just that. I'm worried about missing my captain's exam because we won't get back to Dalcon on time."

There was something else. He could tell by the shadows in her beautiful violet eyes. "And?"

"And if I'm away from my troop much longer they'll declare me AWOL."

Luke took another sip of coffee. "You've got a good excuse. Surely they'll judge each case on the circumstances?"

"No second chances." Janaya shrugged carelessly but Luke could tell it bothered her big-time.

The toast popped up with a loud splat. Luke stood to retrieve it. He placed a slice on the plate in front of Janaya and settled back in his seat. "No point worrying about it. You can't do anything until Dad and Hinekiri return."

"But, Luke. What if something happens to Hinekiri? What if she dies? It will be all my fault."

Janaya looked at him with tear-filled eyes. His heart wrenched in his chest. Weeping females made him nervous but in this case, he wanted to help. He stood and walked around the table to squat at her side.

"Sweetheart, if there's one thing I've learned in my life it's that you can't force another person to fit the mold you design. You're not responsible for other people's decisions or their actions."

"Maybe." Her voice sounded thick with unshed tears.

"Not maybe. Definitely." Luke tucked a lock of blonde hair behind her ear, his insides shifting with a surge of tenderness he hadn't thought he'd ever feel again. Can the feelings, he thought.

Janaya is leaving as soon as she's able. Besides, he wasn't ready for entanglement with a female again. He needed to simply enjoy the moment because that was all they'd ever have.

Janaya picked up the slice of toast and nibbled off a corner. Just to please Luke. He didn't understand but then how could he? She wasn't sure she understood herself.

"Will it be all right if I go to work with you? Won't it raise more questions?"

"I told them you were my cousin. And if necessary, we can broaden the story." Luke grinned. "How do you feel about being a cop?"

Janaya shrugged again. "Sure."

"Just don't bring out that weapon of yours or tell anyone to poke their fingers in their ears. It makes me nervous when you do that."

Half an hour later they were on their way into town, a companionable silence between them as Luke negotiated the country roads. On the outskirts of town, the traffic became heavier and suddenly came to a stop. When it didn't start moving again, Luke pulled over and they both got out to investigate.

"Oh-oh. Trouble. There's the reporters again," Janaya murmured in a low tone. "They've spotted us."

"Ignore them," Luke said, even though he knew the reporters would be right in their faces before much time lapsed.

They strode along the line of vehicles. Janaya grasped Luke's arm. "Luke, this doesn't sound good. They're alien hunters. They've come to check out the UFO sightings."

"Damn, I thought this would blow over. Let me know if you overhear anything else useful."

Janaya nodded and fell in behind Luke, letting him take the position of responsibility. Luke sauntered up to the van parked at the front of the queue of vehicles. A group of men, women and children sat in a circle on the side of the road around a small portable gas stove. They looked like they were making tea. A crowd of locals stood gaping at them, spreading out into the middle of the road and disturbing the traffic flow into town.

"Have you broken down?" Luke asked, instinct telling him to tread easily before he started to throw his official status around. "Can I help with anything?"

"Who are you?" One of the men stood.

Luke recognized him as the man with the long hair he'd spoken to the previous night. "I'm the local policeman."

"Just the man we want to see. Do you know it's against the law to withhold information on aliens?" The man spoke in a loud voice that carried and reached the locals as well as his group.

Luke laughed. "What aliens? There aren't any aliens in Sloan. That's unless you count the pictures in this morning's paper."

"There were sightings again yesterday evening. I put it to you that this is a conspiracy to hide the truth!"

Mrs. Bates pushed her way to the front of the crowd and planted bejeweled fingers on fleshy hips. "Well, I have to agree with the man. My sister and I saw the UFO last night, but the local police — you — have just fobbed us off with excuses."

Luke groaned inwardly. Mrs. Bates. That was all he needed. And his father and Hinekiri — he could cheerfully murder them for leaving him to face the locals. From the corner of his eye, Luke saw the children of the group handing out pamphlets to the groups of locals who lingered to watch the show.

"If you're not broken down, can you please move along? You're blocking traffic and since it's sale day today there's more traffic than normal." A horn blared at the end of the line of traffic to emphasize Luke's point. "The cattle truck must get through to the sale yards."

"We can't move until we finish our breakfast," the man said.

Luke ground his teeth together. "You will finish breakfast down at the station if the traffic doesn't get moving in three minutes."

The truck driver leaned on his horn again. A loud moo filled the air.

"Are you threatening me?" the man demanded.

Luke looked him square in the eye. "No, sir. I am stating facts."

Luke groaned inwardly when he noticed the truck driver with the load of cattle climb down from his cab. The bandy-legged man stomped up the road and halted in front of Luke.

"Are you going to do something?" he demanded. "Or do you want me to unload the bulls right here and herd them to the sale yards on foot? Make up your mind, man. I don't have time for this crap. I have two more loads to pick up before nine." With each furious word, he sprayed saliva. The aroma of garlic filled the air.

Luke took half a step back to get out of range. He wiped his cheek with distaste and gave silent thanks that he wasn't a vampire. "Go back to your truck, Bill. I'll have the traffic cleared in minutes." Luke waited until Bill had turned and stomped back to his truck. "Janaya, can you move the bystanders on for me while I get traffic moving?" He waited for Janaya to nod assent, prayed she didn't pull out any weapons then walked back over to the driver of the van.

"We're moving," the man said, "but only because we're finished our breakfast. We're heading to the camping ground and once we're settled we're starting an investigation into the UFOs."

A woman wearing a long flimsy skirt stepped up beside the man. "Never fear, Henry," she said. "The truth will out."

It would if Mrs. Bates had her way. Luke glanced across at Janaya as she charmed the locals and persuaded them to move along. He wondered what they intended to do with any aliens they caught.

The woman climbed into the passenger seat of the first van. The man slid into the driver's seat. He wound down the window and leaned out to give Luke some parting advice. "We're not going to leave without conducting a full investigation."

The two vans drove off in the direction of the camping ground on the outskirts of town. The second van backfired leaving Mrs. Bates coughing in a cloud of black smoke. Luke bit back a grin at the poetic justice and turned his attention to getting the rest of the road cleared. Bill honked his horn, again, as he maneuvered his stock-truck down the narrow street and turned left to the stockyards.

"Did I disperse the people in the proper manner?" Janaya asked, a twinkle of mischief in her violet eyes.

Luke checked to make sure no one was within hearing range. "Sure did, sweet stuff."

"Those people are going to make trouble," Janaya said. She produced one of the leaflets Luke had seen the young children handing out.

"They intend to capture an alien and use it for breeding purposes," she read.

Breeding! The events of the previous night flickered through Luke's mind like a movie on fast forward. Breeding! He glanced at Janaya to see if she was thinking the same thing he was. Her expression remained the same—calm with a small smile.

"I...We didn't use—" Luke broke off, the gravity of the situation making him sweat. Sweet heaven! They hadn't used contraception last night. Or this morning.

Luke checked the vicinity for eavesdroppers again. "Can someone from Dalcon breed with an Earthman?" he blurted. One particular Earthman? *Him.*

Janaya frowned and for the first time Luke wished he could read her mind. There were times when the woo-woo factor might come in handy.

"I don't know," she said finally. "Hinekiri would know."

103

Luke's breath eased out. Okay. Perhaps it wasn't such a big deal. Hinekiri had known they'd had sex. She hadn't said a thing apart from letting him know how pleased she was that he and Janaya were getting on so well. Luke thought about sex for a moment and his thoughts wandered to his father. Alone with Hinekiri on the spaceship. His thoughts screeched to an appalled halt. Nope, he wasn't thinking about that. He had his own problems!

"I'll ask Hinekiri as soon as she gets back."

Janaya's lips tightened. "Which had better be soon."

Luke hoped it was soon too but not for the same reasons. They'd agreed this would be a short-term fling. And that's where he wanted to leave the matter.

Luke touched Janaya's arm. "How do you feel about doing some actual police work?"

Interest peaked on Janaya's face and Luke congratulated himself on a great distraction. They returned to his vehicle and drove to the police station. Luke parked out the back and they entered the station via the back entrance.

"Seems things are a bit more peaceful here today," he said.

"When there are no more UFOs, things will probably settle down in town too," Janaya said. "I wish we could contact Hinekiri to warn her to make sure the ship is cloaked before she flies over."

"It can't be helped. We'll face the UFO problem when we have to." He guided Janaya into his office and shut the door. "How about a kiss to help me through the staff meeting I'm about to call?"

"Just a kiss?"

Temptation nipped at him. His cock stirred, tenting his navy blue uniform trousers. Luke took a deep breath. "Damn, I'd like to," he muttered.

Janaya grinned. "Good. Hold that thought until later."

"All right. If you're not going to let me play, you're gonna have to work."

"Spoilsport."

Luke grinned. "You'll keep. Later." He walked through to the reception area. One of the temps manned the desk. "Tony is out trying to catch Mabel. She's run loose through Longford Park and run amuck in the pensioners' vegetable gardens."

"Who's Mabel?" Janaya asked.

"Old man Jacob's goat," Luke said with a roll of eyes. "Believe me, we've had a lucky escape. I spent two hours trying to catch her last month when she made a bid for freedom. Any other problems? Apart from the UFOs."

The receptionist grimaced. "That's all anyone's talking about. I'm glad I work in the police station where it's safe. I don't want to run into any aliens and have scars from being dissected!" She shivered theatrically before she reached for the ringing phone.

Luke chuckled on seeing Janaya's jaw drop. He used a forefinger to close her gaping mouth.

"What planet is she on?" Janaya hissed. "That sort of thing went out with space suits and moon boots."

"I'll take your word for it," he said.

The receptionist hung up. "Luke, two boys have gone missing in the bush on the south side of town."

"How long have they been missing?"

"They were with a group of scouts who camped out overnight. They were missing at breakfast."

"Call the fire brigade boys and we'll organize a search grid." Luke hurried back to his office and yanked open a cupboard to grab out his search and rescue kit. Janaya strode after him.

Chapter Nine

ଛ

Janaya gripped a handhold and hung on tight as Luke drove over the rutted track that wound through bush so thick the sun's rays were kept out. The air smelled moist and fragrant, redolent with moss and ferns and the rich soil.

"How much further?"

"Another ten minutes or so to the summit then we walk up to the campsite where they spent last night. The scout master and the rest of the scout pack are still there."

Two other vehicles were parked at the summit when they arrived. Janaya helped Luke unload ropes, torches and climbing harnesses. They divvied up the gear and prepared to move out.

Janaya halted Luke. "Wait for a second. I might be able to hear them."

She cocked her head, suddenly ultra-aware of the bush sounds. The guttural sound of the plump black bird, with the tuft of white feathers at its throat, sitting on the branch of a nearby tree and the soft, musical tinkle of a stream rushing down the hillside. They'd passed a flock of sheep as they raced up the hill, sending them scattering across the road and she heard their bleats as they grazed on the new grass.

"Anything?" Luke asked after a few minutes of silence.

"No. Wait!" Faint voices carried on the breeze. Janaya tensed and then her shoulders slumped. "I can hear voices but I think they're the scouts. I can hear them calling names."

"Come on," Luke said. "It was worth a try. Once we get up to the summit, we should be able to see more of the hill. The bush on the far side isn't as thick since it's second growth. The trees aren't as big."

106

None of Luke's words made much sense so she merely nodded and fell into step behind him. Despite the seriousness of the situation, she was enjoying spending time with Luke. She loved the way he teased her and the way he looked at her with his eyes dark and glowing—as if he wanted to eat her up. He made her feel warm inside. It was a strange yet comforting sensation. Her gaze drifted down Luke's body, taking time to appreciate him. His movements were swift and sure and he carried himself with a commanding air that appealed to Janaya. A broad set of shoulders, packed with muscle tapered down to slim hips and a truly memorable butt. Janaya loved to run her hands down his body. Her cheeks heated at the thought. Of course, she liked to touch the man anywhere he'd let her.

Despite her regulation fitness, Janaya's breath came in pants. Her clothes clung to her body and the G-thing beneath her jeans dampened with her desire. She hadn't exactly picked the right moment but she wondered what it would feel like to mate outdoors with the heat of the sunshine on her skin. She scanned the area and through a break in the trees saw a small, sunny clearing. Another time, she decided. And definitely before she and Hinekiri returned to Dalcon.

Luke slowed and waited for Janaya to join him. His small, private smile warmed her even more. "The campsite is just over that hill." He pointed to a break in the trees and when Janaya squinted, she could make out patches of bright yellow against the green of the grass. They looked similar to the shelters her bodyguard team used when they were out on training exercises.

Janaya stilled to listen again. Beside her, Luke paused. She could hear the steady beat of his heart and found herself regulating her breathing so they breathed in unison.

"Hear anything?"

Mortified heat rose up to color her cheeks then seeped down to her breasts. Why couldn't she keep her mind on the job instead of mooning after Luke and thinking of the pleasure he sent soaring through her body. A dull, edgy heat pooled between her legs and that annoyed her.

"Janaya?"

"I wanted to be sure," she lied after hurriedly tuning into the background noises instead of fixating on Luke. This time, the shouts of children and the deeper voices of adults were clearly audible. "I can hear the group. The mature humans sound worried," she observed.

"It was cold last night. I know they were well prepared but since we're not sure how long they've been missing, we might be looking at a worse case scenario. Hypothermia."

Luke picked up the pace leaving Janaya to follow. Her gaze drifted to his butt, stuck there like the tiny magnets Luke's father kept on his cooler box. Refrigerator, she corrected herself. His long strides covered the ground rapidly and they soon reached the clearing where the scouts had camped for the night. And that was lucky because her body was on slow simmer and almost at the boil. If they'd been alone for much longer, she might have succumbed to the temptation to toss him on the ground and have her way with him.

"Luke." A big man, wearing eyeglasses, shook his hand with clear relief. "We've been searching since seven this morning. It's as if they've disappeared off the face of the Earth."

Luke speared a glance in her direction and it was easy to read his concern. Torgon. She jerked her head in the negative. The Torgon were after Hinekiri's charts. The rest of Earth's inhabitants weren't in danger unless they got between the Torgon and the charts.

Like Luke.

The thought popped into her head and wouldn't leave. Great. Another person to worry about. She was collecting responsibilities like Hinekiri collected souvenirs from each place she visited.

"Don't worry, Sam. We'll find them. Sam, this is my cousin, Janaya. She's in law enforcement too."

Sam nodded but the worry remained on his freckled face. "Good to have your help. We have to find them. I don't want to explain to Mrs. Bates that I've lost her precious grandson."

Janaya caught Luke's grimace before it smoothed out into a professional mask.

"Don't worry," he repeated. "We'll find them. The volunteer fire brigade is on their way. I'm going to divide the area up into sectors. My suggestion is to get the kids home. Can you organize some of the parents in your group to take them back to Sloan? I'd like you to stay here to coordinate the search and direct the fire brigade boys when they arrive."

Sam nodded rapidly, his eyes blinking behind the glass that covered his eyes. Although the man was worried, Janaya sensed he was pleased to be asked to stay and help. Janaya wondered if he feared Mrs. Bates as much as Luke did. The woman was certainly a fearsome sight when she became riled.

Luke pulled a waterproof map from the pack he wore. "Show me where you've searched."

Sam pointed at the map with his forefinger. "We spent the early evening down by the river fishing for trout. We built a fire and cooked them here at the campsite. Spent the evening roasting marshmallows and telling ghost stories. All the boys were present. I counted them and checked off the roll."

"So they've wandered off during the night or early morning before you got up," Janaya said. She glanced at the young humans who sat in a huddled group in the middle of the clearing with the adults keeping watch. "Have you questioned the boys?"

"Yes." Sam nodded. "None of them know anything."

"Might pay to question them again," she said. "Why don't I start that while you and Sam organize the search grid?" The moment the words were out of her mouth, she paused. She'd taken over! Her eyes widened in shock and she glanced at Luke to read his reaction to her orders. She found him grinning and let out the breath she'd been holding with a slight hiss.

"Go ahead," he murmured, his eyes twinkling.

Janaya ambled over to the boys but couldn't prevent a glance over her shoulder to see if Luke watched. He did. The fact warmed her through. Reassured he wasn't going anywhere, she concentrated on the humans. "Hello." Janaya scanned the circle of small faces. "I'd like to question them individually," she murmured to one of the adults acting as chaperone. "I'm with the police," she added.

"You can talk to them over there," the man said pointing at the campfire and a large log perfect to sit on. "I'll send them over one by one."

Janaya walked over to the log and sat to wait for her first victim. A small dark-haired boy arrived first.

"Do you have any idea where the two boys have gone?"

The boy shook his head. Although he trembled slightly, his pulse remained only slightly elevated. Janaya decided he spoke the truth. She worked her way through the boys, using her enhanced senses to judge if they were lying. The second to last boy wouldn't meet her gaze. His voice trembled and broke before he started to talk so fast his words blurred in one long string of nonsense.

He knew something but Janaya decided to wait for Luke. She nodded when the boy finished telling her he'd gone straight to sleep after the ghost stories. She talked to the last boy and ascertained he spoke the truth.

Luke looked up from the map. "Anything?"

"The boy with the green shirt," she said. "He knows something but he's not talking."

"Sam, would you mind sending him over?" Luke asked. When Sam walked away and was out of earshot, Luke said, "Wanna play good cop, bad cop?"

"Does it involve those steel bands?"

Luke snorted a laugh. "Handcuffs?" Interest, along with speculation, lit his eyes. "How do you like the sound of a private party later? We can use the handcuffs then."

110

"I'd need more details," Janaya murmured.

"Details, I have," he murmured wickedly. "Remind me later. Here's the kid. Follow my lead."

The boy walked with slow, reluctant steps, finally coming to a halt in front of them. His brown eyes blazed with belligerence. "I don't know nothin'. I already told the lady cop that."

"I think you do," Luke said in a hard voice. "And if I don't get the answers I want, I'll have you in jail so quick your head will spin."

"You wouldn't put him in jail!" Janaya said. That didn't sound like Luke.

"Try me," Luke snapped. He slipped a wink at Janaya over the top of the boy's head. "What were Matt and David doing? Where were they going?"

"They were going to look for aliens!" the boy burst out. "They can stick whatever they want in my locker. I don't care. I'm not going to jail! They told me they were going to find an alien and sell it to the UFO hunters."

"Where were they going? Which direction?" Janaya asked, fighting her need to break cover and snarl like a bad cop. It was difficult to hide her distaste.

"Up to the cliffs." Worry and fear pulsated off him in waves. "I promised I wouldn't tell."

"We won't tell," Janaya promised. "But think about this. If something bad has happened and they need help, they'll be pleased that you helped. You'll be a hero."

The boy's face brightened. "Hey, yeah!" he said.

"You can go back to your friends now," Luke said.

They watched the boy run back to the group.

Luke checked his watch. "Let's go. I have a bad feeling about this." He bent to pick up his pack and slipped the straps over his shoulders. "I'll get Sam to delegate search areas when the rest arrive—just in case they're not where they told the kid. We'll take the cliff sector."

Janaya picked up the coiled rope she'd carried up along with a smaller pack. Luke wasn't the only one with a bad feeling.

Half an hour later, Janaya stood an arm's length away from the edge of a cliff. Her eyes were focused on a tall, stately tree while Luke lay on his belly and peered over the edge.

"You're right," he said. "I can see one of the boys at least. I'll take your word that they're both there."

Janaya gulped. The bark on the trunk of the tree was very smooth. Or at least it looked smooth. Whether it felt the same way, was anyone's guess.

"Janaya? Are you listening?"

"Yes. What sort of tree is that?"

"Kauri. And good try but no cigar. Our ropes aren't going to reach that far down."

He was going to suggest she go down there. She just knew it.

The muscles of her stomach trembled. She was way too close to the edge. Janaya took a step back. "No."

"No, what?" Luke said, climbing to his feet and dusting off his hands.

"I'm not climbing down there."

"Of course not." Astonishment sounded in his voice, and Janaya's shoulders relaxed. "You'll fly," he said.

"No!" Memories of her childhood rose up to taunt her—her tantrum because they'd left her toy soldier in the spaceport café; her father's fury because they'd missed their allocated slot to fly and the vicious storm that had swept through the sky just before their arrival at Dalcon. Janaya swallowed and backed even further away from the cliff edge. How could she explain her paralyzing fear to Luke? She recalled the long agonizing hours perched on the edge of the mountain with nothing but empty air beneath while they waited for rescue from the crash site. She remembered her older brother crying then finally falling silent forever and the steady drips of blood that trickled from the gaping wound on her mother's leg. Her father's grief had been a palatable thing even for a child of six cycles. He'd never forgiven her. When rescue had finally arrived, it had been too late for her mother and brother. Her father had suffered broken limbs that gradually mended while she had escaped without a scratch. Janaya knew her father still blamed her for the accident. He'd shouted it was her fault because they'd missed their time slot and become trapped in the storm. And he'd followed that up with blaming her for the death of his heir and his beloved mate.

"You rescued me," Luke said, stepping up beside her and cupping her face in his palms. "You can rescue the boys."

Janaya took comfort from his confidence but not enough to agree to his plan. "The only reason I went over the cliff to rescue you was because Hinekiri pushed me."

Luke's eyes narrowed thoughtfully.

Janaya took one look and took two rapid steps backward. "No. Absolutely not! I can't go over that cliff. I just can't."

"How do you get on as a bodyguard if you're afraid of heights?"

"I am not afraid. I'm a good bodyguard. I would have got that promotion!"

"Of course you would." Luke's face gentled. "All right. Here's the plan. I'll climb down to the boys or as far as I can with the ropes."

The idea of Luke climbing over the rim of the cliff terrified her. She curled her hands around his biceps and held tight. "You can't. You can't climb down there."

"There's no one else to do it," he said simply.

Janaya heard a soft whimper. The sound reminded her of the cries her brother had made while they waited for rescue from the mountain ledge in which their spaceship had lodged. A second cry sent a helpless shudder running through her. A tear leaked from her eye.

"What is it?" Luke said.

Janaya squeezed her eyes shut in an effort to halt the escalating panic. "One of the boys is crying."

"No time to waste."

"Wait." Janaya grasped his shoulder. "I'll do it."

Luke looked down at her, a tender expression on his face. He pressed a butterfly kiss on her lips. "We'll do it together," he said. "A partnership."

A partnership. The idea that he'd be with her while she faced her fears, her memories of the past, made all the difference.

"You can do this, sweetheart."

Maybe.

Or maybe not.

But she couldn't live with Luke's disappointment if she didn't even make the effort.

Janaya grasped his hand tightly and stepped toward the cliff. Her knees started to knock together and when she moved close enough to see over the cliff to the ground hundreds of feet below, panic bombarded her mind.

Janaya jerked back. "I think you'd better push me," she forced out from between dry lips.

"You can face this without me," Luke murmured. "But I have an idea."

"I'll try anything," Janaya said.

"Good." Luke picked up a coil of rope and placed it over his left shoulder. Then he grabbed Janaya and kissed her, taking possession of her lips in a masterful manner that made her forget her wonky knees. He hauled her close to his chest, his tongue thrust into her mouth and she felt his erection jabbing into her belly. He pulled away and nuzzled her nose with his.

"Let's go," he said, and took her hand before calmly stepping over the edge of the cliff.

"This is your plan?" she shrieked.

"You'd better think about flying in a hurry," Luke shouted. "Otherwise we're gonna go splat."

Janaya pictured herself standing on solid ground. That had worked last time.

Their downward plummet slowed.

"I have an idea," Luke murmured.

"Don't. I didn't think much of the last one."

Luke kissed her, slow and lazy, as if he had all day. When they surfaced from the kiss, Janaya found they hovered in the air.

"I knew it," Luke said in a smug, satisfied note. "When your mind is clear of panic, you can fly." He stepped onto a nearby ledge, his arm around her waist propelling her onto the ledge beside him.

"There's the other boy," Janaya murmured.

He lay a few feet from them, one of his legs at an unnatural angle.

"He's not moving." Luke grasped the rock face above the ledge they stood on and pulled himself up to the silent boy. "He's unconscious. Janaya, you take him up to the top and I'll check on his friend."

Janaya gaped in shock. He trusted her with the small human. He wasn't even watching her to make sure she followed his instructions. Her confidence took a flying leap.

He trusted her.

A warm sensation curled around her heart. Without stopping to analyze further, Janaya stared up at the still child. She found herself hovering beside him and picked him up, careful to keep his leg stable as she rose to the top of the cliff. She prayed she didn't make his injury worse by moving him.

"Janaya? I need a hand down here," Luke called.

A trace of fear unfurled inside then she concentrated on Luke. She closed her eyes, held her breath and stepped over the edge.

"Over here."

Janaya kept her eyes firmly shut but followed the sound of his voice. "Keep talking." Please, she thought.

"Have I told you how sexy you look?"

Janaya heard the smile in his voice. "No."

"Pretty eyes."

Janaya's eyes flicked open when she found herself brushing his body. "Is that all?" she whispered.

"Nah."

His grin was infectious and brought an answering smile in her.

A soft moan broke the spell that shimmered between them.

"How about taking this little guy up to the top then coming back for me? He's drifting in and out of consciousness."

Janaya gathered the small pliant body into her arms. "I'll be back soon."

She shot upward and placed the boy on the ground well away from the edge of the cliff. The sound of approaching voices hastened her actions. Janaya leapt over the cliff and shot down to Luke.

"Quick," she muttered. "We have to hurry. It sounds like the rest of the rescue team is nearly here."

"Give me a kiss first. You deserve one," he said, and nuzzled the soft skin of her neck.

Janaya groaned. The sound of the voices became louder. "We don't have time for this."

Luke dropped an open-mouthed kiss on her collarbone. "You're right." He placed his hand in hers. "Do your worst, sweetheart. Throw me around."

"Slam you into a tree more like," she muttered. "That might knock some sense into you. Do you know what they do with aliens?"

"No, but I know what I'd like to do." He moved her hand over his bulging erection. "I hope that none of the rescue team notices my hard-on."

Janaya seized him by the scruff of the neck and yanked upward.

"Whoa!"

They slammed into the ground with enough force for the air to whoosh out of Luke and winded him.

"I'm sorry!" Janaya ran her hands down his legs and body to check for broken bones. "Are you all right?"

I sure as hell would be feeling fine if I had you poured over the top of me.

Janaya gasped and sprang about to face the three men that had appeared from the thick bush that covered most of the hill. "We managed to get the two boys but Luke got slammed against the rock face when we were getting him up," she blurted. Her cheeks heated despite her best efforts to remain unaffected by their untimely arrival.

To Janaya's relief, Luke sat up and took over the conversation. "Have you got the portable stretchers? One of the boys has a broken leg. Both seem to have concussions. We'll have to carry them out."

"We've only got the one with us," one of the men replied. "I'll radio down for them to bring up another. The rest of the men aren't far behind us."

Between them, they seemed to have smoothed out the story. The men seemed more interested in getting the boys to medical attention, Janaya thought with relief.

She felt edgy with the adrenaline pulsing through her body. Her gaze met Luke's. They blazed with an inner fire that matched the licking flames inside her. She stepped from one foot to the other and a zap of current shot from her clit where her G-thing massaged the tender spot. Janaya sucked in a deep breath. More than anything, she wanted Luke. She wanted to feel his cock pounding into her pussy. She wanted him full stop.

Chapter Ten

ཀྵ

An hour passed before the second boy was safely transported down from the cliff top and handed over to the ambulance officers. Janaya bent over to toss the boy's hat into the ambulance. Luke couldn't help admiring the rounded cheeks of her butt faithfully outlined by her tight blue jeans. Unfortunately, every other red-blooded male in the vicinity noticed too. Luke barred his teeth at the ambulance driver but the kid smirked, blew him a kiss and carried right on looking. He couldn't have that!

Luke stomped over to Janaya and arrived in time to hear a chat-up line. He curled his arm around Janaya's waist in a clear statement of possession before he remembered they'd told everyone they were cousins. *Shit.*

He jerked away but still narrowed his eyes to slits of warning. "You ready to go?" *Man, that had sure sounded cousin-like. NOT!*

"I could do with a shower," she agreed, a trace of teasing in her violet eyes.

Whoa! Down boy, Luke thought when his body reacted with the same possessiveness his mind had tried. At least wait until they were alone.

The ambulance pulled away and the members of the volunteer fire brigade waved and drifted off to their respective vehicles.

Luke tapped Janaya on the shoulder. "Let's go."

They walked to his Land Cruiser together. Once in the privacy of the front seat, Luke kissed her, eating at her mouth as though he hadn't touched her for months. His hands moved to

119

her breasts, tracing their shape beneath the tight green t-shirt. When Luke finally pulled away they were both breathing hard.

Janaya's eyes glowed. "How long will it take to get home?"

"I know a shortcut," Luke promised and he took off in a cloud of dust.

"This is quicker?" Clear disbelief shot Janaya's brows toward her hairline. Her head thumped against the ceiling as the vehicle scrambled through a series of muddy potholes.

"Yeah." And it had the added advantage of keeping away from town. Probably—no—definitely the best plan when all Luke could think of was getting her into his bed again and the delicious things they could do to each other.

He sped down a back road past the Sloan camping ground.

"The UFO hunters are still in town," Janaya said.

Luke scowled at the two old vans parked under a trio of kauri trees. "I just wish they'd piss off and leave us alone." *And they might have if Dad and Hinekiri had flown to Africa in the middle of the night instead of five in the afternoon when every man and his dog were watching.* But he didn't say it out loud since he didn't want to upset Janaya again.

"The press is still hanging around town too. That was another good reason to drive home on the back roads. Besides, this is the scenic route. See that river through the totara trees over there?"

"I see it."

"I caught my first trout in that river when I was six. Haven't had much time to fish since I moved back home." A trace of regret coated his voice. "Maybe next weekend." *When you leave and I need something to occupy my time.*

Luke slowed at a give way sign and turned to the right, pulling up behind his father's house with a screech of brakes five minutes later. He leapt out of his vehicle and when Janaya reached his side, he dragged her through into the kitchen and slammed the door on the world outside. They stared at each other for a long heated moment. Without taking his gaze off her flushed face, he undid the buttons of his blue uniform shirt and discarded it on the floor.

Janaya snickered but he noticed the way her eyes darkened. "Someone's in a hurry."

"Yeah." Damn straight, he was in a hurry. At the moment. But maybe later he'd leaf through Janaya's copy of the Kama Sutra. Not that he was likely to run out of inspiration but trying a new position or two sounded like fun.

Janaya sashayed up the stairs in front of him, the sway of her butt attracting his appreciative eyes. She peered over her shoulder and winked. "Don't forget the honey and the whipped cream."

A slow grin spread across his face when he remembered their last session. Luke made an abrupt about turn. Sounded like a damn fine plan to him. He thundered up the stairs and arrived in his bedroom aroused and out of breath to find Janaya flicking through the pages of the Kama Sutra.

"Is that possible?" she demanded pointing at an entwined couple. Fascination and curiosity combined along with a frown to give her a really cute look.

Not for the first time, Luke felt something give in the region of his heart. He shied away from the elusive emotion and concentrated on the book. This was about fun. Nothing more. Nothing less. He tilted his head to study the picture she pointed at. It was difficult to see which legs belonged to which partner. Even stepping up beside Janaya and looking at the illustration right way up didn't help.

"Don't know," he said finally. "But we can sure as hell try." A leer claimed his lips as he imagined Janaya entwined with him, arms holding him so tight they felt like one.

"Not straight away." Janaya's tongue dipped out to moisten her lips. After placing her book on the bedside table, she heaped up his pillows and leaned back to study him with an expectant expression. "Strip for me."

"No music." Luke groaned inwardly. *Weak, Morgan. Weak.*

"If that's all you're worried about, I can do music." She hummed a few bars then started to sing an unfamiliar song in a low husky voice.

Luke hesitated, feeling decidedly stupid and more than a little embarrassed at the idea. But determination showed in her eyes and when he thought of the possible payback…he changed his mind. Besides, with his shirt lying on the kitchen floor, there wasn't much clothing left to strip off.

The need to please her made him start his striptease. Janaya continued to sing in a low, sexy voice that plucked at his sexual buttons. A little out of breath and very turned on—the fly of his navy uniform trousers was starting to strain under the pressure. His hands went to his black leather belt. With a shake of his butt, he started to get into the spirit. He unfastened the buckle then realized he'd tip arse over teakettle if he didn't get things in the right order.

Shoes first, idiot.

Luke grinned at his near miss. Somehow, he needed to even the playing field, make her as hot as jalapeno pepper. Then they could burn together.

As he stooped to deal with his bootlaces, he raked his gaze over her curves then rose higher to her eyes.

Janaya's heart jolted. Her pulse pounded at the intense passion in his eyes. The words of the Dalcon song came out of her mouth automatically, which was a good thing. Her nipples tightened at his heated look and her body ached for his touch, for the ecstasy to come. The Earthman removed his boots and peeled off his black socks. One sock landed near his boots and the other draped over the back of a wooden chair. His hands moved to the belt that circled his waist then ripped it from the loops and dropped it to the floor at his feet. The hiss then the thud of the buckle striking the floor stalled her breathing. Excitement lurched inside her stomach. Soon, she'd touch and trail her fingers over his muscled abs but for the moment she'd savor the ripple as he moved, breathe in his sandalwood scent and let her imagination roam.

The male sauntered past the bed, spun about with a devilish grin and eased his zipper down. Every trace of spit disappeared from Janaya's mouth. A pale V of flesh showed between the parted fabric. The words of the song faltered. She swallowed then picked up again, humming this time because the words had fled her memory.

Luke ambled past the bed again and turned with a definite swagger in his step. His lazy appraisal sent an urgent message to her brain. Touch. Hurry. Her clothes clung to her aroused body, hugging her skin like a lover. Too many clothes. Way overdressed for this party.

The trousers slid down his legs and he stepped out of them leaving him standing before her in a pair of silky black shorts. They tented in the front and, once again, her musical accompaniment faltered.

"You're very good," Janaya whispered, giving up on the humming.

"I'd like to be bad."

"Show me."

He waggled a finger at her. "I think not. This is your show…"

"A challenge?"

"Yeah." Luke whipped off his silky shorts and lay back on the bed beside Janaya but not close enough that they touched. She felt his heat through her clothing and saw his goofy grin.

Janaya gave a confident nod. "Close your eyes. No. Wait. I need your scarf."

"It's in the bedside drawer." Interest and definite approval colored his expression.

Janaya opened the drawer and tugged out the soft silk. Leaning over him, she covered his eyes and tied it at the back. His tongue traced a wet path over the upper curve of one breast. A shudder of pleasure jolted clear to her toes. Janaya closed her eyes and swayed toward him in anticipation of his mouth suckling her breast. Instead, he taunted and teased her. Licking. Nibbling and licking again.

"Feels good," she murmured. Maybe she'd do some licking of her own. Bending over him again, she reached for the bottle of runny honey. She planned the move so her T-shirt covered nipple passed right over his lips and lingered to tempt him. When his mouth closed over her offering, a soft sigh escaped. A flood of heat dampened her panties and sent a flush storming across every inch of her skin. Too many clothes, she thought hazily. Slowly, she moved away, the tug on her breast sending a corresponding jolt spearing straight to her clit.

Janaya wrenched her clothes off so quickly a button dropped off her jeans. Leaving them in a heap, she flicked open the pop-top of the honey. Where to start? His nipples, she decided. The honey dripped from the bottle, slowly at first as it dripped onto the flat disc then with a liquid splat that had a river of honey heading for his belly button. Luke flinched. Janaya giggled and quickly bent to round up the golden honey with her tongue. A breathless groan escaped Luke. His hips jerked off the bed with each sweeping lap of her tongue, his cock jabbing at her thigh.

For a second, Janaya was tempted to hurry her game along. A memory of Santana intruded, making her frown. No, she'd take it slow and torture both her and Luke. Eventually, Hinekiri would return and they would leave Earth. Janaya applied a thin drizzle of honey to his lips and as an afterthought carefully painted her breasts with cobwebs of honey. Finished off with a blob of cream that would be the perfect offering, she thought. Suiting action to thought, she grabbed up the aerosol can and yanked off the top. A loud hiss broke the silence as she applied an artful swirl of cream to cover her nipples.

Luke chuckled, squirming restlessly on the bed. "The suspense is killing me, sweetheart. Care to hurry things along?"

"Hmmm," Janaya mused. "No. I don't think so." Elation and a much deeper emotion she didn't care to examine curled through her when she bent to lap the honey off his lips. He moved his lips beneath hers, devouring her softness and fighting to cleanse the honey away first. The sweep of his tongue across her lips sent tiny shivers of desire racing through Janaya. Her nipples throbbed in a silent demand for his touch. His hands stroked across her belly then gripped her hips as his cock batted against her upper thigh. Instinctively, she squirmed down his body to align his shaft with her weeping entrance. Later, she'd try slow. Janaya sank down, filling her emptiness with his cock. She squeezed her eyes closed and concentrated on the slick feel of him as he filled her, the deep and stretching sensation that made her long for more. The scent of sandalwood and sex filled her every breath and his uneven gasps told of his enjoyment as she swayed above him.

A sudden awareness made her eyes pop open. Luke grinned up at her, his eyes uncovered and the scarf lying across the pillow.

"That's cheating," she whispered, biting her lips against a dart of pleasure on a downward stroke.

"All's fair in love and war. Besides, look at you." Husky approval rippled through his voice and shone in his eyes. In that moment, Janaya felt beautiful. She felt like a female instead of a sexless bodyguard who killed to protect. She glanced down at her breasts—the place Luke's eyes seemed riveted and saw the cream had moved despite her lazy pace. Her nipples peeked through the cream while the globes of her breasts glistened, shiny with honey.

"Mine," he said.

Janaya's heart skipped a beat before she managed a nod. "Yes."

His hands reached for her hips and he grasped them, directing her next downward move on his cock. Faster. Harder. Janaya sucked in her breath, feeling as though she were poised on the edge of a precipice. The need to jump was a compulsion. Her inner muscles clenched. She closed her eyes again and concentrated on the tingle in her nipples, the rich aroma of honey. Luke plunged upward into her pussy, nudging against her clit with each surge. Pinpricks of pleasure danced across the back of her eyes and waltzed down her body. Her cunt contracted and suddenly her world shattered into a climax that lifted her from her body, shattered her soul and curled up inside her heart as a memory to treasure. Forever. Forever, Luke.

Slowly, leisurely, Janaya returned. Luke's cock still filled her impossibly full. Excitement rose afresh. This time, this time she'd watch him as he exploded inside her in a rush of greedy satisfaction. Her eyelids flickered and she saw Luke studying her with an intensity that made her freeze. Abashed, she shied from his gaze.

"The cream's gone," she murmured.

"There's more where that came from." He lifted her off him.

"Don't you want to come?" she asked, once again confused with the sudden insecurity, the questions that plagued her mind.

Luke chuckled, the sound easing her heart. "That's a given, sweetheart. Turn over for me. Yeah, like that," he said in approval as she crouched before him and presented her back.

Janaya trembled, balanced on her hands and knees before him, in the position favored by the men of Dalcon. Inwardly, she tensed for a flash of pain. Instead, his hands skimmed down her backbone. The whoosh of the honey bottle preceded a warm line of sticky liquid that ran the length of her spine. His warm tongue lapped it up in one long sweep, finishing where her body separated into the two globes of her ass. He palmed the globes, cupping them intimately and blowing soft puffs of air down the crack between. Janaya groaned. She widened her stance presenting the lips of her pussy for the same luscious treatment. A tingle of expectation grew. His forefinger traced down her perineum. A shudder surged through her stomach while her juices wept, telling of her desire and her need for him.

Luke kissed down one rounded butt cheek and lapped at the flow of juices that ran down her leg. "You taste good." He stilled. "I was going to finger-fuck you, but I think that can wait.

You are so ready for me, sweetheart." His heart pounded. His cock pulsed. Fighting the haste his body demanded, he guided his cock into her tight channel, watching his flesh disappear inch by lovely inch. Fully seated, Luke paused to savor his position. He loved—*Hell, no!* He'd decided he was never getting sucked into that bullshit claptrap again. Not after Victoria. He was not setting himself up for the royal screw again. Remember? These days he screwed, he didn't get screwed in the process.

Janaya pressed back against him drilling him that much deeper inside her warmth. He pulled back and surged inside again setting up a rhythm to suit both of them. He cared for her, he decided. That was it.

At his body's insistent demand, he quickened the pace of his strokes, clinging to her shapely body and trying to make it good for Janaya too. Her vagina clamped down hard on his cock. He felt the pressure build inside him as her topple into climax milked him. Furious pumping spewed his seed into her, making his blood run hot and forcing a masculine cry of triumph from between clenched teeth. Spent, he collapsed on top of her, blanketing her with his heavy strength. After long moments, she wriggled and Luke moved off her, separating from her body with a sucking sound. Luke stared down at his semi-erect shaft with something akin to shock. It glistened with her juices and his come.

No condom.

Again.

Luke knew there was a hidden meaning there. Somewhere. He forced his uneasiness aside and curled up beside Janaya, arranging her pliant body so she faced him and her sticky, honey-coated breasts were level with his mouth.

"How you feeling, Janaya?"

"Relaxed," she murmured, sounding close to sleep.

Luke smiled a feral grin. "You go to sleep and recuperate so you're ready for more loving." He eyed at her tempting breasts. "Me, I think it's time for dessert."

* * * * *

The ring of the telephone dragged Luke from a deep sleep. Bleary-eyed, he groped for the phone and fumbled it to his ear. "Yeah?"

"I'd like to interview you for tomorrow's edition of the Sloan Gazette."

"What about?" Luke demanded, picking up a lock of Janaya's hair and twirling it around his finger.

"The rescue."

Luke's hackles settled a fraction. As much as he hated the press, there were times when he needed to overlook his personal feelings and cooperate. "All right," he said. "Down at the station." He glanced at his watch and saw it was early evening. "I can meet you there in an hour."

Luke and Janaya were waiting in his office, drinking strong black coffee when Marcie Montgomery, the local reporter, arrived. The receptionist showed her in.

"Would you like coffee?" Luke asked when the female had taken a seat.

"Not for me, thanks. I've tried this coffee before. It's strong enough to make a spoon salute."

Luke grinned, but the tight sensation inside his stomach that he'd had ever since Marcie Montgomery stepped into his office didn't ease. There was a suppressed excitement about the reporter that made him wary.

"Thanks to you, Constable, the two boys are safe."

"It was a team effort," Luke reminded Marcie. "I wasn't the only one there. My cousin." He gestured at Janaya. "The scout master and the volunteer fire brigade."

"Ah, yes," Marcie mused. She pushed a pair of rimless glasses further up her nose with her silver pen. "But none of them can fly."

Janaya bolted upright in her chair before she regained control. Luke thought he hid his reaction a bit better. "Pardon?"

"One of the boys is adamant that your cousin flew him up to the top of the cliff."

"Me?" Janaya demanded, thumping her chest with her fist.

If the situation hadn't been so serious, Luke would have laughed. The Dalcon native had her reactions under tight control and was in full damage mode. "You've got to remember the kid, both kids, were in severe shock and the one with the broken leg in pain."

"Yet Mrs. Bates' grandson is not one with an overactive imagination."

"I hope you haven't told Mrs. Bates that," Janaya murmured, her eyes full of mischief. She knew how much the woman pissed Luke and his staff off with her petty grievances. "That implies he's lacking."

"When did you learn to fly?" Marcie demanded.

"Hmmm," Janaya said, fiddling with her braid. "I read the manual last week and from memory, I did the test flight on Sunday."

Luke smirked at the expression on the reporter's face.

"Stop kidding around," Marcie demanded. "I know there's something going on in Sloan. I intend to ferret it out. The UFOs were sighted again last night."

"Last night?" Luke blurted.

"No, no." Janaya shook her head. "Last time I heard the UFO was in Africa."

Luke's jaw sagged in shock but the reporter was quicker.

Marcie leapt to her feet. "Laugh and make jokes all you want but I intend to prove that there are aliens living in Sloan!"

The door slammed on her stormy exit, reverberating through the small office along with alarm.

"That went well," Luke said dryly.

Janaya's brows rose. "Not."

Luke shook his head in half admiration, half disbelief. "I nearly had a cow when you told her about Africa."

A gasp escaped Janaya. Her gaze shot down his body. "A cow? How is that possible?"

Chapter Eleven

৪০

Luke picked the Gazette off his doorstep, took one look at the front page story and stomped inside.

"Look at that!" he shouted.

Janaya grabbed the paper from him and smoothed it out on the tabletop to read. *Flying Aliens Land in Sloan?* "At least they have a question mark," she said.

Someone rang the doorbell to the front door and then seconds later, the phone pealed.

"Reporters," Luke snapped. "Slimy bastards."

"And on your day off too."

"It's not funny."

"We can still go on our picnic, can't we?" Janaya gestured at the wicker basket they'd loaded with goodies. "I've been looking forward to it. We don't have picnics on Dalcon."

"I suppose we could creep out the back and walk up to the waterfalls on Dad's land instead of the spot out by the camping grounds." His eyes narrowed in thought. "We could swim. With no clothes on. And do other things." Masculine eyebrows waggled right before he grinned.

"Let's do it. Before the Earth reporter out front decides to check around the rear of the house and blocks our escape route."

Luke picked up the picnic basket. Janaya grabbed the tartan rug. Together they peered out the windows facing the bush-clad hills at the back of the house.

"Can you hear anything?

"It sounds like a woman out front," Janaya said. "I can hear tiny tapping sounds like Earth women's shoes. The spiky heels."

"Marcie Montgomery," Luke muttered, "We do not want to meet her."

They crept from through the back door, Luke taking the time to lock up before they left. Together, they slipped into the manuka, karaka and totara trees that bordered the rear of the property. The sun shone down overhead, sending dappled rays of light down through the leaf canopy. Dead leaves crunched underfoot while a soft breeze stirred the curls framing her face. Janaya tightened her grip on Luke's hand and decided to enjoy the day instead of dwelling on the fast approaching time when she would have to leave.

The torrent of water pouring over the falls was audible long before they reached it.

"My sister and I used to play up here when we were kids. Lily liked to search for fairies."

Janaya's mouth twitched. "What did you do? Play policeman?"

"I wanted to sail a ship," Luke confessed. "I made paper boats and sailed them over the falls."

The dirt and leaf-strewn track they'd followed up the side of the hill ended right at the base of the falls in a small clearing. Janaya blinked against the bright sunlight after the cool shade of the bush then admired the sparkle of the water. The rush of the water as it tumbled over the falls blocked most of her new supersensitive hearing.

Janaya sighed. It was good to feel normal again. "It's beautiful."

"I'd forgotten how peaceful it is," Luke said. "I haven't been up here for a while." He placed the basket in the shade, took the blanket from Janaya and spread it in the sunshine. He settled on the blanket, lying out flat on his back with a yawn. "We can move it later if we get too hot."

"What does one do on a picnic?"

Luke grinned with a flash of white teeth. "One eats lots, swims, maybe explores then takes a nap. And when one wakes up they start all over again."

Janaya stretched out beside him and stared up into the cloudless blue sky. "Sounds very relaxing."

Luke turned over on his belly and plucked a grass stalk to chew. "Like a swim?"

Greedy for new experiences, especially if they were with Luke, Janaya agreed.

Luke sat up again to unbutton his shirt. He removed his boots and black socks then shucked his jeans and boxers. "You going to swim in your jeans and t-shirt?"

"Won't the sun's rays burn?" Janaya removed her clothes a little more slowly, aware of Luke's interested gaze.

Luke shrugged. "I have suntan lotion." He offered his right hand and pulled her to her feet. His hands unfastened her fly and then tugged her jeans over her hips.

"Last one in is a rotten egg," Luke shouted and took off with a whoop.

Janaya was so busy admiring the scenery she forgot the race. She paused at the edge of the waterhole, watching Luke's muscles bunch and flex when he jumped into the water. A cold splash hit her mid-chest.

"Ow! That's cold!"

"Refreshing."

Janaya rolled her eyes. "Freezing!"

Luke swam to the base of the falls and climbed from the water. He posed for a second then disappeared behind the sheet of water that toppled from above. "You won't get to see what's behind the falls." His taunting words floated back to her and propelled her to action. She dived into the water, the cold stealing her breath. She came up spluttering, wiping the icy water and strands of hair off her face. A flash of light on the other side of the stream caught her attention when Luke shouted at her to hurry. Janaya pulled herself out of the freezing water and ducked behind the veil of water to find Luke waiting.

"A cave."

"If we're really quiet we might see glowworms," he whispered, taking her hand and leading her into the dark mouth of the cave.

A few feet into the cave, Luke propelled her around a sharp jagged corner of rock and tugged her back to lean against his chest. In the almost total blackness, she saw several tiny pinpricks of light on the ceiling.

"Glowworms," he whispered close to her ear. "I wanted to show you before we got distracted." His tongue flickered out into the shell of her ear, eliciting a tremor of excitement. Then he led her out into the sunshine again, tugging her into the water with him. This time, she was prepared for the refreshing nip of the water but when Luke dragged her into his arms and kissed her the cold was of minor significance. She felt the nudge of his cock and wound her legs around his waist, opening her to his sensual invasion.

"Too soon," he murmured against her mouth. "Let me play a little first." His eyes gleamed as they came to rest on her breasts.

"Now," she insisted. "Then I get to play. I've studied my Kama Sutra in greater detail. Just thought you should know."

In answer, he plunged into her pussy, stealing her breath and smothering her shout of delight by covering her mouth with his. Hard and fast and exactly the way she wanted it. Orgasm shuddered through her with gratifying speed. Janaya held tight and let the mind-blowing rapture sweep her away.

They played and laughed then crawled from the water to collapse on the tartan blanket and dry off. Luke produced a small towel and after he blotted the worst of the water away, he produced a bottle of lotion.

"Lie back," he whispered with a wicked yet purposeful grin. "Let me make love to you."

"How can I refuse an offer like that?" Janaya's heart sang with happiness. She watched his concentration as he squeezed a large blob of lotion into his hands and rubbed it lightly between his palms. The scent of flowers filled the air along with something else she didn't recognize.

"It's coconut," Luke said. "I'll show you a picture when we get home."

Home. Janaya's mind seized the word. Back on Dalcon, she lived at the bodyguard quarters in a single room. Whenever she had time off, she stayed with her aunt—if she was around. Otherwise, work doubled as home.

Would her father ever make her feel welcome at the family home? Janaya had hoped her promotion coupled with her joining to Santana would make the difference. Maybe. Maybe not. Luke didn't know how lucky he was to have a father who supported him.

Predictably, Luke's hands went straight to her breasts. Janaya's nipples tightened along with the muscles in her tummy. She held her breath in acute anticipation but at the last second, he grinned and jerked his hands away. They hovered inches above her breasts, so far yet so close.

"Turn over, I'll do your back first." Laughter filled his voice.

The wretch knew exactly the effect he was having on her. Janaya pouted before she obeyed his order. She glanced over her shoulder and considered wrestling him to the ground and torturing him until he gasped deep at the back of his throat and willingly touched her. Right where she needed his hands. The need to have his touch, his hands curving around her breasts, trailing down the silky skin of her belly and sliding over her dew-drenched clit pumped like a fever through her veins. A compulsion to follow through shook her control. And the wretch knew it. She had half turned to rise when his chuckle made her freeze.

"Don't cheat, Janaya. We both know you're stronger." Humor lit up his gorgeous brown eyes. "Be gentle with me."

"Humph," Janaya snorted, fighting the impulse to throw the smug male on his back, straddle his hips and tease him until he whimpered. She expelled a haughty sniff. "I wouldn't think of cheating. It's against the bodyguard's code."

"I'll have to read this code of yours," Luke said with a chuckle.

"Really?"

His soft laugh filled the clearing. "I've discovered I'm curious about aliens."

Luke's interest delighted her because he sounded genuine. It made her think of the future. *If she had one*, she amended with sick dread. She'd have no way of knowing if she'd been declared AWOL and charges laid against her until she faced her superiors. With a tremulous sigh, Janaya subsided onto the blanket and tried not to worry.

"You ready for this?"

"Give it your best shot." Janaya couldn't help but smile as she lay with her head pillowed on her hands. Her mood lightened into anticipation.

Impatience.

Taut expectation.

Prickles danced across every inch of her skin as she waited and imagined what waited. Every sense worked overtime clamoring to give her clues. She felt his muscular thighs when they slid either side of her back, heard the rustle of the blanket as he settled in place and the joyous singing of a small brown bird perched in a tree on the other side of the clearing. Of course, she couldn't see since Dalcon inhabitants weren't lucky enough to have eyes in the back of their heads but the coconut scent drove her crazy with the need to physically hurry Luke along. The Earthman was an evil tyrant.

Janaya sensed his intent to start a fraction of a second before his thigh muscles flexed against her hips. A groan of pure relief escaped when his hands finally connected with her back and slid down, slippery with lotion. A sigh wrenched from her when his fingers kneaded and stroked the muscles in her back. Gradually he worked his way across her shoulders and waist, alternating feathering strokes with more pressure and then kneading his way down her spine. Janaya moaned and relaxed further into the blanket. Luke chuckled and moved further down her body. Janaya sensed him looking at her buttocks and they gave an involuntary twitch. The plastic bottle wheezed a protest when he squeezed more lotion out. His hands rolled and plucked, massaged and kneaded her ass. Arousal replaced relaxation without warning. Each move of his hands shot anticipation to her clitoris and pussy. Janaya tried to widen her legs in a silent plea for him to fill her pulsing emptiness. She wriggled and ached for fulfillment. Another smug masculine laugh filled the air. He knew of her desperate need yet he continued to taunt her with erotic forays closer and closer to her weeping channel.

Instead of giving her fulfillment, he moved down her thighs, massaged her calves and feet until she felt like a puddle again. Janaya didn't think she'd ever forget the smell of coconut. It would forever be entwined with Luke and picnics.

Finally, Luke smacked her lightly on the butt. "Time to do your front."

Janaya turned lethargically and relaxed on her back to stare up at him. Dark, stormy eyes—aroused eyes—met her gaze and it was difficult to miss the erection that rubbed her belly when he straddled her legs. Smugness filled Janaya then. Soon, she'd prod him into losing his patience. He'd catch fire instead of stoking the inferno that ignited in her. She watched him intently with lust and yearning on her mind. Soon, they'd both burn and the flames of passion would consume them.

Luke tilted the bottle up and squeezed a stream of white lotion in a crisscross pattern on her breasts. "I think I'm gonna enjoy this. It's hard to decide where to start." He licked his lips in a rapacious manner but evaded her pouting, needy nipples

137

and breasts to massage of blob of lotion into her right shoulder, his hands tracing the dips and hollows along her collarbone.

Her breath escaped in a disappointed rush. "You know what you said about cheating," Janaya said in a husky voice.

"Yeah."

"I'm thinking seriously about doing it."

"Doing it?" His brows waggled. "Or cheating?"

A reluctant smile tugged at her lips. "I think they're the same thing."

"Hmmm." Luke stilled then bent to snatch a kiss. A hit-and-run kiss that left her wanting. "And what does cheating consist of? What would happen to me?"

Janaya licked her lips while she considered the question. The tormenting ache low in her belly ratcheted upward to a sharp, spiky awareness. "Well…first I'd have to overpower you. And maybe I'd lay you out on the blanket spread-eagled ready for my dining pleasure."

The hand resting on her right shoulder tensed, relaxed and then lowered to absently toy with a nipple. A groan built and her mind fogged. All she needed to do was move a fraction…yes…just like that. Luke's palm curved around her breast and squeezed with exactly the right amount of pressure.

"Janaya?"

"Yes."

"I quite like the sound of that." Luke smiled and her heart went pitter-patter. "Maybe we'll try that another time?"

"Whatever you want," she murmured. "Luke?"

"Yes, sweetheart."

"Please don't tease me anymore."

"Not even a bit?"

Janaya's heart seemed to twist inside her chest. She wanted a snapshot of this moment in time—the exact second when she'd realized she cared deeply for this teasing Earthman. His brown eyes darkened as if he sensed her inner turmoil but his mouth softened into a gentle smile.

"I'll let you cheat another day," he murmured, a promise in his eyes. "But I'm enjoying the teasing, sweetheart, so we'll have to compromise." As he spoke, one hand trailed past her breast and over her stomach. Janaya tensed, her breath coming in pants. But instead of touching her intimately, his hands came to rest on her upper thighs. She lowered her lashes to screen acute disappointment but then Luke tugged on her legs in a silent request for her to stretch them wide apart.

"That's perfect," he said, his gaze on her moist folds.

Janaya's pulse spiked, excitement building to fever pitch at the intent look in his dark eyes. She swallowed, acute expectation making her mouth as dry as the hills that surrounded the Dalcon steppes.

He parted her folds and lapped at her juices, passing close enough to her clit to give her a buzz but not near enough to push her over the edge into orgasm. Janaya lifted her hips in insistent invitation. Luke blew softly. Warm air tickled before he circled her clit with his tongue. Now she had his attention where she needed it, frustration battled with a contrary wish to make her arousal last. He nibbled at her clit and covered the sensitive nub with his warm, moist mouth. A sharp current of pleasure shot to her toes. The warm sweep of his tongue finished her off, sending a mind-blowing, heartrending pleasure surging through her body, her mind, her soul. A series of smaller quakes shimmered through her before she relaxed against the blanket, her body humming with satisfaction. Luke moved his lips over her clit in a lazy kiss then moved up her body to hold her. When he moved his lips over hers in a slow, drugging kiss, she tasted herself on him. His kiss, his taste, sent new spirals of ecstasy swirling and when she felt the nudge of his cock against her leg, Janaya reached down to guide him inside her body.

They both groaned when he slid to the hilt.

Fully seated, Luke paused to brush the hair off her face. The tenderness on his face brought a hot ache to her throat. He withdrew almost out of her before surging home, slow and easy, never taking his eyes off her. He felt impossibly hard inside, each lazy plunge into her heat stoking the fire, making her ignite and flame with passion. Luke kissed her, their tongues mating in a sensual dance. The first stirring of pleasure stole her breath. She tensed as bliss claimed her yet again. Luke groaned his own pleasure and she felt the spurt of his seed deep inside. They held each other, riding the passionate storm until it passed into lazy relaxation.

Luke held her tight. "You make me feel so good," he murmured, low and gruff.

In answer, Janaya kissed him, trying to communicate her feelings with touch, taste and cuddles. One thing was certain. This wasn't a game anymore. This was something more, something profound and life altering. Janaya was suddenly afraid.

* * * * *

They walked hand in hand down the leaf-strewn track, Janaya savoring the closeness between them and the warmth of his hand.

"I had a great day." Luke stopped and kissed her lips, lingering over the job.

"Me too," she said.

Luke helped her over the stile that straddled the fence and they ambled up to the back door. Luke produced a key from his pocket and unlocked the door. The phone rang the minute they stepped inside.

Luke frowned. "Pity the real world has to intrude. I'd better answer in case it's Tony."

Janaya watched him prowl across the kitchen with approval and a tinge of pride. Her man. *Until she left for Dalcon.*

Luke barked a hello then listened to the caller on the other end. "No comment!" he snarled.

Janaya winced at the crash of the phone. "Something wrong?"

Luke didn't answer but stomped through the house. Seconds later, he returned with a newspaper.

"A special edition," he snapped thrusting a wad of rumpled paper at her.

Janaya unfolded the paper. Shock froze Janaya in place. "That's me."

"The bastards obviously followed us," Luke snarled. His gut twisted in fury, anger at the violation of their privacy making him want to lash out.

Kissing Cousins

The headline wasn't so bad but the topless photo of Janaya really pissed him off. Janaya was out of bounds—for his eyes only and not for publication on the front page of the Sloan Gazette.

The phone rang again.

"Leave it," Luke ordered. "I'm going to the station. Damage control."

"I'll come too," Janaya said.

Luke hesitated, knowing from experience how bad things would get.

"We'll do it together," Janaya stated.

Luke's heart leapt. Together. What had he done to deserve a woman like Janaya?

Chapter Twelve

ಏ

"Mrs. Bates, you are free to complain to the censorship board," Luke said through his teeth. His hand gripped the telephone hard enough that his knuckles whitened. "Yes, I am still investigating the UFO matter. No, I am not attending the meeting. Yes, I will let you know if there are developments. Goodbye, Mrs. Bates."

Luke managed to place the phone down gently before he kicked his desk. The roar of pain that shot up his leg concentrated his fury. "Goddamned bloody woman!" he howled.

Janaya leaned back in Luke's swivel chair. "Do you want me to hurt her for you? Maybe arrange her body parts?"

"Good idea," Luke growled. "Visit Marcie Montgomery while you're at it. You'll find them both at the bloody town meeting the UFO hunters organized." He checked his watch. "Starts in exactly five minutes."

Janaya stood and stepped toward the door.

Luke felt his eyes bug. "Where are you going?"

"To punish Mrs. Bates," Janaya said.

His mouth opened then closed. Then he caught the glint of humor in her eyes and sank onto the corner of his desk. "You're kidding."

"Yeah." Janaya wrinkled her nose. "Though personally, I'd like to do something nasty to Mrs. Bates. Between her, the reporters and the UFO hunters—" Janaya broke off abruptly.

"What is it?"

"Torgon. I can hear their clicks as they communicate."

"Holy shit," Luke breathed. That was the last thing they needed. Visible proof for the people of Sloan that aliens existed and were alive and well walking amongst them. "We have to find them before they're seen, before someone gets hurt."

Janaya listened carefully but didn't hear any further communications. "I'm sorry, I can't fix a position for you."

"I have a Torgon weapon," Luke said. His stomach went cold when he recalled the finality of the piles of purple ashes on the ground. "I think we should split up and search."

Luke saw the worry that clouded Janaya's eyes. "We don't have any other option. The people of Sloan are in danger along with my sanity. I don't think I can take much more of the alien paranoia."

Janaya stared at him feeling helpless but unable to think of an alternative. "I'll take the area where I heard them," she stipulated. And hopefully, they were still there.

"Any hints."

Janaya attempted a smile. "Shoot first and ask questions later." *Keep safe. I don't want to lose you.* The knowledge that she would leave soon and lose him anyway followed close on the heels of her first sobering thought. "Take care."

After checking in with Luke's second-in-command, they hurried out the rear exit. Luke drove out of town the long way that took them in the opposite direction to the town hall. Once out of town, he slowed.

"Which way?"

"Let me out here," Janaya said. "I haven't heard any further communications but this is the area they were in."

Luke's face held no expression but Janaya sensed his concern. She squeezed his shoulder trying to communicate her feelings and then leaned in to kiss him hard. She climbed from the Land Cruiser and watched Luke drive off.

The sound of the vehicle faded. The buzz and click of insects filled the air along with the rustle of leaves in the nearby trees and the lowing of a cow. No Torgon. She sniffed and smelled nothing more than nature's aromas—rich soil, green foliage and wildflowers. Worry still tinged her mind and burned in her gut. Instinct told her they shouldn't have split up but what alternative did they have?

Janaya checked the surrounding area for signs of life—Earthman or Torgon. Nothing. She drew a sharp breath and bounded off the ground to land on a rocky outcrop. Still nothing. Janaya drifted back to ground and decided to wander in the direction Luke had left to search.

She rounded a corner and came to an abrupt halt.

"Hello, Janaya."

"Santana!" The Dalcon male stood before her with typical arrogance. His black shoulder-length hair was coiled in the elegant coils of the noble caste. The purple fabric of his suit was so dark it was almost black and another sign of the ruling caste. The male was the stuff of a Dalcon female's dreams.

A multitude of emotions assaulted Janaya. Dismay. Shock. Regret. And guilt. Guilt filled Janaya as she studied the familiar face of the man she intended to join with. She felt nothing for him. Not after loving Luke. The most shocking thought to bombard her was that she no longer wanted to complete the ceremonial joining. She loved Luke. He was the one who made her feel worthy, as if she mattered.

"What are you doing here?"

"Where's Hinekiri? I wish to speak with her."

The Dalcon male refused to meet her gaze. "Hinekiri is not here."

"You lie."

Alarm sounded in Janaya. *Something's wrong with this picture.* Why would Santana travel to this distant outpost to find them?

"I want the charts," Santana snarled. "And I intend to have them."

Ah, now the truth emerged. "I don't think so." Janaya folded her arms across her chest. "The charts belong to Hinekiri."

Fury and distaste chased across his face with startling clarity. "Bah! You're a peasant—a worthless nobody. And now a criminal." His dark eyes flashed with triumph. "You've been announced AWOL. At this very moment they're hunting you like the common criminal you are."

The venom in his voice took Janaya by surprise. She'd known of his indifference but the hate and sheer fury toward her was new.

"You will hand over those charts," Santana stated in a hard voice. "I intend to take them with me."

A tight band formed around her chest and suddenly Janaya had trouble breathing. Thoughts bounded through her head like startled rabbits. Had he ever intended to complete the joining? "Is that why you agreed to join with me? Because of the charts?"

A scornful laugh battered at her pride. "Join with you? Your father was so desperate to rid himself of you he paid me. I needed money so I took it. Stupid bitch. He gave me directions to find you."

Pain struck her hard and deep. Proof of her father's indifference. He'd sold both her and Hinekiri out.

* * * * *

Luke didn't see a single Torgon, not so much as a shiny purple flash of their god-awful suits. He should have felt relief but he had a bad, sinking feeling deep in his gut. Cop instinct kicked in big-time. A black tui burst out of a clump of flax bushes, flying low and barely clearing his head. Luke started then let loose a low, blistering curse. Oh, yeah. Something stunk to high heavens in the town of Sloan.

He prowled down the small, twisting path that ran through the native bush bordering the road, taking care with each foot placement. That bird had acted startled. And it hadn't been him doing the scaring. There! Voices.

Luke eased to a halt behind the thick trunk of a totara tree.

Janaya. That was Janaya's voice. But he didn't recognize the male with her. He decided to wait, knowing his woman could handle herself in any situation.

His woman.

Luke turned the words over in his mind then grinned. *Damn right, she was his woman.*

Janaya's voice rose. The male spoke with a smooth drawl that some woman would find sexy. Luke thought he sounded sly.

"My father wouldn't do that," Janaya insisted.

"Believe it. He sold you out. He doesn't give a shit for you." The male clicked his fingers in illustration.

Anger burned inside Luke. Janaya slouched like a whipped puppy. Her voice held pain and disillusion. Devastation. He ached to hold her, to comfort and tell her how much he cared.

"If I had time," the male drawled all smug and self-satisfied, "I'd take you back to Dalcon myself and claim the AWOL reward."

Luke tensed at the smarmy threat. That wouldn't happen! Not while he had breath in his body. He waited for the right moment to help or intervene should the need arise.

"Try it," Janaya spat.

"All I want are the charts."

Luke watched Janaya freeze. Like a coiled spring, she was ready to attack but the male was too stupid to see it.

The male gestured with his silver weapon. It must have been the moment Janaya waited for. She sprang at the male, one leg kicked up at the weapon. It sailed through the air landing not far from Luke. After checking the clearing, he loped forward to grab the weapon for safekeeping. Janaya's lack of reaction told him she'd known of his presence. Luke stood well back to enjoy the show. It was easy to see Janaya played with the male. Easy for Luke to perceive. However, the alien male seemed a bit on the thick side.

He kicked out at Janaya. She dodged with ease then darted forward to grab the alien's foot while it was still midair. A swift flick of her wrist had the alien male flying backward and landing on his butt in the middle of a blackberry bush. His howl sounded louder than Killer at her best.

Luke stepped closer to Janaya, half expecting her to pull out her weapon and explode the alien asshole into a tidy pile of purple ash.

"You'll pay for this," the alien snarled.

Luke took one look at Janaya and stepped back. The dark purple mist filled her eyes. The male better watch his mouth or else he'd get more than soap.

"Leave, Santana. Go back to Dalcon."

"I'll see you rot in prison," Santana snarled.

A ray of purple fire shot from Janaya's eyes setting light to the dry leaves six inches from Santana's butt. He let out a girlish shriek and scrambled to his feet, backing away from the fire and Janaya. Blood oozed down a cut on his pretty face.

The blackberry thorns, Luke thought. He gave up his internal fight and let a smirk bloom. Couldn't have happened to a nicer bloke.

"Go, Santana," Janaya repeated.

The tired, defeated note in her voice propelled Luke to action. He strode to her side and placed a hand on her shoulder.

Santana glared at Janaya but when she stepped toward him, he backed away with such haste he fell over a punga stump. He cursed, picked himself up and slunk from sight.

"Sweetheart." Luke drew her into his arms and held her tense, shuddering body. A lump bloomed in his throat. He knew she'd wanted to prove her love to her father. But the bastard had thrown her love, her loyalty, back in her face. Luke pulled away to study her face. The color had leeched away leaving her pale and wan.

"Let's go home," he said, concern at the shock-like symptoms bringing a frown.

"I don't have a home any longer," she whispered hoarsely. "My father hates me and my unit is hunting me for desertion."

Luke tightened his grasp on her hand. "You have me. And Hinekiri."

His words didn't draw a positive response. Luke didn't know what to do or how to convince her of her worth. He sure as hell wished Hinekiri was here. She'd know what to do.

He led her unresisting form back to his vehicle and after he tossed the weapons behind his seat, buckled her into the passenger seat. A troubled silence filled his Land Cruiser during the drive to his father's house. Luke helped Janaya out and reached for the front door. It burst open before he could grasp the front handle.

"There you are, son," his father boomed. "Just rang the station looking for you."

"Do ya have any food?" Killer appeared at his father's feet, her black button nose twitching and white tail wagging so fast it blurred.

"Hinekiri here?"

"Yep," his father said, standing aside to let them enter.

Luke led Janaya to a kitchen chair and pushed her down. He placed the weapons on the bench.

"What's wrong with her?" his father muttered.

"She's had a shock. I really need Hinekiri," Luke muttered.

"I get Hine," Killer yapped. She trotted off, her nails clicking on the tiled floor.

Luke took the time to study his father. He was tanned and looked relaxed and fit. "Have a good time?"

His father grinned. "The best." Then he sobered. "We need to talk."

Luke nodded. "Sure, let me get Janaya sorted then we can sit down with a beer."

The click of nails indicated Killer's return. It was the speed of the return that alarmed Luke.

Killer skidded around the corner. "Purple people eaters!"

Hinekiri appeared out of breath but loaded with weapons. "Torgon. Saw them out the window."

Janaya leapt to her feet, seeming to snap out of her lethargic shock and grabbed up a weapon.

"Richard, here's a weapon for you," Hinekiri said. "Remember how to use it?"

"Is water wet?" His father snatched up the weapon and hurried to a window that faced the front of the house.

"Want one," Killer said. "Shoot purple people eaters."

"Not enough windows," his father said. "You guard the doors."

Killer barked. "Okay!"

Luke stared at his father before pushing the release on his weapon. "You understand her?"

"Yeah. Scared the shit out of me the first time."

"Hold your fire." Janaya directed in a hard voice. "I'll give the word."

A tense silence enveloped the room.

"What's Santana doing here?" Hinekiri said.

"He came to steal your charts," Janaya said.

"The bastard! He's mine," Hinekiri cried.

"You'll have to line up behind me," Luke muttered. He wanted to hurt the slimy bastard.

Janaya flicked the release on her weapon. "I'll take out Santana," she said in a hard voice.

"Whatever!" Luke's father said. "Just don't leave me to shoot the Torgon while the three of you blast this Santana into ashes."

"He's yours, Janaya," Luke said. He concentrated on the other targets.

Janaya stared at Santana with loathing. All this time, he'd used her to get to Hinekiri. And her father…

"Get ready," she ordered in a low, terse voice. "Fire!"

Almost as one, the four of them fired their weapons. Three Torgon disintegrated. Santana lost an arm.

"Ready. Fire!"

Three more Torgon fell and Santana lost another arm. He writhed on the ground and Janaya felt nothing but hatred.

"Finish him off, sweetheart." Luke stepped up beside her, sliding a comforting arm around her waist. "Don't make him suffer needlessly."

Janaya knew Luke was right—making Santana suffer wouldn't make her pain go away. Dredging up her professional mien, she aimed and fired.

With their leader gone, the rest of the Torgon milled about in confusion. Hinekiri and Luke's father aimed and fired almost simultaneously.

Richard Morgan let out a whoop. "Bull's eye!"

Hinekiri placed her weapon on the table and walked over to Janaya.

"I'm sorry about Santana."

Janaya closed her eyes briefly struggling for emotional calm. Everything she'd fought for had disappeared from her grasp. Her promotion, her father's love.

Her future.

The onslaught of tears choked up her throat.

"I'm sorry," she murmured, guilt and pain forming a lump of anguish in her throat. She coughed. "I've put you all in danger. Santana knew where to find us because Father told him."

"Your father, my brother, is a worthless rat bag. I've held my tongue all these years because he is your father and I know you love him. But we have to face facts. He's a selfish, devious, overbearing male who wouldn't know the meaning of love and loyalty if it bit him on the big toe."

Janaya tried to laugh but only managed a feeble sniff.

"Oh, Janaya." Hinekiri cupped Janaya's face with her hands and looked deep into her eyes. "I love you, child. You're the daughter I've never had. I've never told you in words because I thought you realized how much I care for you. You're my daughter in every way that matters."

Janaya sniffed again. Tears backed up behind her eyes. No amount of blinking stopped them and soon they poured down her face. "I love you too."

"Good," Hinekiri said briskly, her eyes looking suspiciously bright. "I suggest we celebrate the way we kicked those Torgon asses."

"You're still in trouble for flying off to Africa without telling me," Janaya said.

"At five in the afternoon with a faulty cloaking device," Luke muttered. "You have no idea the trouble you've caused."

Luke's father chuckled. "Rattled a few cages. Thought we might. I haven't had so much fun in ages."

Janaya looked from Hinekiri to Richard Morgan to Luke. Despite their sniping at each other, they were grinning. She knew Luke admired his father and she could see why.

"When is food?" Killer demanded, rubbing her head against Richard's leg. When he acted too slowly for her liking, she gave him a sly nip in the calf.

"Quit that," he warned. "We'll eat now."

He could understand Killer. Janaya cast a speculative glance at Hinekiri. Her aunt was busy beaming at Richard.

"Ah…" Janaya cleared her throat. "Have you two—"

"We don't need to know," Luke muttered, sliding an arm around her waist and tightening his hold in warning. "Too much information."

Hinekiri blushed. "I'll answer anyway. Yes. We have. Richard is coming along on my next expedition. We've come to an understanding."

Happiness blazed from her aunt's face and Janaya was fiercely glad that something good had come from their crash landing in Sloan. Luke's solid presence at her side reminded her of the second thing.

"Looks like we're going to become related," he murmured next to her ear.

"Do you mind?"

"Hell no! Dad needed someone like Hinekiri to jolt him from his rut."

Warmth curled inside Janaya without warning. She hugged Luke and reached up to plant a kiss on his lips. Unconditional love. She'd had it all along from her aunt but was too stupid to realize. And Luke. She stared up into his eyes and every one of her senses leapt in excitement. Oh, yeah. There was love here too if she dared take the risk. Janaya thought about the commitment required for all of two seconds. The decision wasn't difficult. Gut instinct told her life with Luke wouldn't be a gamble.

Luke enfolded her in his arms, clutching her against his broad chest. He smoothed his hand over her hair. "I love you, Janaya."

Janaya blinked away the sudden moisture in her eyes. She felt the solid pound of his heart beneath her cheek and smiled as she cuddled closer.

Dreams did come true. She had a family. She had it all.

Epilogue

ಐ

Janaya snuggled up to Luke's naked body. Sweat dripped off both of them but she didn't care. Relaxed and replete from a thorough loving — there was nothing better. Her thoughts drifted to Dalcon then darted away, too raw to think on the matter with any degree of rationality. Time, her aunt had said, nodding wisely.

"Don't think about your father or Dalcon," Luke murmured. "You don't need either of them."

Janaya pulled away to study Luke's face. "How did you know what I was thinking?"

"Not difficult," he said. "Especially since now and then I get a flash of your thoughts inside my head. It's a bit scary for this poor Earth male."

Janaya frowned. She'd thought it was just her that received his thoughts on what seemed a purely random basis.

"Random. Yeah, that's a good description."

"Scary."

"Yep." Luke picked up a long strand of hair and twirled it around his finger. "It doesn't matter. I still love you."

A pulse beat at the base of her throat and swelled as though her heart had risen from its normal resting place. "I love you too." It was true. There was no other male she'd rather spend her time with. Even when they disagreed on some small matter, she felt connected. Cherished. Loved.

"Janaya?" Luke sat up in the bed and fumbled for the bedside drawer. It screeched slightly in protest at being opened. Muttering slightly under his breath, Luke finally turned the light on. "Ah! There it is." He seized a blue velvet box from inside the drawer and turned to her, an enigmatic expression in place. Then he opened the small box.

Inside a gold ring gleamed. Blue and white jewels sparkled and picked up the light of the lamp. "I love you, Janaya. This is for you—a symbol of my love. Will you bond with me in the traditional Earth way?"

Janaya nodded dumbly, too overcome for words.

Luke grinned and pulled the ring from the depths of the white lining. He picked up her left hand and slid the ring on her finger.

A thousand different emotions twirled like ribbons inside Janaya. She wanted to laugh. She wanted to cry. Tears sparkled on her lashes as she gazed at the ring, the sign of Luke's love. "Will you make love to me? That's the way we finalize joining on Dalcon."

"You bet," he said. "It will be my pleasure." He stroked his finger across her lips, promise simmering in his brown eyes. "What does my future wife think about traveling with Dad and Hinekiri?"

"This place called Alaska sounds like fun. You can teach me how to fish."

Luke pressed a butterfly kiss on each of Janaya's eyelids. "I will. When we have time."

Desire unfurled in Janaya. Pleasure points started to hum.

Without warning, the door shot open and Killer trotted in. She bounded up onto the bed and pushed between them.

"Hinekiri and Richard told me to visit. They busy," Killer said.

"We were about to become busy too," Luke muttered but he scratched behind Killer's ears.

Janaya grinned as the dog rubbed against Luke with a sigh. "I suppose you're going to Alaska with us," she said.

Killer barked. "Might. I hungry."

"You're always hungry," Janaya said.

"Not. Sometimes sleepy." Killer leapt from the bed and trotted to the door then turned back to eye them hopefully.

Janaya's giggle was drowned by Luke's groan.

"Why laugh?" Killer demanded.

"No reason," Luke said, rolling his eyes. "Hell, I'm having a conversation with a dog."

"Good conversation," Killer snapped.

"See you in the morning, Killer," Janaya said.

"Snack?"

"No!" Janaya and Luke shouted simultaneously.

Killer trotted out the door. Then seconds later, she poked her head back through.

"Killer!" Richard Morgan roared. "I told you not to interrupt Luke and Janaya."

Janaya grinned again. Tonight there were no shadows in her heart. Instead, she felt a bottomless peace and satisfaction.

A family.

That's what she had with Luke.

"I leave them," Killer said with a loud yap.

"Good. Go to sleep and give us all some peace," Hinekiri chirped.

Killer was quiet for a moment then Janaya heard her say, "Do ya have any food?"

NEVER SEND A DOG TO DO A WOMAN'S JOB

೫

Chapter One

ഌ

Lily noticed the man straight away. Tall and golden, he prowled down the main street of Papakura like a jungle cat. Proud. Determined. Aware of his surroundings.

Every other female in the vicinity noticed him, too, but he didn't hesitate or seem to take any notice of the admiration. An elderly woman preened, patted her silver hair and promptly dropped her walking stick. The man stooped to pick it up, and she rewarded him with a coy smile. Lily would have bet the old girl's heart pounded. Hers certainly did. A trio of teenage girls put their heads together to whisper then burst into giggles each time they checked him out. Mrs. Pappadopoulos, the proprietress of the kebab shop across the road, rushed out with her straw broom and pretended to sweep her doorstep. Her eyes never left the golden cat. She might have fooled the man but Lily saw through her ploy. A dangerous stud seated at the window booth would boost sales during the slow back-at-work Monday.

Lily shifted on her wooden chair as she stared out the huge, plate glass window that fronted her travel agency. A frown formed between her brows. She could do with some customers to browse through her brochures and bring business. Her bank account was so far in the red it glowed like Rudolph's nose at Christmas time. The bank statements arrived on a daily basis, a not so subtle reminder by the bank manager that her overdraft was at the upper limits of acceptance. Maybe she should hire the golden man to step into her shop? Her gaze swept over broad shoulders and a truly tempting masculine butt. A sigh of appreciation whistled through her lips. Nice view—but not for her.

Lily picked up her pen and aimed her gaze at the flickering computer screen. A scant two seconds later, her eyes were right back on the golden man. He turned. Lily sucked in a loud, startled breath that echoed and filled the travel agency making her aware, more than ever, of the lack of customers. *Probably for the best*, she thought. No one to witness the overweight divorcée making cow eyes at an impossible dream.

Golden man.

An apt description. His curly blond hair grazed his shoulders and shone in the early morning light, the gentle sun picking out highlights that Lily would kill for. Even features were arranged in a tanned face. His dazzling smile was definitely worth a second look. Lily just wished she could see what color his eyes were. Curiosity propelled her need to know. *Maybe brown*, she decided. Her gaze drifted downward. His faded blue jeans were skin-tight, highlighting muscles and bulges with loving care, and one knee peeked out through a rip with each prowling step. A white cotton shirt accentuated his tan. White, Lily noted, bearing not a hint of what he ate for breakfast. She glanced down at her hip-length, cover-all-sins top. Two ugly brown splotches marred the light green fabric. *Yep, definitely coffee splashes*, Lily thought with resignation as she looked up again to follow the man's progress.

The man stopped outside the kebab shop. Mrs. Pappadopoulos beamed and hurried forward to greet her cash fall. She made a sweeping gesture with her right hand toward her best table. The golden man smiled.

Lily's heart skipped a beat. "Holy heck," she breathed in awe. There was a whole street and two footpaths between them yet she reacted to him physically! A tight sensation in her chest reminded her to breathe again.

The teenagers waltzed into the kebab shop, hips swaying, small pert breasts stuck out proudly. Lily didn't blame them.

She realized she'd sucked everything in while glued to the unfolding drama. Not that things moved into place as promptly as she would have liked. And her breasts had never, ever looked pert. Lily blinked rapidly to clear the sudden onslaught of tears. Past history. She was never going there again.

Lily sniffed and concentrated on the scene in the kebab shop. The elderly lady had found a friend, and they both stepped through the door Mrs. Pappadopoulos held open. Once they were over the threshold and safely inside, she shut it so they couldn't leave in a hurry. Lily supposed the oldies could always break out using their walking sticks if they got desperate.

Mrs. Pappadopoulos returned to the golden man. He flashed his smile again, and Lily felt warm all over from just watching the sex appeal ooze from him. The underwire bra she wore nipped at her delicate flesh, and she wriggled uncomfortably. Damn, she was gonna have to break the piggy bank to buy the next size up. Not good.

The golden man said something. Lily saw Mrs. Pappadopoulos's shoulders slump as she spoke in return. The bell on the kebab shop door tinkled merrily as the golden man sauntered out. Lily stared as he crossed the street without checking for traffic. With her luck she would have been run over and squashed flat as roadkill on a Sloan country road. He emerged with nothing more serious than disheveled hair. And dammit, that only made him look sexier.

Okay. Show time over. Things to do. Bills to pay.

But Lily couldn't drag her gaze off him. The view was even better since he was much closer. Chest pains forced her to suck in a breath. Lily stared, mesmerized. An urgent need to touch filtered through her brain. No. No. No! Why was her body not cooperating? The slow prickle of awareness that tightened her full breasts pissed her off. Her mouth firmed and her grip tightened on her favorite, lucky pen. Not again! Never again, she thought vehemently. But still she looked, unable to tear her gaze away from the wide shoulders, trim hips, and…uh…muscular legs. Lily shivered and tried to recall exactly what underwear she'd donned this morning. Just in case she outdid her usual clumsiness and sprawled at his feet. The memory wasn't comforting. A white bra—well, okay, off white with a pink tinge and black granny bloomers. Not—Holy shit! It didn't matter what she wore. Even if the golden cat was interested, she wouldn't let him touch her. No way, nohow was she letting a man close enough to rip her heart out again.

Lily tore her gaze off the male's muscular thighs and barely resisted the urge to check out other bodily bits. The golden man paused outside her travel agency. He saw her through the window and smiled, his brown eyes glowing with an inner fire. Lily's jaw dropped. Her hand started to shake and her silver pen somersaulted through nerveless fingers to do a perfect backward half pike before it landed somewhere under her desk. The golden man reached for the door.

Shit.

Shit!

He was coming in.

What the hell was she gonna do with him? That was assuming she could remember how to speak.

* * * * *

If you hurt my sister, I'll break every bone in your body.

The second Alex caught sight of the Earth woman in the travel agency, Luke Morgan's threat echoed through his mind. The warning had been closely followed by the accompanying threats from Janaya, from Hinekiri and her mate. Alex wasn't forgetting the snarls and yaps from Killer, the dog beast with more attitude than spots. And the opinionated creature had plenty of spots. Alex's amusement dimmed as he recalled the casual dinner with new friends that had turned into a threat-fest and orders to make sure his travel inoculations were up to date. The warning from Janaya, Luke's mate, had been particularly scary since she was an ex-Imperial Guard and knew lots of ways to make a male suffer. As an undergrown male, he'd once sneaked into the Imperial Guard's training hall. The screams he'd heard had featured in his nightmares for weeks after his adventure.

In truth, he had no intention of causing any harm, and they must have seen he was genuine since they'd agreed to send a letter of introduction with him. He peered through the window, catching the Earth woman's attention. That must be Lily Morgan. The woman fit the description he'd been given. She looked pleasant enough with an oval face and a wide, rosy mouth perfect for kissing, but he wanted her brain, her knowledge, her expertise and not a warm place to massage his cock.

He, Alexandre Bellangere, second in line to the King of Dalcon, was sick of being a pampered Prince. Tired of having his chest and ego stroked by palace groupies. Alex refused to go with the flow like his oldest brother and end up a notch on some bimbo's bedpost. Nope. No longer did he intend to be a sex toy paraded around the palace like a trophy. And he absolutely refused to bestow his Royal House of Dalcon mark on any female. He intended to go into trade and become a productive citizen, one with purpose to his existence. His father's decision to match him up with a neighboring female of suitable aristocratic blood had set the seal on his decision to leave.

Alex pushed the door open and stepped inside. Bright posters covered the wall showing enticing views of places on Earth he intended to visit. Places he'd only read about—pyramids, rainforests, mountains. Historical Earth cities. Excitement pulsed inside him. At last, his dream was on the way to reality. Bellangere Grand Tours was about to be born.

"Hello. Can I help you?"

The low, musical voice strummed across Alex's senses. He tore his attention off the shelves filled with brochures, turned to the woman and smiled. The black nameplate on the desk bore the name, Lily Morgan, in gold lettering. This woman was prettier than he'd imagined. The Earth magazine he'd picked up to ease the boredom of space flight had been full of pouting, skinny creatures with jutting bones that looked sharp enough to cut and draw blood. He'd thought the females ugly and definitely uncomfortable for playtime, but this one didn't look like a beanpole. Lily Morgan wore her brown hair tied back from her face with some Earth contraption, and loose tendrils softened her face. She had cute little brown spots sprinkled across her nose and cheeks. He couldn't see how tall the Earth woman was, but she had a pleasing amount of flesh on her bones, good-sized breasts that would fill, nay, overflow his cupped hands — not that he was looking!

Wary blue eyes studied him closely as if he might bite. Alex bit back a wolfish smirk. If he weren't here on such an important matter, he'd be tempted to sink his teeth... Hell, where was his head? Janaya Morgan hadn't looked as if she was joking and quite frankly, he didn't want to test the theory. It was strictly hands off, business only with this woman. Besides, he had goals he intended to conquer.

Alex thrust out his hand in the Earth manner ready to seal introductions, and get down to business. He was excited that his long two-moon cycle of Earth research and careful, painstaking schemes were working without discovery. Not one Earthling had pointed at him or screamed "Alien!" Pride bubbled through his mind. He fitted in, and it would remain that way since the only Earth person who needed to know he came from Dalcon was Lily Morgan.

"Alex Bell," he said. "I met your brother on Dalcon, and he suggested you might help me with a business proposition." When she failed to reciprocate, Alex reached inside his shirt pocket and pulled out the crumpled letter of introduction he carried.

Her mouth rounded to an O. Her hand fluttered to rest on one plump breast. "You...you..."

"Yes?" he asked.

"You're an alien!" she blurted.

Alex tilted his head and surveyed her closely. "Does that make any difference? I assure you I'm willing to pay."

She opened her mouth even further. Her brow scrunched up and the cute little dots on her nose stood out more than ever. Hell, he hoped she didn't scream.

Alex imagined Lily's family rushing to the rescue, his demise at the hands of Janaya, and hurried into speech. "I have access to New Zealand dollars. Please, read the letter of introduction." He'd never considered failing at the first hurdle. Not once. "I'll read your advertising material while you read the communications from your family, then we can talk."

Alex grabbed up a glossy travel magazine before she decided on a reaction. Perhaps if he acted in a non-threatening manner, she'd relax instead of taxing his ears with a screech.

Lily couldn't help but stare. The man was an alien.

An alien.

They sure had a good design team up on Dalcon if Janaya and the golden man were typical samples. Lily realized her jaw sagged open and snapped it shut lest she trap any kamikaze flies. For a moment there, she'd forgotten she was off men. She thought of her ex-husband Ambrose and his boyfriend Garrett and just like that, she was back to normal. Or, as normal as she could be, with an honest-to-goodness alien prowling around her travel agency.

"How did you get here?" she blurted. "Did you come alone? Do you have a ship?" She peered out the front window of her travel agency. Everything looked normal.

"I came aboard a space freighter. The captain dropped me on the outskirts of Papakura and left again. I walked to find your travel merchant shop." He frowned slightly then the lines on his brow cleared. "Travel agency."

Lily nodded. Okay. They stared at each other before she cleared her throat. "The letter?" she murmured.

"Sorry. I got distracted." His smile was dazzling as he handed her a crumpled white envelope. Their hands brushed during the transfer. Lily held her breath, her gaze trapped in his. Time stood still while they stared at each other.

The thump of the door when the mailman entered broke the spell.

Lily tugged the envelope from the alien's hand. He stepped away and reached for a brochure on Australia to add to the one on the Cook Islands he already held. Lily drew a cautious breath. She smelled his scent. Something green and mysterious as a jungle cat. And just as hypnotic.

"Mail, Lily," Jason, the mailman, said in a loud voice.

Lily shook herself back to the present. Jason handed her several envelopes and parked his butt on the corner of her desk. A grin stretched his mouth. "There's a concert in the park on Saturday night. I'll pack a picnic. What do ya say?"

"I—"

"She's busy on Saturday," Alex said.

Jason stood abruptly, his hands curling around his red postbag. "I was talking to Lily."

The tension in her office ratcheted up sharply. Testosterone poured off the two males in crashing waves. Jason stepped toward Alex, his jaw flexing in a belligerent manner.

Lily's heart pounded in sudden fear. They couldn't fight! She had to do something straight away. She eyed the golden man in trepidation. Janaya, her new sister-in-law, could fly. She could toss her husband through a window on a mere whim. No telling what powers this alien had.

Lily rushed between the two men and placed one placating hand on Jason's forearm. A soft growl sounded behind her. Alarm made her hand flex on Jason's arm. "I… Thank you for asking me, Jason, but I have four presentations to finish for Monday. I need to work during the weekend." *Please take the hint. Please.*

"Perhaps another day?"

She nodded and tried to ignore the warmth emanating from the male behind. His spicy green scent filled her lungs. "Sounds...good, Jason."

The golden man's second growl made ignoring him impossible. Lily used her elbow as a weapon without a second thought. The oomph of expelled air brought home the stupidity of her actions. He was bigger than she for a start. And he was an alien. She couldn't forget that part. Silently, she willed Jason to leave, to step away from the danger that warmed her back and prickled her skin.

"Well. Okay then. See you tomorrow." Jason yanked open the door, glared at Alex and stomped out, leaving them alone.

Lily turned slowly and retreated. The intent, determined look on the alien's face made her swallow. She stepped behind her desk, very aware of the large male. Not that it would do her much good if he decided to ravish her or chose to experiment. Aliens were tricky with their powers. Luke had said so although he'd been a bit vague about details. Her father had said so, too. Lily realized she'd made a big mistake by not asking for more information about flying and superhuman strength and anything else alien related. In this case, too much information sounded like a good thing.

Lily gritted her teeth and stared in horror as the male prowled closer. Stupid. Stupid. Stupid. She wouldn't make the same mistake again. "What...what are you doing?" The clear stammer brought a frown. Confidence was the key in dealing with most things. Aliens couldn't be any different. She stood straighter and thrust back her shoulders. "Did you want something?"

He stepped around the corner of the wooden desk and halted a foot from her quivering body. His brown eyes settled on her face then drifted down to her breasts. Her nipples peaked against the cotton of her bra while she was suddenly very conscious of the drape of her top and the fit of the elastic waistband of her black skirt. His spicy scent enticed her to think outrageous things that an innocent human had no right considering. Lily desperately wanted to touch. To run her fingers down his broad chest, grasp his hips and pull him close.

Lily heard a low groan. It had come from her! Mortified color flooded her cheeks, bleeding downward to her neck and upper chest. She couldn't look him in the eye and see the pity on his face. Because that's what she'd see. Men like him didn't look at women like her. Lily didn't think aliens would be any different.

She stepped away from him, away from temptation and further embarrassment. Lily dropped into her swivel chair, ripped the envelope and started reading.

Lily,

This place is amazing. Dad and I are having a ball. Not sure when we'll be back — it all depends on the company Hinekiri is negotiating with to update charts.

We met Alex on our travels, and he spent several days with us before he left for Earth. He seems like an okay bloke and since Dad and I knew you'd welcome the business, we sent him your way. He gave us his word he'd treat you like a lady —

Lily snorted. How did Luke think he could enforce a promise when he was in Dalcon? By ESP?

Janaya had a word with him, too. Don't know what she said but it seemed to put the fear of God into him.

Anyway, he wants to start up in the tour business running tours from Dalcon all over the universe. He'd like to include Earth as a destination so I figured why shouldn't you profit. He's willing to pay big bucks for your expertise. From what I can gather, he wants someone with local knowledge to show him around New Zealand.

Love, your big bro,

Luke

Lily extracted another sheet of paper from the envelope aware of the golden male prowling around her office, picking up brochure after brochure. At the rate he was going, she wouldn't have any left to offer customers. She unfolded the other sheet of paper and frowned at the unfamiliar writing.

Dear Sister,

I hope we're doing the right thing sending this male, Alex, to you. Now that I have a sister, I don't intend to lose her in a hurry. I'm afraid you're stuck with my aunt Hinekiri, and me.

If you feel threatened or need help handling the male —

Well, that was a given, Lily thought. She raised her eyes to his denim-clad butt and shuddered. Oh, yeah. She was threatened all right, but it was her hormones that were the problem. For some unknown reason, Lily couldn't stop looking at him and that made her grumpy. Very grumpy. She would tell him to go to hell. That's what she'd do!

But you can't afford to, a little voice of reason whispered. Not if he's offering business. She put Janaya's letter down and glanced at the man — Alex. "Can you tell me what you had in mind?"

The golden man turned away from the brochures with a slightly glazed look in his amber-brown eyes.

Lily's mouth set in a firm line. Was she that dull and boring? She heaved an inward sigh, thinking that she didn't know what she was worried about. Her virtue was safe from the golden cat. "What did you have in mind? Where did you want to go?" She drew in a deep breath and felt as though she was teetering on the edge of a precarious cliff. "How much are you offering to pay me?"

"I want to see both the North and the South Island. I thought around a month would give me time to research places to stay and visit and sort out reliable contacts. That's what I'd need your help with. As to payment — I can't afford to pay much.

How does one thousand dollars a day sound plus shelter and meals?"

Shock kicked her in the gut, robbing her of speech, but thoughts galloped through her mind. One thousand dollars. A day. One thousand dollars. There were thirty-one days in March. That equated to thirty-one thousand dollars!

"How much?" Lily asked hoarsely.

"It's not much, I know." A frown marred his handsome face for an instant before his brow smoothed out. "Once I start bringing tours through, I'll need help. What about if I pay you a commission as my local agent?"

Lily nodded abruptly, "Where do I sign?" She had to work hard to restrain the celebratory cheer building at the back of her throat. Any sudden moves might scare off her cash cow before she'd signed on the dotted line. She didn't want that!

"I have a treaty with my belongings. I left my bags in a secret hole until we had time to talk. We can discuss the rules and regulations over dinner."

Dinner. That meant dressing up. "Can't we do it now?" Her one good dress was at the cleaners after she'd had a wee accident involving her food and the wandering hands of the man who'd sat next to her at the travel agent convention last month. She couldn't afford to collect it yet. "Or at least discuss the details so we can formalize the agreement tonight." Lily scowled inwardly. Rules and regulations sounded rather daunting.

"Time is of the essence," he agreed in his accented drawl. "Before I left, I had word of an entrepreneur in the Jupiter sector wanting to set up a similar business to what I have in mind. I intend to be first."

Lily's eyes widened. "Just how many aliens are there on Earth?"

Alex grinned suddenly. "Frightened we're going to experiment on you? Perform kinky sexual deeds to see how you work?"

"No!" Lily's cheeks felt as though they had caught fire. The trouble was he wasn't far from the truth. Except in her graphic imagination she was the aggressor. It astounded her that she'd have these thoughts let alone visualize doing them with an alien. "Of course not!" Time to conduct this conversation along official paths. "Tell me what you've done in the way of research. What places did you want to visit?"

"I've spent the last two-moon cycle researching Earth and its people—one of your Earth years. There are many places I wish to visit, but in New Zealand, I'd like to see both islands. Your brother suggested I ask you to take me to the main sites."

Lily found a notepad then searched for her pen. She patted the papers on the desktop before remembering it had somersaulted under her desk. For an instant, she thought about grabbing another pen but superstition propelled her to search for her lucky pen. Lily dropped to all fours and crawled under her desk. A soft choking noise made her freeze. Her cheeks heated anew and a fine tremor ran the length of her body. She didn't want to even start imagining what she looked like from Alex's perspective. But since the damage was done...

Lily ran her hands across the tight pile of the gray carpet in search of her pen. Ah! There it was. She seized the silver pen and backed from under her desk. Halfway out, her bottom connected with something hard. Lily glanced over her shoulder in puzzlement and twisted about to come face-to-face with Alex's legs and manly equipment. Startled and totally flustered, she shot upward. The side of her head connected with the desk. Pain exploded through her head, shooting stars soared past her closed eyes.

"Ouch!" she cried. Shit, that hurt! Lily's hand fingered the sore spot and came away damp with blood.

Masculine hands seized her around the waist and pulled her out to safety. Suddenly she was up close and personal with the alien, her heart thudding loud enough to wake the dead, her senses swamped with him. Lily looked deep into his amber eyes, mesmerized—dazed.

"Are you injured?" His hands ran up and down her body in the most delicious manner. She tried to concentrate on the fact she wore granny pants under her skirt but it was difficult when she stood so close to him. "Where does it hurt?" he murmured.

God, it hurt everywhere. Her breasts throbbed and lower her pussy tingled with longing. Said granny pants felt uncomfortably damp. She shuddered, unable to speak for fear of blurting out her desperate need of him.

"You're bleeding." He stepped away from her, and Lily wanted to protest. Then he yanked off his shirt, and she forgot how to breathe. The need to run her tongue across the broad expanse of his hairless chest pounded through her confused brain. She really didn't like sex, but oh, man, she wanted to do it with him.

Chapter Two

ෂ

Panic of colossal proportions assaulted Alex as he trailed his hands across Lily's silky skin. His cock stirred, pressing against his Earth clothing in an insistent manner that was almost painful. Alex closed his eyes and tried to think of anything but the warm, feminine body he held in his arms. A spasm started in the biggest digit on his right foot. This felt like bonding to him, and he damn well didn't have the time or inclination, even though her hips fitted the span of his hands perfectly. That bloody charlatan of a medical man had given him faulty travel pills. He must have. The pills were meant to stop bonding from happening. The thought pounded through him with relentless truth. One thing was sure—the second he set foot on Dalcon again, he intended to sue. After he'd exacted his pound of flesh from the pompous little windbag. Was it his fault he was allergic to the quills they sourced from Dalcon's fodo bird to inject the travel inoculations? No! The medical man had assured him if he took the pills, he'd be sweet. He'd have no problems with the trace elements in Earth's atmosphere. No problems with illness and certainly no fuckin' bonding for life with a receptive Earth female!

Lily sighed, her warm, moist breath feathering across his chest to hit one masculine nipple. Alex suppressed his shudder of pleasure while he frantically thought of possible solutions. There must be some way out. He hadn't felt the bonding ties until he'd touched her. Maybe if he refrained from touching her again? Swift on the heels of this thought came another. Luke and Janaya Morgan were gonna kill him.

He was dead meat.

Lily edged closer to him and sighed again—a soft breathy sound that sent lusty thoughts roaring out of control. Alex

Shelley Munro

clenched his teeth and fought against the desire to remove her clothes, part her legs and claim her as his mate. That couldn't happen. Despite his royal connections, he had no means of support. Everything he owned was tied up with getting his new business off the ground. If he gave into the need coursing through his veins, he'd be back where he started. A pampered pet for the women of the royal court to paw over. Damn it! He wanted his own identity. He wanted people to look at him and see a self-made man instead of being awed by his pretty face. Was that too much to ask?

The woman stirred again, reminding him of how he'd gotten himself into this mess. She'd hurt herself. Alex inched away and then steeling himself against the jolt of sensation he knew he'd feel, tilted up her head to see the extent of the damage. Blood had trickled from a scrape on her temple down her face and neck. He grabbed his shirt off the desk and started to wipe the blood from her face.

Voices outside the travel agency made him pause. Familiar voices. The sound of the door handle turning made Alex turn. No! He stiffened and waited for the axe to fall.

"What the hell have you done to my sister?" Luke Morgan clenched his fists and loomed over the desk that stood between them. He looked ready to take Alex apart.

The devil-spotted dog bounded into the office with a threatening bark. "Woof! I'll bite him before he eats more blood. Woof!"

"I thought I told you to keep your hands off my sister," Janaya snarled.

Resigned, Alex waited for pain to hit his body. Two more people—Hinekiri, Janaya's aunt, and Richard, Luke's father—crowded into Lily's office. *Great*, Alex thought. The gang was all here.

He was going to die.

Lily tugged from his grasp and straightened her top. Alex's heart wrenched at the separation. But he wasn't fool enough to

174

do anything about it, not with Lily's overprotective family gunning for blood.

"What are you doing here? I thought you were staying on Dalcon for at least another month before you headed off again," Lily said.

"Aren't you pleased to see us?" Luke demanded.

Lily looked confused. "Of course I am, stupid. I just don't understand why you're here."

"We've come to pick up my fishing gear," Richard Morgan said.

Lily's brows rose. "All the way from Dalcon?"

They were lying, of course. Alex knew it, and judging by the expression on Lily's face, she had trouble swallowing their story, too. It had more holes than a fishing net.

"We're finally going fly fishing in Alaska. There's a big fishing contest in Anchorage. I wanted my favorite lures. My lucky lures," Richard added.

"I tried to tell Richard I was going to catch a bigger salmon than him," Hinekiri chirped with a toothy grin. "That's when he decided we needed to come back here to pick up his lures."

Janaya strode up to the desk and scrutinized Lily closely. She winged a glare at Alex. "Have you bitten her neck?"

Trust the bodyguard, Alex thought. She never let go of what was important. They trained the best on Dalcon.

"Well?" Janaya snapped.

Alex took a step back, eying her warily. He didn't like the fire in her eyes.

"What are you talking about?" Lily said. "Alex hasn't bitten me."

Luke stepped up beside his wife and put his hands on his hips. "Then why are you bleeding?"

Killer barked, the hot air expelled heating Alex's leg even through his Earth jeans. "Vampire," she barked.

"I am not a damned vampire," Alex snapped. Royal princes didn't have permanent fangs, for a start. The spotted devil was more vampire than him. Look at the way she was eyeing his buttock flesh.

Lily patted him on the arm. "No one said you were a vampire."

Interesting that Lily seemed to be the only one in the room that didn't understand the dog. The dog stalked closer.

"Tell them how you hurt yourself," Alex muttered, giving Killer a suspicious look. She was awful close, definitely within biting distance.

"I hit my head on the desk when I was getting my pen," Lily said, looking at her feet. Her head jerked up again to glare at her brother and sister-in-law. "You know how clumsy I am." Both her words and her body language spoke of mortification.

Luke laughed. "You hit your head? Klutz. I could never understand how you managed to be so good at bowling a cricket ball when you were so clumsy the rest of the time."

Alex clenched his fists feeling angry on Lily's behalf. He made an instinctive move to comfort then jerked his hand back before touching her. Lily was his employee. His means to make his plans for the future come true. He couldn't afford to touch her again and cement the bond further.

"We told you to have your inoculations," Janaya said with a bite in her voice.

Alex backed up, moving closer to Lily. No way was he stupid enough to let Janaya within striking distance. But then perhaps this wasn't a good move either. His heart felt the pull, the tug of Lily's soul calling. Alex jumped away, glaring at them all. He would not sacrifice his dream.

Lily broke the taut silence. "If you've come back to collect your fishing lures, why are you here in Papakura? Why aren't you in Sloan?"

A perfectly logical question, Alex thought, smothering a smirk. That was his little moon heart. He arched a brow at Luke and waited for the Earthman to extract himself from the hole he'd dug.

"We came to see you," Hinekiri chirped when Luke hesitated. "You're family. Of course we'd want to see you."

Surely, Lily wouldn't buy the blatant lie? Alex narrowed his eyes then groaned inwardly as he glanced at her. The sunshine smile said it all.

"Alex and I were about to discuss our itinerary," Lily said.

Alex bit back a grin. Her words had her family sharing panicked glances although they rallied quickly. And there was a lot of silent communication going on between Luke and Janaya. He couldn't let them talk Lily out of helping him. He needed her.

"Lily is organizing her relief staff, and we're leaving this weekend." Alex met Luke's frown without a flinch. As far as Alex was concerned, this was war. He'd get Lily to help him through fair means or foul. Apart from the bonding. He agreed with her family about that.

"A suggestion," Hinekiri said. "Lily isn't going to get much done with us underfoot. Why don't we leave her to sort out things and meet her in Sloan? Perhaps tomorrow morning?"

"Good idea," Janaya said before Alex could offer an opinion.

Panic jumped up and down in Alex's gut. Quite frankly, he didn't want to let Lily out of his sight in case she changed her mind. With her travel background and her knowledge of aliens, she was the perfect candidate for what he had in mind. He checked Lily for her reaction and froze. For an instant, lust fogged his thoughts—a vision of naked skin and luscious, plump breasts offered up for his tasting delight danced through his mind, leaving him breathless. Wanting. His cock twitching in readiness to follow the thought through.

Hinekiri coughed loudly. "Alex, you can drive down to Sloan with us, and Lily can come down once she's sorted everything here."

His vision dissolved into reality. They were trying to come between him and his goals. There was more than one way to pluck a fodo bird. This was war.

*   *   *   *   *

They stowed his bags and piled into a vehicle called a land something or other. Luke and Killer took the passenger seat and Richard drove. Alex was hemmed in the rear, a potential target between the bodyguard and the explorer. The only weapon he had to protect himself with was an Earth jacket.

Alex clicked the seat belt into place and cast a sardonic glance at each of the Dalcon women who flanked him. Time for the attack to begin.

"I told you," Janaya stated in a hard voice, "to make sure you had travel inoculations before you left Dalcon. I told you of the consequences."

"You informed me of the dangers of bonding and made it clear what would happen if Lily was coerced into a bond with me. I listened to everything you said, but there was a problem. I'm allergic to fodo quills."

"Why didn't you tell us?" Luke demanded, his bronzed face darkening with anger as he glared from the passenger seat. Killer punctuated her displeasure with a low, hair-raising growl.

"I've been thinking about that," Hinekiri said, breaking the sudden tension. "He needed Lily, so he didn't mention his allergy. This business venture of yours must be real important to you."

They didn't know the half of it, Alex thought. If he'd stayed in the palace for much longer he'd have lost every brain cell. And insanity wasn't the done thing for a prince. No telling what indignities the King would have forced on him in the nature of a tonic-fix.

"I've invested a lot of time and money," Alex said in wry understatement. Not to mention run away from home, dodged his bodyguards and spent a fortune on the Driscoll witch spell to disguise his looks. Money well spent since none of them seemed to recognize him as Prince Alexandre. The old crone who'd sold him the spell had assured him he would appear the exact opposite in appearance. Dalconians would see him as dark and plain, the exact same reflection he saw whenever he looked in a mirror now. It had taken a little getting used to seeing a stranger, but he had grown to love the anonymity. Alex considered conducting a test of sorts to ease his agitation but gave up the idea. He didn't want to call attention to himself any more than necessary. "Why did you give me an introduction letter if you didn't trust me?"

"We had second thoughts," Janaya stated with quiet dignity. "And we wanted to pick up some fishing gear. Besides, you told us you had the inoculations covered."

"The medical man prescribed pills."

"Then why didn't you take them?" Janaya muttered, spearing him a look of distaste. "If my sister-in-law must bond with a Dalconian then at least he should have a few looks going for him."

Hinekiri reached past him to slap Janaya on the leg. "Manners! I'm ashamed of you. The male can't help how he looks."

Alex wanted to chuckle and cheer out loud. Proof that the spell was working. "Don't worry. I'm used to it. Looks aren't everything." He just wished that everyone else didn't put such stock in his looks. "And I took the pills. I'm still taking the pills. I've no idea why they're not working. Lily seems pleasant, but I don't wish to bond with any female."

Hinekiri took hold of his chin and stared deep into his eyes before looking at Janaya. "If you ask me the male's telling the truth."

"That's it then," Janaya said. "I'll have to shoot him."

"I haven't done anything." Alex felt his face heat with anger. "I want to do research for my business. I'm not looking for an Earth woman to mate with," he gritted out.

Richard pulled up on the side of the road with a screech of brakes. "I can't concentrate on driving with you sniping at each other. You're acting like children. If you can't behave in the backseat, I'm gonna put the lot of you out and you can walk to Sloan."

Stunned silence met his announcement.

"Looks like rain," Luke said cheerfully.

Richard speared a glare at his son. "One more smart-ass comment and you can go with them."

Killer yapped from her position on Luke's knee. "Yeah," she said. "I have sore head." Her stomach rumbled loudly, echoing in the tense atmosphere of the vehicle.

Alex heard the women sitting on either side of him inhale sharply. He saw Luke stiffen. The expression on the devil creature's face clued him in. She was going to start nagging about food. Again. The dog had a one-track mind when it came to eating.

Killer turned on Luke's lap to peer at Richard. "I hungry. Do ya have any food?"

"I'll put you out to walk as well," Richard growled back, but Alex heard the suppressed humor in his voice. After glaring them all into silence, he moved a lever to indicate he was pulling out onto the road and they carried on.

They drove along in peace this time, leaving Alex free to think about his upcoming trip with Lily. A vision of Lily with her ripe curves and shy smile flooded his mind. Alex's hands clenched, fingernails digging into his thighs as he fought the immediate arousal that slammed through his body. His heart sped, his cock thrust upward, his jeans tenting enough that he was glad of his jacket draped across his lap. His calf protested and throbbed insistently. Alex shuffled his feet to a new position but in the cramped backseat, the movement didn't ease the aching sensation.

Alex concentrated on keeping his breathing slow and even and built a picture in his mind of how his life at the palace would be if he failed in obtaining his dream. Alex exhaled heavily, knowing he had no choice. He would keep his hands off her. It was that simple.

* * * * *

Janaya heard the tap of shoes as her aunt trotted down the stairs, followed by the click of Killer's nails on the wooden floor. She turned toward the door and spoke the instant she saw her aunt, impatient to get a family meeting on the go. "Is he upstairs in his room?"

Hinekiri grinned in a toothy way that indicated secrets and waggled her forefinger in Janaya's face. "You don't have to whisper. His hearing appears normal. Earth's atmosphere hasn't affected Alex like it did you. And just to make sure, Killer and I conducted a test."

Killer yapped agreement. "We say insult—"

Hinekiri grasped Killer's muzzle with her hand and held the dog's mouth shut. "No need to spill the beans."

Killer jerked from her firm hold and bounced out of reach. "What beans? Do ya have food?"

"You ate half an hour ago. Enough!" Janaya said, sending a disgruntled frown in Killer's direction. "We can't leave them alone. You saw how they were looking at each other."

"I remember another couple, not so long ago," Hinekiri murmured, sending a significant look from Luke to Janaya.

"That's different. We're talking about family. Lily to be precise," Janaya said.

"Janaya's right," Luke said. "We don't know anything about Alex Bell. He could be a criminal on the run for all we know." Luke stalked the length of the kitchen. He strode back and stopped beside Janaya, curling an arm around her waist. Janaya smiled. They needed to finish this meeting so she and Luke could get to the good stuff in the privacy of their bedroom.

"I say we leave them to it," Richard drawled.

As one, they turned to stare at him. He calmly sipped from his can of beer.

"Dad, are you out of your mind?" Luke stared in clear consternation. "Lily's vulnerable since Ambrose did a runner with his boyfriend. I don't want her hurt again."

Richard placed his beer can on the tabletop. "You're all forgetting one thing. Lily is an adult. We have to let her make her own mistakes."

Janaya wanted to disagree, but Luke's hand curled into her hip, silently telling her to hold her protests.

"But," Richard said, "as Luke said, we don't know much about this male so as much as I trust Lily to do what's right for her, I think we should ask Killer to stay here to keep an eye on matters."

"Oh! Yes! Good plan." Hinekiri clapped her hands together and blew a kiss to her man.

"Good thinking, Dad," Luke approved.

Janaya paused then nodded slowly at the sheer brilliance of Richard's idea. The spotted dog would make the perfect spy.

Killer stilled then pricked her black ears forward. "Spy?"

Janaya winked at Luke. "We'd pay you, of course."

Killer sat on her haunches and stared at Janaya. "I want collar. One with shiny studs. A black one to go with my spots. And food. Lots of food."

Janaya bit back the grin that ached to burst forth. "That could be arranged."

Killer nodded. "Deal. I agree to spy for collar and food. Start right now." She trotted to the door. "I be like famous dog detectives—Scooby and Scrappy." She disappeared from sight but Janaya heard the click of her claws as she climbed the stairs. "Maybe get own TV show," she said, her bark of satisfaction drifting back down the stairs.

Chapter Three

ဆ

Alex expelled a heavy sigh of relief as the spaceship took off. He stared at the shiny silver disc until the cloaking device slid into place and shielded it from sight. The rumble of the engines faded to silence.

They were gone.

The lot of them, and he was still alive to tell the tale.

Exhilaration galloped through him along with a sense of freedom. Alex inhaled the fresh, crisp air in the hilltop clearing. After the planning and intrigue, he was really on Earth. Although dusk was rapidly turning to dark and they would soon need the torches to navigate the rutted track back to Luke's vehicle, Alex soaked up every new sight. The strange ferns and the tall, stately trees Lily had said were called kauri. A bird called. More pork! More pork!

"That's New Zealand's native owl. It's called a Morepork after the sound it makes." Lily played the torch over the track and stepped over a fallen branch.

Alex turned to smile at her but was careful to keep a full arm's width between them. Despite the simmering temptation, he'd keep his hands to himself, and everything would be fine. No nasty bonding entanglements to stuff up his dreams.

Lily grinned back, and a twinge of need rode him. His heart beat a little faster and a faint film of sweat dampened his forehead. *Hands off*, he reiterated silently. Keep to his plan and his dream would come to fruition. Lily was a complication he didn't need. He'd seen his cousin give up a long-held ambition because of a female. That wasn't going to happen to him.

A loud rustle and the snap of a breaking twig sounded in the bushes to their right. Lily started, let out a faint squeak and promptly tripped on an uneven tuff of dirt. Alex whirled, instinct kicking in. He scooped her up, saving her before she hit the ground.

Lily thudded against his chest, a soft armful of woman. Her generous curves melded against his flesh as though she was designed especially for him. Alex sucked in a deep breath as he tamped down on the searing need that burned his body and had his cock leaping with acute anticipation. She smelled of sweet flowers and woman. She felt like a soft, billowy cushion. Alex closed his eyes while he fought for control. Hell, he could feel the binding ties knitting together into immutable knots. Panic flared, and then she moved in his arms. His eyes popped open.

"Sorry," she said, sounding a trifle winded. Her warm breath puffed against his mouth as she stared up at him. Tense silence reigned as they studied each other.

Let her go. Stand her on her feet and step away. Alex issued the release order to his hands. They ignored the instruction and flexed, kneading the yielding, feminine flesh of her buttocks. A pained groan escaped past his clenched teeth when she pressed closer. The air pulsed between them full of possibilities. Alex thought about the consequences, but with Lily cuddled in his arms nothing else seemed important. Innocent eyes drew him in, teasing but subtle in their goading.

Lily swallowed loudly then her tongue swept out to lick her lips. Another groan built at the back of Alex's throat. Pure enticement. Torture. He lowered his head, wanting to claim her lips, to taste her, and sip and savor more than he wanted his next breath. Lily rose up on tiptoes straining to meet him, her face mysterious in the moonlit darkness. Alex lowered his head a bit more. Their lips touched briefly and then parted.

Another loud rustle sounded right beside them. Alex and Lily sprang apart, both staring at the swaying leaves of a lacy fern.

"Who's there?" Alex demanded when all he wanted to do was curse out loud at the interruption and because he'd left his weapon back at the Morgan house. Only a fool went out without a weapon. He thrust Lily behind him. "Come out with your hands where I can see them."

The silhouetted ferns trembled. Dry leaves rustled. A black nose appeared followed by a black and white head.

"Don't shoot!"

That bloody dog again.

Alex straightened from his protective stance in front of Lily. "Why aren't you on the ship with Janaya?"

Lily laughed, a soft tinkling sound that made him yearn to hold her again. "She's hardly likely to answer you back."

Alex met the dog's sly grin with a frown. Unfortunately, Alex knew the dog could answer him back. Lily was lucky she couldn't understand the devil beast. He glared at Killer, his hands fisting at his sides.

Killer stuck her nose in the air, presenting him with pure attitude. "I needed to use the restroom. I didn't expect them to go without me. Call them back. Tell them to come get me."

Alex opened his mouth to blast Killer then remembered Lily was present. For some reason, no one had seen fit to tell Lily about the dog talking. He wasn't about to break the news.

"She doesn't seem to like you much," Lily observed as the dog growled low at the back of her throat.

And the feeling was mutual!

A loud ring broke the tense silence. Lily fumbled in her pocket and pulled out a cell phone. "This is Luke's phone, so it's probably for him," she said. "I'd better answer. It might be important."

Alex looked on with interest as she juggled the torch and the small phone. Her breasts swayed, drawing his attention and making him wish Killer's timing hadn't been so off. Shaking away the fog of lust, he relieved her of the torch and aimed the beam directly on the keypad. Their hands touched during the transfer. Lily gasped while Alex gritted his teeth and thanked the gods for the dim light since his body was broadcasting signals difficult to miss. His cock ached insistently, as it had since meeting Lily, and his legs quivered in tandem. One look at his raging hard-on and the female would likely run a mile. If he'd been at home, he would have grabbed a female, maybe two, and eased both his intense erection along with the burn of stress.

But he wasn't at the palace. This was a whole new experience.

Lily stabbed a button on the phone and held it up to her ear. "Hello. Luke? What are you ringing me for? Is there a problem?" She listened for a few seconds. "Killer's here with us," she said. "I've no idea how it happened. Are you coming back for her?"

Alex noticed the dog listened as closely to the one-sided conversation as he did.

"But Alex and I can't take Killer with us. Most of the hotels don't allow dogs."

Bloody hell. They were trying to foist the devil creature on them. Time to speak up. "I don't think—"

"Smuggle her into the hotel in a bag! Luke, are you mad? You're a policeman. So is Dad. You shouldn't encourage me to break the law. Besides, how am I going to make Killer stay quiet? Knowing my luck she'll bark at a relevant moment or worse, tear after the owner's cat or...or eat their goldfish!" Lily paused to listen to her brother then handed the phone to Alex. "He wants to talk to you."

Alex accepted the phone from Lily and tried not to react to the jolt of sensation their innocent touch produced. A wry grin twitched at his lips while his erection jerked in reaction, and quite independently from the orders issued from his brain. The other times hadn't been a fluke.

"Luke," he said, a note of caution in his voice.

"I'm sorry to land you with responsibility for Killer. The bloody cloaking device is on the blink again, otherwise we'd come back for her. Just tell her how important it is to be quiet and on her best behavior. She'll listen to you."

Oh, yeah? Alex cast a dubious glance at the dog. "I'm not sure this is a good idea. I'm here on business. We don't have time to watch over your dog."

Killer barked, "I'm not staying by myself. How will I get food?"

Alex closed his eyes. If the bloody dog didn't shut up, he'd give her a demonstration of where she could put her damned food.

"Good," Luke said smoothly. "I'll take that as a yes."

Alex sucked in a breath, ready to tell Luke what to do with his devil dog. "But I don't—"

The phone went dead.

"Damn!" Alex peered at the dog as he handed the phone back to Lily. Funny, he could have sworn the spotted creature smirked.

"It's getting cold. And late," Lily said.

Alex bit back a curse and wrenched his gaze off her plump, kissable lips. But even so, the thought slid into his head. The area was also private. A vision popped fully formed into his mind. And, unfortunately, Lily starred in his dream image. No clothes. Limbs entwined.

A shrill bark jerked him to the present. The dog pushed between him and Lily, forcing Alex to step back. He speared a glare at the furry creature. Perhaps he could sell it to a passing Dalcon trader. Yeah, definitely a solution to ponder.

"I'm not very good in the dark," Lily muttered. "My night vision is terrible."

Killer trotted off down the track. "Follow me. I be good in dark."

"She can't understand you," Alex snapped.

"Why do you do that?" Lily asked her voice shaded with puzzlement. "Luke and Janaya growl back at her all the time, too. She seems to like it."

"You tell her or me?" Killer yapped, coming to an abrupt halt in the middle of the track.

"I'm not touching that one," Alex muttered.

"I have no idea what you're talking about." Lily shook her head, kept walking and ploughed straight into Killer.

Alex snapped his hand out to grasp her upper arm, but the clumsiness was catchy. He staggered on the uneven ground and clutched a handful of luscious breast instead of his target. Startled and off balance, Lily fell, taking Alex with her. Alex twisted his body at the last moment. Lily landed on top, draped across his body like a satin sheet, and his libido went from casual interest to fiery hot in seconds flat. Instead of pushing her away like a male with any sense would, Alex compounded his error by aligning their bodies. Breast to chest. Thigh to thigh. His erection pulsing against her belly.

A heart beat later, that wasn't close enough. Too many clothes separated their straining bodies. Alex slid his lips over Lily's in an openmouthed kiss that exploded on his senses, sucking him into the magical spell she cast. Time seemed to slow. His hearing intensified. Each tiny gasp from Lily tugged at his groin, tightening his cock until all he could think of was plunging into her warm, tight pussy. Alex traced around her lips with his tongue and then giving into temptation, sucked her bottom lip into his mouth.

Lily gasped at the streak of pleasure that shot to her clit. The golden man was kissing her. Her! Lily Morgan. And it sure as hell didn't feel like a pity kiss. Laughter bubbled up inside her until Alex nipped her lip. Lily winced then moaned at the soothing yet erotic swathe of his tongue over her stinging mouth. Her eyelids lowered until a world of pure sensation enveloped her body.

His hard body warmed her, seduced her, and Lily gave into the temptation, exploring, gliding her hands over smooth muscles. She'd missed the closeness of a man holding her, loving her. Lord, she hoped she wasn't acting too desperate. Perhaps she should ease back a little, take things at a more decorous pace. It wouldn't do to look needy.

A wet tongue swiped across her cheek.

Lily's hands stilled. Okaaay. That was a bit weird. Maybe it was an alien thing. Her hands journeyed across broad shoulders.

"Cut that out!" Alex snapped.

Shock sliced deep at his tone, along with hurt. Lily's eyes shot open to see a face full of fur and a pink tongue getting ready to lick her again.

"Good game," Killer yapped. "Play more."

Lily pushed Killer away and attempted to scramble up before the dog barked in her ear again. Her knee connected with Alex's belly, ricocheted and skimmed close to his groin. He grunted and grabbed her forearms, holding her off and away from vulnerable body parts.

They stared at each other. Lily wanted another kiss so badly she shook. She extended her hand and reached for him, but he leaned away. Before she had time to react, Killer darted between them to fill the gap he'd left. Lily groaned aloud when she realized Alex intended to halt the kissing. All right. If she were honest, it was a bit difficult with Killer pushed between their lips. But try telling her body that. Her nipples were budded tight and pressing against her lacy bra while dampness had pooled at the juncture of her thighs. She felt empty. Her body wanted action and her mind wasn't that far behind with the concept.

"Killer, will you get off." Exasperation along with a frown marched across Alex's face as he pushed at the furry body.

Killer barked.

Alex growled.

And Lily started giggling. It was as if they were carrying out a conversation and that was plain stupid. Lily sobered at the thought. Ambrose had always gone on about her flights of fancy. He'd said they contributed to her clumsiness since her head never concentrated on her feet. And he'd always harped on about her weight and the need for a diet.

Lily shook the painful memories away and let her gaze sweep across Alex's face. An alien. And such a pretty one, too. He was nothing like the science fiction characters on the telly with tentacles popping out in weird places. Lily bit her lip. At least she hoped not. She cast a speculative look at Alex's groin and then hurriedly glanced away. Things certainly appeared normal down there. They could… But wait! Here she was all excited, and they were on a dirt track in the middle of nowhere. If she ever got the chance to rip off Alex's clothes, she'd prefer good lighting so she could see every inch of golden skin and hard muscles uncovered. That was assuming his body parts were compatible with hers.

Alex and Killer started growling at each other again.

Lily huffed out an impatient breath and rubbed her bare arms briskly. It was definitely getting cold. "If the two of you are finished, I'd like to go."

The growling stopped mid-chorus. Alex clambered to his feet and held out a hand for her. Instinctively, she took it. He tugged. Lily flew off the ground and smacked into his chest. Alex grunted while Lily's cheeks heated in embarrassment. She was such a klutz. Ambrose would have said it was all the extra flesh making her topple off balance.

"Are you all right?" Lily ran her hands across the cotton fabric of his shirt. "I'm so sorry. I didn't mean to hurt you."

Alex winced, and Lily froze, her hand curving into his pectoral muscle. Then Lily realized she was stroking him like a pet cat. Domesticated, he wasn't. She jerked her hand away as if she'd grasped a hand full of flames. Mortified at her behavior, Lily couldn't look him in the eye. What was wrong with her? Well, okay. She had a fairly good idea. It was the wine. She shouldn't have drunk the third glass that Luke had foisted on her. But wine had never had this effect on her before.

"Lily, please take my arm."

Lily peered through the darkness, trying to read his expression. "Why?"

"We have an early start tomorrow morning."

What sort of answer was that? If he was hinting at clumsiness then he should try telling her something new. Lily stalked past him, heading for the SUV. "I don't need help."

Before she'd taken three steps, she heard him sigh. That pissed her off. He was as bad as her ex. Lily increased the pace, but Alex caught up with her and slid an arm around her waist.

"Humor me," he said. "Please. Besides, I promised Luke and Janaya I'd look after you."

"I'm not a parcel to be handed from person to person," Lily muttered, not in the least mollified. Her family was smothering her via remote control. She might be the baby of the family but she was fully grown—and capable of making her own mistakes. The Ambrose calamity popped into her head. Oh, yeah—mistakes big time.

"I promised to look after Killer as well. And if it makes you feel any better, it's in my interests to look after you. You're my tour guide. I need you."

Humph! Lily wondered if he had visited Ireland on the way to New Zealand and stopped to kiss the blarney stone. He certainly had a silver tongue.

They managed to negotiate the rest of the winding track without mishap. But it was a close run thing. Aware of the warmth of his arm curved about her waist and the spicy masculine smell of him, Lily shivered with the desire tingling through her body. Blood rushed to places that had no business paying attention to Alex's proximity. He was her boss! She was his employee. The thought struck her like a violent blow. No matter how much she was tempted, she must keep things on a business-like footing.

Remember your empty bank account.

Besides, she thought. *Look at the man. He's gorgeous. He wouldn't lack for feminine company. Why would he pick a heavyweight like her?*

Alex pulled away from Lily before he succumbed to the need to throw her on the ground and blanket her curvy body with his. After he'd ripped off her clothes, of course. He shoved his hands in his jean pockets with difficulty. "Do you want me to drive?" At least that would take his mind off sex. Maybe. *Probably not*, he conceded, but it would keep his hands busy.

"Do you know how?"

"Of course I can drive," Alex muttered. Lots of Earth people did it. Besides, he was experienced with the latest in spaceships. Driving a car couldn't be that difficult.

"I know the roads. You can drive tomorrow."

Alex nodded, impatient at being deprived of the experience and annoyed with the surge of need that wouldn't quit. He stepped around the vehicle to the passenger side and opened the door. Killer pushed past without ceremony and jumped inside. Alex barred his teeth, but the dog just smirked and calmly sat on her haunches in the middle of the seat. It was like having a palace chaperon on an outing.

Lily climbed behind the wheel and started the engine. She glanced past Killer to smile at him. "Did you want to walk?"

"Not particularly." Alex leapt into the vehicle and shut the door. The dimly lit cab seemed too private—and full of Lily's flowery scent. The bonding ties pulled tight, jerking his cock painfully. Alex gritted his teeth and prayed for a speedy trip back to the house. Then he'd hit the shower—a cold shower. He couldn't have Lily, so manual relief would have to serve instead.

He peered past Killer to study the way Lily pushed pedals with her feet and used her hand to operate the levers. It didn't look difficult. And maybe if he concentrated on the way Lily operated the vehicle, he might just forget about acting like a Tigus male in heat the minute they arrived home.

Chapter Four

ജ

The privacy of the vehicle abraded Alex's self-control, grinding it away and splintering it piece by stubborn piece. Hormones hopped and his pulse hummed, sending the bonding spell writhing through his bloodstream like a malevolent virus. Huh! It was exactly like a disease without a cure. He was taking pills—lots of them. Hell, he was crunching through them as if they were a pack of Earth sweets.

For all the good it was doing.

Even the damned dog sitting between them didn't dampen the driving need that surged through his veins. He barely managed the short drive back to the house without attacking Lily. Then came the test—trying to act as though nothing untoward was happening while he made it to the safety of his room.

Standing, walking, hell—moving was bloody painful. A pained hiss squeezed from deep down in his gut. Luckily, he walked behind Lily, because he staggered like a geriatric courtier forced into retirement, each step creating friction between his tight Earth garments and his hungry, rampant penis. The palace females teased the males about one-eyed warriors having a mind of their own. Now Alex knew it for fact.

By the time he made it indoors, sweat beaded on his forehead and ran down into his eyes. A fine tremor passed through his clenched muscles.

"Are you all right?" Lily asked as he halted beside her on the doorstep that led to the kitchen. She opened the door and reached around the corner of the doorjamb with the ease of familiarity to flick on a light switch. Concern shaded her voice, and for one heart-stopping moment, Alex thought she was going to touch him.

He jerked away, jumped into the kitchen and scrunched his eyes to slits at the burst of light. "Headache," he gasped out, edging away from her obvious worry. "Don't touch me!"

Lily ignored him, stepping inside and kicking off her shoes, but one look told Alex he'd offended her. He started to explain but was distracted by her colored toenails. Pink. The exact shade of a sunrise on a clear Dalcon morning. The sight was unexpected. Sexy.

Devil's teeth, what was he going to do? Inside the house wasn't much better than the vehicle. In fact, it was worse. The place smelled of flowers, of woman, of her. He couldn't avoid her presence if he tried.

Alex watched the dog trot from the kitchen and turn up the stairs, leaving him alone with Lily. The air thickened, the mood turning sultry and hot.

Man, he hungered for a woman.

This woman.

He'd thought he could control the pounding lust that streaked through his body. But every touch made it worse, and for a man who'd decided on a no-contact rule, he was doing a bloody lot of rule breaking. The urgent need to grab her made him want to howl like a caged tigoth.

Breathing rapidly, Alex's gaze ran from her bare feet and painted nails, up her denim-clad legs, and skipped across the juncture of her thighs to savor the curvy hips. He visualized holding tight and rocking against her, with her, soaring high to mutual pleasure exactly like he'd practiced with his favored consort back on Dalcon. With a sigh, his gaze traveled higher still to linger on lush breasts. Alex imagined tracing the shadowed cleavage with his tongue, molding the luscious curves with his hands and drawing a tight, aroused nipple into his mouth. He couldn't contain the groan that built inside, and it burst forth echoing through the kitchen.

Lily sent him a perplexed look. "Are you sure you're feeling okay?" She reached for him. "Let me feel your forehead."

"No!" Alex snapped, backing up rapidly in distinct panic. "I'm fine. Tired. Just a little. Achy. The atmosphere on Earth is giving me needles and jabs." He had to get out of here. He couldn't fail before he'd even started. "I'll...ah...goodnight! See you on the morrow."

Alex made the mistake of glancing in her direction before he headed for the stairs leading to the next floor. A heartbeat later, his gaze hit her lips, and as if she knew he was watching, her tongue snaked out to moisten the sensuous curves of her mouth. Alex bit back a girlish whimper. The lady knew exactly how to tempt a poor hormone-prone alien.

A soft choked sound made his gaze jerk higher to meet her eyes. They looked dark and mysterious rather than the innocent sky blue he'd admired earlier.

"Good night," she whispered. "Maybe you'll feel better in the morning."

Neither of them moved. Instead, they continued to stare at each other.

Alex knew women liked to look at him even though he tried to ignore the fact. But he had the magical spell that changed his appearance, and still Lily looked as though she wanted to eat him up and then lick him all over for dessert. The hungry expression warmed him—hell, that wasn't the truth. It made him hot. Rhinoceros—no! Horny. The Earth word was horny. It made him feel like a mighty male, and he hadn't felt like that in a long time.

Alex cleared his throat. "I don't think we should follow through on this, Lily."

Under his fascinated gaze, her face went bright red then paled to the shade of his white shirt.

"I'm sorry." Her gaze skittered away and down, ending at her feet. "I'm acting like a desperate woman. You don't want a fatty like me. Don't worry, I won't force myself on you again."

The embarrassed anguish in her voice jerked him upright. She thought it was her! Lily thought he was rejecting her because of her appearance. Didn't she know how beautiful she was? Alex stared nonplussed by her words.

"I'll understand if you want to organize another travel guide."

Her bottom lip wobbled, and she blinked rapidly. Hell, she was gonna start leaking. Alex shuffled from one foot to the other trying to work out what to do. He couldn't touch her—he just couldn't. But then, how could he leave her thinking she repelled him when he was running for exactly the opposite reason?

The soft sob decided it for him. With one step, he closed the distance between them, hauled her against his chest and enclosed her trembling body in his arms. Instantly, the acute pain left his body. His erection softened enough that his cock didn't look like the Dalcon banner flying in the seasonal wind. It was as though he'd appeased the bonding gods, and they were letting up on his poor abused body, rewarding him for good behavior.

Lily fought his embrace, and Alex tightened his arms. "Don't fight." He lowered his head and inhaled the floral scent that came from her hair.

Instead of settling, Lily continued to fight his hold. Alex loosened his grip and pushed her away to arm's length to search her expression.

"I don't want your pity," she snapped.

Alex held back his grin with great difficulty. Lily reminded him of a tigoth cub, all eyes and spitting temper. "I don't pity you. Why would you think that?"

She shot razor daggers at him with her stormy blue eyes, her nostrils flared, and he noted at the back of his mind that her fists were curled as though she meant to inflict serious harm.

"Look at me!" she cried.

Alex knew looking was a mistake, but he did it anyway. He ran his gaze up and down her curvaceous body again before coming to a halt on her pale oval face. "Yeah? What's wrong with you? You're not missing any of the necessary bits." His voice emerged calm and matter of fact, as if he lacked interest and didn't care one way or the other. Nothing could have been further from the truth.

"What's wrong with me?" Lily screeched loud enough to hurt his ears. She widened the distance between them, a pained expression on her face. "I'm fat! What man would want me? My husband didn't. He went elsewhere. To another man!" Her shoulders hunched like a cowering fodo bird that didn't want its tail feathers plucked, and she refused to meet his gaze.

Her husband didn't want her? He discarded her? Shock roared through Alex at the disclosure. Fat? The female scored highly on his mental writing tablet. Body fat to cushion a male. A pretty mouth that made his pulse race, especially when she smiled. She had many good points. He took half a step toward her then stopped at a loss when a broken sob emerged. The only solution that presented itself wasn't that lava hot. But he couldn't think of another.

Alex grabbed Lily before she could strike out with her bunched fists and kissed her. Hard. Unrelenting, until he had to surface for air. By that time, Lily had ceased her struggles and was allowing the kiss even though she wasn't actively participating. Better, but not satisfactory. What now? He studied her, uncertain of how she'd react to his aggression.

"What was that meant to prove?" Lily asked in a quiet voice.

Frustration bubbled up in Alex, and it wasn't all sexual. Someone, probably the stupid-assed ex-male, had done a number on her confidence. They stared at each other in stalemate. He regretted the kiss but only because he hadn't taken the time to taste and explore, to make it memorable for both of them.

"I find you beautiful." Alex lashed out with truth. He stepped behind the kitchen table in the hope it would hide his burgeoning erection. His cock was starting to feel like the sail of a glider-ship being hoisted then hauled in because of fickle winds. Up. And then down. Was it any wonder he felt a little crazed? "Under different circumstances, I would call it an honor to mate with you."

Holy moly. Lily went from depressed and defeated to hot and hungry in seconds. The serious look on his face…he meant his words. Awe whirled and skidded through her mind. She'd thought the lusty feelings had been all on her side. She'd thought…heck, she hadn't thought past her initial attraction because…because she was fat! Overweight. Fleshy. All the superlatives. Ambrose hadn't wanted her so she figured why would anyone else.

Then her mind seized on his words. "What different circumstances?"

"I'm from Dalcon. You're from Earth." Alex shrugged as if his response explained everything.

Lily sniffed. The fibbing toad! She wasn't that stupid. "You're lying to make me feel better. You don't want to make love — to have sex with me."

As she watched, he squeezed his eyes shut as though he were in pain. His impressive chest rose as he inhaled. Then his eyes opened. Blazing with resolve, they pinned her in place even though a part of her desperately wanted to retreat. The golden cat prowled around the corner of the table and halted in front of her. Lily swallowed in sudden trepidation. When she was five, Dad had warned her about pulling a cat's tail. Seemed she was still fascinated by cats but hadn't learned much from the scratches and parental lectures.

"I am not lying," Alex gritted out. "Look." His hands stroked down his denim-clad hips to cup an impressive erection. "Does this look like disinterest?"

Lily froze, her eyes fixed on the spot.

"Feel it," he ordered. "Make sure your eyes aren't deceiving you."

Before Lily had time to blink, Alex grabbed her hand and planted it on his cock. Heat seared her palm, and she jerked her hand away from the fire, panting with a combination of shock and wanting.

Alex laughed without humor, seized her hand and placed it firmly on his erection again. "You wanted proof."

Lily nibbled at her bottom lip while she wondered on a suitable reaction. On the plus side, she was now in a position of knowledge. He was huge. Nice. Very nice.

He stood before her with his arms folded arms across his broad chest. "Say something," he snapped.

"You definitely don't stuff your trousers with socks." A secret smile curved her lips when her fingers flexed involuntarily.

Alex cursed under his breath, and Lily guessed it wasn't suitable for printing in the *Sloan Gazette*.

His cock jumped under her palm, bringing her back to the matter in hand. A nervous giggle escaped. Maybe men and woman fondled strangers and tried parts for size on Dalcon, but she was at a loss as to what to do next. Unless...

The suspicious thought speared into her brain like the arrow from an automatic bow. There was a simple way to prove if he meant what he said.

Call his bluff.

Lily forced away her sudden attack of nerves and insecurity. She'd brazen her way through this and set her mind at rest. Taking a deep breath, she squeezed gently.

Alex's groan reverberated through the kitchen. He backed up rapidly, yanking Lily after him and sat on the wooden table. When his butt hit the flat surface, he widened his stance and pulled her between his legs. Somehow, her hand remained on his person throughout.

Heat rushed to her cheeks while a streak of lightning flashed through her body, the aftermath leaving Lily tingling all the way to her pleasure center.

"Is that it?" Alex asked in a gruff voice.

No, that wasn't all. If he was giving her free rein on his body, then she'd take the opportunity to explore. She might not get another chance.

Alex wanted to curse out loud. If the woman went any slower, he'd come in his pants like he had in his early days of practicing Earth sexual methods. He considered halting her tortuous yet shy exploration but couldn't do it. There was more at stake here than the bonding ties. Lily's self-esteem teetered, and if he weren't careful he'd blow it for her, not to mention his budding business. Alex held back an unsuitable smirk. Nah, he'd grin and bear her ministrations. And perhaps hurry her along.

"Lily?"

Her fingers danced across his straining manhood. "Yes?"

"I'd like to do some exploring of my own."

She hesitated but didn't say no. Alex took that as permission to forge ahead. The idea of stopping now made his head ache anyway. His hands curved around her shoulders then slid inside the gaping neckline of her pale green shirt to glide over the shadowed flesh beneath. Silky skin greeted his touch, but it wasn't enough. Her soft sigh propelled him on, and her hands left his groin to grip the gatoraller leather belt at his hips. Alex withdrew his hands and, before Lily's protests took substance, undid the small buttons down the front of the shirt and slid it down her arms before chucking it behind him. His first actual sighting of female Earth underwear. It appeared different from the pictures he'd seen. Less covering. More spectacular. The lacy bra cupped her breasts, hiding little of her beauty from his gaze. A tiny brown spot decorated the slope of one breast.

"Beautiful," he whispered.

For an instant, she seemed uncertain. Alex leaned over and captured her lips with his. This time he took it slow and easy, caressing her lips before sliding his tongue into the warm cavern of her mouth. She tasted exotic and mysterious with the faint tang of spice mint on her breath. His favorite Dalcon treat. Alex tugged Lily closer, savoring the thrust of her plump breasts against his chest.

"Can I take your shirt off?" Lily peered at him through lowered lashes. "Please."

Sounded like an excellent strategy except that he wanted to see her breasts, fondle her nipples and shape the tempting globes with his hands. The need to explore, to discover shape and texture was a fever in his bloodstream. His hands itched to explore, but his mind blanked when it came to the correct instructions for removing the female apparel. Alex coughed to clear the sudden knot in his throat.

"I'll trade you my shirt for your...garment, then we'll both be down to skin."

Indecision wavered in her face. Alex held his breath waiting for her to say no. He sensed trust was difficult for her, but now he'd crossed the demarcation line from business to personal, he had everything to lose, too.

"Please," he murmured, sliding his hands through her hair and smoothing the silky tendrils. Alex continued the downward move over her shoulders and upper arms, tracing Lily's elegantly curved form. Her skin was petal soft and smelled of the same flowers that perfumed her hair.

"I'll undress at the same time as you," she said.

"You don't have to." All of a sudden, Alex felt guilty. She looked so scared that if he made an abrupt move, she'd probably part company from the ground. He could always go and take that shower.

"No, I want to." She reached behind her back and seconds later the lacy garment fell away.

Alex felt his mouth drop as he stared at her breasts. Perfection. Rose-pink nipples that stood erect and ready for him to taste. The large globes swayed as she edged away, traces of panic coming and going in her expressive eyes. She might regret disrobing, but he sure as hell appreciated the wondrous sight.

"Stop," he murmured. He desperately wanted to touch and took steps to halt her retreat. Alex stood and lifted Lily to place her on the tabletop, making it difficult for her to escape.

"You lifted me," Lily said in clear astonishment.

Alex frowned. "Yeah. I didn't want you to run away." His burst of honesty brought a delighted laugh. Keeping to his end of the deal, he yanked his shirt off and let it fall to the floor.

"Wow," Lily breathed.

"I get to touch first," Alex said, his gaze already traveling the path he wanted to trace with his fingers and mouth, his tongue.

Lily moistened her lips in what he was beginning to recognize as a nervous habit. "I didn't agree to that." She curled her hands around his bare shoulders and drew him close enough that his jeans brushed her inner thighs.

Her shyness combined with flashes of aggression fascinated him. Another time he might have drawn out the teasing but desperation gripped him, directing his actions, prompting him to speed. He'd never wanted to touch, to give and receive pleasure so badly in all his life.

Alex glanced down at her breasts. The pink nipples were distended, silently begging for his touch. The tiny brown spot was like a magnet. His breath hissed out on a sigh. She wanted exactly what he wanted. She just didn't realize how badly.

Leaning over, Alex blew on one nipple. She shivered, and the hands that clutched at his shoulders drew him closer. Alex smiled, and repeated the puff of air across her nipple. He lifted his hand and reverently traced one full globe, circling the nipple with his finger. Although enthralled by her quiver and breathless gasp, the action wasn't enough to appease his driving need. Alex bent and licked across a network of blue veins under her skin, never taking his eyes off hers. His tongue slid across the brown dot. When her hands tugged him closer and her eyelids slid to half-mast, he felt a surge of triumph.

Unable to resist, he sucked a pebble-hard nipple into his mouth and drew hard. While he lavished attention on one breast with his hand, he suckled at the other, glorying in the taste that made him think of cinnamon and exotic spices, the feel of her flesh and the soft sighs she made at the back of her throat.

Alex glanced up and noted the glazed look in her blue eyes with satisfaction. His heart jumped in a leap of relief. The last time he had bedded his consort all he'd seen was gloating and greediness because she'd known that jewels awaited her if she satisfied him in the Earth manner. There was none of that in Lily.

Alex ran his hand over the softness of one cheek and tucked a lock of brown hair behind her ear. He watched her closely, saving the vision to examine later when he was alone.

"More," Lily murmured.

He grinned before bending to kiss her again. She wound her arms around his neck and clung tight, participating with a greediness and genuine warmth that no longer surprised him.

At the back of his mind, he registered a series of clicks, but he'd only started kissing Lily. He'd learned there were lots of ways to kiss a woman, and he'd barely got to variation two.

"Wolf!"

Lily shrieked. Alex jerked away from her with a strangled curse.

"What ya doing?" Killer said. "Do ya have any food?"

Alex spun about and jumped in front of Lily to screen her nakedness. That bloody dog again.

The dog trotted up to Alex, sniffed at his jeans then peered around his legs to check out Lily. Killer stiffened, the fur along her backbone springing to attention. She growled low and mean at the back of her throat then bounded away, staring fixedly at the door that led outside.

"Someone's out there," Lily gasped. "Oh, my God! Where's my shirt?"

Killer barked again and scratched urgently at the door. Alex frowned. He hadn't heard a thing, but then he'd been concentrating on Lily.

"Where is it?" Lily demanded, searching frantically around her and sounding as though she was starting to hyperventilate.

Alex spied the pale green shirt over the far side of the kitchen on the floor. He had no idea how the shirt had ended up there but retrieved it for her. She grabbed it from him, struggling to put her arms into the sleeves while Killer continued with her frenzied barking.

"Go on upstairs," Alex said, taking pity on Lily. Her cheeks matched the color of the red fruits in the bowl on the bench top, and she still fought to match button with the shirt holes. "I'll deal with the visitor."

"But—"

"I'll call you if I need you," Alex promised.

Lily needed no further urging and scurried past him, holding the shirt closed. Alex heard her swift footsteps as she climbed the stairs.

Alex strode to the door and wrenched it open. He darted a glare at the dog as she pushed past to peer into the darkness. "Well? Where are they?" he demanded.

Killer yawned and sat on her haunches. "Gone. I go sleep with Lily," she said, and disappeared back inside.

Alex cursed under his breath. Perhaps he'd take that cold shower after all.

Chapter Five

ಐ

"Lily say time to get up," Killer barked in Alex's ear.

Alex groaned and pulled the blankets over his head to drown out the racket. Unbeknown to Killer, he was already well and truly up. And uncomfortable with it. Seemed like another cold shower was in order before they set off on their journey to Taupo, the first stop on Alex's itinerary.

"Alex, are you awake?" Lily's voice sounded from the doorway.

Alex knew he shouldn't look. Lily and a flat surface in the same room spelled disaster but temptation got the better of him. He emerged from under the blankets and squinted a little against the bright light pouring in the window.

Wisps of hair sprang free from her mane tail, framing her face. Her blue eyes glowed with vitality, and she was dressed in a long black skirt and a red sweater that ended at her hips. Every inch of her skin from the neck down was covered by cloth. Even covered with battle armor, he had to admit she looked tempting.

Alex suppressed a snort as memories of last night rolled through him. Obviously, he needed to work on his seduction skills. He'd lain awake throughout the night, his dick stiff enough to poke out an eye while it appeared Lily had slept the rest of the innocent. *That was what you wanted*, he reminded himself. To be judged on his actions rather than his appearance. But her apparent lack of interest when he was in such agony yanked and prodded at his temper.

"Not a morning person, huh?"

Alex stared. Was this the same woman? This glowing, confident siren bore little resemblance to the frightened woman of last night, the one who had scurried off to bed. She grinned at him, making his heart pump out a double beat. By King Vala. Trouble ahead. How would he manage to keep his hands to himself?

Lily felt the urge to sing but held it in. To her everlasting chagrin, her voice sounded like a wounded bullfrog. Actually, worse if she were being honest. And she definitely didn't want to show off another weakness. Being clumsy was more than enough, thank you very much!

"I've packed a picnic lunch," she said, stealing a look at his blanket-covered form. Damn, not a single limb in sight. Aw, well. Lily threw her shoulders back and firmed her mouth to prevent a grin. Probably just as well. This job for Alex would pay off her debts and leave her a little over to put toward the personalized trip she'd always dreamed of.

"I'll see you downstairs. Coffee's on." Lily heard Alex groan. Not a morning person. The golden man had a flaw. The discovery cheered her. "Don't be too long. We need to leave soon if we want to make all the stops on your list."

Alex stomped down the stairs about ten minutes later with Killer close behind. Lily took one look at the stormy face and shunted a cup of black coffee across the table. Killer trotted over to where Lily sat and barked. Smiling, Lily leaned down to scratch the dog behind the ears without taking her gaze off the golden man. Ruffled and grumpy as he was, he still looked good enough to eat. The alien looked as though he'd go well with chocolate. Sort of like a companion food. And to hell with the diet, Lily thought with an inner smirk.

"Get out of the wrong side of the bed?" she said sweetly, unable to resist.

The dog barked, a weird sounding yap that made Lily stare. Alex merely grunted then picked up his coffee mug. He downed the contents and stood.

"I'm ready to go," he said.

She picked up her empty mug along with Alex's. "Do you want to drive?"

"Yeah."

Lily's brows rose at his surly tone, but she stood, picked up the keys off the counter and handed them to him. "The bags need to go into the car." Lily gestured at the luggage by the door. "Just give me five minutes to give Killer a quick walk."

"Bloody dog."

"Pardon?"

"Nothing."

Lily rolled her eyes. Oh, joy. The surly routine was rapidly losing her sympathy. Still, if it meant her debt was repaid, she could put up with a lot.

* * * * *

The gears ground with nerve-shrieking intensity. The SUV shuddered theatrically as though it were a living beast in pain.

"Do you have your license?" Lily cried when the car swerved around a sheep and almost hit an oncoming stock truck. All before they reached the outskirts of Sloan.

"No," Alex said. His hands gripped the wheel so hard his knuckles were white.

"Then why are you driving?" Lily screeched, pretending she didn't see the one-finger salute from the driver of the stock truck. Frankly, she didn't blame him and thought given the circumstances he'd been restrained in his reaction. "I want to arrive in one piece."

Killer barked in fitting punctuation.

The vehicle shot across the road. Lily shrieked and grabbed the wheel, pulling with all her might so the vehicle lumbered onto the right side of the road.

That stand of kauri trees looked a bit close for comfort. "Stomp on the brakes!" she yelled.

"Which pedal?"

Which… "The middle one! Stamp on the middle one. Now! Do it!"

Killer yelped and jumped off the seat to cower at Lily's feet. Lily glanced out the window, saw how close they were to kauri trees, and wanted to join the dog. They were going to die. Now was the perfect time to act like an ostrich burying its head in the sand.

"Holy shit," Lily muttered, bracing for impact. "The middle pedal. Harder. Now." She glanced at the tree trunks. They were so close now Lily could see the individual leaves on the trees and the patterns on the trunks through the windscreen. The dog whimpered at her feet. Lily knew just how she felt. But at least Alex had worked out the brakes. And the rest of the road was clear of traffic. That was a good thing.

The car hit the soft road shoulder. The wheels spun looking for purchase, and the vehicle slid, turning slightly so it approached the trees sideways.

"I think we're going to hit the tree," Alex said.

No shit. Now there was a newsflash. "I hope you have insurance on Dalcon," Lily gritted out. "Because Luke will have a coronary if you harm a speck of paint on his baby."

"I worry more about Janaya," Alex muttered, stepping on the brakes with all his strength. The vehicle screamed, the stench of rubber heavy in the air.

Lily stared fixedly at the nearest tree. It got bigger and bigger until all she could see through the driver's window was tree. The impact threw her toward Alex and then the seat belt jerked her back. Killer yelped twice. Alex cursed. The engine groaned. Metal screeched as it made contact with a branch. A dull pop preceded the crackle of broken glass.

Then at last the vehicle stopped.

Lily sucked in a breath and gingerly tested her limbs. Everything worked. And at least they hadn't hit hard enough to activate the airbags. "Alex, you all right?"

"Yeah. Will the vehicle still work?"

Lily sure hoped so. "Killer, sweetie. You can come out now. Everything's okay."

Killer poked her head out from behind Lily's legs. She cast a disgruntled look at Alex, and Alex guessed he was in for a tongue-lashing when Killer got him on his own. He checked out Lily. Judging from her set expression there wouldn't be much flesh on his bones for Killer to pick over. His stupid pride had landed him right in the middle of a mess. In hindsight, he should have admitted he hadn't had much experience with Earth vehicles.

"Turn off the engine," Lily snapped.

Alex noticed she didn't call him sweetie. He switched the vehicle off and silence throbbed in the cab. Lily jerked open the passenger side door. Killer sprang out and Lily followed.

Basuko and double *basuko*. Alex flung himself at the door, intent on getting out to inspect the damage. It didn't budge. "*Basukoation*," he muttered, shoving against it with all his strength. Finally, it opened with a protesting groan far enough that he could squeeze out. Pissed, more with himself than anything, Alex climbed out and slammed the door shut. It bounced back and almost hit him at knee level. Alex jumped back and promptly fell over an exposed root. He landed hard enough to smack the air from his lungs. Winded and struggling for breath, Alex lay on the ground and scowled up at the tree canopy and the patches of sky between. He should have followed his gut instinct to stay in bed this morning.

A short yap right next to his ear made him start.

"Car hurt. Luke be grumpy."

"I'll get it fixed," Alex snapped, climbing slowly to his feet. That damned dog was getting on his nerves. If he didn't know better, he'd think she'd purposely interrupted them last night. He pushed past the spotted animal and stepped around to join Lily at the front of the car. Blast, he'd broken the side mirror as well. Alex kicked it out of the way, and it rolled drunkenly underneath the car.

"It doesn't look too bad," she conceded. "I think I should be able back it out from under the trees."

"I'll pay for the repairs," Alex said.

"Damn right you will," Lily stated. She turned to look him in the eye. "Don't lie to me again." She advanced on him, her finger pointing and coming dangerously close to poking him in the chest. "Don't ever lie to me again. I don't like it, and I won't put up with it. I hate people who lie," she ended on a hard note.

Alex nodded, uncomfortably aware of the lie he was living. He focused on the vehicle, deciding a change of subject was in order. "The tree gouged the driver's door. It will have to be repaired before we can leave."

"Maybe I can fix it." Lily stepped past him, grabbing Alex's shoulder for balance as she squeezed between him and the car. Her scent took him from interested to hot and ready before he had time to formulate a countermove to protect himself. It was as though being apart during the night had done nothing to dampen his ardor.

"Door broken," Killer barked.

Alex shot her an aggrieved look. *The dog should try telling them something they didn't know*, he thought grumpily.

While Alex watched, Lily tried to shut the door, but it wouldn't remain closed. "We'll stop by the garage. Hopefully Samuel will be able to fix it for us today."

The cadence of her voice changed when she mentioned the man Samuel. It went soft and dreamy, and she smiled as if an enjoyable memory pleased her. A strange sensation squeezed his rib cage at the thought of Lily and another man. He knew about her ex-husband, but that man was no threat. The ex was downright stupid. This unknown Samuel was worrying.

* * * * *

"We were lucky Sam was willing to lend us his SUV while he ordered the replacement door for Luke," Lily said. "I don't know why you treated him so badly. Are all the males on Dalcon as surly as you?"

"I didn't like the way he was looking at you." Alex had known exactly what was going through the Earthman's mind. And Lily was blind if she didn't see that Sam was attracted to her. He'd had way more than friendship on his mind.

"We went to school together," Lily explained as they drove down the main street of Sloan.

At the back of his mind, Alex noted the trees lining the streets and the colorful red and purple flowers in the plant boxes. "Is this a typical town?"

"Our discussion is not finished," Lily said with a sniff.

"Yeah," Killer agreed. "Lily has more words to tell you off."

"I understand that you're my tour guide, and we need to keep this on a professional basis," Alex said stiffly.

"A pro basis?" Killer barked. "Lily nice lady."

Once again, Alex ignored the dog. No use encouraging her outspokenness. "I've said I was sorry about the vehicle. I've offered to pay for the damages, and I will. Can we please start over?"

The look Lily gave him seared straight to his toes. That bloody sexual awareness again even though he'd taken double doses of the travel pills. At this rate, he was going to run out of pills. His mind sneaked away on him, darting back to the scene last night, remembering the feel of Lily in his arms, the smooth texture of her naked breasts. The taste of her. Alex bit back a groan and stared fixedly out the window at the passing scenery.

"All right," she said after what seemed to Alex an extraordinary length of time to consider his proposal. "But if I find you've lied to me about paying to fix Luke's vehicle or anything else then all bets are off."

Alex opened his mouth to reply then snapped it shut. Best he not answer that one. "So this is a normal town?"

"We'll pass through several Kiwi towns today. You'll get to compare for yourself, but yes, Sloan is fairly typical with a bank, post office and a few shops."

"What is this Kiwi?" Alex asked. He couldn't remember reading about a Kiwi and had no idea what the word meant.

"A kiwi is a flightless bird native to New Zealand." Lily glanced across at him. "New Zealanders call themselves Kiwis. It's an affectionate term."

"So you are a Kiwi?" Alex asked, savoring the unfamiliar word on his tongue.

"Yeah. If we get time, we'll visit the kiwi house so you can see them." She glanced at the guidebook that sat on the seat near Killer. "You should find a picture of one in there somewhere."

Lily indicated to turn onto the motorway south. "Actually, we can take a slight detour and go via Rotorua. It's not far out of our way but there's a kiwi house there. Kiwis are nocturnal," Lily said. "So they keep them in specially controlled environments to fool the birds into thinking it's night rather than day when they normally sleep."

Alex frowned at her professional manner. It was as if she thought to distance him and treat him like a client. Despite his fear of bonding, Alex's irritation blossomed. He wasn't used to being pushed aside, especially by a female, and he didn't like it. *Talk about ironic*, he thought. For a male trying to blend in and go about his business, he wasn't doing such a good job. He had to concentrate on his fledgling business.

"I'd like to see a kiwi. Isn't Rotorua the thermal area?"

"That's right."

"Good, I'd like to visit the place."

"Okay," Lily said. "Check out the guidebook and decide what you're interested in seeing. You can do the tours, and I'll talk details to the site operators and find out about group discounts and that sort of thing."

Alex settled back to enjoy the ride—or tried to. Each time Lily changed gear, her arm brushed his thigh, and as it became warmer inside the car, her scent seemed to permeate each breath he took. He picked up the guidebook, opened it to the section on Rotorua then stuck it on his lap to cover up his blatant erection. This promised to be a long drive, which was why he'd wanted to operate the vehicle in the first place. He'd foreseen this development after the way his body had reacted to her last night. Pity he hadn't been so smart earlier on and chosen a male tour guide.

After they turned off the motorway, they passed lush green pastures dotted with cows, sheep and horses. Alex noticed the small towns they drove through were similar to Sloan, some bigger, some smaller, but each full of what he was becoming to regard as Kiwi character. Now and then, he turned the pages in the guidebook. Lily was right. A visit to Whakarewarewa, the thermal reserve, where they had bubbling mud pools and geysers along with a kiwi house sounded fascinating. Something that would interest his clients.

"I hungry," Killer barked without warning.

"Don't bark in my ear," Alex snapped.

"Wanna smell outside." Killer scrambled into his lap and shoved her nose in the four-inch gap between the window and the frame. Her entire body wriggled with pleasure as she scented the outdoors.

"Smells funny," she said.

The spotted creature was right but Alex could hardly start up a discussion with her without Lily wondering what was going on.

"Aren't dogs strange the way they like to shove their heads out the windows of moving vehicles," Lily observed. "I think we'll stop for lunch soon. There's a picnic spot at the top of the next hill. Killer looks as though she'd like a run."

"Oh, boy," Killer barked. "Rabbits!"

Lily laughed. "Sounds like she agrees with a stop."

Alex shrugged. Lily didn't know the half of it. "I wouldn't mind stretching my legs a bit." And some fresh, Lily-free air would do him a power of good.

Lily pulled up at the picnic spot five minutes later. There was only one other car in the parking area when they arrived.

Alex opened his door, and Killer shot out, nearly unmanning him in the process. With a muttered curse, Alex climbed out and went to the rear of the vehicle to help Lily with the picnic basket.

"Where do you want to eat?" Lily asked. "We can use the tables over there or take one of the walking tracks and find a place in the sun."

No sooner had she spoke than Killer took off down the track, paused briefly and then darted down the right-hand fork.

Alex wrestled the cane picnic basket away from Lily. "I guess we're going the same way as Killer."

Lily pulled a tartan blanket from the back, locked the vehicle, and then fell into step with him. A small bird with a fanlike tail flitted about them while Alex heard the guttural call of another bird in the distance. The situation reminded Alex of an outing on Dalcon with a special female. He'd attended many picnics before he'd grown smart enough to realize the attraction was his status and not his company.

They headed off down the dirt track that wound between mounds of rocks and manuka trees. A series of clicks sounded, and Alex decided it must be a tui. He'd actually absorbed quite a bit of knowledge during the long, sleepless night. The guidebook hadn't put him to sleep, but he'd learned a fair bit about New Zealand.

The track narrowed, and Lily went first. Alex's gaze zoomed to her butt. To his frustration, the black skirt she wore was shapeless, making it difficult to ascertain the female form beneath. The long red jumper didn't help much even though the color suited her. He wished she'd wear a garment that showcased her beautiful curves instead of hiding them. Then again, perhaps not. Other men would ogle her.

Alex thought of the court painters as a case in point. They would offer many gold coins to paint her naked form. He hated the thought of other males seeing her lush curves. The visual that popped into his mind sent his system into full arousal, his cock stabbing against the loose cotton pants he'd taken the precaution of wearing today to lessen the pain. While the thought had been good in theory, in practice he still ached. All over.

The rush and bubble of water filled the air as Alex and Lily rounded the curve in the track. The dim light beneath the trees gave way to sunshine when they stepped into a clearing. Alex caught a flash of white from the corner of his eye as Killer bounded across the swift-flowing water and leapt up the grassy bank on the other side.

Lily slowed to a halt and stared at the water.

Alex caught the look of trepidation. "I'll carry the blanket for you," he said. "You'll be fine. The stones are close together."

Lily gazed at the six stones that jutted out of the water in something akin to horror. This was the stuff of a clumsy person's nightmare. And it wouldn't be much easier wading through the stream. The water would be freezing cold despite the sunny day and the rocks would be slimy underfoot. That was assuming it wasn't too deep for her to cross. "You go first." Her voice sounded faint and more than a little frightened. She wanted to look elegant for once in her life.

Alex speared a look at her but didn't comment. "Okay. Sure." He tugged the blanket from her nerveless fingers and tucked it under his arm.

Lily caught Killer's faint bark as she tore 'round and 'round the small clearing on the other side, her nose to the ground chasing rabbit scents. Then she turned her attention to Alex. He made the crossing look easy despite carrying the blanket under one arm and the cane basket in his right hand. He seemed to glide over the stream, stepping from stone to stone with barely a pause. Suddenly, it was her turn. Lily debated on whether to go back to Sam's car. She could sit and wait for them.

"Do you want me to come back for you?" Alex called.

Lily swallowed, her fear creating a huge knot inside her throat. Yeah, right. Then she'd look stupid and clumsy because she couldn't manage on her own. Memories of her ex crowded her mind along with the jokes and taunts that still haunted her. She inhaled then slowly exhaled. When she glanced down at her feet she saw her hands were bunched into fists. Unconsciously, she'd clenched her fists so hard the knuckles were white. She released them and flexed her hands to stimulate the blood flow. Boy, was she a basket of nerves.

"No. No, don't come back. Set out the lunch, and I'll be there in a few minutes."

Alex hesitated and then turned to walk across the clearing. Lily watched him set the basket down and spread the tartan blanket out on a grassy spot.

Right. She'd finally found a man who didn't think it was woman's work to unpack a picnic. Now all she had to do was cross the stream to get to him. Any child could do it.

Lily sidled closer to the water. It looked…wet. And cold. White water surged around the steppingstones that stuck out of the water like teeth. Where the water ran at a slower pace, it was clear enough to see the gravel bottom. Grass and dark green moss grew on the banks. Lily took another deep breath and forced herself to take the first step. She could almost hear Ambrose's taunts when she'd fallen face-first into muddy water during a visit to his father's farm. "Stupid, clumsy cow," he'd said in his high singsong voice. Of course, that had made her even more self-conscious, and she'd promptly fallen.

She wasn't going to embarrass herself this time.

Not in front of Alex.

"You can do this, Lily Morgan," she muttered in a grim voice.

Lily took another step and stopped with both feet on the second stone. So far so good. Feeling marginally more confident, Lily stepped onto the third stone. Halfway through taking a fourth step, a flash of bright yellow in her peripheral vision snared her attention. Her head turned to track the splotch of foreign color while she placed her foot on the next stone. Cold water seeping into her leather shoe shocked her rigid.

"No!" she gasped, her mind already leaping ahead in horror at the possible consequences.

Lily's body jerked in reaction to her fears. Her foot hit the safe, solid stone then slipped. She'd mis-stepped! She tried to leap the few extra inches in compensation. Her arms windmilled wildly while she teetered on the edge of the slimy triangular-shaped stone. Lily made the mistake of looking down and wobbled some more.

A loud shriek echoed through the clearing as her feet shot from under her and she toppled backward into the water. She hit with a mighty splash. It took Lily a moment to realize the scream came from her. Not that she thought she was in danger. It was more the shock of the icy cold water. It seeped into her clothing, attracted like water to a sponge.

The thump of running footsteps through mounds of dried leaves and grass sounded.

"Lily!"

For a second, Lily floundered in a panic and swallowed a mouthful of water before realizing the water was only knee-deep and she could stand without aid. She scrambled to her feet and stood wavering like a drunken man in the swift current, water dripping from her hair and clothes and down her skin. A shiver worked down her spine as cold flesh met with a cool breeze.

"Lily?"

She looked up at the worry in Alex's voice. "I'm okay. Just a bit wet," she said in a wry voice. "Stay there. No point both of us getting wet." She took a baby step toward the bank, fighting the current and slippery footing and trying desperately not to fall again. A girl's pride could take only so much.

But Alex didn't listen. He waded into the fast-flowing water and reached her side in seconds, making the whole maneuver look simple. His hands ran down her body as though looking for broken bones or bloody wounds. Lily suspected she might have a few bruises tomorrow, but that was all. The only thing that really smarted was her pride. Clumsy clot strikes again.

Chapter Six

❧

Alex swept her up in his arms with an ease that stole her breath.

"No, don't lift me," Lily said belatedly, struggling against his firm hold. Heedless to her pleas, he splashed through the water, heading for the bank and paying not the slightest regard to her strangled protests. "You'll hurt your back. I'm too heavy for you. You can't have sex with a sore back." Lily paused to take a breath. "Well, you could but it would hurt."

"Let me worry about my sexual activities."

Oh, my stars! Burble alert. Lily buttoned her lips to a prim line and tried to ignore the silent laughter that vibrated through his chest.

Alex clutched her a little tighter and halted her uneasy wriggling. But Lily couldn't help tensing, preparing for a spill to the ground. He couldn't carry her all the way to the blanket—not without doing himself an injury.

"I don't want you to hurt yourself," Alex said, as if that explained everything. "Not before I check to make sure you're okay. I mean if you're hurt, I'll have to drive." A teasing grin flirted with his lips.

Lily's mouth went dry. Her breath stalled in her throat. He sounded as if he cared even though they'd only known each other for a few days. Ambrose would have shouted, and he would never have deigned to touch her when she was sopping wet. "Water stains on the designer clothes," she imagined him saying with a sniff.

Alex stepped out of the stream and onto the bank without breathing heavily or a single clumsy stumble. Finally, Lily started to relax and since she was so close, studied his face and savored the sensation of being held against his muscular chest. He hadn't shaved this morning. Exhibit one—his jaw covered with golden stubble. Her fingers itched, desperate to touch, but she kept them under firm control. His brown eyes glowed golden, too. Simply looking made her eyes hurt, and she couldn't help wondering why he seemed interested in plain old Lily Morgan. She didn't think she was misreading the signs. Lily pulled her bottom lip between her teeth while she considered. No, with her track record, she'd better read the signs again. And maybe she'd break out the reading glasses.

Scant seconds later they reached the tartan blanket. Alex let Lily slide down his body until her feet touched the ground. Lily shivered at the erotic sensation—the glide of her soft flesh over iron muscles and hard sinew. She quivered as she traced the sensual line of his mouth with her gaze. Her eyes coasted at will, a sigh of regret building at the back of her throat. Too bad about the layer of clothes that separated them.

"You're cold," Alex muttered. Once again concern shaded his voice, touching Lily and making her feel treasured.

Alex bent to open the picnic basket and pulled out the pack of paper napkins she'd packed. "Get out of those wet clothes," he ordered. "If we spread them out in the sun they should dry before we need to go."

He ripped the plastic that covered the napkins before looking up at her in clear impatience. "Lily, are you listening? Use one of these to dry off your face."

"I can't take off my clothes! There are other people around. You saw the car in the parking area."

"They've gone. They walked down the track, heading for the car park just before you fell in the stream."

The flash of yellow that had distracted her, Lily surmised. "But you'll see me," she muttered, presenting another very important reason for remaining clothed.

"I've seen you before."

"But...but...it was at night."

"The light was on."

Lily felt heat surge to her cheeks. Did he have to remind her? She'd been trying not to think about last night because every time she recalled the feel of hands on her breasts, her mind danced ahead thinking impossible ideas. Yeah! Totally improbable notions about a future with an alien.

"That was an act of insanity," Lily said with quiet dignity. "It's not going to happen again."

Alex snorted, his brows rising in challenge. "You don't have time to get an illness. Strip." His gaze drifted over her face and then lowered to halt on her breasts.

Lily knew exactly where his thoughts had stepped. To the same past she was thinking of. Last night! The heat in her face told her she'd blushed even hotter and harder. His sly grin informed of his liking for the reaction — both the blush and the peaked nipples. In an act of self-preservation, Lily folded her arms to hide her telltale nipples. Then she lifted her chin and met his golden gaze. Unfortunately, she managed negligible nanoseconds before shyness hit and her eyes lowered to focus on the blanket.

"Lily, what are you waiting for?"

"I can't do it. I can't take my clothes off — "

"I dare you," he purred.

Lily's head jerked up in time to catch the small smile that flittered across his mouth and the laughter that lit his golden eyes. "Fine," she said in a hard voice.

Let him face the consequences. Tummy rolls. Drooping boobs. Cellulite. Especially cellulite.

She peeled the wet woolen jumper over her head before she lost her nerve. Once it was off, Lily held it in one hand procrastinating, and frantically wondering what to do next, while trying to hide her scantily covered breasts.

"Don't stop there." Alex tugged the jumper from her hands and turned to drape it over a scrubby bush. "Are you still dressed?" he said when he turned back. Both the challenge and the smirk remained, driving and fuelling her need to best him in this small pissing contest.

Lily let out an impatient huff. Impossible man. Fine. She'd give him the full show. Her fingers went to the side-button closure on her skirt. The wet material meant an undignified struggle, but finally the button came free and she slid the zipper down. The skirt slithered down to sag around her hips. Great. What now? Lily cast a quick, uncertain look at the alien. Either she lifted the skirt over her head and gave Alex a free dimpled thigh show, or she struggled to get the wretched skirt over her hips and risked losing her panties at the same time. Neither alternative appealed. But at least she'd hunted out a pair of decent panties this morning. They even matched her bra and didn't come close to the granny category.

"Shut your eyes," she instructed in a firm voice.

A faint bark sounded in the distance. At least Killer was enjoying herself playing with rabbits. Lily bet the fluffy bunnies were having about the same amount of fun as she was.

"My eyes are closed." Amusement shaded his voice, but she could tell he was determined.

Lily grimaced. "Glad you think it's funny." She shimmied her hips until the open zip strained with a slight cracking sound. On the plus side, she had spare clothes in the vehicle should she damage the zipper beyond repair. Sucking in her tummy, she edged the black cotton down her hips a little more and gripped the elastic band of her panties. The seams strained and creaked a protest. Just a little further, she thought with a silent prayer. Lily tugged harder and suddenly the skirt cleared her butt and hips to drop down around her ankles. Her underwear tried to follow, but Lily kept a firm, one-handed grip on the elastic band.

"There, that wasn't so difficult."

Lily gasped. Even though she wore underwear that contained more material than many bikinis, one hand darted up to cover her breasts and the other her pelvic region. She stepped back, away from his grin and tangled her feet in her skirt. Strike two for the clumsy clot.

As usual, Alex moved quickly and caught her before she hit the ground. Their eyes met, gazes held. Messages passed between them but in a foreign language Lily wasn't fluent in. After all, the man had his hands on her tummy rolls. And Lily was very conscious of those hands. How was she expected to concentrate? She attempted to wriggle away, but those hands followed like pesky magnets. It took Lily a while to work out he wanted to help her stand.

When they were both standing, Alex frowned at her, his face so serious that she started to shuffle self-consciously. "Are you all right? I mean the way you fall over—"

"I'm clumsy!" she snapped. "Haven't you—" She broke off as a thought hit. Both Janaya and Hinekiri were elegant and in total control at all times. She'd picked that up in the short meetings they'd had to date. Alex...well, he was a smooth, well-coordinated cat who prowled everywhere with unconscious grace. That was it! Dalconians had obviously bred the clumsy gene out of their race.

"So you're not ill?"

"Just fat and clumsy!"

Alex's frown turned to a scowl. "You keep trying to force me to think in the way you feel I should. I am grown. Capable of making decisions without aid. You are desirable to me."

It was the passion in his voice, more than the words that snagged her attention. No one spoke like that unless they had suffered. The thought gave her pause. "Um, should we have something to eat?"

"You change the subject."

Lily waggled her eyebrows like a comedian attempting to make the crowd laugh. "Yeah!"

Alex steered her toward the blanket and pressed on her shoulders in a silent bid to make her sit. "I do not find this laughable. Dry your face while I hang your skirt on the bush to dry."

Following orders, Lily sat and dabbed absently at her face and hair with the paper napkins. What had happened to Alex that made him so sensitive and touchy about appearance? No matter how she shaped her thoughts, nothing made sense so she gave up and sat back to enjoy the view.

Alex had his back to her as he bent to drape her skirt over the low growing bush. His trousers cupped his butt, outlining hard gluts when he bent and stretched. Just as he turned, Killer's shrill bark rang out. Lily's faint smile was echoed on his face even as he shook his head, negating whatever thought had filled his mind. Then he prowled toward her, and Lily couldn't help the sigh that drifted from between her parted lips. She really liked watching the alien.

"Will your hair dry like that?"

Lily's hands rose to touch the sodden ponytail on her nape. Until now, she hadn't been aware of the drips of water steadily flowing down her back and onto the blanket. She went to tug off the red band that held her hair.

"Let me," he said, his smoky voice searing right through her.

If she let him touch her, she'd crave more. Lily turned her head slowly and presented her back despite her inner fears. Yep, weak. Definitely feeble. A sad, sad woman.

Alex was a large man, but his hands were infinitely gentle as he worked the fastening from her hair and combed his fingers through the wet locks. He used his fingers and thumbs to massage her head, probing, soothing aches and releasing tension she hadn't realized she'd had until she wanted to puddle into the blanket.

"Feel good?" he whispered next to her ear.

The languor leached from Lily with a jolt. She tensed. He'd see her belly rolls if she wasn't careful. She straightened so quickly she hit him in the face.

"Careful," he said, rubbing his abused nose with a rueful grin.

"I'm sorry," Lily said, mortified at yet another exhibit of her clumsiness. Good thing it wasn't catching. "Do you want coffee? I made a thermos." If she busied herself with lunch then maybe she'd forget her lack of clothing. Yeah. And as her brother Luke often said, maybe cloven-hoofed animals would fly.

"A coffee sounds good," Alex murmured lazily. "I have developed a liking for this Earth drink." He lay back on the blanket, apparently at ease with the world and her tummy rolls. Or perhaps they were so ugly he didn't like to look. That sounded a more likely scenario.

Lily pulled two orange plastic cups from the picnic basket and balanced them on the ground in convenient small hollows. The rich scent of coffee filled the air when she clicked the black pourer top open. Alex had closed his eyes and was so silent, she wondered if she'd bored him to sleep. His soft breathing battled with a noisy tui flying from tree to tree and the faint sound of Killer's barks. *The golden cat didn't even snore*, Lily thought. Apart from being distinctly antisocial in the mornings, she hadn't discovered any flaws.

"Stop looking at me."

Lily started and righted the wobbling thermos before staring at him suspiciously. Did he have a third eye? Now depending where it was, that could be considered a flaw.

"I'm not looking at you," she said.

"Yes, you are. I can feel you looking."

No answer for that. "Here's your coffee."

Alex propped himself up on one elbow and balanced in an elegant pose while he drank his coffee. He took a sip. "Perfect," he said with a satisfied sigh.

For a moment, there was a contented silence then Alex said, "Take your underwear off so that will dry, too. No need to feel uncomfortable for the rest of the day."

The coffee Lily had in her mouth spewed out in shock. She wiped her arms and legs while she glowered at Alex. "No."

"And if I dared you again?" he said in a smoky voice.

"And nothing."

"I'll have to help you disrobe then," he murmured, his golden gaze prowling her body.

No mistaking that look for anything but wicked. Oh, my stars! He licked his lips.

"You and whose army?" Lily snapped, trying desperately to concentrate and not let him distract her.

Alex sat up then, a predatory expression on his tanned face that scared the shit out of her. The golden cat barred his teeth, and Lily saw they looked sharp and dangerous.

"No," she said faintly, scuttling backward like an awkward crab missing a leg.

"That sounded like a challenge."

Excitement-tinged panic soared through Lily, sweeping to every nook, touching every inch of her body.

"It's for your own good, Lily."

The devilish glint in his golden eyes made her snort. "How do you figure that?"

"Lily."

Meeting his gaze made her melt, a sweeping, whooshing sensation low in her belly. How did he do that? Make her feel like a rebellious child. Make her want to obey.

"Come here," he whispered.

Lily inched closer to temptation.

"I'd never hurt you."

He couldn't promise that. Men always hurt her.

"Lily, trust me."

In Lily's experience when people said, "trust me" in that sincere tone, it was time to scamper. But something in his expression halted her retreat—a yearning in him that matched the want hidden deep inside Lily.

Alex closed the remaining distance between them. He touched her, his hands warm on her cool shoulders. One long, elegant finger traced along her collarbone then came to a rest on her pale blue bra strap. He twanged it lightly, a faint smile on his lips.

"This is very pretty." He skimmed one hand down her stomach, grazing the top of one breast on the way, and came to rest on the elastic waistband of her panties. "Matching. Nice."

Lily felt color bloom in her cheeks. They might be nice but she was beginning to regret the impulse that led her to donning her prettiest set of underwear this morning. Lily was sure her granny pants would have turned him from his determined course. Namely—to get her naked.

His finger danced along the frilly edging that stretched around her hips. Lily shivered even as she concentrated on keeping her belly sucked in. Suddenly she didn't feel so cold. And she wasn't disinterested that was for sure. Between her legs felt hot. Moist. And sticky, dammit. Her body had taken control of her mind. Again.

"Lie back," he whispered, the sound low and sinful.

Somehow, she found the itchy blanket at her back and her view from a different perspective. Fluffy clouds danced across the sky. A flock of birds fluttered overhead, chased by the bossy tui. A soft breeze played with the leaves of the rimu across the other side of the clearing, setting the long droopy strands rattling.

And then there was Alex.

His spicy scent sang to her senses, reminding her of moonlit nights and the cool shade of native bush on a hot day.

"Turn over," he whispered.

A block of potter's clay in his hands, she turned over without demure. She lay there in acute anticipation, wondering what his next move would be. Her stomach danced with nerves while her clit tingled without mercy. Lily wriggled uneasily and wondered whether to clench her bottom or not.

The warmth of his hands on her back came as a shock. She jerked, but he held her in place exerting gentle force. His hands swept across her shoulders, trailed down her spine. Then his fingers dug into tight, tense muscles, stroking, soothing. Lily eased out her breath and melted under his ministrations. He massaged her toes, her feet, her calves and thighs.

"Lift your hips," he whispered.

Mindlessly, she obeyed then tensed abruptly when he whisked her panties down her hips and legs. Silence reigned while Lily screwed her eyes shut and waited for a reaction. She felt him move and understood. But then, to her astonishment, he returned to his massage. His hands smoothed and stroked her butt. The rustle of his clothing indicated he'd moved closer. Lily wasn't sure how he'd missed seeing the size of her butt from where he was. Ambrose had told her it was large so often that she believed.

Lily couldn't quell the urge to look over her shoulder. He was looking all right, but that wasn't horror on his face. She held her breath as Alex leaned down and kissed her.

Right on the butt cheek.

Lily turned away to hold back the slight hysteria that rose, tickling the back of her throat in the fight to emerge as a nervous giggle. Well. That certainly gave new meaning to the saying "kiss my ass".

Chapter Seven

ဢ

But what was he going to do next? That was the question that begged an urgent answer. This was uncharted territory!

To her astonishment, Alex kissed her backside again then kneaded her butt cheeks, his hands shaping and alternatively stroking until Lily quivered inwardly and her pussy wept in approval. Alex kept touching, stoking the fire that made her long to grab his hands and direct them to her achy clitoris. She could almost forget that her ass was naked and bare to the world. Almost.

Birds sang. The water in the stream bubbled its way across the clearing. Sun beat down on her bare skin, heating her outside while Alex worked his charms and warmed her inside. He trailed his hands up her spine, his nails raking the skin hard enough to bite. Lily bit back a shiver of ecstasy at the sensual taunting. Positively sinful. The scratch of his nails felt so damned good she wanted to purr. Heck, she was purring. Each breath she exhaled sounded rhythmic and in time with the rush of the stream and his kneading fingers. Without warning, her bra gaped open, spilling her breasts from the lacy binding. Her heart jolted in anticipation, her nipples tightening to rigid peaks against the soft cotton cups.

"Turn over," he murmured.

Lily hesitated and then against her better judgment turned. With a devilish grin, he whisked her bra down her arms and tossed it on the garment-draped bush. Her gaze jumped to his face, ready to flee if she read derision in his eyes. Being naked in the great outdoors raised her vulnerability, especially since the alien remained fully clothed.

The heat in his brown eyes was approval but tinged with something else that jerked at her insecurities. Lily's hands darted up to cover her breasts, but he caught them and placed them back at her sides.

"You're just as beautiful as I remembered," he said, seeming to stroke her breasts with his eyes. "Don't try to hide."

Stories of experimenting aliens flashed through her mind and uneasy with the total exposure, Lily attempted to read him, trying to second-guess his intentions. His eyes glowed, more golden than brown, and they seemed to change color as she studied him but gave away none of his thoughts. Lily breathed out a frustrated sigh. She didn't think he was lying. But she'd been wrong before.

"I have to taste you," he breathed.

Suiting action to word, he leaned over to sip at her mouth. Slow, lazy kisses that left her wanting a deeper penetration. Lily reached for him, twining her arms around his neck and tugging him close to force a proper down and dirty kiss so she could taste him. The sort of carnal kiss she'd always craved from Ambrose. The sort of kiss she'd hungered for and never received. But then her naked breasts squashed against the cotton of his shirt, reminding Lily of her vulnerable position. Naked versus fully clothed. Lily tensed the length of her body, shock at her exposed state kicking her in the gut. Public sex. Where was her head? Ah-ah. Dumb question. She'd been blindsided by the thought of sex after such a long dry spell. But even so...

"I can't believe I'm doing this," she muttered.

Alex pulled away enough to stroke his fingers down her face. "Don't fret," he murmured in his husky voice. "Let me pleasure you."

"Plea...pleasure?" Lily's toes curled in reaction while she felt moisture gush between her thighs.

"Please, let me touch you, Lily. I need you."

If he'd said anything else, she would have refused. But to be needed. That was different. An enticing lure for a woman who'd failed to hold her man in the past.

"Are you sure?" Lily infused her words with a silent plea for reassurance. Under his hot, hungry gaze, her legs trembled and her stomach roiled with the force of the panicked butterflies stampeding inside.

Alex smiled then, obviously picking up on her hesitation. "I don't do anything I'm not sure about. Don't over think, Lily." His hand wandered downward and lazily circled the nipple of her left breast. A trail of goose bumps surfaced in the wake of his touch, nudging her desire higher. Making it difficult for her to refuse.

Lily swallowed, while she battled the need to grab him and direct his mouth to her nipple. Last night had given her a taste of how the sensation would feel. She recalled the wet, moist warmth of his mouth and the tug that shot to her pussy when he'd drawn her nipple deep into his mouth. Now, she wanted more. Craved more, but she was terrified to verbalize the needs that coursed through her body.

What if he laughed?

Ambrose had called her a slut the only time she'd suggested where he touch her. But even being knocked back hadn't stopped her fantasizing. Besides, when a male looked like Alex, it was natural to wonder. And Lily gave her mind full rein. She wanted him to kiss his way down her body, part her folds and tease her clit until she tumbled into orgasm. Lily panted, feeling suddenly scorching hot from the top of her head to the tips of her toes.

He wouldn't know if she didn't tell him.

"Alex?"

"Hmm?" He planted a kiss in her cleavage and nuzzled the curves of her full breasts.

"Stop teasing. Kiss me."

"Teasing? Me? I don't think so."

Lily felt the silent laughter in him and was about to protest when he kissed his way up the slope of one breast. Her eyes drifted shut to relish his ministrations.

His fingers tangled in her damp hair. The light massage he gave her scalp sent a frisson of pleasure surging through her veins, but still he teased her, fondling, stroking and kissing every part of her upper body apart from where she needed his touch most.

"Alex," Lily said in a stern and very un-Lily-like voice. "Please kiss my nipple."

Alex lifted his head to grin. "Moon heart, I thought you'd never ask."

At last. Lily relaxed against the blanket, closed her eyes and waited for the warmth of his mouth, for pleasure to drug her system. *I wonder what a moon heart is*, she thought dreamily. She felt a quick tug on one nipple and promptly forgot about moon hearts. The sensation repeated on the other and then…nothing.

Her eyelids flew open, and he could see the clear consternation in her blue eyes. Alex wanted to laugh but manfully held back his inclination. At this stage, Lily wasn't ready to be laughed at. She needed tender wooing… Wooing! Hell, just listen to his thoughts. He shouldn't touch this woman. His only excuse for the constant contact was that it helped ease the painful throb in his groin and in the rest of his limbs.

Alex sucked in a deep breath, the faint tang of her arousal an aphrodisiac to his raging hormones. His erection tightened to a painful intensity that told him to quit with the teasing. He couldn't handle much more of the petting without wanting to take it further, to free his cock and surge deep inside her cunt.

A shiver rocked him clear to his toes. Man, he wanted inside so much his hands trembled, his palms sweated. But that just wasn't gonna happen. He wouldn't let it. Focus, dammit.

"Alex?"

"Yes?"

"Please don't make me beg."

A chuckle escaped. Even though the teasing tormented him, too, watching Lily lose some of her stupid inhibitions thrilled him to the inside of his bone structure. The Earth woman was so beautiful. At the back of his mind was a vision—he'd drag her off to the nearest cave, have wild tigoth sex, and not let her leave until she bore him a child. Alex snorted. A bit presumptuous of course, but that was the way he felt—for the first time in his life. And it scared him to death because the timing sucked dragonbird eggs. His father wanted to match him up with a suitable female. Eventually, he'd have to join and bestow his mark, probably on the female his father chose, but not before he'd proved his worth.

Lily's nipple puckered up as though silently begging his touch. Unable to resist, Alex covered the tip of her breast with his mouth, laving her nipple with his tongue. Her soft groan boosted the pleasure he gained from touching her silky skin. Alex sucked lightly to test her reaction. She bucked beneath him, her hands tugging insistently in a silent bid for more. So he'd give her more, he decided.

Alex pulled away from her breast with a soft slurping sound to survey his handiwork. Her nipple looked wet and glistened in the sun. A soft blush highlighted her cheeks while her lips glowed red from his kisses. With her hair loose and disheveled, she appealed to him on every level. Lily reminded him of Marisee, the famous Dalconian consort. Marisee's portrait graced the wall of the salon in the castle. Rumor said males dueled for her favors, and the court had gone into mourning when she died. Lily had the same look—like the women in the Renaissance paintings depicted in his Italian guidebook.

"Alex?" she whispered, gazing at him through lowered lashes.

"Just lie back and enjoy." One of them might as well gain satisfaction from the experience.

Using his tongue, Alex licked around the rim of her belly button in sweet agonizing circles that wound desire inside him like a tight coil. She tasted of spices, reminding him of the small square sweets his nurse used to give him when he was an undergrown. But that was where the memory ended. Lily made him think very grown-up thoughts, and he thanked the gods he was grown.

The small indentation quivered under his tongue, he heard a soft gasp. Alex moved further down her body, splayed her thighs and moved into the gap created. Short, dusky curls guarded her sex. Different from Dalcon females. The difference intrigued him, and he tugged the dark curls, brushing his fingers through them to test and memorize the texture. Her excited scent teased at him. Alex breathed deeply and parted her slick folds, the juices of her arousal making her swollen clit shine like a lamp in the broad daylight.

Pretty — and so appealing.

Raw need raced through him, and as if she sensed how his control balanced on a sword's edge, Lily shifted restlessly beneath him, inflaming his stiff, erect tom to extremes. Alex swallowed, tension curling tightly in his stomach. At the back of his mind, he noted his hand trembled as he reached out to touch a small dewdrop of arousal. Unable to resist, he slid a finger over her clit in a teasing, passing foray. He glanced up her body to see the wildly beating pulse at her throat and the way she'd caught her bottom lip between her teeth. Her body arced upward, to keep the pressure on her clitoris.

"Please don't stop," Lily whispered. "Please."

"I won't stop," he promised. God, he couldn't now if he tried. Her response was genuine — so different from the palace consorts. Lily tempted him because she was so sincere. Not a hint of greed shone in her eyes.

He set about exploring, soothing her with his touch, tormenting and gently biting the soft contours of her lower body. Alex's tongue darted out to taste the soft skin of her inner thighs. Lily murmured something soft that he didn't understand but the jerk of her hips enabled him to hazard a guess.

He splayed one hand over her belly, holding her still while he lapped across her clit. Her juices tasted of the same spice that coated her skin. Delicious. Each foray of his tongue across her clit pushed his own arousal higher until his heart pounded against his rib cage.

Lily groaned long and hard, her body straining against his palm holding her still. Along with the desperate need that coursed his body, Alex felt a sense of achievement.

"Alex, I need…I need more," she gasped.

On hearing the entreaty in her voice, Alex dropped his hands to cup her buttocks. He lifted her to his mouth and licked in slow, languorous circles around her swollen, weeping clitoris.

"Alex," she pleaded, her thighs trembling.

Lily felt the slow slide of his tongue across her aroused flesh. Frissons of excitement shook her. Her mouth felt dry as sun-scorched earth during a drought. Every bit of moisture in her body pooled between her thighs. A shimmy of current danced from her clit spreading outward in the promise of more to come.

A small cry escaped as she rose upward to meet his lips. One finger slid into her cunt, filling an emptiness she hadn't been aware of. His finger plunged into her pussy then pulled out, only to return, each languid move timed to coincide with the lap of his tongue across her clit. The fire built. Lily strained against his mouth and questing tongue, every bit of pressure on her swollen bud propelling her higher until she thought she might fly.

"Oh, Alex." Lily squeezed her eyes shut and concentrated on the tiny burst of stars that danced across her lids. An almost painful shock darted from her center, gathering momentum. Explosive. Intense. A sob broke at the back of her throat. She swallowed dryly, hips jerking, body shaking at the strength of the orgasm that rolled through her.

As her pussy contracted and jumped beneath his mouth, Alex's cock throbbed mercilessly. The bloody thing seemed to have developed a mind of its own. His tom wanted in. Alex mentally gritted his teeth and lapped at her flower nectar, battling the lust that hammered at him.

Gradually, Lily's spectacular curves and soft body relaxed beneath his touch. She sighed and when he glanced up, he saw her eyelids flutter open.

"That was amazing. Can we do it again?" Then Lily clapped a hand over her mouth, her eyes big and blue, staring at him over her fingers in shock.

Her breathless question and wide-eyed reaction drew a strained chuckle. "I'd love to," Alex said, but he didn't tell her though he'd love to fuck her, he wasn't going to go a step further. Well, okay. Maybe just a bit of petting to soothe the nip of the bonding ties.

He glanced at the Earth timepiece strapped around his wrist. They'd already been here over an hour.

"I guess we don't have time," Lily said with a regretful sigh. Then she brightened. "Maybe later?"

"I think I've created a monster," Alex teased.

The blood drained from her face without warning, leaving ghostly cheeks. "You don't have to," she said quickly. "I'll understand—"

Alex stopped her words with a hard kiss followed by tongue action. He shuddered inwardly at the desperation that stalked his body. How the hell was he going to keep his tom out of her delicious pussy?

Killer's bark sounded, closer than the previous times he'd heard her.

"Lily? Alex? Where you?" she called. "You hiding? I find!"

Damn, he should probably urge Lily to dress before the devil creature arrived. Killer seemed very protective of Lily, and Alex figured she wouldn't be too happy if she saw he had Lily naked. He stood without haste and plucked Lily's ice-blue underwear off the bush.

"Dry," he said in a satisfied tone.

Lily accepted the silky garments from him. "I suppose we should go. We still have a way to drive."

"There's no hurry," Alex murmured. He heard Killer crashing through the undergrowth and the odd bark.

"Ouch! Prickles!" she yelped.

"I'll check to see if your clothes are dry enough to put on."

"I'll be putting clothes on regardless," Lily said primly. "You never know who might see."

Well, ain't that the King's truth, Alex thought, considering Killer's possible responses. He ripped his gaze off Lily's spectacular curves with difficulty and wandered over to the bush to get her clothes. When he turned back, she'd already donned her underwear. A pity.

Alex handed Lily her skirt and jumper. "Still damp."

"Never mind. I'll change when we get to Rotorua. There's Killer," she said looking past him. "Killer! Over here, sweetie. Can you grab her so she doesn't wander off again?"

Killer trotted up to them with pink tongue lolling, her teeth bared in a doggie smile. She spotted Lily and froze. "You take Lily's clothes off," she barked.

The dog was accusing him!

Alex opened his mouth to deny the charge then cast a dubious glance at Lily. Shit, he'd have to bite his tongue, and the spotted creature knew it.

She stalked over to him, muttering in low barks. "Doesn't happen on TV. People keep clothes on. Difficult case. Hold out for more food next time." She prowled closer to Alex, the hair along her spine rising as she glared at him. "Meddling alien."

Nope, Alex thought, wondering what on earth the devil creature was burbling about while keeping a wary eye on those teeth. *There was nothing sweet about Killer.*

* * * * *

237

Killer muttered in a low nonstop growl for the ten minutes it took for them to drive into the city of Rotorua. Alex tried to ignore the lunatic ravings, but it was difficult with the dog's wet nose poked into his side and the grumbles directed to his ear. A bit like a smoking shooter except this weapon had sharp teeth.

Alex stared out the window at the lake and attempted to shut out the droning yaps coming from the devil creature. Lily seemed happy to concentrate on driving.

The dog leaned on him when they rounded a corner and whispered a low threat, "I tell Janaya on you."

"She's in Alaska." Alex wound down the window to blow the dog smell out of his space. A wave of sulfur hit him, and he glimpsed steam from a vent in the middle of a fenced off reserve. Although he'd read about the smell in Rotorua, he hadn't expected it to be quite as pungent.

"What's wrong with Killer?"

"No idea," Alex muttered.

"You know," Killer snarled. "Lily no clothes. Janaya be angry. She shoot."

Alex suppressed a shiver of horror and adjusted his trousers just to make sure he was intact. A nervous reaction. Shooting was the least of his problems where Janaya was concerned.

"Perhaps she needs a run." Lily pulled up outside the Whakarewarewa Thermal Reserve. "I'll drop you off here."

Alex opened his door and Killer jumped out.

"I need food," she barked.

"Killer, you stay with me, sweetie. They don't like dogs in there."

"Huh!" Killer sniffed in clear disdain. "I have talk with Alex."

That didn't sound good. Alex pointed to a sign. It bore a dog with a big black cross through it.

"Someone graffiti on dog," Killer snapped.

"That means no dogs," Alex countered. And to prove it, he strode up to the ticket booth. "Can I take my dog in?"

"Not his dog!" Killer yelped. "Meddling alien!"

"Sorry, sir. No dogs allowed," the young woman in the ticket booth said.

Alex smirked. Damn it felt good to best the devil creature.

"Don't want to go in anyway," Killer sniffed. "Smells bad like rotten egg. I want real food." But she kept peeking through the gate each time it opened to admit another visitor. Alex didn't try to hide his grin. The dog wanted to explore so badly her shiny nose twitched.

"I'll take memories." Alex patted his brand new image machine. "You can see them later tonight."

"Of course I will," Lily said in a puzzled tone. "Killer can come with me. Is an hour long enough? We can make it longer but it's still an hour's drive to Taupo, and you'll want to see some of the other sights."

Alex waited until Killer jumped back into the vehicle and shut the door.

"Not fair," she barked. "They racist. I complain."

"You certainly do," Alex muttered, forgetting for a split second about Lily.

"If I didn't know better, I'd think there was something wrong with you," Lily teased.

"There is," Alex said, slapping his hands over Killer's ears before he continued. "If you count walking around with a hard-on tom."

"Alex," Lily gasped.

He grinned, taking great pleasure in the bright color that sped to her cheeks.

"You can't say that in public."

"I just did. Ow! Cut that out," he growled as the dog gave his hand a sly nip so he'd uncover her ears.

"You talking about me," Killer accused.

"Overgrown-up talk," Alex countered.

"An hour," Lily said, cutting across the flurry of barks that erupted after Alex's pronouncement.

Alex stepped back from the SUV and watched as Lily drove away. Immediately, his heart thudded in panic and his pulse spiked. That bloody bonding manure-shit again. Man, it vacuumed being an alien on a foreign planet.

He purchased a ticket with the plastic money that Lily had assured him was New Zealand currency. The woman in the ticket booth didn't blink an eye, but Alex was used to using gold and jewels as currency.

He walked through the gate and negotiated a turning gate. Gravel crunched beneath his feet, and a sense of anticipation burned his gut along with the uneasy jolting of the bonding ties. This was what he wanted, and it really felt as though he were moving toward success.

The time flew. Alex watched the carvers use chisels to create the intricate wooden carvings that decorated the meetinghouse and storehouses used to keep food up high from pests. A warrior greeted his group with the traditional Maori challenge. The man pulled so many weird faces, Alex wondered if he had an aching belly. He took several photos of the man's graffitied—no—tattooed face and jotted shorthand notes that would tug his memory later tonight when he wrote them up in a more logical order. The bonding mess with Lily was scrambling his language prowess. He must concentrate.

Alex followed the gravel paths, listening to the guide until a young Japanese woman tried to strike on him. He brushed her off firmly with a polite no, thank you, he didn't want a massage, and wandered off on his own.

The strange kiwis with their long sharp beaks and short, stubby fur-like feathers fascinated him. They ran around in their artificially created darkness using their beaks to dig for worms in rotten logs. Then there were the geysers. Pohutu, the largest, erupted high into the air on schedule, spewing large quantities of water and steam. Mud pools, cooking pools, and the brainpot pool that was supposedly used to cook the heads of enemies in times past. Alex snapped photos of them all. He glanced at his timepiece and saw to his horror that almost two hours had elapsed. Picking up the steps, almost jogging, he pushed past the tourists throwing coins into the water for young children to retrieve. Alex burst through the exit, catching sight of the bright blue car immediately. Killer bounded over to meet him.

"You take picture?"

"I'll show you in the vehicle," he promised.

"What about Lily?" Killer asked, shooting a quick glance behind her to see if Lily was close enough to hear. "She think you crazy."

Alex snorted at that. "I think it's too late for control damage now." He paused briefly, frowning, before stepping up the pace. Control damage didn't sound right, but he'd puzzle out the different meanings of Earth words later when he was alone.

"True," Killer conceded. "We go now."

Alex jogged over to the car. "Sorry I'm late. Time got away on me."

"No problem. I think you'll be pleased with some of the info I've collected for you. The owners of the hotels I went to have offered some great deals although I'm not sure about parking for the spaceship. Where would you like to go next? There's the Agrodrome where they have performing sheep. We could take a boat trip out on the lake and visit Mokoia Island where the lovers Hinemoa and Tutanekai defied their parents and met, or there's the Buried Village—"

She sounded nervous, her words spilling one over the other while her gaze danced everywhere, never settling. Alex found her edginess endearing, and he fought the urge to draw her into his arms and kiss her. That would solve her doubts, but get him into a heap of trouble. Alex wished he could get his hands on her ex-husband. The worm. Then a thought hit. Perhaps he wasn't behaving any differently. Ultimately, he'd leave, and Lily would be alone.

"You choose the sights to visit," he said.

Five minutes later they were on the road again, driving through streets advertising places to stay and their facilities. Thermal hot pools, cable television, children's playgrounds. *Something for everyone on any budget*, Alex thought, and scribbled several notes.

Lily pointed out the adventure sports available for any daredevil clients he might have. "I don't mind waiting while you zorb," she said, slowing as they passed signs depicting a large clear plastic ball rolling down a hill with a person inside. "Or you can bungee jump. I told you about that the other night. Remember jumping off a bridge with elastic bands attached to your feet? That's the private spa pools where you can have massages and treatments." Lily showed him the entrance.

Alex jotted more notes, feeling truly excited about the range of excursions he'd be able to offer. They had nothing like this on Dalcon.

Lily drove through the Government Gardens with their beds of colorful annuals and the mature trees, her mind only half on the job. The rest of her mind was stuck firmly on their lunch stop and what had happened. She'd…they'd… Lily pulled up in the parking area near St. Faith's Church so that Alex could see the old church and where the boats sailed to Mokoia Island.

Alex had…they'd…she'd had her first taste of oral sex. A grin puckered her lips. Alex had done the tasting. But whatever, his tongue on her had made her want to fly. And she had. Lily cast a speculative glance at Alex as he sauntered across the car park with Killer yapping at him nonstop. What would it feel like to taste him, to hold him in her mouth and pleasure him? A funny shivery sensation made her stomach swoop and plunge as if she were on a fairground ride. She wanted to learn. If only Alex would let her. The problem was he seemed to switch on and off like a tap, confusing the heck out of her.

She glanced at him again and saw that two young women had stopped him to chat. Jealousy wiped the pleasant buzz from her system, and she glared at the women through narrowed eyes. Although they had stooped to pat Killer, that wasn't where their attention was centered! The tall, slim one with the midnight-black hair was close enough that her tits brushed Alex's arm.

Lily only relaxed when she saw Alex shake his head. Both women glanced at her and then turned back to Alex. *Probably wondering what a fat cow was doing with the golden cat,* Lily thought with an indignant sniff. All the happiness and confidence that had built during the day seeped out her shoes. Who was she trying to kid? She and Alex were as different as Dalcon and Earth. They would never have a future together.

Chapter Eight

ଥ

They ended up staying the night in Rotorua and spending most of the day exploring and trying out the many activities available. Lily grimaced. Alex had done the quality testing—she was strictly a two-feet-on-the-ground kinda girl, especially since her clumsiness challenged her more than enough to fill her need for adventure. She glanced across at Alex's enthralled face as he stared out at the scenery. The alien's enthusiasm was contagious, and she'd allowed him to dally until late afternoon before putting her foot down and demanding they leave for their next stop.

When they arrived in Taupo, the trio of mountains on the far side of the lake was barely visible in the rapidly closing dusk. Acute disappointment bloomed in Lily, but she promised herself she'd get up early in the morning and walk along the edge of Lake Taupo so she could savor her favorite view to her heart's content.

"Our hotel is down the end of this block." Lily slowed to give way to the stream of approaching traffic then turned into the parking lot. She parked in the last remaining spot and switched off the ignition.

"Looks full," she said. "Lucky I've booked."

They climbed out, and Alex collected their bags from the back.

"Do you want your boots?" Lily asked, seeing them still sitting in the rear.

"No, leave them there. I won't need them tonight."

"Do we have food?" Killer danced around their feet in a four-footed frenzy.

"Later," Alex muttered. "Not now. You're attracting attention. Do you want to get kicked out?"

Lily shook her head. The two of them were at their growling again. Weird. Just plain weird. "I'll go and check in."

Lily left them to their barking contest and pushed open the door to the reception area. It was a plush room with thick carpet that her shoes sank into with each step. A grandfather clock ticked off the minutes in a loud, regal manner from the far corner. Almost seven, she noted. After the long, eventful day, she was ready to kick off her shoes and relax. Lily joined a queue of four people and let her mind wander. Of course, it didn't really wander. Like a magnet, her mind seized on Alex as the topic straightaway. Lily feared she was setting herself up for a huge, body-crunching fall and long-lasting heartache. But that didn't stop her thinking what if.

"Next, please!"

Lily jerked from her reverie to find the middle-aged woman behind the reception desk glaring at her. "Sorry," she murmured, stepping up to the shiny wooden desk. "I have a booking for Morgan."

The woman consulted her register then looked up over the rim of her glasses. "You're late."

"It's only just gone seven." The grandfather clock chimed noisily the instant Lily said the words.

"We hold the rooms until six unless prior arrangements are made. Next, please."

Lily stood firm, and the woman glared at her anew. "I am sorry we're late. Do you have other rooms available? Two singles."

Behind Lily, the door from outside opened with a well-oiled sigh.

"No dogs!" the woman shrieked.

Lily winced and turned to silently signal Alex to take Killer outside. Luckily, he appeared to understand her eye rolls and gestures.

"We don't have any singles left," the woman said. "All we have is a double."

"Can you recommend another hotel?"

"It's the middle of school holidays and the mountain-to-lake run is being held this weekend. Rooms are scarce. You won't get one. Next, please."

Still Lily stood her ground. The thought of driving 'round and 'round looking for rooms wasn't appealing. "I'll take the double."

"Is that your dog?" the woman countered.

"Yes, but she's booked into the kennels." Lily held the woman's stern gaze, trying really hard not to blink or look away. Just as she was about to glance at her shoes, the woman inclined her head.

"Very well. Fill out this. Credit card, please."

Lily took care of formalities and finally received two keycards in return. She turned away and let her breath ease out in a relieved hiss. Thank goodness, dragon lady had believed her about Killer. Now all they had to do was smuggle her into their room. The change of rooms was a bit of a pain since she'd been looking forward to soaking in a hot bath and an early night. But on the other hand... A slow grin spread across her lips. Perhaps this was the ideal opportunity to show Alex how interested she was in learning about the alien way of doing things. Specifically, their sex lives and his anatomy.

* * * * *

"No! Not going in bag."

"You'll have to," Alex said. "Dogs aren't allowed in the rooms."

"Undignified," Killer sniffed, glaring at the large leather bag with a look of pure dislike. Her tail trembled just enough to show her displeasure.

"Do you want food?"

"Food?" Killer's eyes brightened and the wag of her tail increased to a frenzied speed.

"You can only have food if you get inside the bag."

Killer sat and stuck her nose in the air. "No."

Lily returned from exploring the room. "It's a nice room," she said. "And fairly big so we won't trip over each other."

The sharp jerk of his cock reminded him that tripping was the least of his problems. But at the moment, Killer rated a little higher than the bonding ties.

"Killer won't get in the bag," he said.

"If the woman at reception spies her, we'll lose our room. The hotel management will have us out so quick our heads will spin. Killer will have to get into the bag."

Alex backed away from the stubborn dog with an elegant hand gesture. "Be my guest. You tell her."

"She won't understand," Lily said, advancing on the dog.

The bloody dog understood too much for his liking. He folded his arms over his chest and settled back against a brick wall to watch the unfolding drama. This oughta be good.

Killer growled low and mean at Lily, and turned around to present her butt in full-out revolt. Alex smothered his laugh by turning it into a cough.

"Told you," he said.

"I stay in Sam's car," Killer said. "After I have food."

Alex watched with amusement as Lily grabbed for Killer, aiming for the scruff of her neck. At the very last moment, the dog darted out of reach. Lily tripped and saved herself from a fall by snatching at the back of the vehicle but still managed to knock her knee on the tow bar.

A loud thud sounded, and Alex winced in sympathy. That must have hurt. "You okay?"

"Fine," Lily gritted out. "What are we going to do about the dog?"

In the glare of the car park lights, Alex caught the sheen of tears in her eyes and saw the shadows beneath her them. Lily was tired. "Why don't we leave Killer in the vehicle? I'll feed her and take her for a walk before we go to bed."

"I suppose that will have to do," Lily said.

"What number is the room?"

"Room 206." Lily handed him a keycard. "I might go and soak in the spa bath, if that's okay."

Alex nodded, not trusting himself to speak. His gaze zapped to her butt, watching the sway of her hips as she walked away. He didn't want to imagine her naked in a tub of scented water. It was bad enough that they had to share a room. Alex bit off a savage curse and glared at the dark, star-studded sky. If he peered hard enough, he was sure he'd see the Goddess of Dalcon and Tigus wetting herself with laughter. A snort erupted at the thought. The planet of Tigus might appreciate the waterfall. Before he'd left, they'd been complaining of the lack and petitioned the King for a water ceremony.

After seeing to Killer's many and varied needs, Alex stopped in at the hotel restaurant and ordered a room service meal for both of them. Wanting to try some of the New Zealand specialties, he picked out roast lamb with tamarillo sauce and a selection of vegetables. Then for after, he chose cheese and crackers along with a selection of homemade chocolates. The maître d' recommended a bottle of wine and suggested they make coffee or tea up in the room. Lily had looked so exhausted down in the car park, and he had notes to write so the suggestion sounded *basuko* fine.

He slid the keycard into the door with slight trepidation, even though his heart beat in fierce delight at the thought of seeing Lily again. Perhaps there was a temporary bed he could use. What did they call them? Oh, yeah—a couch. It was either that or the floor since he dare not risk sharing the bed.

Lily's special floral scent hit him as soon as he stepped inside the hotel room. Then the sight of the bed grabbed him by the throat, demanding attention and consideration.

It was big.

It looked soft and luxurious.

And Lily lay in the middle asleep. With her eyes closed and her face relaxed and open, she hardly looked older than an undergrown. As he watched, her eyes flickered open. They were a beautiful blue that reminded him of the lakes they'd seen today—sometimes light blue and innocent and at other times, dark, stormy and mysterious.

"Sorry, I didn't mean to wake you."

"That's all right," she said, her voice low and seductive. "If I sleep now, I won't sleep later tonight."

Bloody hell! He didn't want that. If two people lay awake in the small hours of the morning, chances were their minds would take a sharp turn into trouble. Not that his mind wasn't in the territory already. He sighed inwardly and wished he'd checked in at reception instead of Lily. He'd have intimidated the dragon lady into giving them their rooms.

"I ordered room service. I hope that's all right with you," he said, more to ease the rising tension in the hotel room than to impart information.

"Really?" Lily sat up, treating him to a flash of thigh before hurriedly smoothing down the thin cotton robe that she wore.

Alex frowned. "Yeah, but we can go out if you want."

A wide smile stretched her lips, highlighting a cute set of dents beside her mouth that he hadn't noticed before. "No, dinner in the room is a great idea."

Her voice strummed along his nerves, playing him like a master court musician. And the way her eyes caressed him... Alex suppressed a violent shudder and concentrated on keeping his hands tightly clenched behind his back.

A knock on the door was a welcome interruption, and Alex answered with alacrity. A young man wearing a white uniform wheeled a trolley into the room. He unloaded the covered plates from the trolley along with stemmed glasses and the bottle of wine, and set the table ready for them to eat. Alex watched in silence as he placed the final item on the table—an apricot rose-flower in a glass vase.

"Thank you," Alex murmured, handing the man a money-note on the way out.

The door clicked softly as it closed, while the wheels of the trolley squeaked until the man reached the bank of lifts.

"That smells wonderful," Lily said. "What did you order?"

"The man in the restaurant recommended the lamb." Suddenly Alex wished he'd never thought of the idea. All he'd wanted was to make things easier for Lily. But right now, from where he stood, it felt as though he was knee-deep in trouble. The setting was romantic and, dammit, that wasn't what he'd intended at all.

"Let's eat," Lily said, still beaming.

Alex tried not to look directly at her as he gestured for her to sit. He pulled out a chair and seated her then strolled around to sit opposite with a calmness he didn't feel. Every breath he dragged in overloaded his senses with Lily's scent, torturing Alex with reminders of how much he wanted her. The bonding ties felt like a rope around his neck, slowly tightening and squeezing his willpower. The idea of giving in was a seductive song in his mind. But he refused to give in to it. No messy emotional entanglements for him. No, majesty! He intended to remain free to pursue his dreams. No way did he intend to tie himself to a woman only to find that she changed the minute she discovered he was a royal prince. He chanced a glance at Lily. Hard to say if she would be like that or not, but he didn't intend to take the risk.

"Is there something wrong with your meal?" Lily asked. "You're frowning at your plate as though it's full of worms."

Alex jerked his eyes off the roast lamb and looked at Lily. A soft glow made her eyes particularly beautiful. He stilled at the emotion he saw in them — deep and mysterious. Her expression reminded him of the palace consorts when they managed to wear him down and drag him off to bed.

Please don't let her chase me, he thought. Heck, he had to get a grip on himself. With the spell the old crone had given him, he was as ugly as a newborn undergrown. But Lily was a problem because she seemed desperate to prove her value. And that bloody ex-male of hers. He'd mucked up her self-confidence and now she'd decided to test her wiles on someone safe. Him. Well, cometflash — she'd picked the wrong male to test her wiles on. And he sure as hell wasn't feeling safe.

"What did you think of the sights you saw today?"

When Alex risked another glance, he saw her normal, cheery expression. An innocent set of blue eyes framed by wisps of brown hair combined with a sprinkling of brown dots on her nose and cheeks and a gentle smile.

Take her at face value, he decided. He thought of all the sights he'd seen and immediately his enthusiasm bubbled and plans filled his mind with a pleasant buzz. "I want to include Rotorua on the itinerary," he said. "There are so many different things to see. We don't have anything like that on Dalcon. Or on the neighboring planets."

"Are you trying to appeal to adventurous travelers?"

"Not necessarily. I'd like to offer alternative activities in each stop-off point. And I'd like to cater for both male and female clients."

The discussion carried Alex past his awkwardness and suspicions, letting him relax and float all his budding ideas past Lily. By the end of dinner and the bottle of wine, they'd mapped out the stops for Rotorua and worked out a list of possibles for Taupo.

Lily cleared away the plates, stacking them outside the door for room service to collect later. She stepped back inside the room and engaged the security lock with a metallic snap. Alex felt as though he'd been incarcerated with temptation.

"Do you want to use the bathroom first?" she said.

The tension inside him ratcheted sharply upward. Alex's mouth curled into a wry grin. It seemed the minute he forgot to focus on his dream, visions of Lily and sexual relations started to crowd his head.

Okay. Lily could go first. He'd continue with his planning on paper then go take a cold shower, massage away some of the sexual tension and by the time he came back out, Lily would be asleep.

Simple solution.

He forced a smile. "You go first." His gaze darted to her cleavage as the cotton robe she wore gaped. Round, soft curves tempted him to close the distance between them. The little brown dot on her breast beckoned. A whimper built at the back of his throat. Alex bunched his fists and concentrated on deep, easy breaths. By the Goddess, he hoped she was quick because he really needed that shower.

Lily had switched off the main lights and only a single bedside lamp burned when he exited the shower, dressed in a short robe provided by the hotel. Good. She seemed to be asleep. Alex eyed the couch. It looked a little short, but he'd make do.

"Alex?"

Damn.

Lily sat up and patted the expanse of bed beside her. "I hope you're not thinking about sleeping on the couch."

"Yes, I was," Alex stated baldly.

"That's silly. The bed is huge."

But not big enough.

"No, I don't think so."

Lily's eyes narrowed. "I don't bite."

"But I'd like to," he muttered in an undertone.

"Get in bed."

Bloody hell. Alex sat and perched on the edge of the bed. Not a terribly masculine pose, but he was running scared. Her voice had turned masterful but sultry with it. A lethal combination.

"We have a lot to do tomorrow. You need a decent night's sleep. "

"I'm not going to sleep if I'm in the same bed as you." No point pulling his punches.

"Good," Lily said, clear satisfaction in her voice. "We can use the time to explore each other."

Fuck. He'd stepped right into that one. Trouble was how did he get out. "I don't think—"

"No thinking required," Lily said sweetly. Her breasts rose and fell abruptly. "Just lie back and think of Dalcon."

Chapter Nine

🎵

A dare.

Lily's heart thudded so loudly it was a wonder Alex didn't pounce on her fear and issue a return challenge. She needed to act before he called her bluff and climbed off the bed. Quick! But what should she do?

Alex made a move as if he might try to escape. Lily bit her bottom lip. Did she disrobe? Did she jump him? What? Heck, this whole situation was plain embarrassing. She might be female and she'd had sex before, but she still had no idea how to successfully seduce a man. At least she didn't need to worry about contraception since that was sorted. As long as he didn't have any nasty diseases, the pill should suffice.

Then he turned to face her, an anguished expression on his beautiful face that tore at her heart. He was going to move.

Ditch the nightie later. Naked later. Judging by the look on his face, she needed to work on persuasion first. In the light of the bedside lamp, determination laced with something that looked suspiciously like fear replaced the anguish. No, that couldn't be right. Why would he fear her?

She looked again. Alex still looked as though he'd make a run for it at any second. A picture of a wrestler sailed into her mind. Oh, yeah. She could imagine jumping him all right. And luckily, he was big and solid, because otherwise he was in danger of being flattened by her chunky form. From the corner of her eye she saw the muscles bunching in his calves.

Emergency! Lily launched herself across the bed before Alex moved so much as another muscle. A wall of hard muscle flattened her breasts before his hands manacled her wrists and held her away so they no longer touched. She fought back taking him unaware and threw herself at him again. Lily bumped her nose on his shoulder so hard her eyes smarted, but it was worth the pain. Alex's arms came around her, clutching her tightly.

His robe had loosened during their struggle, and Lily smiled as she nestled closer to his naked chest but took care to hide her jubilation. The battle wasn't won yet. His hands gripped her upper arms with an almost painful intensity before he pushed her away to search her face intently. The man looked every inch the predator as his eyes bored into her, transfixing her with his golden glare.

Panic rose to savage Lily. He was going to push her away after all! Lily stopped fighting the strength in his arms and went boneless. As she'd gambled, he let up on his grip and she went in for the kill.

Seduction.

Lily was willing to use every weapon in her arsenal because she couldn't take much more of the physical push and pull games. She ached for him, his full possession. Lily wanted the slow slide of his cock massaging her deep inside her womb. Whenever she glimpsed his chest, she wanted to lick and bite at the golden, hairless flesh. She wanted to tease and torment the flat discs of his nipples. The taste during their lunch break yesterday had left her hungry.

So, this was a test for him. If he really meant it when he said he found her attractive, now was the time for him to prove it.

Lily kissed him, sliding her lips over his in a slow dance of seduction. Alex stilled, his mouth was motionless beneath her questing lips. No. No! Her mind screamed her frustration and helplessness. This wouldn't work if he didn't cooperate. Lily put everything she had into the kiss, moving her lips and tracing the seam of mouth with her tongue. Still he remained motionless. She gulped inwardly as she rained kisses on the corner of his mouth, across his jaw and pondered failure. A block of clay had more animation. Ambrose had kept telling her she lacked sex appeal.

Moving her kisses down his neck, Lily paused to enjoy the soft, tender skin below his ear. Was it her imagination or had Alex tensed? Lily swallowed. Maybe Ambrose was right about her sex appeal. Or the lack of it. Tears formed at the back of her eyes and she squeezed them shut, trying to save embarrassment. Lily pressed another moist kiss across the pulse point below his ear then scraped her teeth over the same tender spot.

A low heartfelt groan cracked like a whip in the quiet room. Lily froze. Her heart pounded. Her eyes popped open.

Then she repeated the move. Slower. A bit more bite. Yeah. Her breath hissed out in celebration. That was a definite groan. Lily sucked, drawing on his neck. His hands gripped her shoulders tighter, drawing her close and allowing her free rein. Lily drew on the same spot for as long as it took to mark him. The idea of the golden cat prowling about with a hickey—her mark on his neck—thrilled her. It smacked of possession but that's exactly how she felt.

Lily wriggled closer to kiss his mouth. This time was better. Her mouth met warm, responsive lips. Masculine fingers threaded through her hair and hands cradled her head. Lily moaned softly, writhing against him in silent demand.

"We shouldn't." Alex nibbled at her mouth. "Do this."

Time to pull out all stops. No way was he stopping while she had breath in her body. Lily tugged free, whipped her nightie over her head and sat proudly naked, despite her inner anxiety.

A vein throbbed at his temple. His hands clenched and unclenched.

"You're so beautiful." He touched one nipple with the tip of his finger. Lily trembled, closing her eyes against the zap of spine-tingling sensation that shot to her clitoris. Unbidden, her hand reached to soothe the achy, almost painful jolt. The feeling intensified as her finger cruised over her clit.

"I have to touch you. Can I touch?"

Lily's eyes fluttered open to see him watching her hand avidly. She nodded, suddenly breathless at the hot gleam in his eyes. She felt a swooping pull in her lower belly. Her vagina contracted sharply. Feminine juices gathered beneath her finger.

"My turn," Alex whispered, his voice low. Smoky.

Oh, my God! Hot flags of color exploded in her cheeks as she realized what she'd just done. She'd touched herself in front of Alex.

"Did it feel good when you touched yourself?"

How did he do that? Read her emotions before she knew them herself. Lily's gaze dropped to the hand that rested on her thigh. Her juices coated her finger and it shone. Her heart thudded hard as if a fist closed around it, squeezing tight. This was the new, go-getter Lily. She didn't lie. "Yes." Lily's chin lifted. "I liked it."

Alex shifted, repositioning both of them on the bed so they reclined fully. Then he leaned over her and traced a finger across her lips. Lily opened her mouth and sucked his finger inside, closing her lips around it and soothing her tongue over the tip. Their eyes met and held.

"Lily." Her name came out as a low groan, coated with passion and possibilities.

Teasing now, Lily gave his finger a final lick then released it with a loud smacking sound. She hoped the next thing she had in her mouth was his cock. A shiver shot through her sensitized body at the thought. "You have way too many clothes on." The words burst from her in a low breathy voice. A sexy voice. Surely, that wasn't her?

Alex stared at her for a long drawn-out moment. He propped himself up on his elbows then swung his legs over the edge of the bed. His hands went to the tie at his waist. "Not for long." Lily licked suddenly dry lips as Alex stood. The huge bulge at his groin drew her attention.

"For me?"

"There's no one else here," he said, his tone rough as he dropped the robe on the floor.

He was naked beneath. Lily sat up, and her breath eased out with a hiss. His manhood thrust out proudly about level with her fascinated eyes. He was different from Ambrose in this department, too. Bigger, but that wasn't a problem since she was built to take big if she wanted. The biggest surprise was the lack of hair.

Enthralled with the discovery, her hand reached without volition to touch the silky smooth skin that surrounded his cock. Oh, the equipment seemed the same—just different.

"I have hair." Lily gestured at her groin. "Do you shave? Or wax?" Eek! Lily winced at the thought. That would take more balls than she had.

"Dalconians don't have much body hair. Are you gonna touch?"

Lily's gaze shot to his face. His lips were drawn back in a pained expression, and his eyes glowed a deep golden color that was mesmerizing and beautiful enough to tempt a saint.

She was no saint—not in her new bad-girl guise. Catching and holding his gaze, Lily licked her lips. Slowly. Completely.

"Stop teasing," he whispered hoarsely. "I'm holding back by a woolo fiber. Touch me. Feel what you do to me. I'm shaking."

Lily's gaze zapped to his cock. "Whoa!" She scrambled away to stare in half horror, half fascination. That was a bit...unexpected!

Alex stilled. "What's wrong?"

"You...you've turned blue!" The sudden need to laugh quivered through her like a glass of tickly champagne. Alex's...thing... She peered a little harder. Not just his thing... "My God," she muttered. "It's the exact color of a baboon's bum!" As Lily watched, his cock shriveled up and the blue color faded upward before vanishing. She blinked then closed her eyes. When she reopened them, all she could see was a flesh-colored cock. "Wow!" Lily grinned up at Alex. "Do that again."

Every muscle in his body—apart from his cock—tensed. "I am not a man-toy. I will not go up and down for your viewing pleasure." He sounded decidedly testy.

Oops. She'd hurt his feelings. Lily stood and ran her hand across his shoulder in silent apology. But she couldn't resist a quick downward glance to see what his cock was doing. To her acute disappointment, the answer was nothing. It was just there and looked like a normal penis.

Alex shrugged off her touch and stooped to pick up his robe.

Panic replaced Lily's humor. "Alex, wait. I'm sorry. I just didn't expect…" She trailed off, valiantly fighting the laughter that gurgled up inside.

"You're laughing at me."

"No! Please. I really want to take this further." One look at his clenched jaw told her that all the words in the world wouldn't soothe his injured pride. Action—that's what she needed. Lily stood on tiptoes and pressed a kiss to his tight mouth. She rubbed her breasts against his chest and groaned at the exquisite sensation of her nipples dragging across the golden skin. Suddenly, the mouth she kissed softened and kissed her back. Okay. Good. Lily caught herself before she aimed her eyes at his groin. Nope, she couldn't do that. Not yet. She needed to get him in the mood again and then, this time, she'd explore the alien aspects of his body without the passion-killing remarks about baboons.

Lily continued to kiss and pet Alex until they both shook with pent-up need. She backed in up to the bed and pushed him off balance, falling on him before he could object. They toppled to the bed together, Lily dropping on top of Alex's muscled body.

"Alex?"

"Yes?"

Lily frowned at the cautious note in his voice. "I'm gonna look now," she said, her heart thumping with acute anticipation. "Do you want to tell me anything else before I look?"

"Madam, I assure you I am quite normal."

The pique had appeared again, and Lily rushed to reassure him. "I'm not implying you're abnormal! But you are from a different planet. I just wanted a bit of warning in case there was…um…something else?" She punctuated her words with kisses because no way did she want his cock to shrink before she got a good, close look at his blue balls.

"There are a few small differences," Alex finally admitted after a long stretch of cranky silence. "But I have studied Earth and know the correct way to proceed—"

"You've studied sex?" Lily blurted. "Then it sounds like you can teach me." She paused, her mind working at top speed. Maybe, discovering the differences as they came along would be fun. As long as there was nothing dangerous… Lily thought about the color blue. A pretty color. Her eyes were blue. "As long as there's no danger involved," she said slowly, catching and holding his gaze, "then I'd like to discover the differences as we proceed."

"You trust my word?"

The scowl on Alex's face was fearsome, but it didn't deter Lily because she did trust the alien. He'd shown her nothing but kindness so far despite her insecurities. "I trust you and would like to proceed." *My stars, that sounded formal*, Lily thought. The need to laugh nipped at her tonsils but she bit her bottom lip and refused to let the gaiety pass into the open air.

Alex continued to scowl, and Lily's heart slammed nervously against her ribs. *Please don't say no. Please don't say no.*

"I would never hurt you, Lily, but if you change your mind, all you need to do is tell me and I'll refrain from touching you again."

Lily laughed gleefully inside and allowed a tremulous smile to curl across her lips. "Thank you. Can I look now?"

Alex gave a stiff nod. The need to appease her curiosity was huge, but Lily proceeded with caution. She could feel his cock stabbing against her inner thigh as she kissed her way down his body. The journey felt long but it was really only a matter of thirty seconds before she reached the action department.

"Wow," she whispered when she came eye to eye, so to speak, with Alex's snake.

Looking impressively large, the huge bulbous head was swollen and a dark royal blue. Apart from the gorgeous, unexpected color, the snake looked similar to her ex-husband's. Lily stroked her hand down the blue exterior, noting the darker veins that ran under his skin. Entranced, she touched the tiny slit at the end. Alex jerked, and a soft groan sounded. Feeling bolder, Lily traced the length of his cock, enjoying the tactile smooth feel of him yet fully aware of the contrasting steel that ran beneath the hot, blue skin.

For her. All for her.

When her hand stroked the tip again, a tear of pre-cum appeared. Without thinking, she bent to lick the pastel-blue drop away. Alex jerked beneath her mouth and she heard a muttered curse. Lily froze then decided if he were that upset with her, he'd leap away to the other side of the bed. To test her theory, she lapped across the head of his cock. Like a giant blue lollipop, she thought with a hidden grin. His scent surrounded her—spicy and green, reminding her out the outdoors on a crisp, sunny day. But the taste of him was better—addictive, and even better than she'd imagined. Must be the blue coloring, she thought with a wicked smirk.

Alex jerked away from her without warning. Lily held her loose hair back from her face and looked up at him. His broad chest rose and fell rapidly as he stared at her with his strange golden eyes.

"You're a witch," he whispered. "You must be. I've never felt like this before." He moved rapidly, rolling her body until he loomed over her. "I hope you're ready for me, moon heart, because I can't wait any longer. I'm gonna come any second, but I want it to be in you."

Lily wanted to object since she'd only started exploring the big blue, but he parted her legs almost roughly and ran his finger around the rim of her cunt. The sensation rocked Lily and changed her mind about protesting. Plenty of time for the big blue. Another curse escaped him as Lily arched against his questing fingers, bringing a grin of delight to her face. His touch fuelled her desire. His words thrilled her heart. And she wanted him just as fiercely. Then he moved over her, his hard, blue cock replacing his fingers as he pushed slowly inside her aching womb.

Lily propped up on her elbows, watching his blue flesh disappear into her pussy. Amazing. Then she forgot about anything other than how he felt inside. The sense of fullness—it was as if he was her other half. Alex filled an emptiness she never knew she had. Lily lifted her hips, offering her body silently. With a muffled curse, Alex withdrew then surged back until he was fully seated.

"More," Lily muttered, writhing beneath his body. "Faster." Her body was primed after exploring the big blue, her juices making it easy for him to slide into her cunt. But she wanted…more.

Alex gave a strangled laugh. "I'm trying to go slow. To give you time to catch up with me."

"I'm ready," Lily insisted. She ground her clit against the base of his cock, squeezing her eyes shut at the sparkles of awareness that resulted. Close. So close to a repeat of her lunch stop experience.

Alex sucked in an audible breath, his chest expanding and abrading her breasts. The tingles echoed in her clit. He withdrew slowly from her vagina then surged back with a speed that made her blink. In. Out. Lily clutched at his shoulders, her body picking up the racy rhythm instinctively. His cock seemed to grow bigger, longer inside her, filling her impossibly full.

She squeezed her eyes closed concentrating on her senses — the spicy masculine scent of him, his soft grunts as he surged and withdrew, the slick, sweaty feel of their bodies as they moved together. And most of all, the burning fire at her loins. Colors, bright and intense, orange and red, flickered like fast-moving pictures at the back of her eyelids.

"Yes." Lily squeezed the words past gritted teeth. The fire roared, out of control, flames burning her clit, singeing. Explosive. Glorious. Alex surged inside her, filling her deeply and grinding against her. Her womb contracted so hard it was painful, clenching against his cock. Alex jerked, driving into her body with a frenzy of short, quick strokes. Impaling her. Pushing her onward. Upward. Over.

Shockwaves clenched his cock, massaging him, making Alex impossibly hard. Goddess, he hurt. He'd never, ever wanted to fuck so badly in his life. Lily convulsed around his tom, small whimpers emerging from her sexy mouth. And just like that, he lost the tiny amount of control he still exerted over his wayward body. Cum spurted from his cock in powerful jets. On and on until he thought it would never end. Pleasure-pain seared the length of his body until he shook with it like a lone tree in a fiery comet storm. And throughout the catastrophic experience, Lily clutched him tightly, as if she'd never let go, never let him fall, her cunt squeezing him with never-ending ripples.

"Devil's teeth," he gritted out, riding the storm, seizing the pleasure like a greedy man. Finally, his body quieted enough that his other senses kicked him. Feeling awakened and refreshed, he lazily surged into her body. Lily sighed, lifting her hips to meet him. Instantly, he was hard again. Ready to fuck some more. Except this wasn't fucking, a small voice murmured at the back of his mind. He'd gone and bonded with her. Deep down, he knew it but shied away from the concrete commitment. Too late to fret now. The deed was done. He'd go with the situation and enjoy in a fashion as he always had. Worry about the consequences later.

Alex continued with his lazy tempo, surging then retreating.

"Feels so good," Lily murmured, her hands sweeping in languid circles over his back then lower to grab his ass. "But it would feel better if you kissed me."

Guilt cut him deep. He'd selfishly seen to his own orgasm and was busy priming his cock to meet his body's ravenous demands. Lily had come, but perhaps she was too sore for more?

"Did I hurt you?" he asked, kissing a slow trail of kisses around her mouth. He pulled from her womb and turned to lie on his back, lifting Lily to rest on top of him.

Lily grinned suddenly and fluttered her eyelashes at him. "My hero," she cooed. "I can't get used to the way you can lift me. Ambrose—"

"Don't talk about him," Alex said. "This is about us. No one else in the bed except the two of us." The feel of her soft curves pressing into his chest and lower in his groin made him twitchy. He wasn't sure if the second time would be any slower. Maybe he should gun for the third?

Lily lifted up on her elbows to study his face. The impish grin remained, and Alex decided he liked this side of her. Fun. Playful. Confident. And sexy as hell. She rose up further until her thighs slid to either side of him and she straddled his hips. Her breasts swayed in front of his face during the maneuver, and he opened his mouth to capture a nipple.

"Uh-uh," she said with a chuckle as she evaded his mouth. "I want to explore."

"Oh? I'm ready for that," he said. The glint in her blue eyes made him grin. He'd never experienced this sort of bedding before. Playful had never entered into the scheme of things. It had all been about satisfaction and jewels, but Lily didn't seem to expect anything from him. Instead, she wanted to give, and he floundered a little with the new situation.

Lily feathered her hands down his chest, and a corresponding twitch moved his cock. He gritted his teeth.

Unbeknown to Lily, tease time was gonna be short. She paused to finger one of his nipples, rubbing it then pinching. Alex felt the nip clear to his toes.

He moved suddenly, dumping her in the middle of the bed. Lily bounced, a surprised squeak escaping.

"Did I tell you I'm not very good at sharing my toys?"

Lily's eyes widened. "You have toys?"

Nope. No toys. But her breathless anticipation made him decide to find some pronto. The Earth manuals had explained sexual toys and aids—a whole chapter so he shouldn't have problems working them out. "No, it means I'm bossy and like my own way."

Lily tried to scramble to a sitting position, but he snared both hands in one hand and placed his weight on top of her wriggling body.

"But, Alex," she said, laughing when he skimmed his fingers down her rib cage. "You haven't given me a chance to touch you. I want to check you out some more. How can I search out differences if you won't let me look? Have you changed back to flesh color?" A delightful blush covered her cheeks, and he was pleased he hadn't gone with his instinct to switch off the bedside lamp. He'd have missed the flush of arousal on her silky skin. Alex glanced down at his blue tom. Still very aroused and very blue. On the other foot, it might have spared his pride if he'd turned off the light. She'd laughed at him and compared him to a baboon bum. Alex recalled pictures of those creatures with their ugly, matching faces and bottoms. He sobered, and wondered if she'd be laughing later.

"After," he promised. "I'm too close to the edge."

Still holding her hands above her head, he brushed a line of kisses across her collarbone then angled down to suck the tip of her breast into his mouth.

"Let my hands go," she demanded. "I need to touch you."

By St. Jupiter, he needed that too, so he freed her hands and concentrated on touching, on learning what pleasured Lily. The slow slide of his mouth against her breast drew small cries from her. Would she cry out and whimper like she had before when he'd pleasured her clit with his mouth? When he slid his fingers inside her wet, moist pussy and thrust slowly in time to his suckling?

Alex grinned against her breast. One way to find out. With one last smacking draw on her nipple, he released the distended bud and kissed his way down her body. Distracted by the scenery on the way, he traced around the edge of her belly button with his tongue.

Her hands clenched in his hair, letting him know she enjoyed his explorations, but Alex didn't linger for long. Her spice mint scent spurred him on. Alex combed his fingers through the short, brown curls that guarded her pussy, tracing around her clit and lower where her juices ran, crying for him. The thought brought satisfaction.

"Alex, you're teasing me." Lily stirred restlessly, her hips moving in small demanding jerks as she sought to encourage him to speed. Her clear, urgent need burned him. His cock twitched, making Alex aware of his hardness. Anticipation throbbed through him, the color of his tom intensifying as his arousal grew. Another extraordinary treat lay waiting for both of them.

First, he blew soft puffs of air against her clitoris. The tiny bud appeared swollen, deep pink with arousal. Alex reached down to her pussy lips and coated his finger in her nectar. The scent alone made him tremble with the need to thrust inside her. Feeling the weight of her stare, he glanced up along her rounded belly and luscious breasts before meeting her eyes with a wicked smile.

"Hurry," she pleaded.

Alex pushed a finger into her slick cunt, her liquid arousal easing his way. He slowly withdrew the finger then pushed in three fingers at once, twisting his fingers until he sensed he'd hit the G-spot the Earth manual had mentioned. When small whimpers of bliss emerged from her, he bent to sweep his tongue lazily across her clit.

Lily shuddered, her legs stirring restlessly on the bed. "Alex, come inside me," she pleaded.

Alex couldn't have denied her request if he tried. "Only if I can hold you."

"A different position?" Interest shone in her face.

"Yeah." Alex rolled her over on her side so she faced away from him.

For an instant, Lily worried about how big her bum would look but the thought faded when she felt the scorching heat of his chest against her back. His erection pressed against the crease between her butt cheeks. Her heart thudded an erratic beat. A frisson of excitement brought a fresh spurt of juices flooding between her legs. Lily wriggled, pushing against his cock.

Alex groaned softly. "Are you always this impatient?"

Lily grinned over her shoulder at the golden alien. "Only with you."

"I've created a monster."

"Suck it up," she whispered, low and throaty.

"Oh, I intend to," he promised. His arms went around her, his hands curving around her breasts and squeezing just enough to cause a frisson of sensation that trod the line between pleasure and pain.

"Lift your leg for me, moon heart."

As she followed his whispered instructions, Lily made a mental note to ask about moon hearts later. His blue cock slid home smoothly then he gathered her tight against his frame and rocked in small, gentle moves that pulled her into magic. He nuzzled at her neck and pinched her nipples again. Hard. The ache shot through her, coinciding with Alex's rocking motion. Pain coalesced into intense rapture. Alex quickened his rocking, stroking against her core. Lily felt minute ripples deep inside.

She bit her lip, pushing her butt into Alex so he could angle inside her easier.

"Close?" he whispered against her ear.

"Yeah," she murmured, savoring being balanced on the tightrope of ecstasy.

Alex nuzzled behind her ear and nipped the soft skin there. He rocked against her and deep inside her, she felt his spurt of semen. Her clit jumped in response, and Lily tumbled into an orgasm that shook her clear to her toes. As she lay there, savoring the aftershocks, Lily pondered his blue cock and semen.

The big blue.

There was obviously a lot more to this alien than she'd suspected. Her mouth tipped up in a smirk. The possibilities were intriguing to say the least.

Chapter Ten

ဆာ

"We've nearly got him! I told you the tracking device was necessary."

Mattio ignored his younger cuz. If Jabot hadn't been makin' eyes at the sloe-eyed bim in the bar, they wouldn't have had to chase the prince to this godforsaken outpost in the middle of nowhere. Always fuckin' up. His parents should have christened him Jabot Fuck-up.

Mattio glared up at the fizzing electric lamp. It cast a white light over the car park, bleaching the bright color from the parked vehicles and making them appear the same color.

Earth! The backward blue planet was a boil on the backside of the galaxy. Why Prince Alexandre had traveled here when he had all the riches of Dalcon at the snap of his fingers—Mattio had no idea. Probably chasing a willing cunt—bah! Just like the older prince, Alexandre's brother. No matter. Mattio didn't want to know. All he wanted was to capture Prince Alexandre, knock sense into the prince's blockhead and hie back to Dalcon before the King found out his precious second son was missing. He didn't intend to muck up so the King could renege on his promises.

Jabot pointed the tracking monitor around the car park in a slow sweeping motion. The low-pitched beep erupted into a frenzy when it passed a square vehicle.

"Over there," he shouted.

"If you talk slow and don't shout, you won't break into that pissy squeak at the end of your sentence." By St. Jupiter. Stuck with a dumbass undergrown. Mattio rolled his eyes toward the stars. What had he done to deserve such punishment?

"It's coming from that square-high box."

"Vehicle. Didn't you listen to all the Earth speak tapes I gave you?"

"Boring," Jabot whined.

"Might mean the difference between success and failure." Mattio worked hard to keep his voice even. He'd learned that shouting or cussing made the undergrown sullen. Although he'd keep the thought in mind for the trip home. Sulking was better than talk. The incessant chatter on the way to Earth had done his head in.

"The prince isn't in the box vehicle."

Mattio thumped his cousin on the shoulder. "I'd be bloody surprised if he was. Earth people do not sleep in their vehicles. He'll be inside the building…" Mattio fumbled for the correct Earth word. "Hotel," he said finally.

Jabot turned toward the hotel, ready to find the prince.

Mattio grabbed his forearm and jerked him to a halt. "By St. Jupiter! Where the hell are you going?"

"Prince Alexandre—"

Mattio exerted enough force to make his dumbass cuz concentrate. "Use your brain. There are hundreds of rooms in the building. It's night. We can't burst into every room until we find him."

"Why not?"

"Because we can't." Mattio cuffed his cuz across the head. "We'll wait here until morning and grab him when he leaves the hotel."

"I don't wanna stay here." Jabot's bottom lip stuck up in a pout.

Mattio counted to ten in Earth speak. It took a great deal of concentration, but he still itched to hit Jabot when he'd finished. The medical man had told him to cut down on stress. How was that possible when he had to deal with Jabot the nincompoop? He reached into his travel suit pouch and retrieved a relaxation wafer. Mattio slid it under his tongue and focused on his cuz.

Jabot glanced around frowning then looked at him in a sly way that never failed to wind him up. "Can we sit in the vehicle?"

Mattio sucked in a calming breath just like the medical man suggested and considered the suggestion from all angles. Not bad. Finally, he gave a grudging nod. "Good idea." After checking the area for signs of life, he led the way to the vehicle. The tracking monitor went berserk when they stopped beside the blue vehicle. Mattio checked for onlookers again then plucked a Dalcon knife from the sheath attached to his survival belt.

Jabot pushed his nose up to the windows of the vehicle. "Can't see inside."

"No matter." Mattio shrugged. He walked up to the back and inserted his knife into the lock.

"Try it first," Jabot suggested.

As if, Mattio thought, but if he didn't try the door, he'd never hear the end of Jabot's complaints. Mattio glanced at Jabot as he tried the handle. A sharp click sounded and the silver handle gave. *Well, blow me*, Mattio thought in astonishment. He turned his head to grin at his cousin. "It's open."

"Told ya."

Mattio tugged the door fully open and peered inside. A white blur erupted from the corner. A mouthful of teeth and fangs flashed in front of his shocked face. Mattio backed up rapidly but was hindered by Jabot hovering at his back, trying to see inside.

The thing kept coming, making harsh sounds loud enough to attract unwanted attention.

"What is it?" Jabot shouted in clear panic.

"How should I know?" Mattio snapped, trying to turn and run. His feet tangled in Jabot's. They hit the ground with a bone-crunching thud.

"Woof!"

A gust of hot air flooded his face. The demon fastened its teeth on his arm and stood over him, and shaking and growling until the teeth bit deep.

"Get him off me!" Mattio shrieked at his cousin.

"I'm not going near that creature. No, sirree!" Jabot darted out of sight behind another vehicle.

The demon growled low and mean. "Woof!"

Mattio wrenched his arm away, timing his move for when the creature opened its mouth to speak. He scrambled to his feet and backed up, his gaze on the creature in case it charged.

"Woof! Wolf!" The creature stalked closer, its brown eyes seeming to bore into him and sapping his strength.

"Run," Jabot called from his position of relative safety.

For once, Jabot made perfect sense. Mattio's heart beat with fear as the demon advanced. He kicked out with his foot. Sharp teeth snapped, barely missing his boot. Mattio's store of courage seeped away, and he turned tail and ran as fast as he could. Seconds later, he flattened himself against the side of the vehicle where Jabot hid.

"Is it chasing?" he gasped, struggling for breath.

"I think we're safe. It looks like it's going back inside the blue box."

For once, Mattio didn't try to correct his cousin. He slumped his shoulders and concentrated on taking deep breaths while his heart settled. When he finally straightened, he scanned the car park to see if they'd attracted attention. They were safe. He couldn't see another living soul but could have sworn he heard laughter.

* * * * *

Alex stirred beside her and Lily turned her head to watch him while he woke. Despite the lack of sleep the night before, Lily felt rested and relaxed. A grin curved her lips. Alex had shown her things last night she'd never experienced before. And she wanted to do them all over.

"Good morning." The husky voice broke the silence.

Lily sucked in her stomach and laughed, ill at ease with being caught gawping. "You're awake."

"Yeah." Alex stretched out a hand and smoothed it down her cheek.

Wow. Waking up with a lover was different from a husband as well. The alien looked as though he wanted to eat her. Lily blushed. All over again.

A thump on the door of their room jerked Lily upright. The white cotton sheet dropped to her lap.

"That will be breakfast." Alex climbed out of the bed and stretched without a self-conscious bone in his body.

Lily wished she'd learned how to whistle. When she pursed her lips and blew, she usually ended up spitting. But oh, boy! If ever a situation called for a whistle, it was this one. "Alex, wait!" She gestured at his blue hard-on.

The thud on the door sounded again. "Room service!"

Alex grinned and tugged a pair of jeans over his morning-stiff tom then sauntered to the door. When he waved the room service attendant into the room, Lily let out a squeak and hid under the thin sheet. She didn't relax until the trolley wheeled out and the door shut.

"Safe to come out now," Alex said.

Lily emerged from under the sheet. Her gaze zapped straight to Alex. One glimpse and every trace of spit evaporated from her mouth. The man appeared beautiful even at this time of the morning. Golden stubble decorated his jawline, which seemed a bit strange to Lily considering he didn't have any other body hair. But whatever, it made him look sexy and she longed to run her hands over him. While he poured coffee, her gaze drifted over his smooth, muscular chest and downward to rest on the unsnapped fastener of his jeans. A pale strip of skin showed, a fraction lighter than the color of his chest and belly.

Lily wanted to run her tongue along that strip of skin so badly she trembled.

He prowled across to the bed and handed her a mug of coffee. She was about to put the coffee aside when she noticed the expression on his face. Serious. Maybe even worried. Lily swallowed to combat the tight, dry sensation that seized her throat. Perhaps now wasn't the time to lick him.

"I'll hit the shower," he said. "We need to leave soon. Killer will need a walk."

Lily found herself nodding. The man was back in work mode. It was as if he'd placed her firmly in the past to concentrate on his project. Her stomach swooped with sudden nerves. Did he regret last night? Had she turned him off in some way?

Lily gulped her coffee but ignored the food in favor of grabbing a robe and starting her packing. By the time Alex emerged from the bathroom, she was ready to go. All she needed was a quick shower.

They walked from the room together, stopping at reception to pay and then headed for the car. As they rounded the corner and headed for the car park, Lily noticed the back door of their vehicle was wide open.

"The back door of the car's open! Did you leave it like that?" she demanded.

"No." Alex frowned. "I shut it. Maybe Killer pushed it open."

"I hope she hasn't wandered off. Luke and Janaya will never forgive me if something happened to Killer."

They rounded the back of the vehicle together at a fast trot.

Killer leapt from the vehicle when she saw them. "Alex. Alex!" she shouted. "Men break in. Try to dognap me. But I chased them way. Bit one. Taste very bad!" She paused to wag her tail. "Do ya have any food?"

Lily felt her mouth drop open. The…the dog had talked. Killer talked! Shock made her wobble. Lily grabbed Alex's arm for balance while she stared at Killer in shock. "Am I awake? I understood every bark she made."

"Food?" Killer yapped at Alex impatiently. "Do ya have any?"

"She really talks," Lily muttered in a dazed voice.

"Of course I talk—" Killer broke off mid-bark to stare at Lily. Then her gaze snapped to Alex. She growled a menacing warning. "What you do to Lily?"

Lily clutched Alex's arm harder, struggling to cope with the concept of a talking dog. "We have food in the front." She marched to the driver's side, keeping her eyes on Alex and the talking dog. "Time. I need time to assimilate," she muttered to herself. "Time to work out if I need locking up in a straitjacket."

"I haven't done anything to Lily," Alex snapped. That crafty smirk on the dog's face made him nervous. He peered past Killer into the back of the car. "If you bit the men, where's the blood? You're exaggerating!"

"No!" Her eyes shifted off him momentarily before she looked back. "We talk about you. You know steak?" Killer demanded. "Favorite food. Steak." Her eyes narrowed. "You give steak, I not tell Janaya. Might like shiny tag and collar, too," she added, considering Alex carefully.

"I didn't do anything."

"Must of," Killer countered. "Luke and Richard didn't understand till they slept—"

Alex snapped out a hand and held the dog's muzzle shut. He suspected he didn't want the knowledge Killer was about to impart. Hell, he didn't want to think about what he and Lily had done to each other last night. Because it made him picture the jaws of a trap snapping closed. Even if the bait tempted, he must resist. He needed to shut the dog up. The last thing he needed was Killer spilling her version of the truth. He maintained his hold on the dog's muzzle while he contemplated a solution. Killer snarled and tried to shake free.

Lily returned to the back of the vehicle with a small foil pack of dog food in time to witness the undignified tussle. "What are you doing to Killer?"

"Trying to shut her up," Alex snapped, giving the dog a look of intense dislike. The blasted devil creature tried to blackmail him. Damned cheek!

"Let her go. She's only little. Here, Killer, sweetie." Lily ripped the packet open and tipped it into a dog's plastic bowl she'd retrieved at the same time. She set it down on the ground and filled a separate bowl with water.

Alex let go and stepped back warily. Hell, Killer might be little but she had attitude enough for six—make that a herd of dogs! Or whatever sets the blasted creatures came in.

Killer sniffed the meal before snorting in a disdainful manner. She plonked her butt on the ground. "It not steak. Want real food."

"It's that or nothing," Alex snapped. "Tell me about the two men."

"They taste bad."

"So you said." Alex stifled his impatience. "What else?"

"They smell bad, too."

"Killer can tell us on the way to our first stop," Lily said in a placating tone.

"I not finished food," Killer said.

"I thought you didn't want it."

"I changed mind." Killer stuck her nose in the air.

Infuriating creature. Alex left Lily to deal with the spotted devil and stomped around the vehicle to the passenger side. The locks didn't appear tampered with. He climbed in and shut the door. The bloody dog could get in Lily's side.

Five minutes later Lily opened the driver's door, and Killer leapt in.

"You buy steak later."

"No," Alex said.

"Lily said," the dog barked.

"I promised her steak if she behaved," Lily said as she buckled up her seat belt.

"You're safe then," Alex muttered, spearing a sardonic look at the creature. "She couldn't —"

The dog pounced, grabbed his arm and bit him. Hard.

"Quit that." Alex batted Killer away. His gaze was snared by the sight of a blue mark the size of a New Zealand ten-cent coin that had appeared on the back of his hand. He stared in disbelief then whisked it out of sight. Perhaps the dog wouldn't realize the significance of the blue mark. "Or you can get out and walk."

"Dognappers will get me. You be sorry then."

"That's debatable." The spotted devil hadn't noticed.

"Stop it the pair of you, or you can both walk," Lily snapped.

Alex and the dog looked at each other.

"Must run in the family," Alex growled in a low undertone to Killer.

Killer grinned to reveal a row of sharp, white teeth. "Yeah, like Richard," she said. "Don't forget you owe steak. I not forget."

* * * * *

Mattio and Jabot spied on the couple from the café across the road.

"That's not the prince," Jabot said, loud enough that several Earth people turned in their seats to stare.

"Quiet," Mattio instructed. He glared at each of the interested parties until their gazes dropped then picked up his glass of juice.

"But it's not him." Jabot shook his head. "That man hurts my eyes when I look. Prince Alexandre is beautiful."

Mattio had to agree with his cuz. The dark-haired man was butt-ugly. Of course, it could be a wig, but the man's features were hideous, and he limped like a wounded tigoth. It looked as though the man had one leg shorter than the other. Jabot was right. The man was not the prince.

"What do we do?" Jabot asked.

"Follow them. They're the only lead we have."

"I don't like this dumb planet."

For once, they were in total agreement. Mattio stood and Jabot followed suit. "We must follow them," Mattio said. "The only alternative is to travel back to Dalcon and admit to the king we've lost his second son."

"He'll chop off our heads. I like my head. Saraphero likes my head, too. She kissed—"

"I'm rather attached to mine," Mattio agreed, cutting in before he heard details of his cousin's perverted sex life. "So, we go with plan B. We'll follow them, and when the opportunity presents, we grab them, torture them and extract the truth."

* * * * *

Lily started the engine and drove through the town. A taut silence reigned inside the vehicle until the dog started to whisper a series of terse comments when she thought Lily wouldn't notice. Alex tried to tune her out, but it proved difficult since every second word seemed to be Janaya. Occasionally, Killer threw in steak as a variation.

At the entrance to the town, Lily pulled into a parking space near the lakefront and switched off the ignition. "Killer, if you don't quit with the whispering, I'll ship you back to Luke."

Killer snapped her mouth shut so quickly Alex wanted to laugh.

"This is a good spot to see the mountains when the day is clear," Lily said. Without waiting for him to answer, she exited the car and left Alex and Killer staring at each other in consternation.

"I behave. Tell Lily." Killer jumped on his lap and nudged at his arm. "Open."

Alex sighed and did as she ordered. Killer jumped out and trotted down to the lake's edge to Lily. Alex shut the door and went with her.

"Have to stay," she muttered. "Have job. I good. Want collar real bad."

Alex shook his head. He had no idea what went on in that creature's head, and he sure as hell didn't want to change that. He strode across the dew-wet grass to join them.

"Killer, did the men say anything? You haven't seen them before?" Alex asked.

"No." Killer wagged her tail. "But I know them if I see again. One short and wide. One tall."

"Probably opportunists," Lily said. "We're lucky Killer scared them off." She cast a sideways glance at Killer. "I can't believe I'm talking to a dog."

"I can't believe I talk to a human," Killer mocked.

"Do the mountains have names?" Alex asked hurriedly. Anything to avoid the impending squabble. "Will we drive closer to them today?" His words drew Lily's gaze. Instantly, his body reacted, his cock sprang into primed-for-action mode. Bloody hell. He placed his hands in the relevant region then whipped them away. No point drawing attention to the problem.

"Your pants too small," Killer said.

Too late.

Lily glanced down, giggled and clapped a hand across her mouth.

Alex was going to kill the dog. And damn the consequences. Walking wasn't difficult. You just put one foot after the other and eventually you arrived. He could walk from here to Wellington if he had to.

Lily peeped over her hand, her blue eyes flashing with amusement.

"This is your fault," he muttered.

Her brows rose. "My fault?"

Alex's skin felt too small to fit his body. Heat from the early morning sun intensified the arousal that boiled through his body. If they hadn't been right near a kid's playground, he would have jumped her. Alex cleared his throat, his gaze resting on the curve of her lips. "Oh, yeah. Definitely your fault."

"Maybe you should have a swim." She gestured at the rippling surface of the lake. "Feel free."

Alex snorted. "The cold shower this morning—" Damn, that wouldn't help matters, admitting how much she turned him on.

"Why you have cold shower?" Killer asked.

"None of your bloody business."

"If the two of you are finished arguing we could drive to the falls then check out Huka Lodge. Who knows, we might even meet a film star or two. The Queen of England and the President of the United States have stayed there. Expensive," she said, "but if you want a luxurious night, the Lodge is a great option."

"Good idea," Alex said. "Let's go."

He spent the next hour scrawling notes and talking to staff at the lodge. He found the woman who showed him around both friendly and knowledgeable, and he left with her business card along with several brochures.

"What do you think?" Lily asked as they drove back through the town, and headed south.

"I was impressed," Alex admitted. "I'd like to have the tour stop here. As long as we can find parking for the spaceship."

"Lady look at your butt," Killer said.

"That's not all she looked at," Lily said in a tight voice.

"What lady?" Alex said. "I didn't notice." And he hadn't. Why would he look at another woman when Lily was around?

"Believe me, she looked you over," Lily retorted, but to his relief, she didn't sound quite as irritated. "Did you want to stop anywhere else before we leave? The prawn farm or we could watch the bungee jumpers."

Alex shook his head.

"Okay, I thought we'd drive down the Desert road and head toward Wellington. We can stop at Martinborough before we get to Wellington."

"Ah, the wine growing area. Sounds good."

"Will we stop for food?" Killer barked.

"Yes," Lily said, pulling a rueful face at the dog. "I can't get used to talking to you."

"I don't have a problem talking to you," Killer said.

"Don't try arguing with her," Alex said. "You won't win."

"I be good," Killer said. "But we need to stop for walks."

Despite three stops during the drive to the bottom of the North Island, they arrived in Martinborough mid-afternoon.

"There are some wonderful places to stay around here. I wondered if you'd like to stay here for the night instead of driving into Wellington?" Lily grinned. "That way I can try some of the local wines without worrying about driving."

Alex shrugged. "Sounds good to me. There's a sign for accommodation. Do you want to try there?"

"Looks like they have room to park a spaceship." She glanced across a snoozing Killer. "I presume you intend to camouflage the spaceship? Otherwise, you'll have UFO hunters following you about. As well as government agencies."

"You haven't asked many questions so far. I didn't think you were interested."

"Not interested?" she blurted, coasting the vehicle to a stop. Lily's mouth worked soundlessly as though she couldn't work out what to say. Then she glanced at Killer and clamped her hands over the dog's floppy ears in case she was awake. "I was too busy trying to work out how to jump you," she confessed. "And how to check out your blue equipment without looking too pushy. I'd like to watch the color change as it happens this time."

"Yeah?" Alex felt a dopey grin on his face, even though the openness of her words brought a sliver of guilt. In three weeks, he intended to leave. He wouldn't change his mind no matter what Lily might say. Or the temptation she presented.

"Yeah."

Killer wriggled free from Lily. "What you say?" she demanded. "I can't tell—"

A sudden suspicion bloomed in Alex. "Are you spying on us? Are you reporting back to Luke and Janaya?" A quick glance at Lily confirmed that she was just as taken aback as him. And her eyes were narrowed as though she agreed with the possibility.

"Me?" Killer yapped, a peculiar sound that could have been a laugh or something more sinister. "Me dog. Me no spy!" Killer puffed out with indignation. "Here." She sidled up to Alex with a challenge in her brown eyes. "Frisk for spy tools. Won't find any."

Alex's brows rose.

"Search," Killer insisted.

"I don't think that will be necessary," Lily said in a strangled voice.

Alex felt his lips twitch as he manfully held back laughter. He sensed if they laughed, Killer would revolt and their problems would multiply.

"I not spy." Killer met his gaze then glanced out the window. "Ohhh!" she yapped sounding breathless. "Oh! Look at him!"

Alex caught sight of a fluffy black and white dog gamboling behind his owners.

"The Border collie?" Lily said.

"Yeah," Killer said with a loud doggy sigh. "I'd sure like to sniff his bottom!"

Lily made a choking sound. When Alex glanced at her, he saw her face was red and scrunched up, and her beautiful breasts jiggled up and down in silent laughter.

Alex chuckled and opened the door. "'Way you go," he said. "I'd hate to stand in the path of true love."

"Oh, boy!" Killer leapt out and trotted in the direction of the Border collie. "What chat up line?" she muttered. "Yeah. Might work."

"I'm frightened to watch," Lily said dryly.

"We're not going to watch," Alex said. "I have other plans for us."

Chapter Eleven

ൠ

"Sounds good." Lily peeped up at him from between lowered lashes. She hoped they were on the same page. Her page was book marked on sex.

"Excuse me, is that adorable little dog yours?"

The young blonde was slender, yet had plentiful curves, and Lily hated her on sight.

"You can't be talking about our dog," Alex said.

"Definitely not cute and adorable," Lily agreed, surprised but pleased by the way Alex coupled them together.

"Are you staying here?" The blonde fluttered ridiculously long lashes at Alex and ignored Lily's presence.

Lily felt like asking her if she had something in her eye but pushed the catty remark aside. "I'll check us in."

"Two rooms," Alex said.

Lily felt as though he'd struck her. And the young woman's ears perked up at the revelation. She stepped right into Alex's personal space and tipped back her head to gaze at him with sultry, I'm-yours-if-you-want-me eyes. For an instant, Lily's lungs froze up then she dipped her head in a curt nod and wheeled away, heading for reception. Alex hadn't meant what he'd said earlier about having plans for the two of them. A sharp pain speared through her chest as she pushed through the door leading into the reception area. She'd had a great time with Alex so far. Maybe she should leave it at that.

"Hello, can I help you?"

Lily organized two rooms then sucked in a deep breath and walked outside to join Alex. The young woman had several friends, and they clustered around Alex like ravenous children fighting for afternoon snacks. Except, none of them had childlike expressions or the innocence to go with the age.

"Lily, there you are." Alex slipped an arm around her waist and tugged her close to his side. "We've been invited to dinner and a dance."

"How nice," Lily said faintly.

"It's quite an occasion," one of the young women said.

Even better. She had nothing suitable to wear.

"Thank you for the invitation. We will see you later tonight." Alex's mouth curved in a devastating smile, and a wave of jealousy flashed through Lily. She wished the smile were for her.

"Bye!" they cooed.

Alex propelled Lily to the rear of the car. "I'll get the bags, darling."

"Dah...darling?"

"Are they gone?" Alex whispered.

Lily peered around the vehicle and saw the girls had wandered off. "They've gone."

"Thank God. They wouldn't leave me alone. I thought they were going to rip off my clothes." He shook his head in a bewildered manner. "I don't understand why."

Lily suppressed a snort. The man was gorgeous. A hunk. A babe. Or whatever the current vernacular was. "I can't go tonight."

"Why not?"

"I don't have anything suitable to wear. You heard them. It's going to be dressy. All my clothes are casual."

"Buy something."

"I don't have the money to buy a new dress," Lily said with dignity. "I don't mind not going. You go by yourself."

Alex frowned but didn't argue. "I want to have a chat with the owners about accommodation. What are the room numbers?"

"Rooms six and nine." Lily tried to hold back her wince at being pushed aside.

"I'll let Killer know," Alex said. "We'll take room nine and give Killer the other. At least they're not next to each other. I wouldn't put it past her to spy through the keyhole."

A chorus of joyous barks rang through the car park. Lily turned in time to see a streak of white whip past followed by a black blur. But all she could think of was Alex and his casual room allocation. They were sharing a room. The other room was for Killer!

* * * * *

"What a great afternoon," Lily said. "Aren't you glad we decided to stay here?"

Alex couldn't help smiling. After visiting four different vineyards and tasting several vintages, he had a pleasant buzz. Lily was smiling and a little giggly. He liked this uninhibited side of her. Possibly, she'd acted like this before her ex-male had done a number on her self-assurance. "I think Martinborough will make a great stop for my tours. I talked to Janet who owns the place. They own the land around here. It's perfect to land the tour clients. I was thinking we could use Earth transport and bus the clients into Wellington from here."

Lily twirled a lock of hair around one finger. "Once you unload the passengers here, you could send the ship over to Nelson and use the ferry to cross the Cook Strait. Maybe arrange for a bus to meet your group on the other side."

"Good idea. Let me grab my notebook." Alex grabbed up a pen and his book to note the details Janet had given him plus Lily's suggestions. He checked his Earth timepiece. "Dinner is in an hour."

Lily dropped on to the large double bed and lay back against the pillows. "I guess I'll have an early night."

Not if he had anything to do with it. With her rosy cheeks, lazy grin and innocent blue eyes, she was more temptation than he could bear. His cock twitched as the bonding ties writhed inside him. He wondered if Lily knew about bonding then tossed the thought aside. Bit late now. His gaze lit on the blue mark. The bloody thing was on the move and had reached his wrist. Everything that could go wrong was happening to him on this trip. Despite taking the pills the medical man had prescribed, his immunity hovered around nil. But still he kept taking them. He hated to think how he'd feel if he stopped taking them totally. Alex prowled toward the bed, intent on taking a kiss. Maybe more.

Someone knocked on the door. Ah. Janet had come through for him. He hurried to answer, eager to see what she'd arranged.

"Janet said you're waiting for this." The young girl stared so hard Alex wondered if he'd grown a second nose.

"Thanks," Alex said, accepting the large package. He tried to act pleasant even though he felt like demanding the girl to spit out her problem with him. Good thing the spell was working. Perhaps he'd grown a couple of warts since he'd topped up the spell last time. "Please thank Janet, and tell her I'll fix her up tomorrow morning." Alex stepped back inside the room, shut the door in the moronic girl's face and dropped on to the bed beside Lily. "This is for you."

"A present?"

"Yeah. Ready for a shower?" Alex asked. "I thought we'd take one together."

"To...together?"

"Yeah," Alex said. "I need help scrubbing my back. And my other bits," he added. Shock zapped across Lily's face. She hadn't expected his suggestion. Her wide blue eyes and rounded mouth clued him in. A grin stretched his lips because it felt damned good keeping her guessing. Anticipation rippled through Alex as he wondered about Lily's reaction to her gift. He hadn't purchased the dress as a test, although her reaction would be interesting. Alex thrust aside his memories of the greedy palace consorts and grabbed Lily's hand. "Ready?"

Lily stood, and Alex saw her bottom lip, caught between her teeth—a dead giveaway of her uncertainty. Obviously, a physical demonstration was in order to persuade her he was serious.

Alex dropped her hand and whipped his gray shirt off. His jeans dropped to the floor with a thud, and he stepped free completely naked. Lily's breath emerged with an audible hiss, and the blue of her eyes darkened. He glanced down at his tom. That had darkened, too.

"Lagging behind," Alex mocked lightly in challenge. "I'll start the shower."

He sauntered into the bathroom. Her gaze drilled between his shoulder blades then he heard the soft rustle of fabric and grinned, whistled softly and flicked the shower on. His cock jumped while his balls tightened in acute anticipation. He couldn't wait to slide inside her warm, tight pussy again.

Alex grabbed two small bottles of shower gel off the counter and stepped under the warm water. It cascaded down his face and back while he waited for Lily to gather her courage.

Finally, after what seemed long, tension-filled minutes, the door to the glass cubicle opened and closed. Feminine arms slid around his waist, breasts nudged his back. Alex turned in the circle of her arms and smiled, barely managing to keep his greeting casual, when savage and devilish nipped at his heels.

"About time you arrived."

"Oh, yeah?" An impish grin darkened her eyes. "Now I'm here, what are you going to do with me?"

Ah, the brave Lily had arrived. Alex grinned inwardly, smoothing locks of wet hair away from her face. So beautiful, he thought, all humor falling away. He'd regret leaving Lily but there was no other way. As long as he didn't falter and mark her… Alex traced her full, pink lips with his forefinger — his heart thudding harder, faster than it had mere seconds before. His hands dropped to cup her breasts, feathering fingers across her pink-colored nipples until they tightened, distending in a silent plea for suckling. Lily shifted restlessly, her eyes echoing her body's entreaty. *All in good time, my love.* Alex nuzzled her neck, scraping the pulse point beneath her ear. Her fingers curled, nails digging into his waist, while a tiny shiver worked through her tense body.

"This isn't back scrubbing," Lily murmured in a breathless tone. Her eyes were closed and her head thrown back.

A muscle ticked in his jaw, her words and presence eroding his control more than he liked. "No, this is more fun." He tweaked her nipple, pinching before ducking his head to soothe the ache with his mouth. Essence of spice mint surrounded him, pulling at his control, spurring him onward to culmination. And Lily didn't help with her responsiveness.

She groaned at the back of her throat and leaned back offering her breasts, giving him better access. Full trust. The concept humbled him.

In the privacy of the steamy shower, the world narrowed to Lily. Warm water streamed over their bodies, over silky limbs and luscious curves. His senses wallowed in tactile pleasures and scents. In Lily.

Lily's busy hands darted over his body, exploring, charting bundles of nerves and pleasure points, but never coming to rest where he needed her touch most. His bright blue cock ached for handling, ached to possess. To dominate and be dominated.

Alex kissed her, thrusting his tongue deep into her mouth in a facsimile of the act his tom wanted so desperately. Nimble fingers skimmed down his length. His breath hissed out, his hands tightened compulsively on her breasts.

Her fingers stilled, an inch short of the swollen, royal blue crown of his cock. "Did that hurt?"

An anxious note played in her words, and he sought to ease her fears. That bloody ex-male hovered over her like an invisible specter. "Hell, no!" Her hand had fisted around his shaft, and Alex instinctively pulled away then thrust into her fist. "That feels great," he murmured, his eyes drifting shut to savor the sparks of passion, the spill of hot pleasure that threaded through his veins. He was so close, another thrust or two and he'd lose his swimmers. "Please continue."

Reassured by his words, Lily's hands busied loosening her grip on his cock and drifted to tease his tight, achy testicles. Alex gritted his teeth. A heartfelt groan escaped. She froze but Alex was prepared and guided her hand back to his cock.

"Don't stop, moon heart."

Lily stroked his length then circled the swollen head. "Can I taste you? I'd really like that." She peered at him through the droplets of water that coated her lashes, once again uncertain and diffident.

His throat closed up with a knot of emotion. Alex had to clear his throat before speaking. She was like two women in one body—sometimes bold and sometimes diffident and insecure like today. "I'd like that, Lily. Very much."

Her shy grin twisted his insides. His instinct was to hold and comfort and build her confidence yet contrarily, he ached to take control. Alex had never felt so torn. Or confused.

Lily knelt in front of him with the warm water still cascading over both of them. She took his cock in her hands and held him firmly. When she glanced up at him, Alex thought his heart would pound right out of his mouth. The hot but shy expression in her blue eyes worked like the most expensive aphrodisiac currency could buy. Muscles in his stomach quivered as he watched her tongue poke from between parted lips. Impossibly, his cock swelled further, lifting toward his belly and closer to Lily's lips. He was tempted to guide her mouth to him and ease his tom into the moist warm cavern. Greedy hunger made him tense. But instinct counseled him to patience, and he held himself in check. Let Lily take her time. The satisfaction would be greater for both of them.

Slowly, so slowly Alex had to bite back a groan of protest, Lily closed the distance between her tongue and his cock. Watching was the most incredibly erotic thing he'd ever experienced. The swathe of her tongue across the royal blue head of his cock hazed his mind with pleasure.

"Lily." Her name was a greedy entreaty to continue. Every emotion he daren't put in words swelled inside his chest.

Her pink lips opened and wrapped around the head of his blue cock. The contrast in colors made his pulse hammer. Moist heat surrounded him. Satisfaction mixed with pure lust. Blood rushed to his groin. Lily soothed the head of his shaft with shy forays of her tongue then started to suck, her cheeks hollowing. Alex jerked, his hips thrusting without volition. Deep shudders swept him. Awestruck, he dragged in a deep breath, while a storm built and struggled to release. He was going to climax. *Basuko.* He'd wanted to last a bit longer. Alex tangled his hands in her hair and held on tight.

"Lily, I can't wait much longer. I…"

Lily's mouth worked on him again. The pressure grew in his cock, his testicles. His legs trembled. "Lily."

Her tongue flickered over the very tip of his cock. His hips jerked until his cock went deep, touching the back of her throat. Holy Hannah! He thrust again, trying to keep his strokes slow. Shallow. But Lily gripped him firmly. Her cheeks hollowed once again, her hands massaged his balls then crept around to caress his ass. Her finger ran down the cleft between his butt cheeks.

Alex's control ebbed. Felt good. So good. He quickened his thrusts. Harder. Deeper. Faster. Lily deep-throated him. Pressure built to unbearable levels. He couldn't hold back any longer. One final thrust and his seed spewed from his cock in long, never-ending spurts. Alex tried to pull free, but she clutched him tightly, swallowing his seed until he ceased fighting and simply enjoyed.

When his cock stilled, Lily raked her tongue across his sensitive tip then slid her mouth free and stood on tiptoe to kiss him. Slow, drugging kisses. Alex tasted his essence as she slid her tongue across his teeth and probed the sensitive skin of his inner mouth. His cock jerked, twitching with renewed vigor, clamoring for the clamp of her womb squeezing tight, milking his swimmers.

The water was visibly cooler and Alex flicked the tap off.

"I haven't washed," Lily protested.

Alex laughed. "The water's gone cold. I'm sure we can occupy ourselves until it heats again." He hoped that was the truth because she'd only taken the edge off. He wanted to ream her until she cried her pleasure out loud.

Alex bent to suckle one breast, raising the heavy globe up to his mouth for better access.

"Alex!" she whispered.

Control, already on a tight leash, strained for freedom. He bit down on her distended nipple, and she writhed against his mouth. Alex backed her against the cubicle wall and lifted her, opening her core for his possession. Her cleft shone with dew, and just like that Alex's control snapped. He thrust inside, impaling her, driving upward and slamming into her with powerful strokes. Bent on ending the agonizing pain, the unrelenting pressure in his cock, his thrusts were fast. Frenzied. Stabbing into her wet, slick cunt.

Lily tensed then shuddered, squeezing, clamping his shaft until the line between pain and pleasure blurred. His seed shot from him in an intense, scalding wave.

At the back of his mind, Alex worried about how good Lily felt with her curves plastered against him. Her chest rose and fell, and the musky scent of sex filled the air. But most disturbing was the flash of thought. That they could have a future. Together. For a nanosecond, he lost sight of his dream, and that perturbed him more than anything.

* * * * *

"I can't go out tonight." Lily couldn't help staring at Alex as he exited the bathroom. A hint of spicy citrus followed him, and she breathed deeply before allowing her gaze to wander his muscular body at will. In the tight, black dress trousers and white shirt, he'd attract a lot of attention tonight.

Lily wasn't sure she was ready to cope with that. And there was no way on Earth she'd leave the room looking like this.

"Why not?"

Lily huffed out an impatient breath, and gave the dress a sharp downward tug. Couldn't he see? "This. It's tight." Her hands gestured at the clingy red fabric that stuck to her body like super glue.

Alex prowled toward her, his eyes flickering the length of her body. A lazy smile bloomed as his gaze made the return journey. And suddenly frissons of carnal excitement inflamed her body, her mind. Danger, Will Robinson! Danger. Her greedy body jumped in anticipation on seeing the hot promise in his golden eyes.

He captured her hands before she knew what he was about and stepped back. "Let me look at you."

"Please don't," Lily muttered. "I can't go out like this."

"No," Alex agreed.

Hurt engulfed Lily at his pronouncement. Hadn't he heard about white lies?

"You need to take off your underwear."

Lily gaped. He what? "I don't think—"

"You asked me." Alex dropped her hands and stepped close. He turned her around and seconds later, her zipper whined its way down. Alex unclipped her bra and slid her dress and bra straps down her arms. He tossed the bra aside, slid her arms into the dress again and zipped her up.

Lily opened her mouth then shut it when she saw the devilish dare in his face.

"Better," he said. "But room for improvement."

Lily thrust back her shoulders with a bravado she didn't feel. The bodice of her dress clung to her breasts, the silky fabric soothing yet oddly arousing.

Alex bent and tugged the mid-thigh length hem up to expose her matching lace and silk panties. His gaze rose to meet hers. Lily saw the sexy glint in his eyes and couldn't help smiling in response. Then his gaze darkened.

"Oh, no!" Lily protested, half in laughter, half panic. She batted at his questing hands.

"These need to go," he said. "The dress will sit better."

"What are you? A fashion expert?"

"Yes," he answered.

Warm fingers grasped the elastic band that snuggled against her hips and tugged.

"No. No, I don't think—"

"Yes, Lily. Aside from looking better, knowing what you're wearing underneath is a turn-on. For me."

"It's what I'm not wearing that you'll be thinking about," Lily replied wryly.

Alex kept tugging and pulled the black panties down her legs. Taking a deep breath, Lily stepped out of them.

"Ready?" Alex murmured, offering his arm.

Lily took an experimental step, wobbling slightly in the unfamiliar black high-heels. "What if I fall over? I don't want to give everyone a peep show." Heck, she didn't have to pretend her fear. She lived it everyday, bumping into desks, tripping over mats. It was embarrassing. Clumsy-clot Morgan strikes again.

"Lily." Alex kissed her on the forehead then stepped back. "You won't fall or trip. I have every confidence in you."

Alex's faith flitted through her mind several times during the buffet dinner that preceded the dance. At least she'd managed to stay spill-free during dinner. Her flashy red dress remained pristine clean and so far—she'd remembered to keep her knees firmly together. At the thought, her pussy clenched. Alex was right. The cool air blowing on her bare legs and her nether regions whenever she stood was a definite turn-on. She was so ready for his possession, she had difficulty concentrating on her meal. Finally, she pushed her plate away half-eaten.

"Oh, Alex!"

Lily shot a glare across the table at the pretty blonde. The redhead sitting beside him was just as bad. Lily caught Alex's wince and felt the shift of his legs beneath the table as he edged closer to her. She wanted to cheer out loud.

"Would you like to dance?" the blonde asked when the live band started up.

"Thanks, but I promised the first dance to Lily." Alex stood and held out his hand.

News to her. Bemused, Lily accepted his hand and stood. "You don't have to dance with me," she whispered. *Please, don't*, she added silently. On the dance floor, she had all the finesse of a hippopotamus on stilts.

"I want to dance with you."

"On your head," she muttered with a wry smile. "Or most likely feet. You do know how to dance?" she whispered.

"Of course. It was in the—"

"Earth manual," she finished for him. "I'm going to have to see this Earth manual."

They walked out onto the dance floor to join the other couples. Thank goodness, it was a slow song. She didn't need to coordinate her feet in a hurry. She had time to think. A vision of her spread-eagle on the ground, her red dress up around her hips sent a shudder winging through her body.

"Stop thinking so hard," Alex murmured. "I won't let you fall." He drew her into his arms, pulling her flush with his body. His cock pressed into her belly.

"I'm not going to be the one with the problem," she said, winking at him. As she spoke, the lights lowered, giving a more private ambience to the large hall.

Lily rested her head on his shoulder and let the music flow through her body. They barely moved from their spot on the dance floor. The music finished and the band slid smoothly into the next number. Lily and Alex stayed entwined, swaying and rubbing their bodies together. For the first time in her life, she was having fun on the dance floor.

"This isn't a good idea," she whispered, leaning up to reach his ear.

"What's not to like? I have you in my arms—your nipples are stabbing into my chest giving me all sorts of ideas. And that's just for starters," he murmured, his tone wicked and teasing.

Lily didn't have to look at his face to know he had a wide grin.

"I have an idea. Why don't we go outside and explore the gardens?"

Lily's heart pounded at the idea. He wasn't suggesting a walk in the garden at all. When one golden eye closed in a wink, she knew it for sure.

"I'll meet you outside in a few minutes," Lily said. She felt as though she'd leapt off a huge cliff into the unknown, even though being with Alex made her happy. Whole. And feel like a woman.

"Don't be long," he murmured, and he let his hand trail down her back to cup one buttock lightly before stepping away. "I'll be waiting."

A smile played on her lips as she walked from the ballroom and down a brightly lit passageway to the restrooms. Lily pushed through the door and stepped inside. Several feminine voices floated out from the separate but adjacent powder room.

"What does he see in her?"

"I know! She's fat. He's a babe. He could have any woman he wanted."

"She must have some sort of hold over him."

"Like what?"

"I don't know—maybe blackmail. Maybe he works for her parents and like he has to be nice to her."

Lily's hands clenched at her sides. They were only saying what she'd thought. But hearing the thoughts out loud made them real. And they hurt so much. Then, she thought about the way Alex had shifted toward her when the women came on to him.

"But did you see the way they were dancing?"

"I know! Like she was all over him."

They didn't have that quite right. Alex had held her close without coercion. They were wrong. She knew it and that was all that mattered. With blazing cheeks, Lily stalked past the gossiping women. Her high-heels beat an indignant tattoo on the tiled floor as she pushed open the door of the stall and locked herself inside. She heard loud whispers then a series of footsteps as the two young women beat a hasty retreat. It took longer for the temper to fade from her cheeks, and her color still ran high when she walked proudly down the passageway and outside into the cool night air.

"What took you so long, moon heart? I've been waiting." Alex took her hand and drew her into a small walled garden to the left of where he'd waited. The scent of roses drifted from four ceramic containers and the stronger, more pungent aroma of rosemary came from a nearby hedge. A row of small colored lights edged the footpaths, lighting them enough for safe navigation by evening strollers.

"I walked in on the two girls that we sat next to at dinner. They were gossiping. About me. And you." Anger built inside Lily again. She should have said something instead of letting them burble on. She should have let loose with a cutting remark. Lily sighed, unhappy and angry with herself more than anything. It was always so much easier thinking up clever, witty, sarcastic remarks after the event.

Lily's anger bled through even though she aimed for calm. Casual.

Alex grasped her shoulders and backed her into a darker corner where the light from the fairy bulbs didn't penetrate the shadows.

"I've told you before. And this is the last time I intend repeating it. You are not fat. I find you beautiful."

With each crisp, snapped word, Alex shook her. Lily stared, unable to tear her eyes away from his stern, almost savage expression.

"Do you understand?" Another shake. "Do you?"

"Yes," Lily whispered, and she was starting to believe it.

"Good." Alex took her lips in a hard, bruising kiss that rocked Lily to her toes. She held tight, riding the roller-coaster kiss, both giving and taking. Their tongues swirled together in an intimate dance, tasting. Mating. The heated kiss sent urgent messages to the rest of her body. Her breasts tingled against the silky fabric of her bodice and the tiny nub above her cleft pulsed and dewed.

Lily ran her hands through Alex's long blond hair, reveling in the intense kiss that felt like a stamp of possession.

Alex pulled away slightly and ran his hand down over the silky fabric to reach bare skin at the hem. His fingers skimmed back up tracing bare skin and only pausing when his fingers encountered the tight curls that guarded her pussy. "You're so wet, so ready for me."

Lily swallowed. The man looked like sex on a stick. Women watched him, but he kissed her. How could she not want him?

His finger slid along her cleft, parting her folds. Probing her intimately. Lily threw her head back, squeezed her eyes shut and thrilled to his possession. As his finger danced across her clit, light enough to tease but firmly enough for her to feel a pleasurable jolt, Lily thanked the stars for Earth manuals. Alex pulled back then thrust one finger inside her slick channel. Lily bit her lip, trying to contain the building whimper of pleasure. They were in a public place. Anyone could walk into the walled garden at any moment. But the thought didn't stop the escalating ecstasy that swirled through her aroused body. It made her hotter. A second finger joined the first, filling her, stretching her pussy, but it wasn't enough.

"More," she whispered. Lordy, she sounded like Oliver demanding more food. She sounded like Killer. "I need you. Inside me."

Alex pumped three fingers inside her and skated his thumb over her aching clit.

Voices sounded on the other side of the brick wall where they stood.

"Hell, Lily. You make me so hot," Alex muttered. "I can't resist."

Did he want to? Lily thrust the thought aside to mull over later.

Alex pulled his fingers free with a soft squelching sound. Lily bit back her instinctive disappointment. Maybe Alex wasn't as turned on about sex in a public place as she seemed to be. No doubt later the notion would horrify her, but right now, she was ready to touch herself, bring herself to orgasm.

Her hand cruised down her leg as the thought formed.

"Turn 'round," Alex said in a rough voice. "Put your hands against the brick wall, where I can see them."

When Lily was slow to follow the order, Alex placed her hands on the wall where he wanted them.

Hot waves of lust swept through her belly, a contrast to the hard, cold brick beneath her palms. Lily trembled, her breathing ragged. Rapid. She heard the rasp of his zipper and the rustle of fabric. Then she felt cool air on her buttocks. Lily gasped, her heart double pumping in acute anticipation. Her skin prickled and her clit throbbed without mercy, swollen and ready to explode.

"Bend over a little, moon heart. Yes, that's it." Smoky desire throbbed in his voice, pooling blood in her nether regions and sending her pulse racing. His erection nudged at her buttocks. Mindless longing made her push back against him. She felt him position his cock at the mouth of her pussy then with one seamless thrust, he entered her. Her womb contracted around him. Feeling pleasantly full and thoroughly decadent, she clenched her vagina, gripping his cock tightly with her inner muscles. Alex's breath emerged with a soft hiss. He withdrew then thrust slowly, filling her sweetly.

Voices sounded again. Closer. Lily held her breath, waiting, desiring Alex's next slow thrust with every fiber of her being. He set a lazy pace, as if they had all the time in the world. His fingers cupped her breasts, stroked her nipples, keeping up his slow, easy thrust and retreat. Lily strained against him, savoring the slap of fabric against her bare buttocks. Her clitoris pulsed and burned as she balanced on a precipice.

The voices moved closer, Alex increased his pace. Lily could hear the crunch of gravel beneath shoes, the soft chatter. She was so close to coming. So close.

"Oh, Goddess," Alex breathed close to her ear. His hips jerked, the pace quickening. Lily bit back a groan as fireworks burst behind closed eyelids. Alex thrust once more and she roared into orgasm, the pulsing of her clit going on for endless minutes. The footsteps sounded almost directly behind them. Alex pulled from her pussy and tugged her dress down in one quick move. Alex zipped himself up then he yanked her into his arms and kissed her as if he'd never let her go.

"Oops! This corner is taken," a masculine voice said. "Sorry." Footsteps retreated and faded.

Alex kissed her until they were both breathless and panting. He pulled away and brushed her loose hair back from her face. A soft grin played on his lips as he tugged a handkerchief from his trouser pocket and handed it to her to clean up.

"How about if we head back to our room?"

Lily's heart raced, and she couldn't help smiling in return. "Sounds like a good plan to me."

Chapter Twelve

ຂວ

They ended up staying two more nights, exploring the area and each other. *Time well invested*, Alex thought. He watched Lily and Killer through a huge plate glass window while he waited in the office for Janet. A smile curved his lips as his eyes lingered on Lily. Neither of them had slept much the previous night. And just looking at her curvy form now made his cock jump. He had to face the truth. He'd bonded with Lily. The thought of touching another woman left him cold.

"Sorry to keep you waiting, Alex." Janet touched his arm in a familiar manner that raised a frown. Women kept doing that. Looking at him as though he were a piece of…that Earth stuff. Yeah, chocolate.

"You've got my contact details, Alex? My business card?" Janet smiled and her eyes twinkled with a flirtatious glint.

Her personal attention gave Alex the flying wonkies. He reached for the cream business card, taking care not to make contact in any way. Chocolate was highly overrated. Alex would take Lily any day.

"Thank you. Lily and I will be in contact," he said. Janet's smile didn't falter. Puzzled, Alex lifted his hand in farewell. He cast a furtive look at his reflection in a small mirror as he headed for the door. His appearance didn't seem any different from the refection he'd seen this morning when he'd dragged a comb through his hair. Dark hair. A scar and pitted skin. Big nose. Blue eyes. Nope, he bore no resemblance to the prince.

"Hey, guys. Ready to go?" he asked. After the days exploring the lower North Island, he was eager to see the capital city and head for the South Island.

"Hey, Alex!" Killer barked. "I say goodbye to Maxwell. One final bum sniff." She trotted over to a sleek Border collie on the other side of the car park.

"I know more about Killer's love life than I wanted to hear," Lily said dryly. "The wee dog is smitten."

"If she stops talking about food for five minutes then her love life is a good thing."

Lily smiled, although Alex thought it was a trifle forced. She'd acted preoccupied ever since breakfast. She hadn't eaten much either. A shudder worked its way down his body without warning. Like an omen. Alex surreptitiously crossed his fingers behind his back to negate the hovering bad luck. Yet still, the back of his neck prickled. He turned, trying to keep his manner casual, and surveyed the parking area. Nothing struck him as out of place.

"We're booked on the mid-day ferry crossing," Lily said, "so that gives us time to do a little more sightseeing around the city first. Do you have a list of places you want to visit?"

The burning itch at the back of his neck continued making him edgy and unsettled. He climbed into the passenger seat, leaving the door open for Killer to clamber inside. Nope, still nothing out of place. As Killer jumped over his legs and settled in the rear seat, Alex decided the problem was his conscience. Despite the bonding, he still intended to leave. Pursuing his dream meant the difference between self-respect and defeat. It was about pride, too. Unfortunately, Lily had only entered his life one week ago. The battle for pride and self-respect was much older and very important to him.

* * * * *

"I don't like this," Killer whined. "The floor moves."

"It won't feel so bad once we're up on deck in the fresh air," Lily said patiently.

Alex wanted to wring the bloody dog's neck. Once they'd left Martinborough, she started right in on him, throwing Janaya

303

and her prowess as an Imperial guard in his face. Alex was all for tossing the devil creature overboard. But in the interests of peace and his sanity, he suggested the one thing that would take the dog's mind off her uneasiness at being on the water. "There's food upstairs."

"Food?" Killer's tail gave a half-hearted wag and her ears perked up as much as a pair of floppy ears could. "Did ya mention food?"

"Yeah, I don't quite believe it myself. Let's go."

They walked past several parked vehicles and still more drove slowly up the ramp to park on the lower deck. The noise grated and exhaust fumes were heavy in the air.

Killer sneezed. Twice. "Don't like down here," she grumbled. "Tickles nose."

"Walk faster," Lily whispered, her blue eyes full of silent laughter. "Before you blow a fuse."

Alex frowned at the unfamiliar saying. Sounded painful to him, so he increased his pace as he led the way up the narrow staircase.

Up on the main deck, the exhaust fumes were replaced by the tang of the sea. White birds wheeled through the sky, other passengers chatted with excitement and waves caused by other boats surged and retreated with soft swishes against the side of the ferry. A sense of wellbeing flooded Alex as he curved his arm around Lily's waist and balanced on the deck. Perhaps bonding with Lily wasn't the worst thing that had ever happened to him. For the first time in years, he felt content within himself. *Something to consider*, he thought.

"Food. You promised," Killer yipped.

"What would you like?"

Killer cocked her head. "Maybe pie. Steak pie. Or sausage roll. They nice. And like biscuits. Ice cream good. Maybe—"

"One steak pie coming right up," Alex interrupted. Hell, if he let the dog choose, they'd be here all day. He joined the line at the self-serve counter, purchasing a pie for Killer and coffee for him and Lily.

Lily guided Killer to a corner table and sat.

"Boat moving," Killer said.

Lily ran her hand over Killer's glossy coat in a soothing manner. And it wasn't just to soothe Killer. She didn't mean to, but every time they went out in public together, she watched other women eye Alex. Then she became nervous and anxious and it colored the way she acted.

"Who Alex talking to?" Killer asked.

Lily's stomach roiled, and it had nothing to do with the swell that rocked the ferry. The dark-haired woman who talked and laughed with Alex was beautiful. The green-eyed jealousy monster nipped at her self-confidence. Yet again. Her hand slowed, finally coming to a halt on Killer's back.

"Don't stop," Killer said, nudging against Lily's leg in an insistent manner. "What you look at?"

"Alex." His name came out before her brain engaged. Lily bit her lip and hoped Killer would refrain from commenting.

"You like Alex?"

And maybe the sun would stop rising each morning.

"He's okay."

"You share room."

"Yeess."

"What you do?"

Holy heck. "We...um...talked...and then...um...slept." And a whole lot of censorship in between.

"Hmmm," Killer said, peering at her closely. "Then why you look tired?"

"Alex snores."

"Moon heart, here's your coffee," Alex said.

Talk about great timing. "Oh! Thanks." She caught sight of the dark-haired woman standing almost right behind Alex. Lily placed her hand on Alex's arm in a statement of ownership and smiled up at him. She caught the astonishment then resignation as the woman turned away. Unladylike triumph shot through Lily as she restrained a smirk.

"Here's your pie, Killer." Alex pulled the pie from its brown paper bag and placed both beneath the table. Then he sat opposite Lily and smiled at her, his lips curling up at the very corners. His attention was solely on her—Lily didn't see him so much as glance at any other woman. Her heart flip-flopped as she remembered making love early this morning. Lily fidgeted on the hard plastic chair, recalling memories of her and Alex. Naked skin. Entwined limbs. Slow, lazy strokes. Moisture pooled between her legs, dampening her panties at the thought. Lord help her, she was ready for another go-round with his sexy blue equipment. A smile curved her mouth at the thought. She was becoming addicted to the big blue.

"How long to ground again? Don't like."

"I'm not buying you another pie," Alex snapped.

"Why not? Janaya—"

Lily couldn't help her grin. If she pretended hard enough, they sounded like a family. Mom. Dad. Bickering kids. The grin died a rapid death. Something she wouldn't have because Alex intended to leave. Killer cuffed Lily's leg with her paw. "Lily, how long?"

Lily glanced at Alex's watch. "Another two hours."

"Two hours! Need 'nother pie. Need strength to earn collar."

"All right. All right! I'm going," Alex muttered, giving the dog a dark glare. She talked a load of gobbledygook sometimes. "You know I read they eat d—"

"Alex!" Lily protested. "Killer doesn't need to know that."

After Killer ate her second pie, they wandered around the deck—some of the time hand-in-hand. And not at her instigation. It was Alex who picked up her hand and retained possession. He didn't notice the adulation and silent whispers of the team of netball players. When the coast of South Island came into sight and they were almost in the port of Picton, they made their way back to the lower decks where their vehicle was parked.

"Door open," Killer said.

"Hell, the dog's right," Alex said, quickening his pace. He jerked the door of the vehicle fully open and cursed softly. "Some of our bags are missing."

Lily peered into the back of the vehicle then searched the vicinity. Other people were returning to their vehicles, ready for disembarking. "How about if we split up and do a quick search in case the thieves have tossed our bags in the rubbish?"

"Shit. Hell. Damn. Fuck." Alex used some of his Earth vocab as he stalked down a line of parked vehicles, his gaze probing any likely drop-off spots for their missing bags. The rest of his anti-bonding pills were in one of the bags along with his top-up spell from the crone. He probably wouldn't miss the pills since they hadn't worked too well. But the spell. That was a problem. The old crone who had sold it to him had said he needed to administer the spell in exactly three weeks. More than two of the weeks had gone. As Alex stormed up another row, he searched for solutions. There weren't any. He'd have to finish up with Lily before the spell wore off or she'd see him in his normal guise. It wasn't the worst-case scenario since his research here was almost done, but he wasn't ready to leave Lily either. Dammit, he liked her because she treated him like an equal. Sighing, Alex made his way back to the car.

"Any luck?" Lily asked.

"No," Alex said.

The ferry slowed and the sound of the engines changed as the captain backed the boat into the berth ready for the passengers to disembark.

Lily tucked a lock of hair behind her ear. "We'd better get ready. We can report the theft once we're ashore."

Two hours later, they finished with the paperwork.

"I didn't think it would take so long," Lily said. "But at least we found one of the bags."

Alex shrugged. Minus his pills and the small metal pillbox that contained his spell. Nothing was going to get his spell back. He was doomed.

"When we go?" Killer demanded. "Smelly here." She sneezed, punctuating her remark.

"Might as well head to our next stop." Alex opened the door for Lily and Killer, and they filed out of the Inter Island Ferry office, heading for the car.

"Strange man," Killer said, stopping dead in front of Alex.

Alex took a huge step in his efforts to avoid falling but stood on one of Killer's paws. She let out a screech loud enough to attract the attention of everyone in the vicinity then ran to hide behind Lily.

"Oh, look at that poor dog," an elderly woman said to her husband.

The man cupped his hand over his ear and shouted, "Fog, you say? Do you think they'll cancel the sailing? I can't see any fog."

"Dog! I said dog!"

"But this is a town. Why would they have bog?"

"We go," Killer said.

Alex rolled his eyes. "For once we agree." He turned to Lily. "You want me to navigate again?"

"Please, just until we're on the main road to Nelson."

They managed to find their way out of the port town without any difficulty, and Alex sat back to watch the scenery and catch glimpses of blue water and beautiful sandy inlets. So different from Dalcon's wide, sparse plains.

Killer stirred in the backseat. "Car behind." She poked her head in the gap between the front seats. Her breath wafted across Alex's cheek. "Men behind. Same men at port. Look a bit like men who smell bad."

"Are you sure?" Lily asked, her gaze shooting to the rear vision mirror.

"You watch too much TV. Too many cop shows," Alex muttered. "Look, they're overtaking."

Killer sniffed and pressed her nose against the window as a green BMW sped past. "They following," she stated. "Shifty faces. Not trust. Clever to pass us."

She seemed so certain. And if there was one thing Alex knew, it was that the devil creature had enough intelligence for several males. Perhaps he shouldn't shove her concerns aside so easily. Hell, with the way his luck was running, it was likely the strangers were Imperial guards. The thought made him bolt upright. He squinted, trying to get a good look at the driver and passenger.

"Watch out!" Lily shrieked. "Oh, my God. They're going to hit that cow." She stomped on the brakes. The SUV shuddered. The brakes squeaked. The tires burned rubber as they fought for purchase on the tar-seal road. Finally, they stopped on the shoulder of the road.

Up ahead the cow let out a startled moo. The BMW swerved. Loose metal from the side of the road sprayed, tires screamed, but the driver didn't slow.

"The driver's an idiot," Lily snapped. "He must have found his license in a cereal box!"

"He missed the cow," Alex pointed out.

"Stupid animals." Killer shook her head. "Cows can't talk. Just say moo."

Would an Imperial guard know how to operate an Earth vehicle? Alex wasn't sure. But one thing he was sure of was the need to follow his dream and become a self-made, useful male. He was so close now, he couldn't let the thought of Imperial guards from Dalcon faze him.

"I'll tell you what, Killer. How about keeping an eye out for the men? Let us know if you see them again." Alex caught a glimpse of the speeding green car before it disappeared around a bend.

"Spy?" Killer shook her head abruptly. "I not think so. Bad manners."

Okay, bad choice of words. "No, I was thinking more along the lines of a bodyguard." Ah, better. He saw distinct interest in the dog.

"Like Janaya?" Killer asked.

No, definitely not like Janaya. Hell, one weapon-enthused bodyguard was enough! Alex thought rapidly, trying to find the correct phrasing. He'd heard Janaya muttering about shooting when they'd visited Lily. He sure as hell didn't want to encourage the dog.

Killer peered out the back window as though contemplating his suggestion. "You'd have to pay. Can't do for nothing. Have expenses."

"Pay you?" Alex spluttered. "What expenses?"

Beside him, Lily chuckled. "What's the going rate for being a bodyguard? We're poor. We can't afford to pay much."

"You poor. He not."

"Great," Alex muttered.

"I want shiny tag for collar. Gold. Engraved with name." Killer moved closer to Alex to emphasize her demands.

Alex stared, unwilling to look away first. Eye contact was a big thing in the canine world. He wasn't about to give in and let the devil creature think she was above him in the pecking order. "You don't have a collar."

"I—" Killer snapped her mouth shut so quickly her teeth clacked.

Alex could see thoughts running through her head. He just wished he could read the sneaky creature.

"Janaya promise to buy in Alaska. She bring one." Killer turned away to look at the passing scenery.

"I have a surprise for you," Lily said. "Killer?"

"What?"

"You know your friend, Maxwell?"

Killer sighed long and hard. "Yeah. Dog with nice bottom."

"His owners are going to visit Nelson, too. In fact, they're staying at the campground. You'll be able to visit since it's not far away. Maybe Max can help you watch out... I mean be a bodyguard."

"Maybe. Not sure. Maxwell high maintenance. Lots of bitches look. Be busy. Have to teach them respect."

"Must be where I'm going wrong," Lily muttered. "Oops. I did not say that. Oh, look at the beach down there. What do you say to stopping?"

Since Lily was pulling over anyway, Alex decided to let her change the very interesting subject. He could call her on it later. Alex shot a gaze at Killer. Much later, when the devil creature was preoccupied with her high-maintenance boyfriend. They needed a serious talk anyway. He'd have to tell her he was leaving sooner than he'd planned, especially since Janaya and Luke were likely to arrive soon to collect Killer. Without his top-up spell, he didn't have any alternative. He didn't want recognition before he was ready.

Chapter Thirteen

ജ

"Come on, lazybones," Alex teased. "It's a beautiful morning for kayaking."

Lily nibbled on her bottom lip in the way she often did when she was unsure. Alex found it endearing. He was going to miss her so much. Just the thought made his gut tighten. Three more days then he'd leave. He'd come to the conclusion in the small hours this morning. With Janaya and Luke due back, it was best he left to sort out the other stops on Earth for Bellangere Grand Tours. Janaya would inform on him. It was her duty.

"What if I can't paddle properly and the kayak capsizes? What if I'm a jinx, and we keep tipping over?" Lily asked, a distinct thread of worry apparent in her wrinkled forehead.

"Then we fall in and get wet." Alex laughed at the thought. "That's why we have our swim gear on. And it's compulsory to wear life jackets or else the company won't let you hire their kayaks."

Lily glanced down at her legs and her luscious mouth pulled to a frowning line. "I'm not sure about this bikini. I shouldn't have let you talk me into buying it."

Alex's gaze already lingered on her beautiful body. If there was one thing he wished, it was for her to regain her poise and feel good about herself. The black and silver cloth cupped her curves, showcasing her beautiful body for any male with a little sense. Unable to stop himself, he traced a finger over the slope of one breast then made a foray into her cleavage across the little brown dot. A sharp nip on his calf brought his explorations to an abrupt halt.

"What you doing?" Killer asked, sounding suspicious.

"Lily had a spider on her. Some of them bite."

Lily's eyes rounded but Alex stayed her with a wink. He didn't want her to squeak because of an imaginary insect.

"Where spider?"

Alex wriggled his finger in Lily's cleavage, making her laugh. "I'm not sure. They're fast."

The suspicious look didn't leave Killer's eyes. Alex frowned inwardly. He was sick of being interrogated by the devil creature. Lily thought it was funny, but he was beginning to think there was more at stake here than nosiness. Maybe something sinister that related to Imperial guards and Dalcon.

"Killer, you haven't told us where you lived before you found Janaya and Luke," he said, watching the dog closely.

"Not talk about." Killer glanced away, but Alex couldn't tell if it was guilt or the attraction of the screech from the bird wheeling overhead. He made a mental note to ask Killer a few more questions when Lily wasn't present.

"You coming with us?" he asked instead of the questions that trembled at the tip of his tongue.

"No. Visit Maxwell."

"You'll be careful, won't you," Lily said. "Keep a low profile otherwise someone might think you're a stray and lock you up."

"No one lock me up again," Killer said with the peculiar sniff she used to portray disdain.

Again? Interesting. Alex was about to question her further when a joyous bark rang out.

"Maxwell! He here. Bye!"

"So that leaves the two of us," Alex said, not trying to hide his satisfaction. His last few days with Lily were precious, and he intended to show her how beautiful she was.

Alex and Lily drove to the southern gateway of the Abel Tasman National Park, and parked the car near the information center.

Half an hour later, Alex helped Lily into the double kayak and pushed out to deeper water before climbing in himself. The morning sun beat down strongly, making Alex glad he'd followed Lily's advice and donned a hat. Small waves traveled at a leisurely pace, curling to grow white tips then racing to shore. Alex dragged in a deep breath, the briny tang giving him an odd sense of satisfaction.

Behind him, Lily stroked smoothly with the paddle, just as the instructor had showed them. Alex set a slow pace along the coast. A fish jumped from the water, a quick flash of silver before it dived back into the sea.

"Alex, look," Lily said in an awed voice.

Alex stopped paddling and turned to study the area of the shore she pointed to. Several seals lay on rocks sunning themselves. Without the splash of the paddles, a series of grunts were clearly audible as two seals jostled for position on a wide, flat rock. They watched the seals for around ten minutes before continuing on.

"It feels good to do some exercise," Lily said.

"I thought that's what we did last night. And the night before."

"You know what I mean," Lily said.

Alex imagined her blush and had to turn to check. Beneath the peak of her black cap, it was easy to see the rosy glow in her cheeks.

"Don't laugh at me."

Alex sobered. "I'd never laugh at you, moon heart. You're very special."

Lily's stern expression softened. "You're pretty special yourself. This trip has been so much fun. It hasn't been like work at all."

Guilt sliced deep. If only she knew. Worried that she would read his unease, Alex turned back to the front and started to paddle. His thoughts whirled as he took in the gnarled trees that clung to parts of the coastline and the rocky shore. Being with

Lily was easy. She was generous, giving and sincere. *Basuko.* What a mess.

Alex swallowed and stopped paddling. "That must be the first of the sandy coves that the man in the hire shop mentioned."

"Do you want to stop soon?"

Alex twisted to search her face. What he saw made his gut churn and his cock leap with sudden need. Nothing new there. Her blue eyes glowed with inner fire. She grinned suddenly and winked…actually winked at him!

"I'm not hungry or tired. And I have to say, I'm glad you talked me into trying kayaking. I'm not sure my muscles will thank you for it tomorrow, but right at this minute I'm enjoying being out here." The small dents either side of her mouth made an appearance.

A grin bubbled out into a laugh. "I have a few other ideas — new things for you to experience today."

"Oh, yeah? Like what?"

That was definite interest, and Alex was fiercely glad. At least he'd have memories. "Oh, I thought we'd swim and eat our lunch. Explore some of the small islands. Make love."

"I'm thinking you have a penchant for outdoors, Alex," Lily said sternly.

"I admit it," Alex said, recalling the small, breathy sighs she'd made when he'd taken her against the wall. "But then, so do you."

"Maybe." Lily giggled. "I think I'm learning new things about myself as I go along. I never knew sex could be so much fun." Or so blue!

Sex. Alex's mind stalled on the word, disliking the harsh sound of it when joining with Lily felt so good.

From the corner of his eye, he caught the curve of another sandy beach. Trees surrounded the small bay and outcrops of rocks littered the shore, jutting into the water and creating screens for some areas of the beach. Private. Perfect for what he had in mind. "How about stopping for a break over there?"

"I wouldn't want my muscles to stiffen up too much."

"Moon heart, some of my muscles are stiff already."

Lily gasped and stopped paddling. "I can't believe you said that."

"What? You can't believe you make me want you?" Alex waggled his eyebrows. "Wanna come over here and see?"

"You need cooling down." An evil grin appeared on her face, so out of character that he stared. Which was a mistake. While he gaped, Lily leaned her body weight abruptly to the side.

Too late, Alex realized what the moon heart was up to.

"Wait! Lunch will get wet."

"It's in the waterproof containers."

Alex hit the water with a splash. When he surfaced, gasping for air, Lily was already clinging to the kayak and making sure it didn't drift away. She chuckled when she saw him.

"You know I'm gonna get you for that. I thought you said you weren't a very good swimmer."

"I lied. I can swim. I'm just not too coordinated at times. Your paddle's getting away."

Alex swam to the rescue. He'd lied to Lily, too. While he tried to keep away from the fact, his mind seemed to dive right back to dwell on his lie. And how much he'd hurt Lily when he left without giving her reasons. Or at least reasons that would make sense. After grabbing the paddle, he swam after Lily, who was already dragging the kayak into shore. He helped her pull the red kayak up high on the sand so there was no danger of it drifting away.

"Feel like a swim?" Alex stopped to savor the look of Lily as she raised her arms and wrung the excess water from her hair. Unaware of his stare, she unfastened the life jacket and tossed it on the kayak. Her breasts rose and fell gently beneath the black and silver fabric of her bikini top. Alex's mouth dried. He swallowed to clear his throat. He must have made a sound because Lily glanced at him, freezing when she realized his frank interest.

"Come here," he whispered.

"Why? What are you going to do with me?" Lily moistened her lips.

"What would you like me to do with you?" As he waited for a response, Alex tugged the waterproof compartment from the kayak and pulled out two towels. He spread them out under the shade of a pohutukawa tree. By the time he turned back to Lily, he was ready, impatient for action. Alex closed the distance between them and took Lily in his arms.

It was like coming home.

He held her tight, simply breathing in her scent and memorizing the feel of her pressed against him so later, when he was alone, he'd remember.

Her hands ran across his back and stopped to squeeze his ass.

"Nice," she said with a hint of laughter.

"Oh, yeah?" Alex skated his hands across her ribs in retaliation.

"Stop!" she shrieked, trying to wriggle free.

"One kiss, and I'll stop tickling you."

"One kiss?"

"Yeah."

Blue eyes alight with laughter, she pecked him on the chin. "You didn't say where," she pointed out. Then before he could react, she jerked from his touch and ran down the beach.

Alex raced after her, his longer legs gaining on her quickly. He grabbed her and tossed her over his shoulder. Kicking and screeching with laughter, she protested the whole time it took him to walk up the beach.

"Put me down. I'm too heavy."

In truth, she was a pleasant armful. That damn lump grew inside his throat again. A bittersweet moment. Alex placed Lily on one of the towels he'd spread on the sand. Her breasts rose and fell swiftly, attracting his attention. Alex skated his hand across her bare tummy.

"Nice," he said, echoing her previous comment with a wicked grin. He bent his head and traced the same path with his tongue. Lily moaned softly, her hands tangling in his hair and drawing him close.

Each time with Lily was better, both the anticipation and the culmination. Alex moved up a fraction until his mouth was level with her nipples.

"Alex? Have you ever swum in the sea with no clothes on? I've always thought it would be interesting. An experience."

Alex smiled inwardly. He really liked this Lily—the brave one. She was appearing more often, and he loved that. She'd changed.

"Sit up, Lily."

Lily sat up, a half smile playing on her lips. He'd been so serious today, as if he had something on his mind.

Alex climbed to his feet, the muscles in his belly and shoulders rippling as he moved.

"You've got a bruise on your biceps," she murmured.

Alex frowned at the bruise while she bit back a sigh of pure appreciation. It was becoming harder and harder to remember that they'd have to say goodbye soon. Lily pushed aside the thought. Maybe she could go with him? Maybe somehow they could work things out and stay together.

He extended his hand and tugged Lily to her feet without effort.

"Are we going to explore?" she asked.

"No." His hands went to the waistband of his shorts. He skimmed them down his hips and stepped out of them unashamed and at ease with his nakedness.

Her mouth twitched. But then why wouldn't he be comfortable given his masculine beauty? Despite the in-your-face blue equipment that looked as though he'd been splashed with paint. She, on the other hand, was a coward when it came to disrobing. Lily had felt brave venturing out in the modest two-piece they'd purchased in a Nelson store. Getting naked in the great outdoors ranked right out there.

"Your turn."

"Me?"

Alex appeared somber for an instant before his golden eyes started to twinkle. "A wise man once said that every day you should do something that scares you." His hand skipped along the edge of her bikini panties, his hot gaze never leaving hers. "Strip. I want to make love to you in the sea. We can both try something new."

Lily felt a pleasurable buzz in her lower body, but then that was nothing new when Alex was around. She spent most of the day in an erotic haze. Horny. Hot. Desperately hot for an alien. Who'd have thought?

Slowly, so slowly that the sensual heat seemed to ratchet upward into the burn zone, she reached behind and flicked the closure on her bikini bra.

The black and silver fabric fell away, exposing her pale breasts to the sun.

"I've never gone topless before," she said, sounding a trifle breathless to her own ears.

"You're going to go further than that," Alex promised.

Lily swallowed, her heart slamming against her ribs. Between her legs felt damp and ready for him. She trembled but managed to hold his golden gaze. Just. Deep down, she knew the truth. It was going to be really hard to say goodbye.

The sun warmed her body, the rays feeling good on her bare breasts. They'd probably feel equally pleasant on her bare ass. Lily took a deep breath, hitched in all the parts that needed tucking and tightening then slid her fingers under the band of her bikini panties.

Approval lit his eyes as Lily let the fabric puddle down her legs. Funny, but her heart felt lighter. As if she'd cast off every single trouble along with her clothes. A wry grin twisted her lips. Lily quirked a brow. Here she was—Lily Morgan in her natural state.

"You're beautiful." Smiling, Alex snared her hand and led her across the fine, white particles of sand to the water's edge. "Moon heart, any fantasy you want. Just tell me and we'll make it come true."

Lily felt tears build at the back of her eyes. Pleased, happy tears. She didn't know how to express what she felt in that moment. He really was attracted to her—his penis was starting to transform already.

Alex peered closely. "Please don't start leaking. I didn't mean to upset you. Please, moon heart."

Lily brushed an escapee tear from her cheek and tried to smile away the ache of happiness. "I'm happy, Alex." She reached up on tiptoe and wound her arms around his neck, drawing his head down. "You make me happy." And he did. She grinned up at him and angled her mouth, sliding her lips across his and coaxing him to participate. Tongues swirled together in a lazy-no-hurry exploration of smooth teeth and inner cheeks.

Alex cupped her buttocks and lifted her effortlessly, pulling her flush with his groin.

Lily laughed, fluttering her lashes at him. "My hero."

"Ready for a swim?"

"I'd prefer sex," Lily admitted.

A brief frown flashed across his golden face before he grinned. "We'll do both, but we'd better do the swimming first because it looks like a kayak is heading this way."

Holy heck! Lily spun about ready to scurry for her clothes. She might have gathered the courage to bare all for Alex. But not all and sundry.

Alex scooped her off her feet with a suddenness that made her squeak.

"Don't worry, once you're in the water, no one will notice what you're wearing."

Lily checked out the rapidly approaching kayaks. Three single kayaks, and if she wasn't mistaken, men paddled them.

Alex waded into deeper water.

"Go a little faster," she urged, her eyes on the rapidly approaching kayaks.

"Moon heart, males on Dalcon would pay to look at your ripe, luscious body."

Lily glanced at the pale stretch marks on her upper thighs and grimaced. "Takes all sorts, I guess."

"You could always ask Janaya."

Lily hid her head against his shoulder and bit her lip on hearing his disappointment. "Do we have to talk about Janaya? I know she's married to my brother, but I don't know her well. She's a little scary."

"You don't have to tell me." Alex let her slide down his body until she stood. "All covered up."

Lily doubted that. To her, the water appeared transparent. And... "Oh, my God!" she muttered, digging Alex in the ribs with her elbow. "Look!"

Alex made a choking sound. "Well, bless a fodo bird. That's a new one."

They both stared at his groin. His penis and balls glowed like a blue firefly in the dark.

"I guess I'd better stand in front of you so they don't wonder what the blue light is."

"Must be a reaction with the sea water. I have a better idea," Alex purred. "I could slide my tom inside you—"

"Ahoy there."

Alex lifted his right hand in lazy acknowledgment. "Hello."

With his free hand, he tweaked Lily's nipple. The sharp nip of his fingers sent a bungee cord of pleasure shooting along her nerve endings. Knowing other people were present intensified the thrill. Lily felt her cheeks heat. The color seeped down her neck and spread across her chest but embarrassment didn't lessen the thirst for more. As she sidled closer to Alex, she wondered if her eagerness made her depraved. Another sharp tweak at her nipple sent a groan soaring up her throat. The kayaks were close enough now that she could see the features of the men who paddled them. A yellow kayak stopped closest. The men in the red and blue kayaks stopped to discuss a flock of sea birds on a nearby outcrop of rocks. After another pinch, Alex's hand cruised across her belly and lower, to tangle in her pubic hair.

With her eyes on the man in the closest kayak and a polite smile pinned to her lips, she widened her stance to allow Alex better access. Immediately one finger skimmed downward across her clitoris and dipped into her pussy. Lily drew in a sharp breath.

"Have you been further around the coastline?"

"Not yet," Alex said pleasantly. Beneath the water, his fingers stroked and played, delving in her folds then coasting further up along the sensitive skin of her perineum. "We decided to stop for a break."

Lily shuddered violently, excitement building, her body reaching, striving to reach a pinnacle. The craving got to the agonizing, painful point where she just had to move despite the audience. Her hips tipped forward then back in counterpoint to his massaging fingers.

"We talked to another group who were out here yesterday. They saw a pod of dolphins. I don't suppose you've seen them?"

"Alex." His name came out on a longing whimper. The man in the nearest kayak gave her a funny look, but the slow, agonizing pace of Alex's fingers never faltered.

"We saw a few seals earlier on," Alex said. As he spoke, his thumb traced lazy circles across her swollen clit. His fingers danced in deliberate forays around the rim of her cunt, teasing, tempting, driving her higher and closer to meltdown. Flames licked her nerve endings as she hovered on the cusp of ecstasy. But the emptiness inside needed filling. She desperately needed to be filled by Alex's cock. Now. Before she tumbled. Lily bit down on the inside of her mouth.

How could he act so calmly?

A wave, bigger than the preceding ones, brushed under the kayaks and lifted Lily off her feet. Her upper body lifted, exposing her breasts.

Lily caught a wolfish grin from Alex as his hand whipped out to cover her tight, distended nipples. Then a soft choking noise attracted her attention. The man in the yellow kayak had received a right eyeful, and his gaze was fixed on her shoulders, avidly waiting for the next wave to do its worst.

"We thought we'd laze around here for a while," Alex said. His eyes settled on her mouth, and for a moment, Lily thought he would kiss her. But he didn't. Instead, two fingers slipped inside her tight channel. Regardless of the audience, Lily shifted closer to Alex and wrapped her arms around his waist. The head of his cock dragged against her belly, and the friction made his eyes narrow.

Lily smiled inwardly. Not so unaffected after all. "I hope you see the dolphins," she said. Between their bodies, her hand fisted around his engorged cock, and she rubbed her thumb across the tip.

Another wave rocked them together, and Lily laughed. She acted on her wicked thought, wrapping her arms around his neck and her legs around his waist. Slowly, so slowly, she drew her body close, positioning his cock at the weeping mouth of her pussy and pushing down until she impaled herself. The empty, achy sensation fled, replaced by fullness and promise.

"Ah, I think we'll go."

"Newlyweds," Lily said over her shoulder. She felt Alex's chest rise and fall in silent laughter. "Are they going?" she whispered.

"Yeah."

"Thank God! I thought I was going to combust. I don't think I'm ready to do it in public, but I couldn't seem to help myself."

"That man saw more than I was happy with," Alex growled.

"Just a flash of tit."

"Mine," he said on a slow groan as he grasped her hips, lifted her then eased her back down. "For my eyes only."

Lily loved the sound of his possessiveness. But afraid to let herself hope. Live for the moment, she decided, as gravity and Alex's hands slid her down his erection. Her sensitive clit brushed the length of his penis. The slow slide sent her pulse soaring. Jolts of pleasurable excitement hazed her mind on the next glide down his cock. Her fingers entwined in his hair. "Faster."

Their mouths meshed together in a moist, erotic duel. Each breath came in harsh sounding pants. Alex quickened his strokes. Flesh slapped against flesh. Lily kissed his lips again then angled a trail of kisses down his neck. She bit lightly, and he made a dark sound at the back of his throat.

"Goddess, do that again," he muttered.

A wave pushed against them, and tumbled over her head with a splash. Lily grinned once she'd wiped the water from her face. "Make me come first."

Alex's golden eyes darkened. He rotated his hips and inserted his finger between their locked bodies. A teasing foray across her swollen, achy nub stole her breath.

"Like that?" he asked.

"Yesss."

"How's this?" He swiveled his finger, exerted a fraction more pressure and hot pleasure streaked to her toes. Another deliberate revolution of his finger pushed her over the edge, cascading wave after wave of sweet delight through her shuddering body.

"Good," Lily managed when she could breathe again. "Not bad."

"Maybe I should try harder." His hand toyed with her clit, wringing a twinge of sensation.

Her womb remained pleasantly full and stretched with his thick cock. "Harder sounds excellent."

A growl vibrated through his chest as he barred his teeth at her. "You asked for it, moon heart."

Alex plundered her mouth, ravishing. Taking. He grasped her hips with both hands, withdrawing then surged back into her womb with leashed power that sent a renewed surge of raw need spiraling through her veins.

"Alex." Her hips jerked. Heat stabbed. Lily arched into Alex's next thrust, angling her clit for his intimate touch in the exact place she needed. His cock seemed so long and hard.

He withdrew then slammed back inside her cunt. His groan came from low down in his chest. "Ah, Lily."

Deep inside her sheath, she felt the rapid pulse of his cock, the spurt of his seed. Alex clutched her possessively, with hips still pumping, his head thrown back and face screwed up in an expression of agonized ecstasy. It excited Lily to know she could unravel him this way.

Slowly, he opened his eyes. The flare of languid desire in his golden gaze shot an arrow of heat spearing outward from her clit. One last slide as they slowly rocked together was all it took for Lily to explode into spasms of blissful pleasure.

"Rating out of ten?" he asked in a low smoky voice.

Lily opened her eyes to see a full out grin. "Nine," she said promptly. "Although I'm happy to let you retake the test if you want."

Alex snorted. "Ah, moon heart." He lifted Lily off him and lowered her to her feet before kissing her thoroughly. "You might regret that remark…" One eye closed in a wink. "…when you have trouble walking tomorrow."

Chapter Fourteen

ॐ

The soft twittering of birds outside their cabin woke Lily. She lay, wrapped in Alex's arms, savoring the warmth that emanated from his body and the tangible link to her lover. Her lover. A smile wandered across her lips. She opened her eyes.

"Ahhhh!" Lily ripped herself from the bed and backed away until the wall at her back blocked further retreat. Her heart pounded in a terrified tattoo and lodged halfway up her throat. Dread backed up behind the bottleneck, only squeezing past in tiny incremental whimpers.

The man she'd been wrapped around was not Alex.

"Lily?" The dark-haired man yawned, sat up in the bed and scratched at his hairy chest.

A panicked whimper emerged from Lily's tight throat. "Don't...hurt me."

"Lily! Lily! What wrong?" An urgent scratch came from outside the cabin door.

"Why would I hurt you?"

The rough, gravelly voice sounded nothing like Alex. Lily edged along the wall toward the door, unable to wrench her petrified gaze off the strange man. Killer presented security. And right at this moment, Lily didn't feel safe, but she wanted to. Her hand closed around the brass doorknob. She twisted it, keeping her eye on the stranger in the bed. Holy heck, her limbs were shaking so badly she thought she might sink to the floor. As she watched, the dark-haired man changed. His hair flashed from dark to gold and back. Lily blinked.

"Lily, hurry," Killer barked.

Lily yanked on the handle, the door opened and Killer trotted into the cabin. The dog froze, the hair along her spine rising. A low, menacing growl vibrated deep in her throat.

"I don't know who you are," Lily said, scowling at the dark-haired man and trying to look as menacing as possible with wobbly knees. "And I don't care. Just leave and there won't be any trouble."

"Lily, what are you talking about? Killer, knock that off."

"How do you know our names?" Lily demanded. "Where's Alex? What have you done with him?" As she said his name, the man's appearance flashed from dark-haired and plain to a more familiar golden cat.

A look that might have been anguish sprinted across his face. He rose from the bed and marched across to a mirror. His hand swept across his face. "Fuck."

Killer trotted across to Lily and leaned against her legs. Lily took comfort from the warm, furry body.

The dark-haired man turned to Lily and Killer.

The look was definitely anguished.

"Holy Hannah!" Killer let out a whistle-bark. "Look at the dangly bits on him."

Lily was trying not to. This man wasn't Alex, yet she'd woken in bed with him. She hadn't done the dirty with him. Had she? Her mind did an abrupt u-turn. She was so not going there.

"Lily, look." Killer rubbed her wet nose over Lily's bare leg to snare her attention. "That Alex."

Lily gaped. Killer was right. Alex was flashing—rapidly changing from dark to blond and back.

"Why are you staring at me?" the man demanded.

"Are you really Alex?" Lily said in a faint voice. She had trouble taking her eyes off him. His appearance changed with the frequency of a light flicking off and on. Disconcerting and very weird.

"You flashing, too," Killer said to Lily. Disapproval coated her announcement. "Cover up bare bits."

Good idea, Lily thought then maybe she wouldn't feel at such a disadvantage. She snatched up a robe from inside the wardrobe and fumbled her way into it, tying the belt firmly at her waist.

Killer prowled a tight circle around the bedroom. Her nails clicked noisily on the polished wooden floor, only muted when she stomped across the multi-colored woolen mat. The dog stopped beside the rumpled bed Alex had climbed from. Then she leapt onto the smooth covers of the neighboring bed. The dog's eyes narrowed. Her chest vibrated with an angry growl as she glared at Lily. "You sleep in same bed as Alex."

"Yes." Lily didn't have a problem admitting it, not to Killer.

"Janaya be angry!"

"What's it got to do with Janaya?" Lily didn't have to pretend confusion. She didn't owe her sister-in-law explanations about the private choices she made.

Killer clacked her teeth in disgust and bounded off the bed. "I won't get collar. Won't pay for shoddy job!"

"What collar?" dark-haired Alex said from the ensuite door.

"Oops!" Killer ran for the door. "Me go now. Maxwell waiting." She shot outside.

Either the wind caught the cabin door or Killer gave it a shove because it slammed noisily breaking the tense silence within the cabin.

Lily folded her arms across her chest. "I guess you have an explanation."

"Yes." Alex sank onto the end of the bed—the rumpled one that still bore the scent of their lovemaking.

Lily tried to maintain eye contact, but the rapid changes in his appearance made her dizzy. She had to glance away. "Well, are you going to tell me?"

"I—"

"Wait!" Fear struck Lily without warning. Maybe she didn't want to know after all. Instinct told her she wouldn't like the answers he gave. Uneasiness made her shuffle from foot to foot. "I'm frightened," she confessed, squeezing her eyes shut. "But I guess I knew what we had was short term."

"Sit." Alex pulled out a chair for her. "I'll make coffee and then we'll talk."

The wait did nothing to settle her nerves. This was worse than listening to Ambrose pontificate about why their marriage hadn't worked and why the blame lay squarely at her feet. Unable to maintain calm, Lily jumped to her feet and strode over to the window just for something to keep her occupied. Once there, she pulled up the cedar blinds and stared blindly at the punga ferns and the sparkling sea beyond. Ambrose's voice echoed through her head. Her fault because she didn't have what it took to attract a man.

"Lily, the coffee is ready."

She turned away from the vista, suddenly aware of the pungent scent of coffee beans. She thought she might throw up if she drank a cup of coffee.

Alex set two mugs of coffee on the table along with a selection of pastries.

The pastries sent her stomach wildly lurching. "Where did these come from?"

"They were delivered a few minutes ago. Didn't you hear the door?"

No. Too immersed in the pain of the past. Lily sucked in a slow breath, trying to draw on inner strength. She remembered that Alex had called her beautiful and clung to the thought. But fear still stalked her mind, negating all her efforts for calm. And the way Alex's appearance flashed off and on didn't help. At least the changes seemed to have slowed.

Alex sat opposite. Lily glanced at him then ripped her gaze away to stare instead at her coffee mug. Maybe if she concentrated really hard on the steam rising off her mug, she wouldn't break down and cry. Or throw up.

"My real name is Alexandre Bellangere."

Lily did look at him then. She hadn't expected a false name. "I'm more interested in what's going on with your body. You're switching colors like a traffic light. Is that one of the things I was meant to discover along the way?"

"On Dalcon," Alex continued as though she'd never interrupted, "I am a member of the royal court. It's not the done thing for a male in my position to take up a trade since it's considered common. I wanted—needed—the challenge. And so, I found a way to leave. I purchased a spell that changed my appearance, firstly so I could leave without messy problems and secondly, so I didn't attract attention."

Not attract attention? That didn't make sense. The man was a babe. A hunk with shoulder-length curly hair, golden skin and brown eyes. Then there was the bod. Muscles. Broad shoulders. Six-pack abs. The whole works.

"But you're gorgeous," Lily blurted. "How did you think you'd blend in looking the way you do? Haven't you seen the way women look at you? Not just women my age either. School girls and grandmothers look at you with the same fascination."

Her words startled him, but then he remembered the owner of the kebab shop, the giggling schoolgirls. Janet in Martinborough. "Describe how you see me."

"Tall. Blond. Sexy."

Alex's mind seized on one word. Blond. "Why the hell am I seeing black in the mirror?" he demanded, tugging at a lock of hair. "Are you saying that everyone on Earth sees a blond male? My normal appearance," he mused out loud. "But Janaya and Luke didn't. And neither did Hinekiri or Richard because they didn't recognize me."

"Should they?"

Alex nodded, but didn't go into detail. What had the crone said? People on Dalcon would not see him. He hadn't taken her words literally. He should have. The crone had muttered about not missing a spell or there would be dire consequences, and people would see what they should not see. He should have taken that literally, too. He should have asked the crone about the fine print, the small details, but he'd been so excited to outwit the palace guards that he'd grabbed the opportunity. Now, he risked losing Lily's friendship and love because she could see both visages—his disguise and his true self.

"You can't go outside like that." Lily stalked around the small wooden coffee table and stopped to clench her hands around an upright chair. "How did you keep from doing that before?"

"My top-up spell was in one of the bags that were stolen. I think…I hope it will wear off."

"Then what?" Lily asked in a flat tone.

Ah, bonding. How the hell did he explain that? Hopefully Luke and Janaya—no, Lily had said she hadn't really talked to them about things alien. "You'll agree that we're good together," he began hesitantly. Between the space of yesterday and this morning, Alex had decided he couldn't leave Earth without Lily. Although joining with her would make it difficult, almost impossible for him to return to Dalcon, there were other planets, other galaxies where a pissed, thwarted father couldn't interfere. Of course, he wouldn't have the satisfaction of proving to his father he could be a productive citizen, but he could still successfully run Bellangere Grand Tours. The main thing was whatever he did Lily was there to share it with him. His own Renaissance painting. A painting by Botticelli, just like the one in his guidebook. His heart lightened at the thought. He hadn't admitted it to himself before, but he made the effort now. When he was apart from Lily, he felt as though a slice of his heart was missing. Lily made him whole. There, he'd admitted it.

He only hoped that Lily felt the same way.

"Will you join with me?" Oh, yeah. That was great. Blurt it out before you lay the groundwork. Too late now—the damage was done. Alex stilled, praying to the saints under his breath as he waited for Lily's reply.

Lily started to chew on her bottom lip, and Alex's heart stuttered with instant alarm. The feel of her serious gaze skimming over him, over his body bred panic. "We've bonded," he blurted. "Our souls have recognized each other and have bonded already. Joining is the Dalconian way of formalizing the union." He watched her anxiously—the way she chewed on her lip until it was a deep, rose red. The redder her lips became, the more he worried.

"Explain joining to me. I don't understand."

"I think marriage is the Earth equivalent."

"Marriage?"

Damn, she was still abusing her bottom lip. Alex ached to soothe it, to lie her down and sink deep into her womb. Claiming Lily. Showing her the depth of his feelings, instead of trying to put it into words.

"We're good together." Alex meant every word. This was no comforting placation. Lily treated him like an equal instead of a piece of ass only good for one thing. She never made him feel like a pretty face or an accessory whose only job was to decorate her arm. Her determination and gentleness, her innocence and even her clumsiness were endearing. And her growing feistiness.

Lily made him feel worthy, as if he could do anything.

Of course, his father wouldn't agree, which was why they could never return to Dalcon without some heavy strategic planning and maybe a spell or two.

"We're compatible," he insisted.

"I thought Ambrose and I were well-matched, but we lived a lie." Lily glared at him. "Your version of truth is like elastic. You lied to me about your identity. That's no basis for a relationship."

She didn't know the whole of it. "Will you at least consider it?"

Alex didn't intend to tell her the whole truth until he had to. He didn't want to scare her off with either his identity, his father's position of power or the implications of bonding. She didn't understand yet. "I know you want to travel. We can do it together. We have so much in common." Like they'd bonded. Fate had joined them already.

"I have commitments here. Debts to pay. I can't go off—"

Frustrated with her stance and irritated at himself because he was unable to explain, Alex did the only thing he could think of to turn her to his way of thinking. He seized Lily and kissed her. Hard. Desperately. His lips ate at hers, his mouth moving hungrily before he gentled to nibble on her top lip. When she didn't respond, Alex slowed the kiss even more, persuading rather than demanding. Lily moaned softly and drew closer. Her hands stroked restlessly up and down his back. Their lips moved together, tongues twirling slow and easy, exploring and arousing. A mating of the lips—an act of possession. A statement of intent.

Alex pulled away and stared down into her blue eyes. "Please say you'll think about joining." If he could persuade her rather than lay down the law, he sensed the situation would remain calm instead of flying into volatile.

Lily smiled suddenly and traced a gentle finger across his cheek. "You seem to have stopped flashing."

"Good," Alex said dryly with a great deal of feeling. At least she was still speaking to him. That was a start. "A paper bag over my head would have made sightseeing a bit difficult."

"Not to mention attracting attention." A gamine grin lit up her face. "Perhaps we should work out a disguise for you in case. How do you fancy a dress teamed with heels?"

"Not. I'd probably sprawl on my face and show my knickers."

"I wasn't suggesting you wear panties."

The deadpan look on her face got him—at first. Then he caught sight of a sassy twinkle. "Very funny. Are you eating?"

Alex picked up his mug of coffee and grimaced. "Cold. I'll pour more coffee."

Lily glanced at the plate of warm pastries and the coffee. She shuddered slightly. "Maybe later. I think I'll have a shower." She started for the stairs leading to the master bathroom.

Alex felt the grin that sprinted across his face and suspected it looked suggestive or even plain down and dirty. Instantly his body leapt to lust-mode. Packed. Ready to fire. "I'll come and scrub your back." To his relief definite interest sparkled in her eyes.

"Think you can manage without sex taking hold of your mind?"

"I doubt it."

Lily snickered. "Good. Let's go."

They climbed the wide stairs together to the bathroom. Not one curtain or blind blocked the stunning floor to ceiling windows or the magnificent view of the coast, but anyone using the room remained assured of privacy since they were high up, away from prying eyes.

Alex untied the belt at her waist and hung the robe on a convenient hook. He shrugged out of his robe and hung it next to Lily's. At the back of his mind, he noticed how great the robes looked next to each other. A goofy grin appeared. He was definitely hung up on Lily.

Lily had already turned the water on and stood beneath the six jets of water that sprayed from concealed showerheads.

He had to touch her. The need to touch, to explore her curves was a compulsion inside. Alex soaped his hands with the lemon gel provided by the lodge. A heady scent, reminding him of the palace gardens, surrounded them, intensified by the sultry heat of the morning sun and the warm water pounding over their naked bodies. Alex stepped up behind Lily and cupped her breasts, soaping them carefully with attention to each rounded curve and underside. Her nipples puckered beneath his palms. Lily released a soft sigh and leaned back against his body.

"Feel good?" He ached to mark her with his personal brand, that of the Royal House of Dalcon, so everyone knew, without doubt, they were a couple but she wasn't ready. He'd lied enough—he wouldn't trick her, too.

His erection brushed against the crevice separating her butt cheeks. Insistent need strummed through his body, but Alex resisted knowing the payoff would be so much greater if he waited until they were both delirious with need. Lily's head lay against his shoulder, her wet, brown hair tickling across his collarbone. Contentment settled around him like a plaid blanket. After searching for so long, he'd finally found a home with Lily. And nothing would come between them. Nothing. His hand wandered across her rounded belly, her hipbone, then lower to tease her clit. She was moist, ready for him and the knowledge brought him to his knees.

Lily would wear his mark soon.

Joining with Lily meant more than aimless, casual sex. His heart pounded, and he felt like a raw undergrown having sex for the first time. His fingers shook, his tom swelled to impossible hardness, and his throat tightened with emotion. Pressure built behind his eyes, despite his best efforts. Alex slid a questing finger inside her cunt. His eyelids closed, he bit his lip, but his eyes started leaking regardless.

"Ah, Lily," he murmured, needing to be inside her so badly he trembled. "Turn around, moon heart. Put your arms around my neck." He lifted Lily effortlessly. Her legs twined around his waist, opening her pussy to him in silent welcome. Alex slid home in one seamless thrust, and his eyes leaked salty tears of emotion at the mating with his true mate.

"Lily! Lily! Alex! Alex!" Frantic scratching at the door on the ground level announced Killer's presence.

Alex stilled, deeply seated in Lily.

"Don't stop," she panted.

He felt faint tremors of her womb, clasping his cock.

"Alex! Let me in. Bad people here! Come quick!"

"Shit." Alex bit off the word low with feeling. "Killer's downstairs. She says the bad people are here."

Lily gazed at him through languorous eyes. She clenched her womb and a bolt of lust blindsided him. "I can't hear anything."

"Lily, I want to finish this more than anything, but I don't think Killer is joking." Alex listened intently.

"I can't hear anything," she repeated.

Alex turned off the water and the sound of shrill barking became clearly audible. He separated their bodies with a soft, squelching sound.

"You're right." Lily sounded disappointed.

Alex grabbed a towel and threw another to Lily. He wrapped the white towel around his waist and stomped down the stairs. Killer's barks ceased and when Alex yanked the door open, she shot inside.

"Shut door," she gasped. "Men coming."

"What men? What do they look like?"

"One small. Dark hair. Bit fat. Other much bigger. Skinny."

Alex peered through the door. "I can't see anyone."

"They come," Killer said. "I hear them talk to office lady. One that check your butt."

"A woman with supreme good taste," Lily murmured.

Killer spun around so quickly, Alex was surprised her spots didn't remain behind. She took one look at Lily and growled. "You do thing together. Again! Bad. Very bad. Make Janaya angry at Killer. Not get collar." She turned back to Alex and stalked toward him. "Bad male. You buy Killer collar now! You pay. Price go up." She sniffed. "You buy shiny tag with Killer's name on and collar."

Blatant blackmail. "We'll discuss it later. Where are the men?"

Killer bounded to the open door and planted all four feet in the middle of the doorway as if daring Alex to get past her. "We talk deal now."

A Border collie appeared behind Killer and ran his muzzle across her flanks. "What's wrong, honey?"

"He talks," Lily muttered. "Why does nothing surprise me any more?"

Alex propped his butt against the nearby table and folded his arms across his broad chest. "Well that's fine and dandy! You have the gall to judge me. I'd like to know exactly what you've been up to." His gaze slid over the black and white dog that cuddled up to Killer. That didn't look like a casual relationship to him.

"None of your business," Killer yapped, her nose shooting upward with pure attitude.

"Honey, two men are heading this way. Maybe talk terms later? I'll help." The Border collie eyed Alex. "Will bite for you."

"Alex, you can't go outside like that. You'll cause a riot." Lily's gaze wandered his chest then settled lower to concentrate on his swollen member. "Or a heart attack. Better put some clothes on."

Alex headed for the master bedroom but halted halfway up the stairs. "Your bag's ringing. Have you still got your brother's phone?" That was all he bloody wanted. Add Janaya and Luke to the Earth recipe and things could become a mite tricky.

"It is in my bag. But I'd thought the battery would have run out long ago."

Alex groaned. He felt his world closing in. Doom pressed down on his shoulders. No doubt, Hinekiri and Janaya had something to do with the phone's amazing battery life.

Lily hurried up the stairs after him. Alex's heart pumped in double-quick time. The scent of her arousal drifted to him along with the lemon-grove perfume from the shower gel they'd used. He turned to watch her sashay toward him. The subtle sway of her hips ratcheted up his interest. He wanted to make sweet love to her for the rest of the day.

But it wasn't going to happen. Not yet. He grabbed his jeans and stepped into them. "I'll go with Killer to check out the men while you talk to your brother." Alex thrust his arms into a crumpled denim shirt then strode across the room to plant a swift kiss on her lips before hurrying down the stairs.

Seconds later, Lily heard the clatter of Killer's nails on the floor then the slam of the door when they left. By the time she located her bag the ringing had stopped. Sudden nausea darted up her throat. Lily sank onto the rumpled bed and took a cautious breath. She'd obviously eaten something that didn't agree with her. Her stomach danced uneasily, informing her of the fact. Or it could merely be nerves, she acknowledged.

Alex or Alexandre. His real name sounded exotic. He made all the right noises, made love to her sweetly, telling her over and over how much he cared for her. But caring wasn't the same as love.

Lily balked at jumping blindly. This time she intended to enter a relationship with her eyes open. Especially when the man looked like Alex and attracted attention like Killer craved food. Gut instinct told her there was more to Alex's story. And while he hadn't exactly lied, he hadn't told the truth. Secrets. Lily hated them with a passion.

The ringing of the phone interrupted her unhappy thoughts. She answered, holding the phone to her ear. "Hello? Janaya. How are you? Where are you?"

"We've finished with the fishing and thought we'd come to pick up Killer. Where are you at the moment?"

"We're in Nelson, but we are heading to Kaikoura to go whale watching. You could meet us there."

"Sounds good. Can we go watching the creatures with you?"

The perfect opportunity to ask a few questions. "I'd like that." Perhaps she'd ask a few now. If Janaya didn't know the answers she could find out for Lily and let her know when they met in Kaikoura. "Janaya, have you heard of Alexandre Bellangere?" Lily picked a piece of lint off her robe while she waited for the important answer.

"Prince Alexandre. Sure. He's second in line to the throne."

"A prince?" Lily whispered. "I've been sleeping with a prince?" Alex had lied to her. A prince. She'd had wild, uninhibited sex with a prince.

"You've slept with him? Oh, man. That's gonna cause problems in the royal court!"

Lily's belly roiled. "What sort of problems?" The sensation intensified. She swallowed rapidly trying to dispel the nausea that churned for release.

"Are you sure it's the prince? Have you got the right name? Last I heard the King had arranged a joining for Prince Alexandre. Citizens end up in the dungeons when his majesty is annoyed."

"I'm sure," Lily whispered. "He told me this morning."

Janaya's shriek of horror nearly deafened Lily. "At least Alex is taking his anti-bonding pills," Janaya muttered after her shriek had died away. "Maybe we can salvage the situation. We'll come immediately. I'll talk to the Prince, get him to see sense and escort him back to Dalcon. Maybe the King hasn't noticed he's not at court. He might think he's holed up with a consort... By the Goddess, I'm sorry. I...um...didn't mean... Shit!"

A burst of excited chatter sounded on Janaya's end. Lily's stomach rose and fell like a roller coaster ride at a fairground. A fully fledged ache started at her temples. "What pills are you talking about?" He'd said his supplies had been in one of the bags that were stolen. This did not sound good.

"The pills to stop him bonding with an Earth female. For some reason, our psyches are compatible, and we bond if the circumstances are correct. It's like soul mates."

"He asked me to join with him."

"Holy shit!" Janaya shrieked again.

Lily held the phone away from her ear until she heard the feminine shrieks replaced by a calm voice of reason. Luke — her brother.

"Did I hear right? You've bonded with the Prince?"

Lily explored the uneasiness she felt inside. "If that means I hurt like hell whenever I'm not with him and I can't wait to have sex — "

"Stop, cupcake. TMI."

"It might be too much information, but I have to talk to someone. I guess you bonded with Janaya. You know how it feels," Lily muttered.

A rueful laugh drifted down the line. "Yeah, I know. Believe me, I know. I take it you can talk with the dog?"

"Yeah. Talking dogs. Who'd have thought?" Then Lily remembered something else. "But I hear it's more a case of spy dogs. You and Janaya will buy that dog a collar. The best damned collar in the shop," she ordered.

Luke chuckled. "We've already packed it."

"And don't think the subject is finished with. I have a long memory." Lily attempted to swallow the huge lump in her throat but it stubbornly remained. "He lied to me, Luke. Alex lied to me." The pain she felt inside echoed in her voice. "I wouldn't join with him if he was the last remaining male on Earth. Or Dalcon!"

Chapter Fifteen

She had no future with Prince Alexandre. None whatsoever. The man was a liar. It was difficult to get past that.

Lily tossed her clothes in a soft canvas bag and zipped it shut. Dressed and ready to go. All she needed to do was wait for the prince and Killer. Uneasiness assailed her gut. Her soul craved Alex, but she slammed the thoughts away and concentrated on what she needed to do to get through the next week. A few days in Kaikoura. A few in Christchurch, Dunedin and Queenstown then the drive home. She could make it. If she kept things on a business-like footing and they slept in separate rooms. No long, leisurely lunch stops. Lily shoved aside the pangs of loneliness. She'd get through this if she took things one day at a time.

"Lily! Lily!" Killer barked. "Men gone. Maxwell and I chased. Bit on bum."

"Taste bad," Maxwell growled.

Lily turned to the tall, handsome man that had ripped her life apart. "Did you see them, Prince Alexandre?"

"Yeah, I... You know," he said, his voice expressionless. "Janaya must have told you."

"Lies have a way of coming back to bite you in the bum."

"I can explain—"

"I don't want to hear. I'm packed. I'll check out and wait for you in the SUV."

Lily walked away, her chest tight, her heart pounding. Concentrate on breathing. One day at a time.

The drive back through Nelson was completed in silence. Alex had tried to explain for a second time but Lily had shut him down.

"I don't want to leave Maxwell," Killer said for the third time in as many minutes. "I sick. My heart hurt."

Alex patted the dog on the head. "You'll see Maxwell soon. His owners are driving down to Kaikoura the day after tomorrow."

"Janaya and Luke are meeting us in Kaikoura," Lily said as she concentrated fiercely on the road ahead. She would not cry. Even if her traitorous heart ached. She aimed to hide her inner turmoil. Alex—the prince—did not need to know how much he'd cut her inside, how badly her wounded self-confidence bled.

"Janaya and Luke stay till Maxwell come?"

Lily sighed. "I don't know. You'll have to ask."

"Is that vehicle following us?" Alex said without warning.

Lily checked the rear vision mirror. "It wasn't there last time I looked. We're almost at the Wairau Valley. We'll check out a few of the vineyards so you can decide whether the tour stops here or at Martinborough."

Lily navigated down narrow roads, passing rows and rows of grape vines, as they wound their way to the first vineyard. The leaves were still green but had a tinge of color, of yellow and orange on the edges. Winter was on the way.

* * * * *

"That was the prince."

"About bloody time," Mattio muttered. The prince had led them a chase, and he was tired of it. He couldn't wait to leave this wretched outpost.

Jabot wound down the window and pulled his weapon out of hiding.

"What the fuck are you doing?" Mattio slowed and righted his mad swerve so the hired car returned to the correct side of the road. Taking one hand off the wheel, he drilled Jabot in the ribs with a pointed finger.

"Ow! Whatcha do that for?"

"Dumbass. How are you going to explain to the king that you've shot his son? Get the tranq gun out. But don't shoot until I give the word. We have to pick our time and location."

"But I wanna go home," Jabot wailed. "I don't like this place. No fuckable women. Food's crap. And the devil creatures." Jabot shuddered and paused to glance over his shoulder as though he expected one to jump from the backseat.

The dumbass. Mattio couldn't wait to get back to Dalcon and ditch his cuz. If things worked as planned, he'd never need to worry again. He'd have people to carry out his wishes instead of doing other people's dirty work. And it would happen. Success was so close he could taste it.

"Right," Mattio said. "Here's the plan. We follow them for the rest of the day until we find out where they're staying. Then tonight, we'll use the tranq gun, shoot the prince with the tranquilizer dart, call up the captain and get him to meet us with the spaceship. We'll be back in Dalcon before much longer."

"Females," Jabot said with a beatific smile.

"Make sure you follow my instruction or else you'll be off to the palace dungeons. You won't see daylight, let alone a receptive female."

* * * * *

"Did Janaya say what time they would arrive?" Alex asked to break the silence. The silent treatment was making his head hurt. He missed the smiling, happy companion of the previous days. And nights. A shudder worked down his body and seemed to end at the tip of his aching cock. Hell, what was he going to do if she wouldn't change her mind? He'd had no experience of this type of situation before. A female had never turned him down. Torment ate him up at the thought of Lily denying him the right to join with her. He had to make it right — he just had to.

"She said after dark so they were less likely to be seen by UFO hunters. They'll ring when they arrive, and I'll go and collect them."

Lily pulled into the parking area of a small beachside motel.

"I'll check in," she said.

Alex winced at the slam of the door. "That went well." He turned to Killer. "What am I going to do? She won't talk to me unless it's related to business."

"You stuff-up. Should have told truth."

"How could I?" Alex demanded.

The driver's door opened. "How could I what?" Lily asked. Without waiting for his answer, she started the car and drove down a narrow road that petered out by a cabin. She pulled up outside the small building.

Alex climbed out to stretch his legs and rid his lungs of Lily's spice-mint scent. It didn't work. Looking skyward, he stretched again. Suddenly, he shot upward, about half the height of his legs into the air. His panicked grasp of the vehicle was the only thing that kept him from flying higher. Alex looked down. What the *basuko*? He took a deep breath and let it ease out. He'd noticed his hearing and sense of smell had improved since stopping the pills, but flying? Alex tugged himself back down until his feet were firmly planted on the ground.

Lily climbed out of the driver's side and glared across the roof of the car.

"I've said I'm sorry. I've tried to explain, but you won't let me."

"All right. Explain."

She didn't sound happy about listening, but Alex sensed he wouldn't have another opportunity. He cautiously let go of the vehicle and only started talking when he was sure he would remain Earthbound.

"Life at the palace is hard to describe. As a prince in line to the throne, I have everything done for me. My position means that both males and females in the court vie for my attention."

Lily narrowed her eyes. "Charming. I imagine that means hot and cold running women."

"Palace consorts. They jostle amongst each other trying to sleep their way to a position of power within the court."

"I do not intend to join that group."

"That's the point. I never asked you to." Alex started to pace to settle his agitation.

"Fine, we both know where we stand." Lily swung about, her black skirt swirling up to display her legs. Distracted by the sight, Alex almost missed his grab for her arm. He tried again, his fingers curling around her upper arm as he jerked her to a stop. "I love you, Lily. I've never said that to another female before. I want to commit to you." He swallowed. He wanted to mark her.

Lily wanted to believe. But how could she trust him? That was the crux of her problem. "No, I can't," she whispered. She blinked rapidly but tears still squeezed past her lashes.

"You're treating me the same as all the palace consorts do. A male with a pretty face—worthy to fuck and brag about the deed later to your friends. I have a brain, dammit! I'm worth more than a fuck to brag about." His hands fisted and for an instant, Lily thought he might take his anger out on the SUV. She tensed—ready to make a grab for his hand if he showed the slightest sign smashing in one of the blue panels.

"I'm going to sort out my notes," he muttered finally. "Where's the key?"

Wordlessly, Lily passed him the key. "I thought I'd go for a walk along the beach. The owner said there is a shop where we can buy food supplies. Remember I told you that motels have cooking facilities?"

Alex moved his shoulders in a whatever shrug and grabbed up his hardcover notebook from the front seat. Without another word, he headed for the motel unit and disappeared inside. His reaction ignited her temper.

Blast the man. He was the one who'd lied. And look at the way he attracted women. What if she let him capture her heart then he walked away? History repeating itself. Pain burned through her at the thought. Dammit, he had already ensnared her enough that she experienced severe uneasiness when they were apart. The anxiety only eased when they were together again. Already, her stomach jumped uneasily. Alex's fault again, but this time for a different reason. Lily was beginning to suspect the queasiness she'd experienced lately was a symptom of pregnancy. Now wasn't this a fine and dandy mess?

Killer bounded about in front of Lily, distracting her from her painful worries. "Food for me?"

"Sure." Lily nodded absently. "Do you want to walk on the beach with me?"

"Oh, boy! Chase stupid white birds!" She bounded off down the well-trod track that led to the beach, leaving Lily to follow more slowly.

While Killer amused herself chasing seagulls, Lily mooched along the beach. She stared blindly at the waves rushing to shore. Tears blurred her vision. Lily dashed them away. When they kept coming, she sank onto the sand. The sudden move made her stomach lurch uneasily, and she pressed a hand to her belly.

Something cold and wet touched her arm. "Lily, what wrong?" Killer squirmed close until she was sitting on top of Lily. The weight on her stomach made the queasiness worse. Bile rose up her throat and she turned abruptly away to vomit.

"Yuck," Killer said, stepped away to a safer distance. "That catchy?"

"We're in trouble if it is," Lily said. "I think I'm pregnant."

Killer stared at her long and hard. "I be in trouble now. You carrying evidence I failed. Definitely, get no collar. Bad. I very disappointed in you."

"You materialistic beast!"

"Maybe so. Make you laugh."

All amusement seeped from Lily. "What am I going to do? How can I keep the interest of a man like Alex?" She laughed and the sound didn't hold an ounce of humor. "The man's a prince. I'm ordinary—a commoner. How do I compete?" The tears started flowing again.

"Put his trousers on same as other males," Killer observed. "One foot then other."

Lily gave a hiccuping laugh. "Maybe."

"True," Killer insisted. "Maybe other females prettier than you, but you beautiful inside. Very nice person. Maxwell think so, too."

Lily was touched. She stroked a hand the length of Killer's spine and flexed her hand until the little dog wriggled in canine ecstasy.

"You missed spot."

"So sorry." Lily's laugh came easier this time.

"Alex say people judge him by face. You too. You do same as all other females."

"No, I don't. I—" The accusation sank in and stopped Lily mid-sentence.

"Do too."

"Maybe I should talk to Alex again."

"Good idea," Killer said. "We go food shopping now?"

Lily rose and brushed the sand off the back of her skirt. "What do you think of baked beans?"

"Prefer sausages. You tell Alex have trial period. Get to know each other better. Take things slow. That what me and Maxwell do."

Lily grinned at the idea of taking romantic advice from a dog. Even weirder, the dog's opinion sounded promising. Sensible.

An hour later, Lily opened the door to the motel unit and stood back for Killer to enter. She shut the door and carried the shopping over to the kitchen area.

"I think we bought more than we needed," she said unloading eight cans and placing them on the Formica counter.

Footsteps sounded behind them, and both Lily and Killer turned.

"I was starting to worry." Alex stroked the back of his hand over her cheek. "I missed you."

"Lily did thinking," Killer said. "Food. Can I have some?"

A thump sounded on the motel door.

Lily glanced at her wristwatch. "That can't be Luke and Janaya. They said they'd ring."

"Probably motel lady to look at Alex's butt," Killer said.

Alex's brows rose. "Do you want food?"

The thump sounded again.

"I'll get it," Alex said.

Lily chuckled as she ripped open a sachet of tuna and forked it out onto a plate for Killer.

He opened the door and immediately wanted to slam it shut again. His past colliding with his future. His bodyguards. Damn, that was all he needed at the moment.

"It's a delivery for me." Alex stepped outside before Lily could ask questions and closed the door behind him.

"What are you doing here? This isn't a good time."

"Not a good time," Mattio sneered. "Too bad, bro. Too bad."

Alex stared. "What did you call me?" Alex glanced across at Jabot and saw he was nonplused, too.

"Never mind." Mattio pulled out a weapon. "Over there." He jabbed the air with the tranq gun. "Jabot, get the cuffs."

"Huh?" Jabot blurted.

"Get the cuffs and put them on the prince."

The male was stark raving mad. Barking. Alex saw it in Mattio's pale eyes. The devious cunning of a male balanced on the edge.

"Why?" Jabot wanted to know. "He's the prince. You don't tie up a prince. If the King hears, he'll have a raving fit."

"Just do it!" Mattio snarled.

Jabot looked undecided, his gaze darting from his cousin to Alex and back. Tension made Alex's heart pump faster. What the hell did he do? He didn't know. But he needed to do something quickly before Lily stepped outside to investigate.

Mattio gestured with the gun. "Over there by the tree."

Alex backed away. Keep him talking. Flying would look good right now. He glanced skyward and did a half jump but he landed back on the ground without mishap. *Basuko.* "There's no need for the gun."

"Every fuckin' need!" Mattio roared. "All my undergrown years were spent in your shadow. Then they gave me the job of bodyguard, treating the position as though it was an honor. Bah!" He spat, a globule of saliva landing at Alex's feet. "No more. With you out of the way, the King will have to acknowledge me. His third son."

"Son?" Alex echoed.

A shot rang out. Alex staggered, and he felt a sudden numbness in his left shoulder. He gripped his shoulder, pressing down and trying not to panic. Panic sped the heart and would send the drug surging through his body. At least it hadn't been one of the weapons the Imperial Guard carried or else all that would be left of him would be a pile of ashes.

"You shot the prince," Jabot said.

"Dumbass! He's not going to leave voluntarily."

"But he's the prince." Jabot sounded confused.

Alex struggled to remain standing. He needed to keep his wits about him. He didn't like the way Mattio was waving the weapon around.

From the corner of his eyes, he caught a flash of black. While Mattio's attention was on Jabot, he casually scanned the vicinity. Hell! Lily and Killer. He opened his mouth to shout a warning then clamped it shut when Lily signaled him.

Instantly, he feared for Lily. If anything happened to her… Alex shuddered, his heart cramping at the thought of life without Lily. He wouldn't be able to live with himself. Alex felt himself drifting in and out of consciousness. He must stay awake.

Lily and Killer separated and both disappeared from sight. Alex lost focus of his eyes for an instant. It was obvious the plan was surprise attack, but it might work better if he knew details. "Son?" he repeated trying to distract Mattio. "What proof have you got?"

"Proof," Mattio spat the word as though it were something disgusting. "I've got blue balls. What other proof is required? I gave the King proof but he refused to acknowledge me because my mother was a slave."

Confusion pounded Alex. A brother. "But the King would have needed to mark—"

"Of course, he did. How the hell do you think my balls are blue?" Mattio snarled.

"You've got blue balls?" Jabot whispered in awe, his gaze shooting to Mattio's groin. He gave an envious sigh. "Mine are orange."

Without warning, Killer appeared from the bushes right near Mattio and Jabot. She sank her teeth into Mattio's calf.

The male howled. He kicked out trying to dislodge the dog. Jabot edged away, his eyes rolling back in his head. Alex searched for a weapon, frantic to take advantage of the situation.

Already, he could feel the numbness of the drug crawling through his chest. His legs wobbled like a newborn.

"Alex! Down."

On hearing Lily's voice, he dropped instinctively. A strange whistling sound flew past his ear. Something hit Mattio in the head with a solid thunk. He dropped like a rock to the ground and didn't move again.

Jabot kept backpedaling, his mouth wide open with an expression of horror.

"Alex, you okay?" Lily called.

"Man down!" Killer barked. "Good job." She trotted over to inspect Alex. Killer nuzzled his shoulder, and Alex couldn't prevent a pained groan. "Alex hurt," she said as Lily ran to join them.

"What did they shoot you with?" she gasped, running her hands over his body checking for wounds.

"Tranq gun," Alex muttered. "Not too bad. Need to sleep it off."

"What about him?" Lily gestured at the lifeless form on the ground not far from them.

"Is he dead?"

"Unconscious. I hit him in the head with a can of baked beans. My cricket skills came in handy."

Alex laughed, but it hurt like hell. "My hero."

"Put cuffs on," Killer advised. "Give him to Janaya."

Lily picked up the silver cuffs that lay on the ground. When she looked more closely, she saw there were two sets.

Killer peered around her knee. "One for feet. One for hands."

Lily fumbled her way through putting them on then dragged the man into the motel unit.

"He's still breathing," she announced, "but he'll have a hell of a headache. Are you sure you're going to be all right?"

"Just need sleep."

"Lucky I'm strong," Lily said, with a trace of good-natured humor. She helped Alex to his feet, staggering slightly under his weightier frame.

"Thank you, Lily. Most females would have cowered in the background and let Mattio take me."

They wavered their way to the unit. Once inside, Lily directed him to the main bedroom.

"I'm not most females."

"I know." Alex leaned on her with more weight, his legs barely functioning. "That's why I have the good sense to love you."

Alex dropped to the bed, his legs going all wobbly. He bounced lightly on the mattress, tried to fight the weakness that disabled his body then gave up the fight and subsided to lie against the pillows. His eyelids wanted to close — the drug in the tranq gun drawing him closer to sleep.

"Love me to join," he managed. No, that wasn't right. "Love me?" His eyes closed even as he strained for her answer.

"I love you, Alex. We'll talk when you wake up." Lily grasped both his shoulders and shook. "You will wake up?"

"Moon heart." Alex felt himself smile, he felt Lily's hands dig into his shoulders and decided he was the luckiest male in the world. Lily loved him.

Chapter Sixteen

∞

Warmth surrounded Lily. She smiled sleepily, sensing the heat emanated from Alex. A soft snore erupted near her ear. Smiling again, she arched against his naked form, savoring the slide of her breasts against his smooth chest. Her nipples contracted to hard buds as she rubbed against him. His slow, regular breaths reassured her of his good health. Life was good. Maybe she could entice him into waking, give him a few explicit pointers and let him take it from there. Oh, yeah. Sounded like a fine —

"Bloody hell!" a feminine voice shrieked. "Luke, come see this!"

Lily jerked upright with a scream then scrambled beneath the blankets when she saw her brother and Janaya in the doorway. She sure as hell hadn't advanced to sex in front of other people. Especially people she knew. Family. That other time in front of the man in the kayak had been an accident that she wasn't ready to repeat.

"What are you doing in bed with the prince?"

Lily twisted to stare at Alex's broad shoulders — his broad, naked shoulders, and let her hand flutter to her mouth in pretend astonishment. "Oh, goodness." She turned back to her brother and Janaya and batted her eyelashes. "Is he a prince?"

"Cut it out," Luke said. "Janaya told you about him. He can't join with you. His father will never allow it. You'll get hurt."

Lily ignored the implied questions. "What are you doing here so soon?"

"It's after eight. It's dark out," Luke said, a trifle defensively Lily thought.

"You were going to ring," Lily pounced on the sense of guilt her brother harbored. Nothing like wrong-footing him to gain an advantage.

"Ah, Janaya's here. Good." Alex touched Lily's leg under the blankets and sat up in the bed. "Janaya, could you deal with Mattio? He's cuffed in the other room."

"What happened to your shoulder?" The horrified tone of Janaya's voice drew Lily's attention to the large blue area on Alex's left shoulder. The bruise. It had moved. How strange. She leaned over to finger the discolored area, gently watching Alex for a reaction. His wince brought a shaft of anxiety. He'd said he'd be fine. What if he'd lied?

Obviously sensing her agitation, he leaned over to kiss her lips, ignoring the low growl from Lily's brother and the squawk of outrage from Janaya. Even Luke's warning for his wife to keep her weapon holstered didn't raise much more than a blip of interest.

"I'm fine, moon heart. I'll prove it soon," he whispered. Lily shivered at the promise in his eyes and tried desperately to quell the sudden spurt of nausea in her belly. She closed her eyes and counted to ten, willing the show of weakness away.

Alex turned his attention back to Janaya. "Mattio zapped me with a tranq gun. He's claiming he's a son in the Royal House of Dalcon."

"Fool," Janaya muttered, jumping to attention. Imperial guard mode, her brother called it. Lily thought she looked plain scary. "That's treason. I'll deal with him." She stormed from the room.

"Perhaps you could help your mate," Alex said. "You don't want her to do anything she might regret. Tell her Mattio should have help from us. Tell her he has blue balls. She'll understand what needs to be done. He has a partner somewhere. He shouldn't give you any trouble. His name is Jabot, and his balls are orange."

Lily suppressed a grin as Luke hesitated. His mouth opened to ask questions then he obviously changed his mind and stomped after Janaya.

Alex waggled his eyebrows at Lily. "Alone at last."

Unaccountably, nerves joined the queasiness in Lily's belly. "I love you," she blurted. "I'm sorry for judging you by your appearance. I don't like it when people do that to me, and it won't happen again." Words tumbled out in a rush as she steeled herself to tell him of her suspicions. "I really love you, but could we go a little slower? It takes time to adjust to the idea of loving a prince. Could we work on your business together and make it a team effort?"

"Will you wear my joining symbol?" he demanded, seizing her right hand and pressing a kiss along the inside of her wrist. "I want to mark you."

"I...yes," she whispered, acknowledging in that moment that the trial period of courtship she was suggesting was not really necessary. "Do I want to know about marking? It sounds barbaric."

Alex repeated the kiss on her wrist and her insides twisted. Deep in her heart, she sensed he really was her other half. Why else did she feel this way—expectant and happy, and full of anticipation at the future? But now came the difficult bit. How would he react? "Um, Alex?"

"Yes, moon heart?"

"I have something I need to tell you." Fear jostled with the sense of wellbeing for a few seconds before she gathered courage. Alex said he loved her. Everything would work out all right. "I think I'm going...we're going...to have a baby." Lily peered at Alex closely, trying to gauge his reaction. Her heart slammed against her ribs, and she had to swallow to ease the dry lump in her throat. "Say something. Please."

"A baby? Our baby?"

Lily nodded.

"How? Why?" His mouth worked and nothing came out.

"Sex can and does produce babies," she said wryly, "although it shouldn't have with me being on the contraceptive pill."

"My anti-bonding pills didn't work either. Perhaps it was something in the spell the old crone sold me."

"Maybe. Alex, the baby?"

"Our baby," he mused. To Lily's astonishment, a lone tear trickled down one tanned cheek. "A baby sounds wonderful. Perfect. We're going to have a baby!" he shouted, his golden eyes glowing with excitement and such pleasure that Lily grinned and felt her own eyes mist over.

"Will your father disown you?"

"Moon heart, I think you've managed the one thing that will make him come 'round." He grinned. "I don't know why I didn't think of it myself. For years, he's wanted a grandundergrown to dangle on his knee. I'll call him from Janaya's ship tomorrow. I'm fairly sure he'll forgive me if it means a royal undergrown in the family. A baby," he murmured. He tugged the blankets from her bare belly and leaned closer. "You're beautiful now, moon heart. But I can't wait to see you ripe and swollen with our undergrown." Alex pressed a kiss to her belly than licked and kissed a trail up over to her breasts to her smiling mouth. "You make me whole," he whispered. "I couldn't be happier."

A scratch sounded at the bedroom door. "Lily, Lily! You tell Alex 'bout baby yet?"

"Baby!" a masculine voice roared from the other room.

"Oops," Lily said in a small voice.

The door crashed open, smashing into the doorstop and shuddering to a stop with a solid thud.

"Hi, Dad," Lily said, clutching the white sheet to her chest. This bedroom was like a railway station. It was only the solid feel of Alex's arm around her shoulders that kept her from ducking under the blankets to hide.

Hinekiri, Luke and Janaya crowded into the bedroom, too.

"Did that dog say baby?" Richard Morgan demanded. "Who the bloody hell are you?"

"No," barked Killer, peering around the corner of the door.

"Yes," said Alex. "Prince Alexandre Bellangere at your service."

Her father ignored the royal announcement and cut to the important part. "Well, which is it? Get your stories straight. Did you get my daughter pregnant?"

"Richard, there's no need to shout. We can all hear you perfectly well," Hinekiri chirped. "I'm sure they can hear you on Dalcon. They won't need to make a royal announcement. You've already done it."

"Lily and I are having a baby," Alex stated in a clear, firm voice. "And we are joining."

"A baby," Richard said. He whirled on Killer. "What sort of a spy dog are you? You were meant to stop this very thing from happening!"

Killer stepped into full view and puffed up indignantly. Her fur lifted along the back of her neck. "I did excellent job. Janaya already pay me. Too late now. Not give back."

Lily bit her bottom lip. Now was not the time to laugh. Alex squeezed her shoulder under the cover of the blankets, and Lily felt the silent laughter in him as they both gazed at Killer's shiny, new collar. It was made from black leather and had red stitching running down both sides with a row of silver studs in the middle. There was no doubt the collar was a work of art.

"It's a beautiful collar," Lily said. Joy bubbled up inside her as she cuddled up to Alex.

"I go show Maxwell." Killer trotted to the door then turned and winked. "I have hot date. Don't wait up."

"I don't believe my ears," her father muttered. "Finding out that dogs talked was a shock but they have a love life?"

Hinekiri shunted Janaya and Luke from the room before turning her attention to Richard. "Perhaps we could leave Lily and Prince Alexandre to their privacy," she suggested.

"But...but..." her father spluttered.

"The damage is done," Hinekiri chirped with a wink at Lily. "We can plan the wedding tomorrow."

"But he's an alien," Richard said.

"I'm an alien," Hinekiri said with a distinct snap in her voice.

"Oh, yeah. Right. Sorry." He allowed himself to be directed from the room.

"Congratulations," Hinekiri said and she too left the room, closing the door firmly after her.

"You have a great family," Alex said. "They care about you."

Lily pushed Alex back against the pillows and leaned over him, letting her breasts rub against his chest in a suggestive manner. "They'll be your family, too. I'll remind you of this moment when they start telling you what to do."

"But they love you."

"Yeah," Lily said. "Enough chatter. I think we're guaranteed privacy for the rest of the night. What say we make use of it? Maybe you can explain this mark. It sounds intriguing."

"A good plan." Alex wrapped his arms around her and kissed her. Lily melted inside, feeling so happy she wanted to cry. Dreams really did come true if you believed hard enough. Lily believed with all her heart.

The kiss changed in a subtle manner, the pressure increased and something sharp pressed against her lips. She jerked away in surprise. At the same time, a pulse sprang to life against her breast. It felt like the wings of a butterfly flapping between them.

"What's wrong?" Alex murmured, his voice husky and notes lower than normal.

The vibration increased.

"Eek, it feels like there's an insect in the bed with us." Lily tugged away from Alex's grasp and brushed a hand over her breast. She glanced down and stilled. "Um, Alex?"

"Yesss?"

Lily's head jerked up to see his face. "Holy moly!" She scrambled away from Alex and stared, her disconcerted gaze alternating between the mobile bruise that now rested over his heart and his—no other word for it—his fangs. "Um…Alex… I'm warning you now. If you say, all the better to eat you with, I'm gonna pitch a screaming fit and run." Her voice shook, and Lily didn't mind admitting she was slightly freaked. She shifted her legs toward the edge of the bed, ready to scramble to safety if he so much as pointed his fangs in her direction.

"Lily. Trust me."

Lily's eyes were drawn to his fangs. They extended downward past his bottom lip, looking sharp enough to draw blood. Her blood. As she watched, a brilliant blue flooded the milky white fangs, and gradually the white faded entirely. Black humor bloomed up inside Lily. The big blue strikes again.

"Lily." His words sounded different, but then why wouldn't they with those bloody huge daggers poking from his mouth?

Lily swallowed and backed further away. Her legs tangled with the bed linen, and suddenly she ran out of bed. An undignified shriek escaped as her arms clutched at empty air. But before she hit the ground, Alex caught her securely in his arms. Tenderness filled his golden eyes, and he smiled at her as he placed her safely in the middle of the bed. Lily frowned. At least, she thought it was a smile. It was a bit difficult to tell with the sharp objects in the way ruining the line of his beautiful mouth.

"Love you, Lily." Alex held her gently in his arms, rubbing his hands up and down her naked back until her startled heartbeat calmed. "Always love you."

"Are you going to…?" Lily swallowed. "Bite me."

"Yesss."

Lily's eyes widened. Not quite the answer she'd expected even though the evidence was right in front of her eyes. "You could have lied!" she mumbled, unable to take her eyes off his brilliant blue teeth. Slowly, she reached out an unsteady hand to touch one fang.

The heat from the fang seared her fingers. Then, he hissed, his startled reaction making Lily jerk her hand away in a hurry. Surreptitiously, she checked her fingers. Okay. All present and accounted for.

"What's happening?" she demanded in a terse whisper.

"Mark. Pleasure. Trust. Lily."

The fangs seemed to have reduced him to single words. A shiver racked his muscular body, and worry replaced her fear. "Are you going to be all right? Should I call Janaya?"

"Need you," he forced out with a groan. He writhed on the bed, and Lily saw to her horror that the blue from the bruise over his heart was spreading outward at a rapid pace.

"You're turning blue all over." Curiosity bloomed in her. "Does it hurt?"

"Need you. Now. Kiss me."

Lily cast a doubtful look at his mouth. It didn't look quite so sexy and tempting as usual with the sharp protrusions.

"Lily." The heartfelt groan that followed his plea galvanized her to action. She leaned over his shaking body and pressed a cautious kiss to a flat, blue, masculine nipple. When he didn't attack her with his teeth, she relaxed a little and trailed kisses across his broad chest. The contact soothed both of them. Lily let the uncertainty about his fangs float away and concentrated on giving them both pleasure.

She trailed her fingers across his pastel blue skin in fascination. Her tongue flicked out to tease the circumference of his belly button, dipping inside then lightly nipping his muscular belly with her teeth.

Alex's tortured groan throbbed in the air between them. "Again. Please."

Lily scored her teeth across his flesh then tugged the cotton sheet away from his body. A grin escaped. "The big blue is bluer than normal."

Alex snorted his amusement and reached out to caress her breasts, cupping one plump globe in each hand. His thumbs massaged both nipples, and Lily felt a liquid gush between her legs.

"Trust. Me?"

Lily's eyes drifted to his fangs. She loved him. He was the father of her baby. Her gaze traveled upward to meet his eyes. The silent pleading she saw made up her mind. "I trust you, Alex. You are my love. I trust you with my heart and soul."

The worry in his golden eyes faded, and his lips curved up in a positive, definite smile. She was certain this time since she glimpsed the whole fang from root to tip. Lily squeezed her eyes shut. She trusted him, but they were two big suckers.

Alex leaned over her body, his chest brushing sensitive nipples. She felt his erection brushing the entrance to her womb and shifted to allow him better access. Her body trembled, but it was no longer fear and she opened her eyes again. Alex kissed one breast. The scrape of a fang across her skin brought pleasure instead of pain. A repeat of the caress doubled the exquisite sensation. Lily's heart thundered while each of Alex's kisses made her hotter than she'd ever felt before. The lap of his tongue across her breast made a pulsating ache spring to life deep in her pussy. She ached for Alex's possession. Her hips shifted. A groan emerged.

"Please, Alex. I need you inside me."

"Frightened?"

She shook her head. The strange thing was that the fear had left her as soon as Alex started to pet and stroke her skin. A shudder drifted through her as he kissed his way down her body. The sight of his golden head between her legs brought a gush of juices. She stirred restlessly, yearning, seeking Alex's touch. His possession.

"Ready?" he asked in his fang-altered voice.

Lily nodded. As ready as she'd ever be. She only hoped it didn't hurt too much.

Alex grinned up at her, apparently enjoying her apprehension. Then he parted her legs and blew across her clit. The moist air sent a rush of pleasure shuddering through Lily. He scrapped the fangs across the soft skin of her inner thigh then soothed the bite with a lash of his wet tongue.

"Lily." Her name came out on a sigh.

Alex moved back up her body and kissed her gently. The fangs pushed against her lips, the heat from them immense and startling.

"Lily," he said again. His cock surged past the wet entrance of her womb, filling her completely and totally. His eyes glowed with an unholy blue light as he pulled from her vagina then thrust home again.

Lily sucked in a tiny breath, the ripple of her orgasm almost on her with just two thrusts. She trembled, moving with Alex, fighting for release. He felt impossibly big inside her, larger than he had ever felt before. He lowered his head and sucked on one taut nipple.

The pull at her breast pushed her over the edge. Pleasure, immense and satisfying, surfed through her body. Lily felt the dig of his fangs on the slope of her breast.

Alex cried out. Deep in her womb, his seed spurted long and hard. Pleasure hummed in a never-ending stream through her body.

And then he bit her.

His fangs sank deep into the slope of her breast. A drawing, swooping sensation shot the length of her body. Her clit convulsed, her womb clamping at Alex's cock. White-hot pleasure hurled her from her body into a place where the present didn't exist. But she wasn't alone. Alex soared beside her, his tom hard and thick inside her pussy. On and on the pleasure went, building, increasing until she didn't think she could bear it. Starbursts flickered behind her eyes. Alex held her tight, safe, and they rode the storm together until the lightning and thunder calmed and the world was right again.

Lily came to herself slowly, feeling Alex's heart thudding against her breasts. Her eyes flickered open even though she didn't remember closing them. She smoothed a lazy hand across his mouth.

"Your fangs are gone."

"Yes." Alex lifted away from her upper body. A slow smile curled across his handsome face.

"What?" Lily whispered, quietly pleased that the forbidding fangs had disappeared.

"The mark." Supreme male satisfaction coated his purr. "We are mates for life."

Lily glanced down at her breast. On the upper slope where he'd bitten her, a blue mark glowed. When she studied it more closely, she saw it was the size of a fifty-cent piece. The swirly pattern reminded her of a Celtic design.

"I have one, too."

And he did, on his chest in the same place she did. It was the exact size and color of the one that decorated her breast. "A matching pair of bookends," Lily said dryly. To her relief, his skin had returned to a more normal color, and he didn't look like a character out of a children's storybook any more.

Alex shook his head in silent denial. "Mates."

"Is it always like that?" The pleasure still rippled through her womb like a series of fireworks in a display.

"No idea," Alex said in a cheerful tone. "It's never happened to me before. Never will again," he said with a careless shrug right before he pressed a lingering kiss to her open lips.

"Explain," Lily said as soon as he lifted his head.

"Marking is a once in a lifetime thing. I will never mark another female. Physically, it's impossible while we both live. I'm afraid you're stuck with me."

Which wasn't such a bad thing, Lily thought with a rush of pleasure. Suddenly, the idea of growing older seemed less daunting. With Alex at her side, she could face anything.

Her hands drifted over his chest to finger the blue mark that glowed on his pectoral muscle. It felt rough beneath her fingers and a little hot to the touch. It reminded her of a brand.

"So, you'll never go blue like that again?" Her gaze wandered down to where their bodies were still joined. His skin appeared normal again, golden against the blue of the mark.

Alex brushed the hair off her face and grinned. "Moon heart, I'm afraid you're stuck with my blue tom and the mark." His hand drifted down to touch the blue mark on her breast. The trail of his fingers across the mark made her clit pulse in a startled leap of enjoyment.

Lily sighed, and the sigh was based in happiness. She could think of worse things than living with Alex and the big blue.

Enjoy An Excerpt From:
SEX IDOL

Copyright © SHELLEY MUNRO, 2006.
All Rights Reserved, Ellora's Cave Publishing, Inc.

ဢ

"We'd better get ready," Sasha said.

She didn't want him. Indignation made him push her away but the soft flush on her cheeks changed his mind. She wanted his baby. She liked kissing him. Sasha must feel something for him. Antonio wished he could fathom what she really wanted from him.

They strolled side by side into the small backstage room specially set aside for the next competitor on stage to warm-up and prepare. Antonio noticed the technicians give Sasha's naked body a few sidelong looks. Several of the others were naked too, but it seemed to Antonio that they were paying particular notice to Sasha. Damn, why hadn't they grabbed robes? He winged a glare at the nearest offender and placed his body between Sasha and the man's leer. Sasha's bag hid some of her, and at least there would be spare robes, provided by the sponsors, in the waiting room. They sure as hell weren't heading back to their dressing room without them.

"Name?" a security guard demanded.

"Antonio Perez and Sasha Greenacre." Antonio watched the man carefully in case he ogled Sasha, but the appreciative glint in the man's eyes told him the security guard swung the other way. The sly pinch on Antonio's ass as he passed confirmed the supposition. Sasha's virtue was safe but Antonio wasn't so sure about his.

Antonio caught a whiff of sanitizer spray when he stepped inside the room. Cleaned instantly by the housekeeper droid for their use to warm-up or whatever else it took to prepare for their onstage performance. A large screen showed them the action on the stage if they wanted to check out the opposition. Sasha ignored everything to rifle through her bag. She muttered before giving a small cry of success and pulling a plastic jar out.

"I've brought some body glitter with me. It's something new I've been experimenting with. If we choose the nighttime backdrop, you know the one with the deep blue coloring that comes with stars and the moon. The lighting they use with that backdrop should highlight the body glitter."

"All right. What about positioning on stage?"

"I'll take the chair." She stopped abruptly and pointed at a small speaker.

The room was bloody bugged. God knows who was listening in. It could be management or other competitors. "Warm-up time," he said abruptly.

Sasha went into his arms, following his cue without protest. Her hands glided down his chest to tease his cock. She traced the baby-soft skin of his balls before running her fingers from base to tip. "You look so much better without all the body hair. You feel better too. Did it hurt?" Her eyes were full of silent laughter.

"Yes, it fuckin' hurt," Antonio muttered, wondering what the hell she was going on about.

"Do you think we're being watched as well?"

"Possibly."

The two-minute warning bell sounded.

"We'll have to risk it." Sasha pulled away and grabbed up the jar she'd set on the bed beside her bag. She screwed the top off and dipped her forefinger into the thick pink cream. "I'm going to do a quick pattern on your chest and back."

The one-minute warning belled peeled out.

"What about you?"

"Here. Dip your finger in and make some swirly patterns on my back and butt." As she spoke, she rapidly traced around her breasts, down her belly and lower body. "The glitter will shine in the light."

A knock sounded on the door before it opened abruptly. "You ready in there. On in one minute."

An officious-looking woman with hair pulled tight in a bun and old-fashioned horn-rimmed glasses tapped a pencil on her chart. "Which of the categories are you performing first? I need to tell the compere."

"Self-pleasuring," Antonio said.

"Why are two going onstage?" she demanded, stepping in front of Sasha.

"There's nothing in the rules to say two competitors can't go on stage. They can't touch each other, of course," Sasha stated. "But there's nothing else to prevent a competitor and partner being on stage at the same time."

"We'll see about that," the woman said. She stomped over to the registrar and spoke him with much gesturing in their direction.

"Are you sure?" Antonio said.

"I'm sure. Shush, she's coming back."

"You can both go on stage but the slightest infraction of the touching rule will result in disqualification," the woman said. "Wait for my signal and you're on. Background music— slow, medium or fast?"

"Slow music, please," Sasha said. "A ballad."

She sounded nervous again. Antonio wanted to take her in his arms and kiss her, soothe away her fears. Couldn't happen. Not here in front of everyone. Instead, he reached for Sasha's hand and squeezed it briefly, trying to put everything he felt into that one touch.

"Did you hear about the Irish man who broke his leg?"

A faint smile replaced the anxiety in her eyes. "No."

"He was trying to tap dance and fell into the sink."

Sasha grimaced. She'd forgotten he used to tell Irish jokes to scare away her nerves. "You've told worse."

"I'm mortally offended." Antonio grinned. "Ready to go on stage?"

Sasha gave a clipped nod. "Showtime."

"Next up is Antonio Perez," the compere shouted over the cheering crowd. "And his drawn category is self-pleasuring." A round of wild applause filled the stadium.

"Antonio! Antonio!" a group of fans screeched from the front. They waved banners and one of the more adventurous flashed her breasts.

"Still got your fan club," Sasha said dryly.

Antonio grinned, taking heart from her tone. "Let's do this then we can go back to the dressing room and work out how to fit the carrot into our act."

He strutted onto the stage in performance persona with Sasha at his side. Confidence grew and he flashed her another grin.

When the audience saw both of them, they became silent, aware that something out of the ordinary was about to happen. Their faces and every action were recorded and beamed onto huge screens so everyone in the audience could take in the smallest detail.

Sasha strutted over to a chair and fell into the comforting cushions in a relaxed sprawl, just as they'd discussed. With her blonde hair mussed and the light catching the body glitter, she looked like a wanton angel. His angel.

Enjoy an Excerpt From:
MAKE THAT MAN MINE
Copyright © SHELLEY MUNRO, 2005.

Found in the anthology
MEN TO DIE FOR
Also Featuring
Denise A. Agnew

&

Ravyn Wilde

His mouth worked, but no words came out, then before she could take another breath, he grabbed her. Their lips smashed together and parted just as quickly. Jack jerked away from her, and they stared at each other, both breathing hard.

"That was not a kiss," Emma said breaking the pregnant silence. Frustration washed through her, leaving her feeling totally cheated. The mission she'd set for herself was going to be trickier than she'd first envisaged.

Jack scowled. Emma supposed he meant to frighten her like he scared everyone else he came into contact with. It wouldn't work. She was on to him. "Come here. I want to show you how we should kiss in public."

When he didn't move, she closed the distance between them. She placed her hands on his shoulders. They were tense. Like touching blocks of cold rock except for the dragon tattoo. For some reason that was hot. "You're very cold."

"Get it over with." Jack's eyes flashed with enough temper that she knew not to push him any longer.

She stood on tiptoes and gingerly pressed her lips against his. He didn't move but he didn't cooperate either. Time to move this experiment along. Emma opened her mouth and brushed her tongue across the seam of his mouth. A groan rumbled deep in his chest. *Oh, yeah!* Score one for the home team. Working on pure instinct, Emma moved her lips persuasively against his. She nibbled his bottom lip, then soothed the nips she'd inflicted on him with a swathe of her tongue. Jack's arms came around her without warning, tugging her off-balance so his muscular chest flattened her breasts. He tipped her head back and moved his lips over hers with an expertise that made her toes curl. She gasped taking in his masculine taste, a hint of mint and the tang of the sea. He tasted so good—better than she'd ever imagined.

Then his tongue slid inside her mouth, and she was addicted. Her breasts peaked against her bra as their tongues slid together in a sensuous dance. Jack pressed her closer and to her delight, she found he was interested. *A hard-on.* With a subtle twitch of her hips, Emma pressed against his sizeable erection. Her eyes fluttered shut to savor both the sensation and her triumph. Emma Montrose had turned on big, bad Jack Sullivan.

Why an electronic book?

We live in the Information Age—an exciting time in the history of human civilization, in which technology rules supreme and continues to progress in leaps and bounds every minute of every day. For a multitude of reasons, more and more avid literary fans are opting to purchase e-books instead of paper books. The question from those not yet initiated into the world of electronic reading is simply: *Why?*

1. ***Price.*** An electronic title at Ellora's Cave Publishing and Cerridwen Press runs anywhere from 40% to 75% less than the cover price of the exact same title in paperback format. Why? Basic mathematics and cost. It is less expensive to publish an e-book (no paper and printing, no warehousing and shipping) than it is to publish a paperback, so the savings are passed along to the consumer.

2. ***Space.*** Running out of room in your house for your books? That is one worry you will never have with electronic books. For a low one-time cost, you can purchase a handheld device specifically designed for e-reading. Many e-readers have large, convenient screens for viewing. Better yet, hundreds of titles can be stored within your new library—on a single microchip. There are a variety of e-readers from different manufacturers. You can also read e-books on your PC or laptop computer. (Please note that Ellora's

Cave does not endorse any specific brands. You can check our websites at www.ellorascave.com or www.cerridwenpress.com for information we make available to new consumers.)

3. *Mobility*. Because your new e-library consists of only a microchip within a small, easily transportable e-reader, your entire cache of books can be taken with you wherever you go.

4. ***Personal Viewing Preferences.*** Are the words you are currently reading too small? Too large? Too… ANNOYING? Paperback books cannot be modified according to personal preferences, but e-books can.

5. ***Instant Gratification.*** Is it the middle of the night and all the bookstores near you are closed? Are you tired of waiting days, sometimes weeks, for bookstores to ship the novels you bought? Ellora's Cave Publishing sells instantaneous downloads twenty-four hours a day, seven days a week, every day of the year. Our webstore is never closed. Our e-book delivery system is 100% automated, meaning your order is filled as soon as you pay for it.

Those are a few of the top reasons why electronic books are replacing paperbacks for many avid readers.

As always, Ellora's Cave and Cerridwen Press welcome your questions and comments. We invite you to email us at Comments@ellorascave.com or write to us directly at Ellora's Cave Publishing Inc., 1056 Home Avenue, Akron, OH 44310-3502.

THE
☥ ELLORA'S CAVE ☥
LIBRARY

Stay up to date with Ellora's Cave Titles in
Print with our Quarterly Catalog.

TO RECIEVE A CATALOG,
SEND AN EMAIL WITH YOUR NAME
AND MAILING ADDRESS TO:

CATALOG@ELLORASCAVE.COM
OR SEND A LETTER OR POSTCARD
WITH YOUR MAILING ADDRESS TO:

CATALOG REQUEST
c/o ELLORA'S CAVE PUBLISHING, INC.
1056 HOME AVENUE
AKRON, OHIO 44310-3502

Make each day more EXCITING With our

Ellora's
Cavemen
Calendar

www.EllorasCave.com

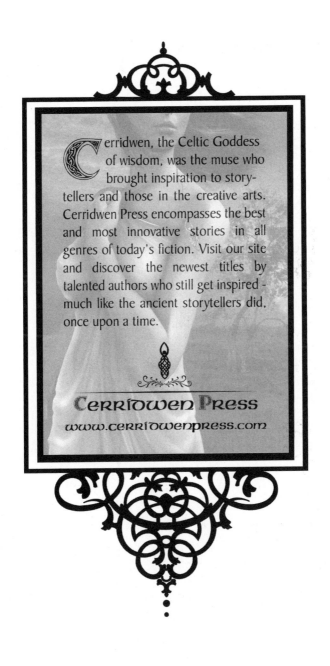

erridwen, the Celtic Goddess of wisdom, was the muse who brought inspiration to story-tellers and those in the creative arts. Cerridwen Press encompasses the best and most innovative stories in all genres of today's fiction. Visit our site and discover the newest titles by talented authors who still get inspired - much like the ancient storytellers did, once upon a time.

Cerridwen Press

www.cerridwenpress.com

Discover for yourself why readers can't get enough of the multiple award-winning publisher Ellora's Cave.

Whether you prefer e-books or paperbacks,

be sure to visit EC on the web at
www.ellorascave.com

for an erotic reading experience that will leave you breathless.